CRAVING CASSIE

Visit us at www.boldstrokesbooks.com

CRAVING CASSIE

by

Skye Rowan

2022

CRAVING CASSIE

ISBN 13: 978-1-63679-062-6

This Trade Paperback Original Is Published By
Bold Strokes Books, Inc.
P.O. Box 249
Valley Falls, NY 12185

First Edition: November 2022

Credits

Editors: Victoria Villaseñor and Cindy Cresap
Production Design: Susan Ramundo
Cover Design By Tammy Seidick

Acknowledgments

I've always had my heart set on writing a book, and the characters of Siobhan and Cassie have followed me around for longer than I can remember, so when Radclyffe took a chance on me, it truly was a dream come true. The team at Bold Strokes have been fantastic with their support and advice, making my first book a pleasure to write. I owe so much thanks to Rad, who believed in me from the start and knew exactly when to step in. My next shout out is to the wonderful Vic, my amazing editor, who worked tirelessly to ensure this novel was the one I wanted to write. She helped me to find my author voice and encouraged me to believe I was the one who knew my characters best. This book would not exist without her words of wisdom and motivation. I will be forever grateful to her for the time she put into this, the encouraging Zoom calls she made when I was lost and her endless positivity and support.

There are friends I need to thank for helping along the way too. Vikki for reading my very first version and telling me it was way too long; her honesty was just the inspiration I needed to start again and get the job done! Jacqui for listening to my constant agonizing over character decisions, bad jokes, and wacky ideas and for being there and being interested. Finally, to my amazing partner Nic, for putting up with my "writer quirks." I couldn't have done it without her, especially in the middle of the night, the time I picked to bump heads with myself and deliberate my writing choices. There are no words for how much I appreciate her.

Dedication

For Nic,
It's such a wonderful thing to love.

CHAPTER ONE

"Not sure a stick of Brighton rock was quite the look I was hoping to master," Siobhan Carney murmured as she pushed an unruly lock of hair behind her ear and smoothed down her crisp, navy pencil skirt. She questioned her choice of shirt: a striped sunset orange with capped sleeves under her navy blazer, but there was no time to change her mind—or her attire—yet again. She'd have to accept looking like a stick of seaside candy.

Although rush hour was over, every traffic light she approached had the audacity to turn red right on cue, allowing her nerves more time to build. Her stomach somersaulted each time she thought about the possibility of being late, and heaven forbid her leg would stop shaking.

Now that Park Place was to be her permanent workplace, she knew she needed to consider taking the Tube into Canary Wharfe. It would be the quicker option, especially moving through central London, but this morning hadn't been the time to tackle Tube travel with other pressing issues on her agenda.

With the rearview mirror as her ally, she checked and rechecked her teeth for lipstick stains and made sure her hair was still presentable.

She entered the building's rotating doors and proceeded to the elevator, taking it up to floor thirty-five. It wasn't her first time in this building, but this time things felt different. She'd dedicated herself to this company. She'd earned this promotion. And she desperately needed it.

A woman dressed all in black approached Siobhan, and she instantly regretted her choice of color, fumbling around with the buttons on her blazer to fasten it. The woman, who was at least a foot shorter than Siobhan, had a face pinched like a Cornish pasty. The crinkles across her forehead spoke of a permanent frown and her eyes narrowed as she spoke.

"Are you Mrs. Carney?" She barked the question, looking like she'd rather be dining with Dracula in the darkest depths of Transylvania. "Unusual name." The woman stared at the form in front of her, as if staring alone would help it make sense. "Seeahban."

"It's an Irish name and it's pronounced Shivon." She offered her hand and was met with a stilted handshake.

"I'm Julie, Ms. Townsend's secretary. Soon to be yours too, apparently." Julie's gaze rolled over her like a car navigating a speed bump. "I've been instructed to take you to her office."

Julie turned and led at such a rapid pace that Siobhan struggled to keep up, questions racing through her mind. In particular, she wondered if the Ms. Townsend she was referring to was really who she thought it might be. Finally, she fell in step beside Julie, recognizing the importance of getting this woman onside sooner rather than later.

"I'm glad they sent you to meet me. I don't think I would have found my way alone."

"Maybe I should draw you a map? Ms. Townsend has no tolerance for incompetence. You'd do well to remember that."

Siobhan got the feeling she was about to be swept up in a perfect storm, much like Dorothy on her way to Oz. "I know. I'm not—"

"You know? How do you know her?"

"I know *of* her. Anyone with any interest in investment banking knows of Cassie Townsend. She's the most successful investment banker the company has ever produced and comes with quite a rep—"

"Before you continue singing her praises, let's see how you two are getting on in a week or two."

"How we're getting on? I'm sorry, have I missed something?"

Julie huffed, making a big fuss out of stopping in the corridor before turning to face Siobhan. "Didn't you get the brief?"

Siobhan shook her head, her stomach turning. No brief meant she was already a step behind. A position she didn't intend to be in for long.

"This is your first investment role. When the managing directors see potential in someone, they like to partner them up with an experienced banker. There's no one better than Cassie in terms of success and experience, you've got that right. So the plan is simple.

You'll train with her until you're well acquainted with the role and ready to work independently. There's only one problem...I'm sorry, I really shouldn't say anything more."

Julie's smug grin would usually have bothered her, but Siobhan's excitement overshadowed any apprehension about this news. Learning from the best in the business was an opportunity that didn't come around every day and one she intended to make the most of. Julie resumed walking, her pace still unnaturally quick, as if she couldn't wait to dump Siobhan at Cassie's doorstep.

As they passed other employees, some smiled at Siobhan, but most regarded her with what could only be described as *Better you than me* sympathy.

The least promising look came from Julie, who eventually showed Siobhan to a seat in an office space immediately outside Cassie's, where she now perched, twisting her wedding ring as if it were a cap on a tube of toothpaste that she couldn't get open. Julie took up a seat at the desk opposite, making herself at home in a way that could only indicate this was her usual workspace.

It was clear that Cassie wasn't a safe subject for conversation. Perhaps Julie would prefer to talk about herself? "So," Siobhan asked, "have you worked here long?"

"Long enough to recognize a poisoned chalice when I see one."

Siobhan nearly choked on the deep breath she'd just inhaled. "Poisoned chalice?"

"This is the first time Cassie has *ever* been asked to train someone. There's a reason for that." Julie stared at Siobhan as if she expected her to fill in the gaps. When Siobhan merely blinked at her, Julie glanced around, as if she expected Cassie to be looming behind her or lurking in shadows. "She's not exactly a people person. In fact, she's pretty impossible to work with and I'm just her secretary. I'm not sure what the thinking is behind pairing the two of you up. I can't imagine her having the patience to teach you anything." Julie paused for effect, "About investment banking."

"I think you've said enough." Siobhan pulled on her wedding ring so hard it dropped to the floor. She reached down to retrieve it and when she looked up, she noticed Julie's mouth was agape, her chest puffed up like a bird, feathers about to explode. "Really," Siobhan bristled, putting up a hand to stop her. "I've heard enough."

Ignoring Siobhan, as if she had been invited to elaborate, Julie said, "You do know she's a lesbian?"

"What?" Siobhan rubbed her sweaty palms together, confused that of all the information Julie could have imparted on her, she had chosen this. "I think everyone is entitled to a private life."

The door to Cassie's office opened.

"Good luck," Julie whispered, giving Siobhan a thumbs-up that seemed more like a middle finger.

A lackadaisical voice floated out of the office. "I'm guessing this is the earliest you've ever been late?" There, oozing cool, leaned against the doorframe, arms folded across a fitted black shirt, stood Cassie Townsend.

Siobhan glanced at her watch. She wasn't late at all. Desperate to regain her equilibrium after Julie had thrown her completely off balance, Siobhan took another deep breath, rolled her shoulders back, and maneuvered her mouth into a smile to display a confidence she didn't truly feel. Cassie didn't smile back. Hoping her hair still looked sleek around her face, Siobhan stood and followed Cassie into her office.

Inside she encountered Cassie's lavish décor. Good—she'd have something else to look at besides Cassie's don't-fuck-with-me expression. She tried not to appear awestruck, but everything in the office demanded her attention: the wall-to-wall windows showcasing a glorious view of the city, which included the winding river Thames with tourist boats passing by like they had all the time in the world. Unlike Cassie, apparently.

Two large pieces of artwork decorated the walls, one immediately capturing Siobhan's attention. Two towering rock formations crept out of the ocean amidst color and vibrant beauty. She was instantly taken back to her childhood summers. She had always loved the ocean, sitting in the front seat of her mum's car listening to showtunes as they traveled the Ring of Kerry together, just the two of them. She smiled at the memory.

"Am I interrupting something?"

Siobhan was startled into the present, Cassie stealing up beside her, arms still folded, eyebrows raised. Faint heat crept into her cheeks that she had been caught out so early in their interaction. "Sorry. I was just admiring the colors of the ocean here. It's an incredible piece of artwork. I'm Siobhan."

Cassie turned around and slipped back towards her desk, reclining in her chair and kicking her feet up. She pointed at herself. "Cassie. But you can call me Ms. Townsend."

"Pleased to meet you, Ms. Townsend." Siobhan held out her hand, which Cassie took, shaking it with more force than Siobhan had expected. "I'm looking forward to working with you."

Cassie drummed her fingers on the desk. "About that, I don't share my space. You can work out there." She pointed to where Siobhan had just come from. "I've asked Julie to organize a desk for you. I should've asked her sooner, but today sort of crept up on me." There was no apology in Cassie's tone. "I'm meeting a client later this morning to run through some financial projections. I really don't have much time for this."

"That's okay." Siobhan shuffled from one foot to the other and back again, questioning whether she meant now, or ever. "I can help Julie sort my space out. I'm meeting with—"

"There won't be any meeting. Your training is my responsibility. Welcome to the deep end. I hope you make a splash when you're thrown in. For my sake."

Cassie couldn't have looked any less thrilled than if she'd been asked to hike across the desert for a morning Starbucks, only to find they'd run out of milk. Siobhan's excitement at being partnered with the best the company had to offer was deflated by the fact Cassie saw her as nothing more than a burden.

"I'm pretty capable," Siobhan said. "I'm sure there's lots I can make a start on. I'm a quick learner, and since you won't have to show me things twice, I won't impose on your time unnecessarily."

Siobhan was sure she saw the corners of Cassie's mouth twitch upward, but as quickly as it came, it went. She watched as Cassie picked up a document and scowled at it. She had never seen anyone glare at something so inoffensive with such animosity.

"Here." Cassie offered her the document. "This would be a good place to start."

"Thanks." Siobhan hoped her smile conveyed her willingness accurately. It was rebuffed in no uncertain terms. Siobhan's eyes drifted down to the document, then widened in surprise—her feelings mixed. "This is the pitchbook for your meeting today."

"I can't think of a better way to learn than on the job. Can you? But you're only there to observe; you mustn't get involved. That's my one direction. I'm thinking you'll accompany me today, gain some insight, read the other pitchbooks, then by the end of the week you'll be ready to handle client meetings on your own. Right?"

Siobhan nodded. "I'll take them home to make sure I'm up to speed."

"As long as you don't lose them." Cassie pulled open a drawer and pulled out a packet of cigarettes. "Any questions, just ask."

"Right, because approachable is your middle name?" The moment the comment left Siobhan's mouth, she longed to retract it. How on earth had she let it out into the world in the first place?

"Wow."

Siobhan watched Cassie's posture stiffen and braced herself for the imminent scolding. Instead Cassie pocketed her lighter and made for the door. When Cassie brushed past her, Siobhan saw her drop her cigarette and, with an irritated sigh, bend to retrieve it. "Much like these cigarettes, I come with a warning." Cassie stared pointedly at her.

"That thing about your approachability. I didn't just say it out loud, did I? Because that would be ridiculous."

"Yes, and you said it with such conviction too." Cassie angled her head. Her eyes seemed to linger. "Have I met my match?"

"I'm not in the habit of starting fires," Siobhan returned, hoping humor would help.

"Nor I extinguishing them."

When Cassie arched an eyebrow this time, Siobhan turned back to the towering rocks depicted on the wall, wondering if now was the time to throw herself off them.

"Canon Beach."

Siobhan flinched with both the shock of Cassie's voice sweeping over her shoulder and her presence so close behind. "It's in Oregon. You seem to like the painting."

"I love the ocean. This painting has reminded me how much. We're lucky here in London; we can be at the coast in an hour."

"Perhaps that explains the outfit." Cassie's mouth twitched again as Siobhan stared nonplussed, waiting for an explanation. "You look like a stick of rock." Cassie sniggered at the striped shirt sneaking out despite Siobhan's failed attempt to keep it hidden under her blazer.

Damn it. She should have changed after all. "Not everyone pulls off black with such aplomb."

Cassie's eyes lit up. "Compliments indeed. Actually, my sister lives in Broadstairs. The views from there are spectacular, especially where the jagged cliffs reach out into the ocean. Not that I have time for frivolous, whimsical things like *enjoying the view*. I'm far too busy being a sensational investment banker."

"I was just thinking the same. Not the sensational investment banker bit," Siobhan quickly clarified. "Happy to leave that to you." She cringed, hearing herself laugh. "I was actually thinking that I should make more of an effort to take the kids to the seaside."

At the mention of her kids, Siobhan saw Cassie's expression harden, her mouth downturned in what Siobhan could only read as perpetual disapproval.

"I really need to smoke this cigarette." Cassie waved the cigarette as if it were a magic wand and exited her office.

When Cassie was gone, Siobhan began to analyze their first meeting. Things hadn't exactly gone to plan. She'd told her new mentor that she was unapproachable. Despite being on time, she'd been on the receiving end of an accusation about arriving late. Cassie hadn't exactly welcomed her with open arms. And yet…there'd been a hint of something in Cassie's smile, small and swift though it had been. Not that she needed to evaluate their interactions in such minute detail. They didn't have to be friends, Siobhan just had to learn all she could, as quickly as she could. This working relationship had to succeed.

With one last sweeping glance of the room, Siobhan retreated to the newly acquired desk that Julie motioned towards, flung herself down into her seat, and flipped open the pitchbook.

CHAPTER TWO

Pull yourself together, Cassie-nova, she's a happily married woman."

"I said she wears a wedding ring. That's not the same thing." Cassie grinned. "Anyway, whether she's a stunner or not makes zero difference to the fact it's been a week and it's a pain in the arse training her."

Cassie sat in her usual seat in the lively café, where she and Helena often put the world to rights. It was her favorite place to unwind after a hectic day at the office. In truth it was also one of many places she found it effortless to pick up women.

At that thought, Cassie looked at the barista serving their table. She quickly looked away and hunched over, suddenly engrossed in the mosaic pattern on their table, studying it like it was a Picasso. The younger woman, whose pain was evident in the crease of her lovely brow and in the down-curve of her full lips, slammed Cassie's drink down in front of her. The coffee pooled on the table, clearly satisfying the barista's need to express her distress. Before Cassie had an opportunity to respond, the barista stalked away, as if she couldn't escape fast enough.

Helena's eyes narrowed. "Tell me you didn't."

"I didn't." She did her best to look innocent.

"And I rode in on the Tube with Gentleman Jack." Helena rolled her eyes.

"Ahhh, Suranne Jones. Now she could serve me pancakes dripping in maple syrup, stark bollock naked." Cassie pretended to swoon, hoping she had dodged the conversation. No such luck.

"I can't believe you slept with Laila! Is there anywhere we can go without awkwardly bumping into one of your conquests? I just want to be able to enjoy a cup of coffee without receiving daggers."

"They aren't aimed at you. Besides, it just happened. It was an accident."

"Of course, like it always *just* happens. I know *I'm* always accidentally falling into bed with women, especially ones who make the best caramel macchiato in town."

"It was weeks ago and it really wasn't anything to write home about. I have no idea why she'd be pissed off with me."

"If I were to hazard a guess," Helena dramatized her deliberation by tapping her nose and scrunching her brows, "you didn't call."

"I never call."

"Need I say more? You have women queuing up, when I can't even get a date. What is it about one night with Cassie Townsend?"

"I'm not giving away my trade secrets."

"I guess that explains why we've been frequenting that other place recently for our coffee and catch-ups. When was the last time you slept with anyone there?"

Cassie pressed her hands over her heart, leaned to the side, and pulled a face much like a dying dog. "You wound me." She sat back up in her chair. "Besides, you know I have a marvelous time ruining everything."

"Just putting it out there: I love this place, so if you could refrain from shagging anyone else who works here, huge bonus points are available."

"I told you I've sworn off women. Cross my heart." Cassie mimicked the gesture.

"I know." Helena was clearly trying not to laugh. "You're focusing on your career, or so you've told me, and yet here we are, about to delve into why you shouldn't enjoy this attractive married woman."

"I think it's time for a cigarette."

"Oh, no, you don't." Helena held her hand to keep her from getting up.

Cassie slumped back into her chair, cursing how well her best friend knew her. She thrived off their easy camaraderie and quick banter, especially considering there were few other people she would consider giving the time of day to, but sometimes Helena knowing her so well could be vexing.

They had met at university in Bath and formed a firm friendship. It always made her laugh when she thought back to how they had first gotten to know one another, arguing over who would make the greatest female James Bond: Jodie Foster or Gillian Anderson. Cassie knew Gillian had it in the bag, but the debate had been heated and Cassie had loved Helena dearly ever since.

Throughout their university years, Helena had played wingwoman to Cassie's Lothario, but those days were over now. Helena had tired of Cassie's antics long ago. Of course, this hadn't deterred Cassie from her purpose, but she had to admit it wasn't as much fun these days. Coupled with the fact that the pool of available, willing women was lessening as her reputation worsened, it was little wonder she needed a break from sleeping around.

Then there was the elephant in the room, which they never, ever, talked about. Helena had always been attracted to Cassie. Short of a drunken fumble, Cassie didn't think they had taken things any further, but she could never quite be sure, since alcohol had been such a popular pastime in their early years together. She wanted to give herself enough credit that had she woken up next to Helena, she would have remembered such a disaster. Given that she had no memory of any such blip, she was pretty sure they'd never done the deed. But Cassie knew if she suggested that they hook up and ride off into the sunset together, Helena would be more than willing, but she just didn't see her that way. Besides, Cassie didn't do relationships; she was far too committed to her career for that to ever happen.

"So come on then, tell me about this stunner Siobhan."

Cassie scowled. "For some ridiculous reason, my boss deemed it wise that I take on a trainee. I don't work as part of a team, never have, never will."

"They obviously think you're the right woman for the job. You ought to find that flattering, right?"

Helena always saw the positives in any situation, much to Cassie's frustration. She was the only person Cassie knew who would find the box of doughnuts empty and instead of falling into a full-on sulk, would see it as an opportunity to begin a new health kick.

"Not really. If she's shit, then it reflects badly on me."

"And if she's fucking fantastic, that also reflects on you, right? But that isn't an option?"

"I find approaching any situation with the view that everyone else is incapable works best for me. If I'm honest, she seems to be showing promising signs, but it's early days. It's not often you get brains and beauty."

Helena harrumphed at the perceived affront. "Now you're just talking shit and you know it."

"Look, I have to be successful. It's the only thing that matters to me. If Siobhan puts that at risk, it isn't going to work between us. I think it's safe to say this isn't my skill set. Honestly, it's draining me already. Plus, I don't have the time. I have way more important things to attend to than babysitting an amateur."

"You wouldn't regard it as a success if you trained her to be as brilliant as you are? That wouldn't get you the recognition you're always longing for?"

Cassie cocked her head, processing the idea. A destiny devoid of uncompromising success was bad enough, but... "What if I do my job too well and her talent surpasses mine?"

"Then you would burn up in roaring flames, taken by the devil himself?" Helena mocked her. "Give the woman a chance."

Cassie wilted in her chair. "She called me unapproachable, right to my face."

"Well..." Helena played with her napkin, not making eye contact. "She's not wrong. You have been known to be slightly frosty on occasion."

Cassie waved off the compliment. "I'm a busy woman. I don't have time to pick up her mistakes left, right, and center. She's an inconvenience."

"Yeah, I'm sure looking into those dreamy brown eyes will be a real inconvenience for you."

"Blue, actually. The color of forget-me-nots, if you want a precise description."

"Quite frankly, I'm stunned you noticed the color of her eyes. Do you even know what color mine are?"

"Red," Cassie said, "like a clown's nose. Why would I notice that about you?"

"The point I'm making is that I don't think you could tell me the eye color of any of the women you've slept with. Laila, for example?"

"Not a fucking clue," Cassie admitted, swallowing the lump forming in her throat. Helena had a point. Siobhan's expressive eyes and the warmth they radiated had been ingrained in her brain all week. "And this means what, exactly?"

"You tell me," Helena said, but Cassie simply shrugged. "I've not seen you all starry-eyed over a woman before. It's disconcerting."

"I am in no way starry-eyed over anyone, it's not my style. I'm simply appreciating a good-looking woman. *That's* my style."

"And do we know more about said good-looking woman?"

"She's not terribly forthcoming about her personal life, though I can't say I've shown that much interest."

"You must at least know who put that ring on her finger."

"Well, considering she's Mrs. 2.4 Children, I think we can assume there's a husband out there. Plus, I've studied her walk."

"You mean you've been perving on her arse."

Cassie directed a cutting look towards Helena, folding her arms. "Look, she doesn't have the Sapphic strut. We both know what that means. She's straight."

"Which just adds another level of challenge, right?"

"Did you miss the part where I said she's a nuisance, nothing more? Like I said. She's attractive, but I'm not interested."

"The lady-killer doth protest too much, methinks." Helena winked at Cassie, who felt her cheeks heat, despite her best efforts.

"Oh, please. It's not like I've welcomed her with open arms. She probably hates the situation as much as I do. I bet she dreads walking through that door every morning."

Cassie paused to consider this. Was this how she wanted Siobhan, a woman who was new to the job and trying her absolute best, to feel? She shook off the tiny niggle. After all, Cassie was doing everything she had been forced to and Siobhan was improving as a result.

"Just admit you're intrigued by her, and I'll shut up."

"She's a pain in my right royal arse. If you take that to mean I'm intrigued by her, then who am I to disagree?" It was time to change the subject. "Are we going out tomorrow night?"

"Actually, in an unexpected turn of events, I have a date."

Cassie ran her hand through her short hair. She didn't want to appear too pleased for Helena, but this was brilliant news.

"Could you try to look a tiny bit disappointed?"

"My heart is shattering into a thousand pieces." Cassie grinned. "Let me just grab a dustpan and brush."

"Advice on outfits? I know you find it impossible to believe I could pull off sexy, but that's what I'm going for. Any tips would be greatly appreciated, especially from the woman who masters it without giving one ounce of fuck."

Cassie rested her chin in her palm. It was her turn to tap her nose and feign thinking as if she were making an important decision. "Jeans and a simple shirt."

"Do you even want me to get laid?" Helena glared at her.

"It's top of my list. I just think less is more. You can't go wrong with tight-fitting jeans and that black and white patterned shirt. I mean Siobhan rocked up looking like a neon tube of toothpaste and still managed to look hot." Cassie took a moment to reminisce. "And I mean head-turning hot. She's got those classic dimples you know I like."

"Thank goodness you've brought her up again. In the fifteen seconds since you last uttered her name, I'd nearly forgotten about her existence."

"You're such an irritant." Cassie was more irritated with herself for being uncharacteristically invested. *No, not invested. Interested.* "So where are you meeting this woman? Is this a totally blind date?"

"Not totally. We've been chatting on an app." She held up her hand to stop Cassie's protest. "I know you're cynical about apps, but we don't all have the power to walk into a bar and attract women like a human magnet. I'm getting good vibes, and we're only meeting for a few drinks. You're just annoyed because you'll have to go out on the pull alone."

"Actually, I was planning on curling up with pizza and a bottle of wine."

"Well, if I do need a Wonder Woman-style rescue, you can be on call. If you could rock up in the full outfit, eagle motif headband included, even better."

"Oh, but I don't have the right image. Dark, flowing locks, stunning blue eyes."

"Sound familiar?" Helena quirked an eyebrow.

Cassie squirmed under her scrutiny. "Shall we talk dos and don'ts for tomorrow night?"

"Are you imparting dating etiquette? Is it even dating, what you do?"

Cassie shrugged half-heartedly. "Maybe you should ask Laila."

"Last time I checked, she didn't seem overly enamored with your manner, your...what shall we call it...aloofness?"

"Just because I don't want to wake up next to the same woman for the next fifty years of my life does not mean I am aloof."

"She's looking our way again." Helena nodded to where Laila stood behind the bar, staring directly at Cassie like she wanted to string her up on a butcher's hook.

"She needs to move on. It's not like I promised her the world. It was just a shag. Nobody likes someone who seems too keen."

"Are you going to keep that advice in mind?"

"It was aimed at you. As brilliant as my advice is, I don't need to follow it." She didn't need to worry about being too keen on anyone. It never happened.

"Of course, I forgot. You're not stubborn, your way just happens to always be better."

Cassie swatted Helena with a twenty-pound note, then threw the note onto the table. "Good luck."

She rose, kissed her on the cheek, and exited into the evening, smiling at the realization that her best friend had a better chance of getting laid this weekend than she did. Throughout the years Cassie had always enjoyed the biggest slice of the cake, but it was time for Helena to have her moment, and she wasn't going to deny her that.

Perhaps Cassie could simply swear off women forever.

The thought made her anxious and she brushed it away. This was a short-term abstinence, anything more was unrealistic. She didn't need to swear them off forever. She just needed to keep herself from the chaos and entanglements of anything real.

No problem.

CHAPTER THREE

"Quad biking!" Dylan bounced up and down, waving a poster in Siobhan's face.

"Hello to you too."

"It's only an hour away and you get to go over mudslides and race through the forest. You could even take a quad out with us if you're brave enough."

"I'm assuming we're talking about birthday parties here?" Siobhan grinned at her son's enthusiasm. "Of course I'm brave enough!"

"You're home!" Neave skipped through from the living room. "Check this out!"

Neave cartwheeled down the hall like a Catherine wheel, all sparks and energy. "That's one of the moves I added to my routine today. Like it?"

"Like it?" Siobhan pretended to consider the question as she scooped her daughter into a hug. She squidged Neave's nose. "I love it!"

"And you love quad biking too, right?" Dylan asked.

Siobhan wrapped her arm around her son, pulling him closer. "Give me the poster and I'll take a look."

Dylan leaned on the banister, grinning. "So that's a yes?"

"How can you think about quad biking on an empty stomach?" Neave grumbled. "My stomach's practically talking!"

Your father couldn't feed you? Siobhan fought the urge to shake her head in disgust. "I'm sorry I'm late. It's been a busy day. The lady I work with is a little intense."

"What's *intense*?" Neave asked, wide-eyed.

"Someone who takes things a little too seriously."

Neave nodded, as if she understood exactly what Siobhan meant. Maybe she did.

"Well, we can't have you two turning into the characters in *Funny Bones* now, can we? How about I get dinner ready and you can show me another dance move as we wait?"

"Want to see the Worm?" Neave threw herself onto the floor in preparation.

"As the creator of the move, I would love to see it." Siobhan couldn't contain her laughter as Neave wiggled along the floor into the kitchen.

"Mum, you did not invent the Worm." Dylan waved his hands dismissively.

"Clearly you've never seen me in action on the dance floor."

"You haven't been near a dance floor in the last hundred years." Dylan grinned at her.

Although he had a fair point, Siobhan decided to rise to the challenge—or rather, descend to it. She flung herself onto the floor and managed to impressively pull off the Worm, rising and falling with about as much elegance as an elephant trying to twerk. Neave burst into laughter, tears streaming down her cheeks, and Dylan creased over, his eyes nearly popping out of his head.

"What on earth is all this racket?" Matthew came to an abrupt standstill, his feet planted right in front of her, so that she had to look up at him.

She noticed his lip curled in thinly veiled disdain and picked herself up from the floor, clearing her throat. She ruffled Dylan's hair before heading for the fridge to start dinner.

"Mum was just busting a move," Dylan said with a shrug, rubbing his eyes.

"I bet *you* can't move like that," Neave teased him.

"I can't think why anyone would want to move like that," Matthew muttered, flopping into a chair at the kitchen table.

"Those who can, do. Those who can't…complain." Siobhan used a tone that would amuse her children but not incite her husband.

Matthew was too busy scowling at the night's meal choice to notice he'd been insulted. "Are we really having freezer food for dinner on a Friday night?" he asked as she poured chicken nuggets and oven chips onto a tray.

Siobhan blew out a deep breath before responding. "I'd love nothing more than to prepare a home-cooked meal for everyone, but after ten busy hours in the office, I just don't have the energy."

"We're playing at Oak Park tomorrow," Dylan piped up, looking about as enthusiastic as his father, although for an entirely different reason, Siobhan suspected. "Spurs are at home, so Dad said you'd take me. We don't have to go if you don't have the energy."

Siobhan touched her son's cheek. When it came down to it, it was her standing out on a muddy field in the freezing cold, Saturday after Saturday, knowing full well Dylan's heart wasn't in it. "It's not a matter of my energy, love. It's a matter of your interest. Dylan, do you *want* to play football this weekend?"

"No," Dylan said. "I don't want to play football any weekend. Or any weekday. It's cold, muddy, and boring."

Matthew's mouth dropped open like a drawbridge. "He can't just quit mid-season. I've paid his subs for the year! We need to instill commitment in him."

"We need to support his interests," Siobhan said evenly, "not force him to do things he isn't interested in. He's gone along with it because he wants to please you, but he's nearly eight years old, Matthew. He's old enough to make his own choices."

"Are we going to let the six-year-old make her own choices too?" Matthew mocked her. "If she wants to go scuba diving or start sumo wrestling, are we going to give that our stamp of approval as well?"

"Mum is," Neave said. "You're just going to stamp your feet." She began to stamp around the kitchen, impersonating her father brilliantly.

Matthew glared at Neave, who quickly grew subdued, then shifted his scorn to Dylan. "Perhaps you're just too girly for the game."

"Thinking that way is just so old-fashioned," Dylan said, then glanced at Siobhan. She gave him a reassuring wink and he beamed back, buoyed by her support.

"It's also really dumb," Neave added. "Lots of girls in my class play football. Sometimes I even go in goal."

"Then perhaps *you* should play football tomorrow." Matthew's sneer was like something from a comic book. It wasn't meant to be funny, but it definitely missed the mark.

Neave shook her head. "I have to be in the mood."

"Well, since you've all decided you aren't going to football tomorrow, what *are* you going to do instead?" Matthew asked.

Siobhan thought back to the beginning of the week and the painting of the ocean in Cassie's office. She had missed trips to the seaside and couldn't think of anything more appealing right now than a day at the coast with Dylan and Neave. Even better, Matthew would be at the Spurs game and therefore wouldn't have to go with them. "We're taking a day trip to Camber Sands."

Dylan and Neave responded with exclamations of excitement.

"It's hardly beach weather," Matthew pointed out.

Siobhan bit the inside of her cheek. "It will be fun," she said, intent on assuring her children rather than pacifying her husband.

"I'm surprised you even have time for fun. This new job seems to demand all your attention."

Siobhan seethed at Matthew's audacity, not to mention his exaggeration of her current work-life balance. "The only thing that has changed is Fridays. I've taken the kids to school every day like usual. I've gone out of my way to ensure things stay as normal as possible for them."

Matthew pursed his lips and Siobhan was sure he muttered something under his breath, but then he leaned back and let out a deep sigh.

There was a forced pleasantness to his tone as he spoke. "I know you have, and I appreciate it. But I miss you."

Siobhan tried to hide a derisive snort.

"Wait till you see how much," Matthew said, rising from his chair. "Close your eyes."

Siobhan complied momentarily. When she was certain Matthew had left the room, she opened them again, leaning against Neave and enjoying a rare moment of respite.

"Dad's gone to get the you-know-whats." Neave looked pointedly at Dylan, clearly in on the secret.

"Right." Dylan gave her a thumbs-down, but then switched to a thumbs-up when their father returned to the room.

Siobhan quickly shut her eyes again.

"You can open them now," Matthew said, though it sounded more like an instruction than an invitation.

Siobhan laid eyes on a huge bouquet of artfully arranged flowers and a stilted grin on her husband's face. These weren't your usual last ditch petrol station flowers, which made the gesture not only unexpected, but also uncharacteristic. She hoped her face didn't say as much.

"We just wanted to say that even though you haven't been around much for us this week, we still love you."

Only her husband would turn a loving act like flower-giving into a self-serving one intended to amass guilt.

"They're beautiful," Siobhan said with as little acrimony as she could manage. Setting the bouquet on the table, she smiled at her children. "I'm going to go and get changed. Then we can have tea and watch a film together before bed."

"I get to pick the film!" Dylan yelled, racing past his sister into the living room.

Neave chased after him. "Not if I get to the remote first and find Mary Poppins!"

Even Mary Poppins couldn't fix this marriage, Siobhan mused as she began making her way up the stairs. Next week's appointment with her solicitor couldn't come soon enough, especially now that she felt bold enough to set their divorce in motion.

"So you liked the flowers?" Matthew asked, following her. "Because you didn't immediately put them in water."

"Unlike you, they might grow on me," she muttered, noting this was the second inappropriate comment she had spoken out loud in a matter of days. This was a bad habit she needed to curb.

"I thought that—"

"You thought that one bunch of flowers would make up for eight years of absence?" she asked, though it was more of a statement than a question.

"I'm here every day," Matthew said.

"But you're not here for *us*, are you?"

He stopped short, as if deliberating his next move.

Siobhan made hers first. "In eight years of marriage, I've been invisible to you—unless it's been for cooking, cleaning, or childcare. Now suddenly you miss me if I'm not around for a few hours? This couldn't have anything to do with the fact I'm trying to better myself, so you feel this need to throw a spanner in the works?"

Matthew ground his teeth, his face twisting. "Better yourself? You've not exactly been struggling through each day before you took this stupid job. I've built you and the kids a good life."

Siobhan shook her head. "You honestly think you're the sole contributor? Matthew, you contribute nothing. And you certainly don't appreciate what I bring to the table. You don't see anything I've ever done as meaningful, in or outside the home. I exist merely to meet your ideal of a traditional family and, on rare occasions, your mother's approval."

The tips of Matthew's ears turned red. Siobhan had never spoken to him with such candor, usually because he wasn't prepared to listen, but as the thoughts she had suppressed for so long emerged with remarkable ease, she felt the tension in her entire body dissipate. Siobhan held his gaze, unwilling to look away.

Matthew broke eye contact first. "You're tired, you've had a busy week at work—"

"This isn't me knackered from a week in the office; this is me being honest with you—finally—and you won't even acknowledge the truth of what I'm saying." Siobhan could feel tears begin to form in the corners of her eyes. She wiped them away, determined not to cry.

"I'm not listening to this," he said, shrugging off her feelings as if she'd been complaining about the weather.

As she stared at Matthew, exasperated at his incessant indifference, years of unvoiced frustration detonated from within. "Why the fuck are you so disengaged anyway?"

Matthew stared at her like she'd spoken in another language. The answer didn't matter though. He was never going to change or even attempt to understand her grievances. He was oblivious to the debilitating effect he had on her welfare, day by day running her into the ground. Worse still, he didn't understand how he was hurting the children.

Dylan and Neave were the driving force behind everything she did, including—especially—her decision to leave Matthew. That was why she was so determined to succeed in her new position at work. If she could support herself and her children without any help from him, they would all be better off.

Matthew sat down next to her on the bed, looking desperate to backpedal on the last ten minutes of their lives. She tried not to cringe at his closeness.

"You're not particularly engaging either. Most of the time it feels like you dislike me intensely." Matthew's tone was grating in its deceptive gentleness. "Would it help if we spent more time together? I can ask Mam to have the kids next Saturday. We can spend some time alone, engaging in...something."

Although his suggestion was hardly suggestive, the word "No!" left her lips with more force than she intended.

"But it's been so long since we did anything, just the two of us."

"That's what happens when two people have next to nothing in common. Furthermore, I don't want to palm the kids off on your mum. In one breath you're telling me they've been deeply affected by my new job and in the next you're sending them off to Bronagh's."

"I did mention that you might do a Sunday lunch for everyone at hers." He plucked at a thread on the blanket. "We could spend Saturday together doing whatever, and then go be with the family on Sunday."

Siobhan covered her face with her hands, her head throbbing as though a wrecking ball had taken up residence. She opened her mouth to respond but swiftly snapped it shut, opting for dignity over discontent. She walked into their en suite bathroom, locked the door, sat on the edge of the bathtub, and breathed.

No one thing he had done today had tipped her over the edge. The difference today was that for the first time, she had said her piece and it felt liberating, despite the fact she was now locked in her bathroom to escape him. The term divorcée had never held such appeal.

"Siobhan," Matthew called through the closed door, "this isn't entirely my fault, you know. If your feelings had changed like they were supposed to, we might not be playing happy families. We might actually be one."

Siobhan opened the bathroom door, determined to keep a level head as she faced him with the truth.

"And if you'd listened to me all those years ago when I told you my feelings wouldn't change, we wouldn't be here."

"So you'd rather have been there, in rural Ireland, unmarried and pregnant? If I hadn't married you, you'd have been disgraced. I saved you from that fate!"

Siobhan stared down at her knuckles, white from clenching her fists too hard. "My fate was to be with a woman."

"I saved you from that too, chasing after women around the bloody town," Matthew said. "You're welcome."

Siobhan *was* thankful—that Dylan and Neave chose that exact moment to burst through the door, giving her a reprieve. It was evident from the way Dylan rubbed his eyebrow and Neave's wrinkled brow that both children had heard their raised voices.

"Are you ever coming downstairs, Mum?" Neave pleaded. "You're taking forever. You haven't even changed yet."

"I think the chicken nuggets and chips may be burning," Dylan added. "Just saying."

Matthew looked like he too was about to go up in smoke with them. Siobhan almost laughed.

"Matthew, can you please check on dinner while I change?" Siobhan requested as diplomatically as she dared. She sat on the bed, bone-tired, her spirit exhausted.

"Of course," Matthew said with his counterfeit courtesy. "It would be my pleasure."

Once he had barreled out of the room, Dylan sat beside her and wrapped his arm around Siobhan. "Hey, Mum?"

"Yes, love?"

"I've told everyone at school you work in the Gherkin." Dylan puffed his chest out like King Kong.

Siobhan swatted playfully at Dylan, grateful for his distraction. "It's a pretty tall building, but it isn't quite the Gherkin."

"You never know, one day you might work there, and Dad will be even more pissed off."

"Language, Dylan!"

"You could even star on that television show." Dylan nudged her, grinning. "Especially with your terrible dance moves."

"Ignore him, just because he dances like he's waiting in the queue for the toilet." Neave, sitting on her other side, kissed her on the cheek, then her expression turned serious. "Do you think Dad's going to be in a bad mood all night?" Her eyes were wide open now.

"You let me worry about that, darling." It made her heart hurt that her children were so affected by their father.

"Dinner's ready!" Matthew's voice boomed up the stairs.

No one hastened to join him.

"When we go to the seaside tomorrow," Dylan said, holding still in expectation, "will it be just the three of us?"

Neave cuddled closer. "Please?"

Siobhan rolled her head back and forth, smiling. "Yes, just the three of us."

"Great! Because Dad's a dick!"

"Dylan, you cannot speak about your father like that." Siobhan scolded him despite his unerring, if inarticulate, description.

"What's a dick?" Neave asked as Dylan sniggered.

"A rude word we will *not* be using in this house. Now why don't you show us the Robot." Siobhan planted her feet firmly in position and began to move, first one arm, stopping to then move the other. She wobbled back and forth in between, mimicking a machine for dramatic effect. "Work with me here."

Neave did, popping her arms, legs, and torso in an imitation of squeaky hinges.

Dylan buried his head underneath a pillow and kicked his legs. "If this is my punishment, I'll never call Dad anything ever again!"

Neave ignored him in favor of focusing on her dance-off with Siobhan.

For her part, Siobhan threw herself into the routine as if she were rehearsing for a performance. She was glad of the diversion, as silly as it was. Upheaval was coming for the children, there could be no doubt, and the thought of turning their world upside down made her feel immeasurably guilty. In some ways she had failed them by living a lie all these years. Yet if she hadn't made that choice, she wouldn't have Dylan and Neave now and they were her world, the unconditional love she felt for them getting her out of bed each morning. In the long run she knew her decision would benefit all of them, but right now it was hard not to feel like an artist too focused on the brushstrokes that she couldn't see the bigger picture.

CHAPTER FOUR

They say the best things take time."

Siobhan's unpredictable entrance and breathy laughter had Cassie curious as she watched Siobhan stumble into her office, arms sagging under the weight of the box she carried. For a woman usually so well put together, Siobhan looked discombobulated, a frenetic feel to her energy as her humor missed the mark.

"Which is why I'm late."

Cassie took in the sight of Siobhan: ruffled suit, windswept hair, soaking wet coat. To top it all off, she had a stain in the middle of her shirt.

"I cannot tell you how sorry I—" The bottom of the soggy box Siobhan was carrying fell through, its contents scattering across the floor. "Shit!"

Cassie sighed internally. She should help her. She knew she should. "You look like you could use a hand," she said, and didn't offer one. The last thing she wanted was to appear nice. Siobhan had only a meager collection anyway: a photo of her kids, a coffee mug now minus the handle, and a small cactus plant. It was kind of sad, really. "Did you forget we have a meeting with a brand new client?" Cassie asked, stubbing out her cigarette.

"I don't think you should be doing that in here." Siobhan pointed at the ashtray.

Cassie ignored her. "And that you offered to take the lead on this meeting, which I allowed, against my better judgment?"

"It's been one of those mornings where—"

• 35 •

"Here I was, thinking you were blossoming under my direction. Then the honeymoon period ends and you start slacking off." She raised an eyebrow, allowing time for an explanation.

"Please don't doubt my commitment to the role, Ms. Townsend." Siobhan launched into an explanation from where she knelt on the floor, picking up her things—Cassie caught something about her son projectile vomiting in her car, followed by mention of some sort of ambiguous appointment. As per usual, she wasn't fully taking notice. Her mind was on the meeting ahead, and on not looking at the slight cleavage showing in the V-neck of Siobhan's blouse.

Summoning an ounce of sympathy, Cassie crossed to the coffee machine and began preparing an Americano, reasoning that if she rallied to Siobhan's aid, her trainee might not be totally unproductive today after all.

"Here." Cassie handed the drink over to Siobhan, who took a long sip.

"You remembered how I take my coffee?" Siobhan asked, smiling gratefully.

Busted, Cassie bristled. "No. It's an educated guess, though I have been paying attention." Realizing how that sounded, she clarified, "It's my job to anticipate people's needs." Realizing how *that* sounded, she glared at the stain on Siobhan's shirt. "You can't rock up at today's meeting looking such a mess," she said, scrunching up her nose. "Lucky for you, I keep a spare shirt in my cupboard."

"You're very kind, but I don't want to take something you might need later."

"It's no problem. I can go out in this." She indicated her Oxford shirt, the color of midnight. "Helena won't mind."

"Is Helena your girlfriend?" Siobhan asked, then quickly buried her face behind the rim of her mug, her cheeks pink.

"Christ, no!" Cassie felt her own coffee dribble down her chin. She hastened to wipe it away but must have failed to do so discreetly because Siobhan looked like she was trying not to laugh. "I don't have a girlfriend, and getting one certainly isn't on my bucket list of things to do before I die. Eternally free and single, that's me." Cassie wondered why the words felt so empty as she said them. It wasn't like she was interested or wanted anything more than to simply undress Siobhan with her eyes; that was hardly a crime. Anything more was definitely off the table.

"You're more a love-them-and-leave-them kind of woman?" Siobhan's expression was neutral. "Not that it's any of my business."

Right now, Cassie felt like she could conquer the world, despite Siobhan's alarmingly accurate assessment being bang on the money. "You don't hold back, do you?"

Siobhan looked like she expected to be swallowed up whole by Cassie any second.

"Don't worry about overstepping the mark. My reputation has always been something I take great pride in. Does that surprise you?"

"Not really." Siobhan pulled at her wedding ring. "It's just that—"

"You expected someone as charming and enigmatic as me to have a partner," Cassie finished for her, offering a playful grin.

"Well, there must be *someone* out there who can handle a woman with *such* a formidable reputation. Someone who likes a challenge perhaps?"

Siobhan's eyes sparkled with what Cassie liked to call *potential*. "Well, as much as I'd love to sit here, put my feet up and discuss my love life all day, we're due in a meeting." Cassie glanced at her watch. "Very soon."

Cassie pulled out the shirt as promised and handed it over. It was one of her favorites: a cornflower blue Ralph Lauren number with a button-down collar. She often picked it out if she was in a rush, or was heading somewhere for an impromptu date, not that dating had been on her mind recently, since women were off the cards.

"I'll step outside to give you some privacy. I wouldn't want anyone to think that shirt came out of my closet, or worse still, that you did."

Siobhan had already begun unbuttoning her shirt, apparently untroubled by changing in front of Cassie.

Cassie faced away and pretended to study the notes she had made for their meeting. It was practically impossible for them to hold her attention, but she tried admirably, staring at the words so hard they practically jumped off the paper at her. Her fingers quivered. "You've prepared for today? You're confident?" Cassie's eyes never left her notes.

"I'm a little nervous, but yes. I have everything in order."

"As I would expect by this point in your training."

Siobhan fumbled with the buttons on the shirt at the exact moment Cassie gave up and decided to turn around. Cassie found she had to concentrate on tensing her muscles, mentally coaching herself to fight off her arousal before her jaw threatened to hit the floor. Siobhan had a wonderful, toned stomach, and where her hips began, she had well-defined curves in exactly the right places. She only just remembered to breathe as she moved her eyes back up to striking, full breasts. The freckled skin above her breasts looked so smooth.

"You're probably wondering how I stay in shape," Siobhan said as Cassie cursed herself for being so obvious.

"I wasn't wondering anything—"

"My daughter has some fierce dance routines and I've been known to bust the odd move or two," Siobhan said.

"Come on. We should get going. We're already late, and people tend to let their imaginations run a little wild here. Especially Julie."

"In what way?"

"Oh, you know, the usual. Who I've taken on top of my desk this week, that sort of thing."

"I highly doubt that is the sole focus of anyone's conversation." Siobhan brushed off the remark coolly.

Cassie laughed. "Well, where do you stand on that?"

"On what?"

"Being the subject of idle gossip…or…well, you know what the other option is." She threw what she hoped was a teasing look.

Siobhan's brow furrowed in apprehension. Or perhaps condemnation. Cassie couldn't quite tell as she studied her and watched her fiddle once more with that damn wedding ring.

"I think we need to put a stop to this conversation. I don't know what you're insinuating, but if you think I've led you on in some way, then I'm sorry. That was certainly *never* my intention."

"I wasn't trying to…I didn't mean anything by it, it's a habit." Cassie felt the blood rushing to her ears. "A bad habit. You know you *are* perfectly safe with me, don't you?" She searched Siobhan's expression. "You have *nothing* to worry about."

Siobhan's back stiffened, her eyes bulging ever so slightly. Was she insulted or relieved that Cassie wasn't about to come on to her?

"You don't need to keep reminding me of your 'happily married' status by tugging on that thing either." Cassie nodded towards the wedding ring, angry with herself for even caring what Siobhan might think of her. "I'm a total professional."

"Right, let's get going then," Siobhan said, dodging out of the conversation and Cassie's office.

When the meeting began, Cassie's mind was all over the place. She was totally inept at reading Siobhan, and it bothered her more than it should have. A couple of hours later, two more pressing things troubled her. First was the fact Siobhan had absolutely dazzled, winning the client over with the same ease Cassie usually mastered. She had been outshone and she knew it.

What concerned her more was her inability to focus on the task in hand, instead fretting over what she had said to Siobhan and whether she had put her professionalism at risk. She went through life throwing out flippant remarks and not giving them a second thought, but Siobhan's disapproval, if that's what it was, bothered her. She had given up attempting to contribute halfway through their meeting, instead running their previous encounter over in her mind. She had sought out eye contact numerous times, hoping the offer of a warm smile would limit the damage, but every time she tried, she found herself rebuffed.

"Well, you smashed that like an absolute pro," Cassie said, swinging her feet up onto her desk and knocking a pile of folders to the floor in the process. The queen of cool was losing it. She swept her hair off her face and pretended not to notice the mess.

"Thanks. I'm going to start working on the Ryman deal. If you need me, I'll be at my desk."

"Part of your training involves analyzing your performance. We should do that now."

"You just told me: I smashed it like a pro." Siobhan laughed but it sounded forced. Worse still, she made absolutely no effort to fill the awkward silence that followed, instead picking up a folder from the floor and flicking through it as she waited to be dismissed, leaving Cassie no choice but to set the record straight. Well, as straight as she could manage anyway.

"About what I said earlier…I don't really have sex on my desk." Cassie offered Siobhan an almost smile. "There are better places to do it."

"Noted, although it's really none of my business."

"A lot of people make it their business."

"That's hardly surprising considering how…open you are." She looked flustered. "I mean how comfortable you are…in your own skin. I wish I had half your confidence."

"What do you have to be insecure about?" Cassie asked, genuinely curious.

"I need to get back to the Ryman deal, Ms. Townsend." A distant look was back in Siobhan's eyes.

"Shit," Cassie muttered, irked by her inability to make neither head nor tail of Siobhan and further frustrated by the fact she even cared in the first place. "You're not the only one whose particular talent is inserting the whole steel-toe-capped boot into the ever-so-slightly audacious gob."

"We have…It's common ground…" Siobhan stumbled over her words. "It seems…" She bit down on her lip, remaining aloof much to Cassie's annoyance.

"Is that the remix version?" Cassie changed tack, expecting to see Siobhan's body loosen and relax with the joke. Nothing. She reached for her cigarettes, then shut the drawer without retrieving one. "You really did do a commendable job today," Cassie tried again.

"Thank you. Now, if you'll excuse me, I really do need to get back to it."

Cassie picked up a folder and then slammed it down on her desk, irritation getting the better of her. "I thought we'd agreed my middle name isn't actually Unapproachable."

"Did we?"

Cassie couldn't tell whether Siobhan was in accord or if she were just smiling because it was expected of her.

"Then why am I feeling like I've had my wrists slapped? You don't need to look at me with such disapproval. It really was just a joke."

"Look, I'm here to succeed. I know today didn't get off to the best start with me being late, but this job means everything to me," Siobhan offered in a steady voice, exuding calm and focus. "I can't afford distractions."

"Likewise. I plan on running this place one day in the not-so-distant future," Cassie said, feeling the need to assert her authority, despite wondering if there were something deeper under the surface of Siobhan's determination. "My success is inevitable."

CHAPTER FIVE

Siobhan had lost count of the number of tasks she had started and abandoned as she clock-watched that morning. Finally, the clock struck lunch, the appointed hour of her consultation with Cassie, who'd insisted on repeating her review of Siobhan's performance. That in itself was progress. Cassie had given up her lunch hour to speak with Siobhan. She still felt on edge around her because she had no idea what Cassie might do or say next—or more importantly, how she was supposed to respond.

Taking a final calming breath, she knocked on Cassie's partially open door. "Are you ready for me?"

"Armed and ready," came the response as Cassie wielded a plastic ruler, swinging it around her head like a gladiator about to duel for honor.

Siobhan drew her notebook up over her chest, placing it against her heart as a shield for protection, her nerves abating. "Do I need to seek cover?"

"Thank goodness I'm no longer offending you," Cassie remarked, sounding relieved—or at least relaxed. "And I see that you've finally given in to my witty banter."

"Oh, I'm not giving in to *anything*."

Siobhan took the seat opposite Cassie, folding her hands together and circling her thumbs. She had no idea if she was reading too much into the situation, but every time she was around Cassie, she was unsure whether she wanted the flirtation to continue or was frustrated that it hadn't.

"So," Cassie cleared her throat, "we're here to review your performance, remember? No point delaying the inevitable."

Siobhan was conscious of the blush searing her cheeks and chose to avert her gaze. The last thing she wanted was for Cassie to think she couldn't take any form of criticism. She waved the notebook and pen at her. "I'm planning on making notes, Ms. Townsend, so you best make it noteworthy."

Cassie's jaw clenched. "I'm not accustomed to giving positive feedback."

"Well, why don't you have a go and I'll let you know how it goes?" Siobhan said. "If you can forget you're meant to be hating it, you might not be half bad at it."

"Whose performance are we analyzing here?" Cassie tilted her head to the side and pursed her lips, before covering them with her hand.

Siobhan wondered if Cassie was in danger of breaking into a smile.

"Mine would be easy. I'm the best investment banker this company has ever seen and that's saying something. Nothing else needs to be said."

"Aren't you supposed to be giving me positive feedback, rather than yourself?" Siobhan asked, rubbing her eyelid. She noticed Cassie open her mouth to speak, but felt the need to continue. "It's fair to say you've taught me a lot in a short space of time; it's been fascinating," Siobhan admitted. "You've given me some pretty amazing experiences this week, letting me lead on both the Miller and Ryman deals. I appreciate that." She formed a steeple with her fingers and pressed her lips towards it.

Cassie shuffled in her chair before she spoke. "A decent review, thanks. I have to say you've impressed me this week. You *seem* to be able to turn your hand to anything." She appeared to stare out of the window for a moment. "I don't like to admit it, but working with you has been…bearable. Though it does slightly piss me off that you handle clients just as well as I do."

A satisfied smile, followed by a deep chuckle as realization dawned. "Thank you for holding me in such high esteem. It means a lot to know I'm doing a good job." She smiled. "I honestly can't remember the last time I felt appreciated," she admitted, more to herself than to Cassie, who let out an exasperated sigh.

"There's a huge client coming in for an initial meeting next Wednesday," Cassie continued. "Another massive deal. I wondered how you'd feel about working together on it, rather than me running it alone."

"I would love that, Cassie!" Siobhan enthused. Realizing her mistake, she wrung her hands, cleared her throat, and amended, "I would love that, Ms. Townsend."

"You may call me Cassie. I'm hoping we can put that little episode last week behind us. I don't want you to think anything of it."

Siobhan froze momentarily, but she did well to plaster a smile onto her face to hide any disappointment she may or may not feel. The lines suddenly felt blurry. "It's forgotten. Though I hope I didn't make you feel uncomfortable either."

Cassie shrugged. "Not at all. Like I said, witty banter."

"Well, it's great that's all sorted then," Siobhan said, and promptly concentrated on her notebook.

Cassie groaned, startling Siobhan when she launched herself across the room on her leather chair, rolling it close to where Siobhan sat. They were almost but not quite within touching distance.

"Dare I ask who doesn't appreciate you?"

Siobhan's palms started sweating and her knee began bouncing. Marital strife was not the sort of thing one discussed with a work colleague. "I could do with photocopying the files for next week," she said. "I'll look over them at the weekend, so I'm up to speed."

Cassie arched her eyebrow. "They're here." She pointed to a pile of folders, ordered and ready to go. "I asked Julie to photocopy them to save you time." Cassie's attention seemed to drift momentarily, but it wasn't away for long. "Sounds like you don't have plans this weekend, if your highlight is reading these files."

"I have plans. I'm taking the kids to London Zoo." She laughed when Cassie's face scrunched up like the ball of paper she aimed at the waste bin. "I can tell you've never been, because if you had, you would be all smiles instead of glowering."

"Animals and children." Cassie pushed her chair back towards her desk. "My ideal combination."

"What's your favorite animal?" Siobhan asked, ignoring the theatrics.

Cassie glanced at her. "I don't have one."

"You didn't even stop to consider. I reckon even you'd crack a smile at the monkeys monkeying around."

"Ah, yes, maybe they'd be a chimp off the old block." Cassie rolled her eyes.

"Go on, give me your favorite." Siobhan pressed, undeterred by Cassie's apathy. She wanted to get to know the woman beneath the polished, if sometimes rough, exterior.

"If you're going to force me to answer such a ridiculous question, I'd have to say giraffes."

"We like them too! They have a canopy at London Zoo where you can feed them. You pick treats from the herb garden and then you watch them munching away." Siobhan wasn't sure why she couldn't stop talking, but she plowed ahead regardless. "It's quite fascinating. You wouldn't believe the length of a giraffe's tongue."

Cassie sucked in her cheeks, as if trying her best to keep a straight face, but she couldn't hold it together and began to chuckle. "I don't think I've ever met anyone who can speak with such enthusiasm about a giraffe's tongue."

"You should come with us." Siobhan slipped farther down her chair as she realized what she had just said. Her voice weakened. "You might enjoy it."

"If I'm ever in need of the company of rampaging rhinos or horny hippos, you'll be my first port of call."

The lightheadedness and accelerated heartbeat came on without the least bit of warning, and Siobhan was glad she was already seated. The thought of Cassie wandering around the zoo with her, all wisecracks and playful teasing, appealed to her more than she wanted to admit.

"And your weekend?" Siobhan asked, shifting focus.

Cassie ran a hand through her hair. "There's actually a gig that my sister's begged me to go to, but she has terrible taste."

Siobhan's eyes drifted to the new addition in Cassie's office: a Florence and the Machine tour poster, signed by Florence herself, which took pride of place on the wall.

"I'd much rather go with the Flo," Cassie said with a grin. "There's not many women I'd go out of my way to please, but she would be one.

I would treat *her* like royalty." Cassie went all googly-eyed and faked a swoon.

"She's a distinctive-looking woman, I'll give you that, but I'd always go for a blond." Cassie's spine seemed to straighten as she sat up in her chair. Siobhan had her attention now. Her pulse began to race. Why was her tongue running away with her? And why was she thinking of her tongue in tandem with Cassie? *Shit.* "What I mean is, *if* I were going to go for a woman, it would be someone like the West End's leading lady herself, Kerry Ellis."

"The Wicked Witch of the West?" This time Cassie ran both hands slowly through her blond hair, leaving them there for a moment as she smirked.

"She's blond in real life, you know, flowing locks and dreamy blue eyes, not to mention her killer smile. Not that I've paid much attention," Siobhan hastened to clarify, coming back to earth with a bang. "Anyway, what's the gig? It can't be that bad. If nothing else, you'll get to enjoy your sister's company."

"There's no way I'm putting my name to a Drake concert. Eva has a fiancé for shit like this. Besides, she loves a bit of kiss and tell and I've nothing to share."

"It's Eva who lives by the sea in Broadstairs, right?"

"Have you been taking notes?" Cassie stared at Siobhan for longer than was quite proper and then busied herself with a folder full of notes. Siobhan watched, entertained, as the notes rained down all over Cassie's desk in disorder.

"I pay attention. But that's a reason to visit, Drake or not. Take me anywhere I can see the ocean and I'm happy. I took the kids down to Camber Sands last weekend." She bit her lip as Cassie began fiddling with a pen, seemingly losing interest in the conversation. "I mean, there's always an incident with a seagull; this time it involved Dylan and his chips, but—"

"Will your husband be joining you at the zoo?" Cassie interrupted, her tone sharp and forthright. Leaning forward, she added, with more derision than interest, "Does he have a favorite animal too?"

"Matthew and I don't exactly…" She stopped mid-sentence. She wasn't at all sure she should have this conversation now, with someone she hardly knew. "We don't really spend much time together."

Siobhan could swear she saw Cassie's lips twitch at this information. Or was she imagining things?

"Does he work away?" Cassie asked.

"Oh, no, not at all; he's a carpenter with a workshop in Greenhill. We just live very separate lives. Being married to him is a thankless task." Siobhan couldn't understand why she kept divulging information about her life. She was normally very private.

"So it *is* Matthew underappreciating you?" Cassie spun her chair around, probably in another attempt to avoid eye contact, and remained silent so Siobhan could answer. When she didn't, Cassie said, "I liked you better when you were stumbling in late, all presumably happily married. Now I just feel bad for you. But if he doesn't appreciate you, someone has to?"

"I'm not sure what you're getting at," Siobhan murmured, disconcerted by Cassie's assumptions.

"Let's just say if you did have a secret, I'm a pretty good person to divulge it to. Mainly because nine times out of ten I'm not listening." Cassie spun all the way around in her chair, as if to reiterate the point. "If you're having a fling with the postman, who doesn't seem to deliver to you on Fridays, then you can tell me." She stopped spinning at Siobhan's expression. "What's that face for?"

"I'm just surprised that you've paid enough attention to remember me complaining about Friday's post. You pull off disinterest with such aplomb. And for the record, just so we're one hundred percent clear on this, the postman is not my type."

"You have a type?" Cassie poked fun at her.

"Shared interests, the ability to engage in conversation, sense of humor is a big one and of course basic respect. Am I asking too much?"

"So you *are* seeing someone else?" Cassie moved forward in her seat. "I'm a big fan of illicit affairs," she whispered with a wink.

"Is there any other kind?" Siobhan asked, but when she didn't receive a response, she felt it important to point out something else. "For someone who's not keen on being the subject of office gossip, you seem to take a remarkable amount of pleasure in gossiping."

"I—"

"I'm not seeing anyone." Just because Cassie seemed to find this sort of thing exciting, didn't mean she had to display the same mislaid moral compass. "And I haven't really spoken to anyone about my marriage." Her voice faltered as she realized how near to breaking point she was. "In truth, you're the first person I've told." Siobhan blinked away the tears that were forming, hoping Cassie hadn't noticed. "If I start talking now, I won't bloody stop."

Cassie reached out as if to touch Siobhan, but when Siobhan looked at her hand, she rapidly retracted it. "Best not start then or—"

"Eight years of marriage and all I have to show for it is two gorgeous children and a big fucking headache. The kids are the best thing that's ever happened to me, but the rest is just one fucked-up disaster and—" She stopped short.

Cassie resembled a rabbit caught in a snare: leg twitching, gaze darting around the room.

"You don't have to look so trapped. I'm sorry I overshared."

"I don't think I'm the best person to discuss this with. We hardly know one another, and I don't know the first thing about marriage."

"Perhaps in some ways that makes you easier to talk to." Why was she pushing it? She should turn around and leave. She should keep the professional boundary between them. But it felt so good to open up to someone.

There was a long pause before Cassie answered. "Perhaps."

She took it as a sign to keep going. "I only married him because I was pregnant and didn't know what else to do. It was the worst decision I could have made, but he was very persuasive. I was too focused on being pregnant and unmarried to think clearly, but that's my fault. I knew my own mind, even back then, but I wasn't strong enough to carry through my convictions."

"That surprises me."

Siobhan left her seat and walked over to the window. She gazed out across the city, admiring its breathtaking beauty. Tall buildings reaching up to the sky, like sunflowers yearning for light, shared space with buildings that were shorter but more historic. Arrows of sunlight laced through the clouds, suggesting spring was well on her way, and the city seemed to come alive under Siobhan's watchful stare.

"Is that St. Paul's Cathedral from *Mary Poppins*?" She broke the silence, feeling the need to fill the air with something.

"That's the second musical theater reference you've given me today. I love the theater, though I don't find the time to see many shows these days."

When a robust blend of musk and cedarwood wafted into her nose, Siobhan realized Cassie had joined her at the window. "I'm a big fan," she shared, as they stood by side, "but like you, I haven't been for years. My daughter went through a 'Supercalifragilistic' phase. We couldn't even manage the school run without hearing it at least three times. Eventually, my nerves became super fragile." She shook her head, amused at the memory.

"Mine would have snapped like a kite string." Cassie's eyes remained fixed on the landscape. "It's a beautiful building. Have you ever been inside?"

"I'm not really a visiting-religious-buildings kind of person." She began to laugh, mainly at the ridiculous turn their conversation had taken.

"Yet you love gaping at wild animals, who as a rule will no doubt be inappropriately mating!" Cassie gave her a playful nudge. "Religion or sex, I know which I'm picking."

Siobhan swallowed the lump forming in her throat. Her face, neck, and ears all felt impossibly hot, and she had a sudden compulsion to flee the room.

"I'm going to go make a start on reading this, if we're done?" she said, hoping she'd be dismissed before any remaining poise she possessed evaporated like a puddle on a sunny day. "I hope you enjoy your weekend, whatever you decide to do."

Siobhan felt Cassie's gaze drilling into her like a ground auger. She pulled hard on her wedding ring, hoping Cassie couldn't see the sweat forming on her brow. It didn't help when she looked at Cassie and found her running her finger along the edge of her shirt collar.

"Hideous music and awkward conversations," Cassie said. "I can think of better ways to spend a weekend. By the way, you're blushing again. I'll try and ignore that fact."

Cassie turned her back on Siobhan and pulled her chair back towards her desk. She picked up a pencil and scribbled with such force that the tip broke. She flung it down and began to tap her fingers on the desk.

Clearly, she'd hit some kind of nerve. Instead of going back to her desk, Siobhan grabbed her handbag and was about to head into the bathroom, when she overheard Julie on the phone.

"She's been spat out of the dragon's mouth. I've got to go." Julie put the phone down, her eyes narrowing. "You look frazzled," she said, peering over the edges of her glasses to examine Siobhan. "Have you two had a lovers' tiff?"

"We've just done my performance review," Siobhan said, figuring it was the safest answer.

"Ah. She reviewed your performance. That's why you look like you're about to burst into tears. Poor thing. You were always going to be demolished the minute you walked into the Minotaur's den."

"It's not like that between us."

"It's not like that between you *yet*," Julie corrected her.

Siobhan could feel Julie's gaze scorching her suit jacket as she marched up the corridor to the bathroom. Examining herself in the mirror, she wasn't sure what her eyes betrayed, but she raised her eyebrow in disapproval at the rosiness that remained in her cheeks.

Cassie had her on the back foot, divulging things she had never spoken to anyone about, including her attraction towards blonds. Of all the things to say, she cursed herself for her honesty, yet for some reason Cassie coaxed it out of her. She needed to be more on guard, remembering that she was here to do a job, and that she needed to remain professional at all times. There was no point aiming to improve herself and make a new life for her and the children, if she was going to mess up her chances by saying too much. She would say nothing, keep her cards close to her chest and get on with her job. Anything else right now was far too risky.

CHAPTER SIX

Thought you'd appreciate this! Cassie typed into her mobile, captioning the photo she'd taken of the light illuminating the ocean.

The tranquility of Minnis Bay was very different from the buzzing family beach at Camber Sands, but she had a hunch Siobhan would love it here too. Not that she was thinking of Siobhan, but if she were, Cassie couldn't think of a more delightful distraction from the unknowns of the day ahead than her incredibly head-turning hot trainee. When she'd told Siobhan about her weekend plans with her sister, she'd declined to mention she'd also be seeing her mum, and potentially not seeing her dad. That was none of Siobhan's business.

Cassie turned back to her phone, reread what she'd written, and huffed in displeasure, deleting the message before shoving her phone back into her pocket.

Taking a deep breath, Cassie tilted her head back and let her eyes drift shut. The sun was beating down on her face, her skin tingling deliciously under its glorious rays. Now that she was no longer thinking about it, an idea came to her with ease. She whipped her phone out.

Making waves today! she composed quickly, so she wouldn't forget what she wanted to say. Next, she ran through the range of emojis that would best accompany the uncomplicated message. Grinning face? *No, too obvious.* Winking face? *No, too suggestive.* Face with rolling eyes? *No, too self-deprecating.* Giving it up as a bad job, she pressed send, rubbed the sand off her feet with her socks, and strode back to her car.

Fifteen minutes later, when Florence was no longer blasting out and the soft-top was no longer down, Cassie realized she'd spent the whole journey worrying about Siobhan's reply to her message—specifically, if she would even offer one and if she did, what it would say. Would Siobhan appreciate contact outside working hours? Or would she want to keep matters strictly professional? She wondered which prospect was more daunting.

Navigating the walkway to the beachfront property, she had similar thoughts about her father's presence—or absence. She paused at the threshold, wondering if most people knocked on their parents' door or if they simply walked straight in. Her stomach twisted into knots more complicated than the kind used to moor a boat. While waiting on the doorstep, she experimented with a range of facial expressions, from ecstatic to irritable, to the extent that a passerby might have thought she was practicing for a gurning festival.

The door swung open and Cassie's sister welcomed her with open arms, a familiar grin stretched across her face. "What took you so long?" Eva squeezed her like Cassie was a ketchup bottle and she wanted to extract the last dregs.

"I stopped at the beach."

"I told Mum you'd have done that. Come through. She's in the kitchen baking."

Cassie called up her apathetic expression. "And Dad? Is he here?"

Eva hesitated before answering. "Danny took Dad to look at wedding cars," she said, as if their father hadn't gone there of his own free will. "Believe it or not, it's the first thing either one of them has shown an interest in while we've been planning this whole wedding. I'm sure they'll be back soon."

"*Of course* he's decided to go check out wedding cars on the one day I visit. Oh well." Cassie shrugged, not sure who she was more disappointed in: her dad for disappearing or herself for foolishly hoping he wouldn't for once.

Cassie kissed her sister on the cheek. "It's good to see you."

"Cassie, where on earth have you been? We were expecting you an hour ago."

"So, that's the reason Dad isn't here? I'm late?"

A nervous laugh accompanied her mum's next remark. "Were you and Eva talking about the wedding?"

"I'll put the kettle on." Eva pushed Cassie towards her mum. "Give her a hug, she hasn't seen you in ages."

She walked across the room and embraced her mother, if only to hide the lie on her face as she spoke. "I've missed you." She disengaged, glanced at the floor, and began rocking back and forth on her heels.

"Have you?" her mother enquired, but it sounded more like skepticism than jubilation.

"Have *you*?" Cassie shot back.

"You're not even trying," Eva hissed before turning her best smile onto her mum. "Why don't you two go through to the living room? I'll bring the drinks. Did I mention Mum's been baking?"

"Twice now." Cassie made her way into the living room.

She perched on the sofa, the cushions swallowing her up like Cyclops, the one-eyed giant. She stared ahead, the flowery wallpaper playing havoc with her senses and reminding her of those Magic Eye pictures she'd had to stare at for ages as a child until something jumped out, usually something disappointing. Her mother's taste had always appalled her. Her gaze wandered to the photos on the bookshelves: a wedding portrait of her parents when they were young and carefree, a photo of Eva at her university graduation, a picture of Eva and Danny celebrating their engagement. Any visitor to the house could be forgiven for assuming they had only one child.

"What's new with you?" Her mother sat in the armchair opposite. "Are you still—"

"A lesbian?" Cassie finished for her, folding her arms.

Her mother shuffled in her chair, paying more attention to her own comfort than her daughter's petulance. "I was going to ask if you're still in the same office. See how you're doing generally."

"Oh," Cassie said flatly. "I thought perhaps you were going to ask if I'm still unphotogenic."

"What?"

"Look around." Cassie swept out her arms like she was conducting an orchestra. "Is somebody missing?"

"Do you think we need reminding how absent you are from our lives? It's not that we don't have any photos of you. We do, you know we do. We just have them tucked away for safekeeping," her mother stuttered like a bad record. "It's difficult not seeing you."

Cassie drew in a steady breath, using a carefully controlled tone. "It seems Dad's really struggling with it. That must be why he's made such an effort today. I'm right here, he's not." She would never admit how much her father's rejection stung, how she had hoped this visit would somehow be different to all the others; it wasn't in her nature.

"Do I need to remind you what happened last time you two were in a room together? You make things impossible."

This time Cassie swallowed down her anger. She felt like the main character from *Spring Awakening*, about to burst into a raucous rendition of "Totally Fucked." She smiled. Another reference Siobhan would appreciate. It was time to divert the conversation. "Eva said you two were in London last week, in the West End. Anything interesting?"

"*Wicked*. It was incredible. I tell you, you'd give the main character a run for her money; there are some remarkable similarities."

Cassie's brow furrowed. Why did her mother sound so wistful? And why were her mother's eyes shimmering like the sequined jacket Cassie had hidden away at the back of her wardrobe? She chose to ignore her mother's sentimentality. "Thanks for the invite."

"We snagged tickets at the last minute while we were out shopping. Not everything is a personal vendetta against you. You were working, but you're welcome to come with us next time, if you're not too busy chasing after women. You loved the theater when you were a kid."

"There it is, the fault-finding." A range of outrageous quips, designed with the sole purpose of winding her mum up flashed through her mind. Doubting her mum would recognize or respect any of these, she abstained, continuing with the simple truth. "Women chase after me, and if I choose to let them, that's my prerogative."

Her mum scrunched up her face and then released it. "I didn't mean...that came out wrong."

"Apparently, so did I!"

"I leave you two alone for two minutes and come back to find you sparring in a boxing ring."

Eva was doing a fine balancing act, carrying a tray full of hot drinks and cakes, which felt way out of place now. Cassie accepted the drink but had to hold her tongue at the glare that came with it. "We've been discussing Dad's disappearing acts during my visits. And my sexuality." Cassie grabbed the knife, cut herself a slice of cake the size of Great Britain and took a whacking great bite. "Great cake, Mum," she spoke angrily through a mouthful, giving her a thumbs-up. "Can I get some to go?"

"Cassie, please don't." Eva gave her a pained stare.

She slammed her plate onto the table. "You insist on me coming here, make me feel like absolute shit, and then wonder why I don't visit more often? Why do you even—"

"It's not like that." Her mother raised her voice. "You walked in looking for an argument. I get so frustrated with this bloody situation, with both you and your dad. I'm doing my best to acknowledge your choices, trying to crack a joke, keep things light. Your sexuality doesn't bother me, your behavior does. Honestly, Cassie, meeting your expectations of me would be impossible. You asked me when you came in if I missed you? Well, I do."

"Right." Cassie closed her eyes. "You don't mean it any more than I did. Please don't try to tell me Dad does either. It's been a long time since we spoke. In fact, the last words I remember us exchanging were...*I can't believe you're a dyke!* and *Fuck you!* It doesn't take a rocket scientist to work out who said what."

"It was a shock to him, you have to remember that."

"People recover from shock, even shocks that are more stupefying than that." Cassie raised her eyebrows, looking to Eva for support.

"Do we really need to dredge all this up again?" Eva shook her head. "It's not something that's going to get resolved right now."

"Or ever." Cassie tried to ignore the hurt when her sister didn't simply support her. "You always leap to his defense. You justify his behavior by blaming me for mine."

"I'm not blaming you. I just wish..." Her mother paused, as if contemplating how to put one foot in front of the other. "I just think maybe if you made some attempt to settle down, stopped with the performance, it would be easier to take you seriously, to take your sexuality seriously. At the moment all we have is a string of women, half of whom you only went with because they worked for your dad and that was your misguided attempt to get his attention."

"Or get back at him," Cassie said. "That too."

"The point is," her mother plowed ahead, "I want more for you."

Cassie eyed her with suspicion. "If I'd slept with a string of Dad's male coworkers, that would have been acceptable?"

"Did I say that? See, that's the problem here. You and your father are both so stubborn. There's never going to be a breakthrough until one of you becomes more compliant."

"Sorry to disappoint you, but that's not going to be me." Cassie sucked in her cheeks. "I need a cigarette."

"Grab your drink." Eva touched her arm. "Let's go into the garden."

Cassie welcomed the escape, though she did feel slightly guilty watching Eva perform the role of mediator. "You hate having a supporting role, don't you?" Cassie asked, joining her sister on a weathered bench.

"I don't hate being supportive," Eva answered as Cassie took her cigarettes out of her pocket and lit one up. "I just hate being caught in the middle, like Mum."

Cassie swallowed hard. She hadn't exactly looked at it from Eva's perspective. Or her mother's. In her eyes she was the victim and she always had been.

Eva rubbed her temple. "Give that here." She captured the cigarette and took a quick puff, then coughed before she gave it back.

"Better?" Cassie raised her eyebrow, her mouth twitching.

"No. This was a shit idea. I should've come to yours, knocked back a few G and T's, and Drake, here we come. I always think I'm acting for the best."

"And that's why I won't hold it against you," Cassie said, squeezing her sister's arm. "Much. Besides, you know I'd do anything for you, within reason."

"Would you not kick off like this at my wedding?" Eva asked.

"Certainly. Just sit me in another room, at—"

"—someone else's wedding," Eva finished with her.

Chuckling in spite of herself, Cassie took a final drag on her cigarette, the end burning red, then stubbed it out and took a swig of her now cold coffee.

"I'm sorry about Dad."

"Not your fault."

Cassie's backside began vibrating. She practically yanked her phone out of her pocket. When she realized the good vibrations were from Siobhan, she felt a lightness in her chest. *Gorgeous photo, but you aren't really on my level*, the message read, accompanied by a close-up of a giraffe, leaves ensnared in its protracted pink tongue.

Cassie couldn't help but smile at the photo, but she wished it included Siobhan, who was far more interesting than the giraffe. Still, at least she'd texted back. She wasn't about to analyze why it mattered.

"You look like you're knee-deep in a fantasy," Eva teased her.

"It's just a text from a coworker." Cassie whisked her phone back into her pocket.

"From the absorbed look on your face, it must be a female coworker. Tell me it's someone you like. Mum will be made up, she just wants you to settle down."

"I don't *like* her. I just don't mind looking at her."

"You never know, you could like her if you allow yourself to. You had *one* bad experience and ever since then, your natural instinct has been to run."

"Actually, my new natural instinct is to want someone entirely unobtainable. So no, I couldn't like her, because I can't. It's not an option." Why did saying it out loud bother her? She never cared if a woman was unavailable. She simply moved on to the next one. It was tedious, this thinking about someone all the time.

Eva rolled her eyes. "That's your standard excuse for saying it won't ever work out: picking the wrong women. You could try a different approach and look for someone who is both appropriate and available."

"What fun would that be?" Cassie teased her. Of course, Siobhan's appropriateness and availability had been at the forefront of her mind since their conversation yesterday, but her sister didn't need to know that. "Look, there's an attraction there, nothing more. Unless we sleep together. Then there'll be an orgasm there, nothing more. Unless we have multiples."

Eva shook her head. "I wish you'd open yourself up to *happiness* for once."

"You do remember Drake offends my ears. I suggest if you want this arrangement to go ahead, you need to stop needling me." Admonition aside, Cassie found it remarkable how much better she felt after spending just a few minutes outside with Eva. Her sister could read her like an instruction manual, pick the one thing Cassie wouldn't want calling out on, and call her out on it anyway. Cassie loved her for it.

Eva leaned back against the bench. "Remember how you said you'd do anything for me, within reason? Well, is it reasonable to expect you to come back inside and share a civil conversation with Mum before we make a move? Chat to her about the weather if you must, just don't leave things like this. She really *did* want to see you."

"Fine." Cassie sighed. "I'm sure we can discuss the weather in great depth. Just give me five minutes to recalibrate."

Eva nodded and retreated into the house.

As Cassie stood alone in the garden, she wondered how things had turned sour so quickly. Was she at fault in some capacity? Perhaps she didn't even *have* the capacity for normal human interaction. Siobhan certainly thought so. After all, she did say *You really aren't on my level*. Was she reading too much into what had been a simple, friendly message?

Cassie took her phone out of her pocket and prepared to reply to Siobhan's last message, but before she could respond, another text popped up: *Enjoying your day in Broadstairs?*

Cassie tapped her tongue against the roof of her mouth, considering how to describe the day. It was all very…theatrical. *If this afternoon were a matinee*, she typed, *it would be called…*

A surplus of possibilities flashed through her mind like titles on a theater marquee, each one bordered by blinding light bulbs: *Sunday in the Dark Without Mark*, *My Foul Lady*, and her personal favorite, *Anything Goes (Except Lesbianism)*. Reluctant to reveal too much, she finally decided on *Beauty and the Beastly Time*. And an emoji face with a hand covering the mouth.

After taking one last glance at the goofy-looking giraffe, she put her phone back in her pocket and steeled herself for the second act.

CHAPTER SEVEN

D o you fancy a celebratory drink? That deal didn't seal itself."
Cassie perched on the edge of Siobhan's desk, swinging her
legs. "There's a stylish little underground bar just across the road—
Electric Shuffle. Helena and I often bob in after work. You fancy it?"

"Sure. I'll give Matthew a ring, let him know I'll be home late."

"Great!" Cassie pushed off the desk and headed down the hallway.
"I'll meet you there. Just slip down the cobblestone alley. You can't
miss it."

Once Cassie was out of view, Julie came into it. "A personal
invitation from Cassie herself. You really have excelled, unless there's
something you're not telling me?" Julie's eyes narrowed to pinpricks.

"I'm really good at my job." Having shut down Julie, she
proceeded to do the same to her computer. She wasn't about to give the
office gossip any fodder.

En route to the bar, Siobhan reached into her handbag, took out
her phone, and prepared to press *Call*, then hovered in hesitation. A
text message would suffice. Straight to the point, no opportunity for
discussion. Plus, she wouldn't have to hear his voice.

*Dragged out by coworkers to Electric Shuffle for drinks. Please
remember to pick the kids up from after-school club.* She contemplated
adding more detailed directions, but if Matthew couldn't complete
basic tasks like dinner and bedtime, Dylan and Neave were competent
enough to provide instructions. She had no need to feel guilty about
going out.

Upon entering the bar, which wasn't difficult to find considering
there were only three bars in the vicinity and only one to be entered

from a cobblestone alley, Siobhan found Cassie perched on a stool, chatting away to a woman behind the bar. Siobhan couldn't help but wonder how they knew each other, and her mind went blank when she realized Cassie had changed into the very same stylish shirt she had lent out the previous week, and it fit her to a tee.

When their eyes met, Cassie stared back for what felt like an age, then took a long sip of her drink and playfully bit the straw.

Siobhan waited for Cassie to introduce her to the woman she'd been chatting up, but instead Cassie hopped down from her stool. With her drink in one hand and Siobhan's elbow in the other, Cassie guided Siobhan away from the bar, in apparent pursuit of a corner booth.

Siobhan glanced over her shoulder, only to find herself on the receiving end of stiletto-sized daggers from the woman Cassie had abandoned. Well, it answered at least a little of the question as to how they knew one another.

Her phone vibrated. By the light of the old-fashioned street lantern on the table, Siobhan checked her screen. Three missed calls from Matthew and a text. *Have you left yet?* She longed to ignore him, but the fear that he would spend the whole evening bombarding her with texts made her structure a reply. *Just arrived. I won't be back late.*

"I've ordered a bottle of prosecco. Are you hungry?" Cassie took the seat opposite. "This place serves legendary sandwiches, if that's your thing."

"What's not to like about a sandwich?"

Cassie tapped her temple, as if the question demanded serious thought. "Hummus, beetroot, cress, raw onions, rocket, and absolutely any form of egg or fish, to name but a few."

Siobhan raised her eyebrow. "Did you think if you'd invited me out for celebratory sandwiches, I would have declined?"

"I know which side my bread is buttered on," Cassie said. "Though it's not my condiment of choice. Speaking of which, how do you take your chips? The answer to this question could impact heavily on your future."

"With ketchup?" Siobhan squeezed her eyes shut.

"Thank fuck for that!" Cassie laughed and waved to a waiter, who was sauntering over laden with an ice bucket, glasses, and a bottle of prosecco.

Siobhan took the opportunity to check her phone again. This time, there were no texts, just two missed calls and one voice mail. She didn't have to listen to know what it said: *You shouldn't have gone out tonight without arranging childcare.*

"Job done." Cassie surprised Siobhan by getting out of her seat and scooting up next to her in their booth.

"Three glasses? Are we expecting company?" Siobhan asked, dropping her phone back into her handbag.

"Give it half an hour or so and Helena will be rocking up. She somehow gets a whiff of drinks after work and boom." Cassie clicked her fingers. "She's here."

Siobhan was glad they'd have someone else with them. Being in a bar with Cassie felt a little too intimate. "You never did tell me, how was the gig?"

Cassie was about to speak when Siobhan's phone rang again. She picked it up and canceled the call, hoping it would go unnoticed. The last thing she wanted was Cassie thinking Matthew was keeping tabs on her.

"Overrated. My musical tastes are far more on point. Actually, I would rather have gone to see *Wicked* at the theater, but my sister saw the show a few weeks ago."

"I'm desperate to see *Wicked* too," Siobhan said. "We're finding more common ground it seems." Why it was important to have common ground she wasn't sure. Nor was she sure finding it was a good idea.

"The advertising poster is spectacularly Sapphic." Cassie's eyes widened. "Have you seen it? Glinda has to be whispering some sort of flirtatious banter into Elphaba's ear, of that I'm sure."

An image of Cassie murmuring cajoling sentiments into her ear galvanized a rise in Siobhan's body temperature. She hoped Cassie wouldn't notice that she had started perspiring. She focused on her breathing, trying to force a state of calm. "We should go see the show together. Then we'll know for sure." She wanted Cassie to see she could master the same confidence Cassie oozed. Before Cassie could answer, her phone rang again, and once more she silenced the call. So much for confident. She would have to choose between infuriated and infantilized.

"Is that the president of the Siobhan Carney Underappreciation Society?" Cassie asked, not unkindly.

"I'm sorry." Siobhan bowed her head. "He's quite persistent."

"When a woman gets persistent, I just drop her, problem solved."

"If only it were that easy to extract the problematic people from my life." Siobhan sighed. "Should I expect to be dropped any time soon?"

"I wasn't talking about you," Cassie said, sounding almost aggrieved by the admission. "Anyway, how did you two end up together? Was it love at first sight?"

This time it was a heavy sigh. "It was only ever about getting me into bed."

"Apparently that's what my mum thinks I do all day. Chase women into my bed."

"And is it?" Siobhan asked, despite herself. Cassie had pretty much said so herself in her office the other day, and she couldn't help but wonder if she exaggerated her reputation to keep people at bay. But then, maybe it was true, and Cassie's mum was right. Either way, it was dangerous getting any closer to Cassie, that she knew for sure.

"I don't think that's the sort of thing you need to be concerning yourself with." Cassie closed that line of conversation. "I've had enough of the third degree from my mum."

"I'd give anything for one more conversation with my mum. I miss her."

"What?" Cassie inclined her head, her brow creasing.

Siobhan took a deep breath. "She died when I was seventeen, totally out of the blue."

"I'm sorry." Cassie began to fiddle with the handle of the ice bucket. Yet her tone was softer than Siobhan had ever heard it. "I can't imagine how difficult that must've been for you."

"To lose both parents is tough—"

"Both?" Shock was evident in her tone.

"My father died before I was born. After Mum passed, the responsibility for the farm fell to me. We had a lot of farmhands, Matthew being one, and he really worked hard, especially after..." Siobhan steadied herself. "I've known him since I was a teenager. I went to an all-girls secondary school, so he was really the only boy I spent time with. I guess I sought solace in his arms. He had his motives, and I was a mess. It was a really tough time for me and he was there, though I can't honestly say he was a comfort."

"It sounds to me like he took advantage of the situation. That the two of you would never have been together had things been different. It certainly wasn't love at first sight." Siobhan could detect the disapproval in Cassie's voice, but Cassie followed it up with an eye roll for good measure.

"It really wasn't." Siobhan hesitated, scared that she was sharing too much, especially considering she didn't know Cassie all that well. Damn these complicated boundary issues. "I almost managed to hold him off through the whole of my time at Trinity in Dublin. Therein lies the downfall: *almost*." Siobhan's gaze settled on her wedding ring. "I graduated with honors and a baby on the way."

"Here you go." A waitress placed a platter of sandwiches and a bowl of chips on their table. "Would you like any sauces?"

"Ketchup," they both replied at the same time. Cassie raised her eyebrow, a smirk curling the corner of her mouth, as Siobhan tilted her head to the side, unable to prevent herself from smiling back, glad of the distraction.

"So how did you get from pregnant to married? That's a lot of relationship goals in one go."

Siobhan popped a chip into her mouth. "As you can probably tell, it wasn't planned. I'm from a rural village called Slane. You don't go back there unmarried and pregnant, not without becoming the talk of the town. I didn't want them to gossip like that about Orla's only child. I couldn't face tarnishing her reputation. It was so fucking hard."

Cassie exhaled. "That doesn't sound like a great starting point for a marriage."

"Not at all. Before I could start showing, he had me down the aisle and then whisked me over here, where his mother lives. I should never have settled for him—he was wrong for me in so many ways—but my mum wasn't there to talk me out of it. Deep down I knew she disliked Matthew, she thought he was dull and old-fashioned in his views. Turns out she was bang on."

"He couldn't have been wrong for you in *every* way," Cassie pressed, and her insistence both baffled and intrigued Siobhan. "I mean, you must have liked him at least a little back then."

"Not even that much. Honestly, Cassie, sometimes I look at him and I can't believe what I've done with my life. The things he comes out with, his lack of engagement, the way he treats the kids—"

"The way he treats *you*, by the sound of—"

"What have I missed? You ordered sandwiches without me! That shirt looks fantastic on you, Cassie. Is that the one you lent to your incredibly hot trainee?"

"Helena!" Cassie barked. "Helena, this is Siobhan, the head-turning hot trainee," she said, although it sounded more like a correction of Helena's characterization than an introduction between them.

Siobhan felt grateful she was sitting, given that her knees weakened at the mere thought of Cassie describing her as hot, preposterous as it was. It'd been a long time since anyone, let alone a lesbian sex symbol, had acknowledged her apparent attractiveness. She gulped down far too much wine in one go and began spluttering. Maybe now was the time to make her excuses; she could get home in time to put the kids to bed.

"There are worse things she could've said about you," Helena said, grabbing a chip. "I think you're getting off pretty lightly with incredibly hot."

"Can we stop saying incredibly hot?" Cassie performed the time-out action as if she were refereeing the world's dirtiest game of basketball.

"Only if we can start saying head-turning hot," Siobhan shot back. Her confidence kicked into even higher gear when Cassie's cheeks flushed postbox red.

"Now you're just fishing for compliments," Cassie said, her arm grazing Siobhan's side.

Siobhan felt an overwhelming urge to respond to the touch, but she held back. The queen of cool shuffled around in her seat, unbuttoning another button on her shirt, as if the temperature in the room had suddenly spiked.

Siobhan sat up a bit straighter, hoping but not hoping that the height change would afford her a glimpse of Cassie's cleavage.

"You really *are* fishing." Helena teased her, and Siobhan snapped back into a slump. "What else are you doing alone in this booth together with such an outrageous selection of sandwiches?"

"We *were* having a quiet drink." Cassie shook her head.

"Would you like me to work on a more subtle entrance? I can do it again."

"It's probably best if you reveal your true colors straight off. Where is…" Cassie looked genuinely embarrassed, her chin dipping down.

"Riley?" Helena asked. "I'm not ever introducing her to you. You're not casting your 'woman voodoo' over my new girlfriend."

"She's your girlfriend now?" Cassie picked up a sandwich and looked more interested in it than Helena's answer.

"We haven't technically discussed it yet, but we've had three dates. That's as good as exchanging wedding rings."

"Is that a lesbian thing?" Siobhan asked.

"Usually, but with Cassie it's *totally* different. With her it's all sandwiches and women, probably in that order." Helena nodded sagely. "Anything to tell on either front tonight?"

"There's nothing." Cassie's clipped tone sounded like an attempt to silence her friend. "We do not need to be having this conversation right now."

Apparently, Helena was no good at taking cues. "You see, Siobhan, what I'm trying to ascertain is which lucky woman will fall prey to her charms tonight—"

"I've sworn off women, Helena," Cassie hissed, her mouth hardly moving as she spoke. "You know that."

Helena continued, unfazed. "If you're looking for the absolute night of your life, Mrs. Head-Turner, she's the one, but if you want someone to wake up with the morning after, walk away."

"Are we really doing this now?" Cassie glared at her.

"It's fine, Cassie, especially now that I know you like your women how you like your coffee…hot and Irish." Siobhan wiggled her eyebrows and batted her eyelashes.

Helena roared with laughter. Siobhan monitored Cassie for signs she had caused offense. But when Cassie shook her head, there was mirth in her eyes and laughter on her lips. Siobhan felt a spark of delight knowing her one-liner had warranted it.

"Jesus, Mary, and Josephine, I love that accent!" Helena tipped her glass upside down. "This prosecco has disappeared before my very eyes. Another bottle?"

"Anything to get you off my case." Cassie nudged Helena's chair with her foot, and Helena hopped off. She turned to Siobhan, pinching the bridge of her nose. "I'm sorry. She hasn't got an *Off* button."

"I'm learning more by the minute," Siobhan said. "It seems you're the go-to person if one is seeking 'the absolute night' of her life and absolutely nothing more?" Siobhan was shocked at her own forwardness, but the banter between them had created a sense of comfort. Plus, the fact that Helena had chosen to warn Siobhan about Cassie directly had piqued her interest. Did Helena know more than she was letting on? Could she tell Siobhan had the potential to be into Cassie? Was that even an option? Siobhan tried to brush the idea away, but it was always there, just beneath the surface, especially when Cassie made eyes at her, which she appeared to be doing now.

"Why? Are you interested?"

Siobhan's pulse raced, but a few calming breaths helped to hide it—she hoped. "If your ego got any more expansive, it would be the size of Westminster Abbey. Of course I'm not interested. I'm merely intrigued."

Cassie leaned in closer, her eyes softening as Siobhan fell into the eye contact, unblinking. "And why do my lesbian exploits and, it seems, lesbianism at large intrigue you?"

"I was under the impression you're an expert on the subject. I am your trainee, after all."

"If I don't tell you, Helena will give away my best-kept secrets anyway."

Siobhan wondered if she were imagining Cassie leaning in closer, but when the scent of summertime, warm days, and the ocean breeze captured her senses, she realized it wasn't all in her head. She inhaled as deeply and discreetly as possible.

"What Helena's getting at is that I'm pretty much a free spirit when it comes to women. I've always had roving eyes, even at the tender age of ten."

"Age ten? Even *I* didn't start looking until I was around thirteen. Erm, what I mean is, I'm assuming you're using the term *free spirit* because it sounds more sophisticated than *hedonistic?*"

At this, Helena, who had just returned to their table, burst into raucous laughter, trying to speak between chuckles. "Oh, Cassie Townsend. You've got no chance with this one." She held her sides until her laughter subsided.

Cassie glared at Helena, but Siobhan detected a glimmer of a grin too.

"I believe what Helena was hinting at is that I can't imagine being able to function in a relationship."

"Relationships are bloody hard work." Siobhan knew that for certain.

"Which is why I've slept with lots of women but dated none. Too many, in fact. I must've built up resistance to them or something. I'm taking a break now."

"There must have been someone who meant something?"

She was torn between unease about Cassie's aversion to commitment, though she couldn't explain why, and a tinge of jealousy. Siobhan had never had the opportunity to explore her own interest in women, putting it to the back of her mind when Matthew took her to bed. It had resurfaced with a force she hadn't quite expected and a reason she didn't want to explore any further.

When nobody responded, Siobhan took a sip of her drink. As silence swept over them like a dense mid-morning mist, she noticed the awkward glance Helena and Cassie shared. This topic was off-limits.

"What's it like working with Cassie?" Helena digressed. "Is she as big a tyrant as she makes out?"

"Worse." Siobhan went to pat Cassie's knee but stopped herself. It was far too early in their friendship, if they were in fact forming one, for physical contact. She noticed Cassie stiffen, as if anticipating the touch that never came. To compensate, Siobhan leaned closer until their sleeves were touching. "You're not exactly a typical textbook villain though, are you?"

Cassie put her head in her hands. "I've been working so hard on that too."

Helena pointed at Siobhan. "Moving on from villains to heroes. Or, rather, heroines—"

"Here we go." Cassie held up her hand. "I know exactly what's coming next. Take careful consideration before you respond. This *matters* to her."

"She's right; it does matter." Helena steepled her fingers together on the table. "If you were put in charge of directing the next James Bond film, and you made the eagerly anticipated choice to cast a woman, who would it be?"

Siobhan was a little disappointed with the new direction of the conversation, Helena having shifted the focus away from the two of them. She supposed she should be thankful for the respite, but she wasn't. "Am I allowed to hear your choices first?" Siobhan asked.

"Absolutely not," they responded in tandem.

"We don't want to influence you," Helena said.

"Okay. Don't judge me, but—"

"Oh, judgment is the sole purpose of the exercise." Cassie took another big bite of her sandwich.

"The pressure's on then." Siobhan took a pause for dramatic effect. "Sandra Oh."

"Commendable choice," Cassie said as Helena shook her head in protest.

"You can't cast anyone stupid enough to stab Villanelle, rather than do the deed with her, as James Bond. It's nonsensical. My phone's ringing." She pulled it out of her bag. "We'll continue this insane conversation when I return." Helena left the two of them alone again.

Cassie tapped her chest where the button was no longer fastened. "I'm in Gillian Anderson's corner all the way, always have been."

"So you *can* be loyal to one woman," Siobhan said, and for an instant Cassie looked caught between reveling in this disclosure and refuting it.

"Helena's loyalty runs deeper than mine," she said, "and Riley's devotion is even more disturbing. It must be twenty-four-007 with them. At least they'll never be short of conversation, minimal though the topics may be. Did you know that conversation is an art you have to master in a relationship?"

"Matthew and I have got miscommunication down to a fine art." Siobhan sighed.

"What are you going to do about it?" Cassie asked, but her eyes were fixed on something in the distance.

Cassie's directness almost forced her to mention the divorce, but it was too soon to be disclosing that sort of information. Siobhan was about to offer a vague reply when Helena shimmied back over, her face glowing. "Riley's coming to meet us, so you best be on your best behavior, Cassie."

"Talking of unexpected guests, that bloke at the window seems to be gawping at you, Siobhan. Is that the postman with whom you aren't having an illicit affair?"

Siobhan followed Cassie's gaze to find Matthew stationed outside the window. His arms were crossed, his expression was cross, and he was flanked by Dylan and Neave. Siobhan blinked, certain she was seeing things. But then the children waved at her, professing their presence, and fury rocketed through her veins.

"Shit!" Siobhan glanced at her phone, horrified to find she had fourteen missed calls. She shot to her feet. "It's been a great evening. It was lovely to meet you, Helena." She turned her attention to Cassie, hoping her mortification wasn't showing. "I'll see you tomorrow, Ms. Townsend."

A cold sweat formed on her skin as she thrust the door open and approached Mathew and the kids.

"We found you!" Neave launched herself into Siobhan's arms.

"You sure did!" Siobhan replied, kissing her on the cheek.

"Can we go home now?" Dylan yawned, his eyelids drooping.

"Of course, love." She lowered her tone to Matthew as she spoke. "You dragged them out here when I told you I'd be home soon?"

"Speaking of which…" Matthew's gaze roamed past her to where she had been sitting only moments before, enjoying herself and her company. "Aren't you going to thank me for rescuing you from your coworkers, who *dragged* you out for drinks?"

"You couldn't handle the idea that I might be enjoying myself without you for an hour? Or was there an actual emergency?" She stared at him until he looked away, his jaw clenching. No emergency then. Just his ego. But she didn't want to cause a scene, not here. *Yes, thank you so much for dragging me away from them.* She glanced back in the window, and when she offered Cassie an apologetic smile, Cassie returned it, but there was a question in her eyes that Siobhan couldn't decipher.

CHAPTER EIGHT

The best way to avoid a hangover is to stay drunk." Cassie slipped a shot of espresso onto Siobhan's desk.

"Thanks." Siobhan offered her a weak smile. "I know how it must look, but I'm not hung over. I hope you realize I'm more professional than that."

Cassie noticed the dark rings around her eyes, evidence of lack of sleep. Upon closer examination, she saw that Siobhan's eyelids were puffy, her cheeks red and blotchy.

"Are you unwell?" Cassie asked, uncertain what else to say. If Siobhan had, as she very much suspected, been crying, she didn't have the inclination to deal with it. "You seem distracted, unfocused."

"I have a slight headache," Siobhan admitted, her voice cracking.

"How about we take our lunch over to that little square across the road." Cassie handed her a tissue, hoping the gesture sufficed as sympathy. "You look like you could do with some fresh air. It's a glorious day."

"I'd like that."

"Let me grab my lunch and we'll walk down together."

A few minutes later, Cassie found herself nestled in a quiet corner of the square, enjoying the steady sun beating down on her face. She leaned back against a stone wall, the grass underneath soft and spongy. Siobhan sat next to her, a respectable distance between them. Cassie had a slight desire to erase some of the distance but couldn't risk her shoulder being close enough to cry on. "Want to try this?" Cassie offered up half of her sandwich, but Siobhan just shrugged. "Triple-decker

BLT. You can't possibly say no to that." Cassie took Siobhan's hand and placed the sandwich into her open palm.

Siobhan didn't flinch, so Cassie tried not to. She also solemnly swore not to acknowledge the hunger the touch generated.

As she took a bite, Siobhan almost cracked a smile. "To be fair, it is pretty good."

Without thinking, Cassie flicked a crumb from the corner of Siobhan's mouth. "The hazards of sandwich consumption," she joked, brushing off her forward manner. Cassie ran her tongue over her lips, checking for a similar misdemeanor. "So…" she hesitated, deliberating the right degree of indifference to display. "When someone on my team, someone I work closely with, is distracted, their performance affected, I need to know why."

"There's been nothing wrong with my work today," Siobhan snapped.

Cassie sighed. She imagined what advice Helena would give her: *Just because you're heedless most of the time, doesn't mean you have to keep it up when you're in danger of actually caring. Get a grip, be the Tin Man, find your heart.* "Admittedly, that wasn't the right thing to say." Cassie's willingness to accept her mistake startled her. Her tone was softer the next time she spoke; she was learning. "Do you want to talk about it?"

"It's nothing work-related. You needn't worry about it," Siobhan said, sitting upright as if to prove the point.

"Something's going on," Cassie said. "Is it about what happened last night?"

Siobhan's focus drifted off into the distance, her eyes glazing over. "If you mean my husband embarrassing me in the worst possible way, then yes."

"Hey." Cassie stopped herself from reaching out. "You don't have any reason to feel embarrassed. *He* was out of order, turning up with the kids like that." Cassie gave Siobhan what she hoped was a reassuring and nonjudgmental smile.

"That was only the start. He was horrible when we got home last night. Making all kinds of snide remarks. He even asked which one of you I was sleeping with."

"Shit!" Cassie tried to sound horrified when in truth she was thrilled by the mere prospect. Still, she played along. "He's out of order.

Just because he's your husband doesn't give him the right to speak to you like that. And whatever in this world would make him think that you were sleeping with one of us? You're not exactly screaming *lesbian* at the world, Siobhan. No offense."

"Actually…" She took another long pause, as if weighing something up. "I may not be screaming it on the outside, but…" Siobhan blushed London-bus red. "When Matthew saw me at the bar, I must've looked too comfortable in your company, because he started questioning whether there was a revival of my feelings."

Images of fireworks pouring a radiant rainbow across the sky filled her mind. Cassie cocked her head and allowed herself the briefest of smiles. "You did say Matthew was wrong for you in so many ways," Cassie said, "but this way is my *absolute* favorite." She watched as Siobhan's frown gradually grew into an amused smile.

"When I think of everything I've missed out on…" Siobhan tutted, shaking her head. "I mean, who knows what could've blossomed with Kendra Lynch?"

"Kendra Lynch?" Cassie was close to an actual fist pump by now.

"She was the postman's daughter and one of my closest friends. She was also the most gorgeous girl in all of Slane and totally out of my league, though I spent all my days down at the post office, trying to attract her attention and escape Matthew's."

"And where is Kendra now?" Cassie asked. "Do you have an address?"

"Married with five children, and didn't you swear off women?"

"I can probably be persuaded to change my mind for the most gorgeous girl in all of Slane." Cassie tilted her head towards Siobhan, stretching out on the grass and tucking her hands behind her head, her smile unrestrained. "Though we may have differing opinions on who that is."

Siobhan was quick to brush off the remark. "Anyway, now you know why I look like shit: a thundering argument and a night on the sofa."

"You don't look like shit," Cassie assured her. "Not to my well-trained eye."

Siobhan crumpled up the tinfoil the sandwich had been wrapped in and pelted it at Cassie's head. Siobhan smiled, but it vanished in a heartbeat. "When I left the house this morning, Matthew called me a dyke."

The word sent Cassie reeling. "I can't fucking stand intolerance." She bolted upright, her nostrils flaring, as her earlier ease was replaced by agitation. "He shouldn't speak to you like that. Nobody should."

"I'm guessing this anger stems from more than Matthew's words?" Siobhan asked, drawing her knees up and wrapping her arms around them.

Cassie was surprised at the accuracy of Siobhan's observation. Her thoughts spun like a roulette wheel, her gaze flickering from Siobhan's tired, red eyes to her downturned mouth and back again.

Cassie had never found it easy to open up, but if Siobhan trusted her enough to speak openly about her own personal life, it was only fair that she at least try to reciprocate. "Matthew reminds me of my dad." Already, she could feel herself clamming up, her palms sweaty. "It seems they share similar opinions and a particular habit for offensive language."

"Your dad called you that? I can't believe he would speak to you like that. You're his daughter. That's just wrong in *so* many ways."

Cassie had mastered apathy well, but she had forgotten what it was like to see someone else react to his behavior. "We don't need to talk about this."

"You're right, we don't. But it might do you some good to open up. You know you can talk to me about anything. In fact some might say I'm a pretty good person to divulge secrets to. Mainly because, unlike you, I *am* listening."

Cassie gasped, more pleased than perturbed that Siobhan had used Cassie's own words against her. It excited her, the way Siobhan could beat her at her own game.

"You've got one up on my dad, then," she said, dragging her hands across her shirt to dry the perspiration. "He doesn't listen to me. Truth be told, he won't speak to me at all. Whether or not that will ever change, well…I wouldn't bank on it. Actually, that is the one thing we do agree on: investment banking, though I doubt it delights him that I work for his main competitor. He probably perceives it as a vengeful act and maybe at first it was my misguided attempt to get back at him, but I'm beyond that now. I've learned to live with his rejection. Hearing about Matthew's reaction just opened old wounds." It wasn't true. Given how she'd reacted the other day at her mum's house, the wound wasn't even close to healed yet. But that was an admission too far.

"I often imagine what my father would've been like."

Cassie didn't know whether Siobhan had deliberately changed the focus or if it was accidental. Either way she felt grateful.

"May I ask what happened?" Cassie realized that at some point during their conversation, her hand had drifted towards Siobhan's, the sides of their fingers in proximity. Since Siobhan had made no attempt to pull away, she left it there.

"A freak accident with the machinery on his friend's farm." Siobhan's eyes filled with tears, and Cassie shifted her shoulder slightly, in case Siobhan needed to rest her head on it. She didn't. "I can't imagine what my mum went through, having a child on the way and losing the love of her life. I doubt she ever truly recovered. She certainly never loved again. She always used to say my father and I shared many similar traits. I was a constant reminder of what she'd lost and yet she was always there for me. That unconditional love is what I want for Dylan and Neave. And myself."

When Siobhan's eyes met with her own, Cassie almost crumpled under the affection she saw there, but she fought off her initial flight reaction and composed herself. "I've always found it difficult to fit in with my family, even before I came out and World War Three kicked off."

"And why is that?"

"Probably because I go with my instincts, make poor judgment calls, take risks I shouldn't be taking, and do it all without breaking a sweat. I don't have any beige settings."

"I hadn't noticed," Siobhan said, her smile stretching across her entire face. "I was too busy being blown away by how approachable you are."

"Would you like anymore of this?" Cassie waved another hulk of sandwich in Siobhan's direction.

Siobhan shook her head. "Don't you have any restraint?"

"Yes." Cassie reached out, brushing a stray hair behind Siobhan's ear, her thumb skimming the exquisite line of Siobhan's jaw. And then, with a strength of character she hadn't known she possessed, she stopped herself. "More than you will ever know."

CHAPTER NINE

There are two types of people in the world." Cassie dropped a large pizza onto Siobhan's desk, the delicious aroma of fresh dough suddenly making her stomach rumble and her mouth water. "Those who love pizza..." Cassie winked. "And liars."

Siobhan grinned. "Firmly in the first camp. But do your sandwiches know you're seeking nourishment from other sources?"

"I'm not cheating on them, if that's what you're implying." For a second Siobhan thought she'd offended her. But then Cassie's lips stretched into a beautiful smile, one that Siobhan was coming to fully appreciate. "I took a punt on ham and pineapple."

"A controversial choice in Italy, or so I'm led to believe."

"How do *you* feel about fruit on pizza?" Cassie sat in Julie's chair and used her feet to push herself across the room, stopping when she was directly opposite Siobhan.

"Is this another deal breaker?" Siobhan offered a bemused smile before she opened the box, the welcoming aroma enticing her.

"If we were dating, I'd say one hundred percent, but as friends, I could just about let you off." Cassie's eyes twinkled like scattered moondust.

"You don't do dating," she hastened to point out. "But I'll always be happy to share a ham and pineapple pizza with you. It's my absolute fave!" She pulled a slice off, the stringy cheese resisting as it imitated the bubble gum she constantly nagged the children to stop blowing on. Siobhan took a bite, savoring her first mouthful, while trying to control the misbehaving mozzarella.

"Mine too." Cassie laughed, taking up a slice for herself and engaging in a similar struggle. "Moreno's is the best place in town," she mumbled around a mouthful. "I really hope you appreciate what a huge step sharing this pizza with you actually is."

"In truth, I thought you'd dropped it on the floor and didn't want it." Siobhan sucked up a particularly challenging string of cheese.

"You wound me." Cassie placed her hand on her heart before slumping forward onto the desk, an unruly piece of pineapple sticking to her forehead as she looked up.

"You saving that for later?" Siobhan reached forward and peeled it off, dangling it in front of Cassie, who didn't look in the slightest bit perturbed by the pineapple.

"There are many things I could save for later."

Siobhan's stomach fluttered like a flickering lamp, but she decided to let it embolden her rather than frighten her. Something about the ease between them, the banter, had rekindled feelings she thought she had abandoned long ago in Ireland. "How about next week we jump off the ledge together?"

"Meaning?"

"You could come round to mine for dinner on Friday night. The kids and I can take over the kitchen and see what carnage ensues."

"I'm sure your husband would love that."

Siobhan wasn't going to let Cassie's brush-off deter her. "Matthew won't be home."

"I'll think it over," Cassie promised, sounding about as sincere as a postcard proclaiming *Wish You Were Here*. She twisted the pizza crust between her fingers, avoiding Siobhan's eyes.

"If you're really lucky, I might even find one of the great old musical films for us to watch."

"If *I'm* really lucky? Most women would consider you the lucky one, should I agree to come round and have dinner with you, and even luckier if I ever agree to take you out."

"Wednesday nights work well for me, if we're going out," Siobhan answered, too swiftly apparently, because Cassie's eyebrows curved like her pizza crust. "I have no responsibilities on Wednesday evenings." Siobhan backpedaled but she knew it was too late. "Hence why I agreed to work late tonight. The kids stay with Matthew's mum, and Matthew goes to the pub with his friends or to Champions League games if Spurs are at home—"

"And you?"

"I get to take Neave's bed rather than the sofa. And enjoy the peace. That's after doing the shopping, washing school clothes, and tidying the house, of course. If I'm fortunate, I might get time for a relaxing soak or the chance to settle down with a good book. Living the dream and all that."

"So hypothetically, if I were to plan an evening out—"

"And I agreed to come." Siobhan concentrated on her pizza, trying to calm her rapidly beating heart.

"Oh, you'll come and you'll enjoy it." Cassie waved a piece of pizza at her. "Wednesdays would be a good option?"

"I guess it depends how engrossed I am in my latest novel."

"Oh? What are you reading?

"*Tipping the Velvet.* Although I've heard that's *your* specialty."

"Of course, one of many! You should know it isn't the only string to my bow."

Suddenly it wasn't just the pineapple making Siobhan's taste buds tingle. She looked down at Cassie's hand, which was once again resting next to her own. "If the way you seductively suck up cheese that's dangling precariously from the corner of your mouth is anything to go by, someone is in for a real treat."

"Now we are getting personal. Perfecting the whole cheese thing has taken years of hard work you know."

"Impressive. Who knows, if you eat all your meals with this much allure, we might have to make this a regular thing." Siobhan hoped she sounded at least semi-seductive within the confines of their teasing.

Cassie withdrew her hand from the desk and her eyes from Siobhan's, and Siobhan realized, with a combination of pride and panic, that she may have taken things a little too far. After all, Cassie had told her time and time again she wasn't open to anything, which probably included flirting with a work colleague.

Cassie stood up, her demeanor changed, her jaw rooted like concrete. "We should make a start on the presentation." Here she was, functionality and precision, back to her professional best.

"Shall I come through to you?" Siobhan asked, fearing she already knew the response.

"I'll do the figures, you put together final notes for the pitch. We might even get home this side of midnight if we put our minds to it."

As she watched Cassie stride back into her office and shut the door behind her, Siobhan wondered exactly what was going on in Cassie's head and whether despite her protestations, she did see something more than flirtation developing between them. The likelihood was that this would scare Cassie, just as much as it did Siobhan, which could go a long way to explaining why Cassie had just shut it down and retreated into her own space. Just as they appeared to be moving forward into new territory naturally, Cassie would withdraw—without warning, rhyme, or reason.

Siobhan was unsure if *she* even wanted to move into new territory, whatever that meant. Not when Cassie made her feel so on edge and so at ease at the same time. The only conclusion she could draw was that Cassie had misgivings about their flirtations and was concerned that it was unbecoming, unprofessional, maybe even misleading. But Siobhan managed to place it under the category of harmless fun, so Cassie really had no reason to think otherwise, not given her insistence that she had sworn off women for good.

For the next couple of hours, Siobhan worked quietly on the pitch, adding pie charts and detailed graphics to their work, wondering if Cassie planned to emerge again that night. Above all else, she was dedicated to her work, but she had to admit part of the pull of working late had been the opportunity to spend time with Cassie.

When her work was completed, she dithered at Cassie's doorway, deliberating whether to knock. After a moment's hesitation, she pushed open the door and wasn't the least bit surprised to find Cassie puffing steadily on a cigarette, feet up on the desk. Apparently, she had finished working a while ago, and rather than offering to help Siobhan, had chosen to retreat into herself, or so it seemed from where Siobhan was standing.

"You *can* come in." Cassie puffed out a smoke ring.

"That won't be necessary. I've finished the presentation and added the projections. We can take a look in the morning, unless you want to do it now?"

"I'm tired." Cassie yawned as if to prove her point.

"Right, then. Good night." Siobhan turned to leave, but putting one foot in front of the other suddenly seemed difficult.

"Siobhan?" Cassie said her name softly.

Siobhan's curiosity sparked and a craving that caused her breath to rush in and out rose swiftly. She couldn't not turn back. "Was there something else?"

Cassie took a long drag on her cigarette. "Thanks for staying tonight. I appreciate it." Cassie let out a steady, deliberate breath and rolled her head in a slow circle, holding the back of her neck and trying to look casual. It was a decent effort, but Siobhan knew her better, and recognized the crackle of tension in the air. The absolute giveaway was Cassie's foot tapping up and down, seemingly of its own accord.

"You only have to ask and if I can, I will." Siobhan cleared her throat. It was down to her to bring back the laid-back nature of their earlier chat. She needed that; they both did. Formality didn't suit either of them.

Siobhan took herself right into Cassie's office and sat down, looking directly at her. She loosened her collar, crossed her legs, uncrossed them, placed her hands on her knees. She went to reach for her wedding ring, then tucked her hands beneath her thighs instead. "I need your expertise."

Cassie stubbed out her cigarette, wafting the smoke away. "My expertise?"

"You know about cars—"

"I drive a Carrera, if that's what you mean."

Siobhan could tell Cassie was interested, despite her pretense of nonchalance. It almost worked for her.

"Dylan's car mad. He's a huge Formula One fan and he's wanting to go quad biking for his birthday. He's shown me a poster of a place he's found, not too far from your sister's. I wondered if you might fancy it?"

"You're asking me to an eight-year-old's birthday party?" Cassie looked as though she'd swallowed bitter lemons. "I'm still debating whether or not to accept your invitation to dine with your children, let alone party on down with them."

Siobhan's jaw tightened. "I was only asking if you'd come along with *me* to check it out this weekend. It would just be the two of us, and it would give you and Dylan something to talk about *if* you meet him—"

"Why are you even asking me?" Cassie asked.

Siobhan couldn't decide whether Cassie was snarking or sulking. "Is this another aversion? You don't like children, either?"

"I wasn't aware I had to explain my every whim to you." Cassie's face twisted into a smile that seemed half-hearted at best.

Clearly this invitation was a huge blunder. Yet Cassie's behavior didn't sit right with her, and after having spent so many years keeping her opinions to herself, Siobhan knew Cassie wouldn't respect her— and she wouldn't respect herself—if she remained silent.

"Look, I'm not sure what's wrong with you tonight. You have more changes in direction than the wind on a blustery day. I need consistency. If you're incapable of managing that, then we need to keep this purely professional. My job means far too much to me to compromise it by trying to be friends with you when you're going out of your way to make it difficult."

Cassie steepled her fingers and rested her chin on them. Siobhan wondered what on earth had happened in Cassie's life that made lowering her barriers for the simple act of friendship such a struggle, but stopped herself from asking. There *might* be a time, but it wasn't now.

"It's an afternoon of quad biking?" Cassie asked. "Nothing more?" She hesitated, her expression serious. "Because I like messing around with you. I like teasing and joking. But the bottom line is that I'm not into anything serious, and kids are out of the equation. I don't want to lead you on."

Siobhan ignored the deflating expectation and kept her expression neutral. "Banter is perfect, and I'm only looking for a friend. If you can handle friendship, then we're good."

An image of Cassie straddling a quad bike, clad in tight jeans and her leather jacket, steamrolled into her mind. Windswept hair and Ray-Bans completed the provocative look. She tried to refocus her attention, but it wasn't easy, especially when she was busy playing out fantasies she'd only just introduced into existence and Cassie's pouting lips were commanding her attention. She debated whether or not she should feel ashamed of herself. Especially after the shameless lie she had just put out into the world about only looking for friendship. Was this how friends thought about one another? Somehow she didn't think so.

"Even if I wear a leather jacket?"

Cassie's voice seemed to ring out in Siobhan's ears, considering their proximity. Cassie arched her back, thrusting her breasts out in a ridiculous manner, as though she were posing for a men's motorcycle calendar. A shiver shot down her spine.

Perhaps it was the playful ring to Cassie's tone or the warmth radiating from her eyes. Maybe it was even the fact they were alone in the office together late at night, but Siobhan's brain no longer seemed capable of sense. And they'd made it clear where they stood, so a little fun was harmless. Right? "Happy to give special dispensation for leather jackets."

"You like a woman in leather?"

"Not just any woman, I'm quite specific."

"I'll see if Kendra Lynch is available," Cassie taunted her.

"Are you poking fun at me?"

"That ship has sailed." Cassie made waves with her hands.

"Well and truly," Siobhan confirmed. For some reason it mattered that Cassie knew this.

"Any other special requests?"

Siobhan merely shook her head and Cassie sighed. "You might be right about me. I do have more changes in direction than the wind on a blustery day. I'm like an aimless Mary Poppins, practically imperfect."

"But not in *every* way."

Siobhan's breath caught as Cassie reached towards her face. But she drew back before making contact, and when Siobhan exhaled it was with a mixture of regret and relief. She knew it would be all too easy to get lost in that touch, if it ever came.

"Shall I stay until the wind changes?" Siobhan asked. "Or just your mood?"

"Either could be dangerous."

CHAPTER TEN

For a woman usually brimming with self-assurance, Cassie could hardly believe the doubt she felt. Even standing outside Siobhan's front door felt like a huge step, as her stomach performed alarmingly impressive acrobatics. She should be looking forward to spending an evening with Siobhan, she told herself. Then she came back to her opinion that all children were bratty and irritating; Siobhan's were bound to be no exception. In some ways, they were likely to be more tiresome because they were an obstacle in her way; one she desperately needed. She would meet them, they would annoy her, and her attraction towards Siobhan would, as desired, be snuffed out like a cigarette. She lifted her fist to the door and knocked once.

Siobhan answered, looking relaxed in her casual attire, hair tied back off her face, her face devoid of makeup. Cassie couldn't help but admire the sweet, natural look, even though she had promised herself all such thoughts would be banished tonight. Dark blue jeans hugged her curves, and perky nipples protruded through her sunset-colored T-shirt. Cassie forced herself to perform a double take. Siobhan's nipples weren't conspicuous. It was just her wishful thinking.

"I decided I'd take you up on your invitation," she said, as if Siobhan hadn't been expecting her, "because it's obvious you find my company irresistible, which also describes how you look tonight." Cassie rocked back and forth on her heels. "I don't usually arrive at the door dishing out compliments." Cassie clamped her lips shut, vexed that her customary subtlety and sophistication had deserted her when she needed it most. "I'll stop now."

"I think that's best." Siobhan's smile was sweet. "You've already ruined the acclaim. And if you roll those eyes any more, the kids'll be playing marbles with them before the night's through. Dylan! Neave! Dinner's ready and Cassie's here."

Cassie allowed herself to be led into the kitchen, where she put down the bottle of wine she'd been carrying. She stared wide-eyed as she heard the children charging down the stairs like a stampede of rhinos.

Dylan charged through the door first with Neave hot on his heels. "We didn't hear the smoke alarm, so we weren't sure if it was *really* ready!" Dylan spun into his seat, laughing.

"Very funny! This is my son, Dylan, the comedian." Siobhan ruffled his hair as he grinned right at Cassie.

"She's a pretty good cook really." He studied her the way kids do. "She's kept me alive for eight years, though I was hanging on by a thread once after the chicken hotpot."

"Hi, I'm Neave. Don't worry about the food—I helped cook." She sat down next to Cassie, who marveled at her resemblance to Siobhan. They shared the same forget-me-not blue eyes, the same intelligent smile, the same dimples creasing their cheeks.

"Hey." She managed to find her voice, utterly bemused by their open, friendly welcome. How was she supposed to react?

"Please tell me you've driven here." Dylan jumped out of his seat and raced to the window.

"I did mention the fact he's obsessed with cars." Siobhan indicated towards the images of various sports cars fastened to the fridge. "I may also have mentioned that you drive a pretty cool one."

"That's a 911 Carrera, Mum! It's more than pretty cool. Mum doesn't know anything about cars. If you want to talk to someone about speed and engines, you'll have to speak with me."

"Noted." Cassie looked towards the clock, as if the feeling of annoyance she was expecting to experience would kick in as soon as the clock struck 7:03. Normally it would already be in place. What was happening?

"I'm going to drive an orange Bugatti when I'm twenty-one," Dylan said, still looking out the window. "What did you drive when you were twenty-one?"

Cassie opened her mouth to supply a response but found she felt too flummoxed to offer one.

"Dinner is served." Siobhan stepped in, placing a huge pot of chili and four foil-wrapped potatoes on the table. "Cassie, please would you do the honors?"

"That's usually Dad's job." Dylan grabbed a potato. "I like it better when he's not here." Dylan flipped the foil open and indicated he was ready for Cassie to serve him, which she did, far too generously. "Adult-size portions! Thanks."

"You're welcome." Cassie racked her brain for something else to say, but gave it up as a bad job and instead served the rest of them chili as slowly as possible, her hand and the spoon in it trembling like a first-time rider on a world famous rollercoaster.

"Are you nervous?" Neave asked, calling her out on it, while also managing to sound merciful. "Don't be."

The way Siobhan's daughter could read her, at the mere age of six, made Cassie feel exposed and understood at the same time.

Siobhan joined them at the table, where her son was gobbling up food at breakneck speed. "Dylan, do you really have to eat like that? It's revolting! The rest of us civilized beings don't want to watch you eating like a caveman."

"Sorry, Mum," Dylan mumbled, even as he stuffed more potato into his mouth. At least he swallowed before saying, "You know, Cassie, you're Mum's first real friend. I don't think she's ever had anyone over to dinner before. Mum's pretty much a loner. She—"

"Shall we open your bottle of Chardonnay, Cassie?" Siobhan interrupted, her cheeks crimson, but Cassie felt flattered. She smiled to herself. *Happy to be her first in more ways than one.*

"I'm having Fanta!" Neave boasted, holding up her cup as if that were the better choice.

"I'll get you a glass, Cassie." Dylan leapt out of his seat once more and raced over to a cupboard, then strained and stretched and jumped in vain. "On second thought, you'll have to get your own glass. I can't reach that high."

"Too bad you're not a giraffe." Cassie teased him, shocked that articulate words had emerged from her mouth. Somehow, the children's instant acceptance had inevitably put her at ease, although part of her did wonder if they were acting out of character under their mother's direction. Had she laid the rulebook at their feet?

"I think I'd rather be a dinosaur than a giraffe," Dylan was saying, as Cassie made her way to the appointed cupboard.

"I think you'll need this too." Cassie glanced down to see Neave at her other side, holding a corkscrew.

"Don't you just love a child who knows their way around a wine bottle?" Siobhan chuckled, as they all returned to the table.

Another point in Siobhan's favor, Cassie bemoaned, taking a small mouthful of chili. She savored the aromatic flavor. Not only was Siobhan the sexiest woman she had ever clapped eyes on; she was an excellent cook too. Aware that Siobhan's gaze had settled upon her, she felt the need to say as much. "Hot!" Cassie spluttered, her brain not catching up with her mouth in time.

"We can open a window," Neave said.

"Hot food is great." Cassie made a hideous attempt to save face. "Much better than the takeaway I had planned."

"You're lucky Mum cooked for you," Dylan said. "It's usually Freezer Food Fridays."

Siobhan cleared her throat. "That's not strictly true." A nervous laugh escaped her. "I do sometimes cook on a Friday night."

The realization that Siobhan had gone out of her way to prepare a meal for Cassie would take a little time to process, so she filed it away for later consideration.

"Do you have kids?" Neave asked, and the nerves that had been slowly abating started to regenerate.

She fumbled with her knife and fork, sending the latter launching across the table and onto the floor. Dylan burst into laughter.

"Cassie doesn't have kids." Siobhan rescued her, reaching down to collect the mutinous cutlery. "I'll get you a clean one. Or at least one that isn't prone to flights of fancy."

"What about a boyfriend? You look too young to be married, but then, so does Mum and she's married." Neave made a face Cassie took as disapproval.

The candid question came with such wide-eyed innocence, Cassie felt compelled to respond. She met Siobhan's gaze and received a nod of approval. "I'm not married," she said. "And I don't have a boyfriend."

Neave nodded, nibbled on a chili bean and said, "Girlfriend?"

It was Siobhan's turn to send her fork flying across the kitchen. Cassie caught it with the hand she'd been using to drum her fingers against the table and passed it back.

"Neave, love, please stop pestering our dinner guest with personal questions."

"But she answered all the other ones," Neave mumbled.

After that, the conversation ground to a halt, giving Cassie time to reflect on the fact that Siobhan had gone out of her way to cook for her tonight. The children had made it clear that this wasn't a usual occurrence, Siobhan inviting a friend round to dinner. She could read what she wanted to into that information.

Before she could make a decision, Dylan broke the silence. "Who do you reckon would win in a race? You in your Carrera or Hamilton in a Jag F-Type?"

Cassie was delighted by the change of subject and went for it full throttle. "Clearly me! He wouldn't stand a chance. But I'd race him in my Lotus Elise, the car I drove when I was twenty-one."

"Color?" Dylan looked as if his life depended on the answer.

"Silver, of course, just like my current one."

Dylan exhaled in what sounded like immense relief. "Good choice."

"The only choice. No one can argue against silver." Conscious of not leaving Neave out, Cassie turned her attention to Siobhan's daughter. "I take it you're not into cars like your brother. What's your favorite thing to do?"

"Well, I used to like dancing, but I'm not as into that as I used to be."

"Since when?" Siobhan was clearly amused. "It was only a few weeks ago you were throwing shapes around this very kitchen."

"So were you!" Neave vaulted out of her seat. "Mum, show us another of your crazy moves."

"It's embarrassing." Dylan threw his head down on the table. "Mum claims to have invented the Worm."

Ecstatic the focus was no longer on her, she relaxed back in her chair, preparing to indulge herself. "What other moves are you staking a claim to?"

"Do your moonwalk," Neave begged, jumping up and down next to Siobhan.

"Can I just clarify that this is not where I perceived the evening going when I invited you round?" Siobhan bit down on her bottom lip and got into position: head down, foot tilted. "You're only getting this once, so enjoy."

"I intend to."

Cassie had to hand it to her: Siobhan moved with some skill and plenty of attitude. She pulled off the illusion of gliding in reverse with poise, repeating the steps over and over, as if she were being pulled backward by an unseen force while trying to walk forward. The fact that Siobhan's backside, clad in tight fitting jeans, shimmied in her direction, had no bearing whatsoever on her approval.

Neave joined in.

"This is so not cool." Dylan groaned. "Cassie, make them stop!"

Cassie laughed until tears rolled down her cheeks. There was something totally beguiling about Siobhan poking fun at herself, interacting playfully with her children and—potentially—playing up to her audience of one.

When they eventually came to a standstill, Cassie roared her approval, clapping and cheering, "We want more! Actually, scrap that! I'd like to see more; Dylan wants to move to Australia."

Siobhan bowed. "I'm available for bookings weeknights and some weekends."

"You're way more fun than Dad, Cassie," Neave said. "He hates us being silly and gets angry when there's *disorder*." She impersonated her father's stern tone and mimicked his facial expression.

Cassie looked over to ensure she had Dylan's approval too, but he had disappeared.

"He must have gone off to his room so he could die of embarrassment in private." Neave shrugged. "At least we didn't scare *you* off. In fact, you're no longer afraid of us, are you?"

Cassie stared right at Neave, shocked she had been so caught out.

Once more, Siobhan was there to help her out. "You never did tell us what you want to get into next, Neave, now that your love for dance is fading. Not that we've seen much evidence of that here tonight!"

"I'd love to learn an instrument," Neave said as they went through to the living room. Siobhan sat down on the sofa and patted her thighs. For a second, Cassie interpreted that as an invitation, and it was—for Neave, who leapt onto her mother's lap. Siobhan tapped the space next to her indicating *that* was where she wanted Cassie.

But it wasn't where she felt comfortable, she realized, as Siobhan's thigh flanked hers, generating a surge of heat between them. Yet as Cassie's composure evaporated by the minute, she recognized that the attraction both exhilarated and soothed her, so much so that she found herself saying, "I used to play the drums back in school."

"Cassie Townsend," Siobhan gasped. "You dark horse."

"I was a world-beating drummer," Cassie said. "Should've been picked up by any number of famous bands, but wrong place, wrong time."

"Teach me how to play." Neave turned to her, her expression pleading.

"I think Cassie has too much on her plate." Siobhan gently jumped in.

"No, she doesn't. She cleaned her plate at dinner. And it wasn't even a plate. It was a bowl." Neave slid down to the floor and hugged her knees. "If you won't teach me, Cassie, who will? Dad won't pay for lessons."

Cassie didn't know the inner workings of children, but she could tell when she was being targeted for a guilt trip. If Matthew disapproved, what did she have to lose? It might even be fun. "I reckon I might be able to give you a few drumming tips," she relented. "Show you how to spin the sticks, throw them in a dangerous and deadly way, that sort of thing. I think my sister still has the kit somewhere."

Siobhan's dimples creased with her laughter. "Thanks for that, Cass. Just what I need: a rock star in the family!"

A surge of heat crept deliciously through her veins. It was one thing for Siobhan to call her Cassie—everyone did. But no one had ever called her Cass before. Their gazes locked and Cassie knew in this exact moment that if she weren't careful, pretty soon she would end up doing something really stupid.

"Can we take a proper ride out in your car?" Dylan reappeared, fresh from his shame-induced demise, waving a magazine. "This mag has info about some of the best roads to drive in the UK." He plonked himself down next to Cassie on the arm of the sofa. "Let's take a road trip!"

For some reason, these children wanted to spend a remarkable amount of time with her. *Do they really want to hang out with me?*

"Yes!" three voices chorused.

Cassie blinked. "Am I doing that thing you're so good at, saying thoughts I don't want out in the world, out in the world?"

"Wonderfully." Siobhan gave her a thumbs-up.

"Can I take it back?"

"No."

"I see. Well, then, I suppose we can take a road trip to Eva's." Why were these things coming out of her mouth? Siobhan looked like she didn't recognize Cassie. Or like she was seeing her for the very first time. Cassie gulped.

"Is Eva your sister? The one with the drums?" Neave bounded back onto the sofa.

"Yes," Cassie said. "What do you say, Siobhan? Shall we kick off with some drum lessons?" Drums weren't the only thing that would be kicking off if she weren't careful. Her libido was playing havoc with her good sense. Thank God the children were there, although she was unsure whether this was a blessing or a curse. "I'm sure we can visit Eva's at some point, maybe a bit later in the year." Now that she had promised as much, she wondered how long it would be acceptable to put them off. Why hadn't she just said no?

"We do love a trip to the beach," Siobhan said, making Cassie feel truly terrible for her thoughts. She decided there and then she would make this happen.

"My favorite seaside is Brighton," Dylan said. "But I'm not picky. Cassie, have you been on the rides at the pier? Mum took us last summer when Dad was at football." Dylan made a couple of loud snoring noises.

"I'm way too old for rides," Cassie said.

Dylan narrowed his eyes. "Exactly *how* old are you?"

"Way too old to be up in the air and risk losing my tea. When I was a kid, I was addicted to helter-skelters, but it spiraled out of control."

Dylan blew a loud raspberry and Neave giggled. When she glanced at Siobhan, the look she received caused Cassie's head to spin as if she were riding one right now.

"You two have half an hour before bed," Siobhan announced. "Say good night to Cassie."

Dylan went straight in for a fist bump. "See you soon, Cassie."

Neave elected a high five. "We weren't nearly as bad as you expected, were we?"

"Of course we weren't," Dylan said. "We're awesome."

Cassie found herself nodding in agreement and hating herself for it. "It was great meeting you both. Good night."

"Don't even dare tell me you think that went poorly." Siobhan leaned back against the couch, and if Cassie did the same, their entire sides would be touching.

A low ache began developing in her stomach. Even after seeing Siobhan in her role as mum, Cassie was still desperate to get to know her better. Siobhan felt present, real, unlike any woman she had ever known.

Siobhan must have assumed Cassie had taken her threat seriously, because she continued, "It was lovely to see the kids so relaxed in your company. They can feel quite on edge when Matthew's around."

"Remind me again why you're still with him?" Cassie asked without thinking.

"Remind me again why you care?"

"I shouldn't care." Cassie paused, wondering how on earth she was going to get out of this one. "I guess I don't want to see you hurt. You deserve better than a man who calls you a...you know what I mean. I think the kids seemed to like me. Not that I'm suggesting myself as an alternative, obviously." She squeezed her eyes shut. "Jesus."

"I knew they'd like you." Siobhan allowed the change of subject, much to Cassie's relief. "And without any incentive from me. You know what this means, don't you?"

Cassie shook her head. "Do I *want* to know what it means?"

"Knowing you, probably not, but I'm giving you it anyway. It means, sad to say, you must have *some* redeeming qualities."

"Shit!" Cassie rested her head in her hands.

"They're very particular about who they let into their lives, Dylan especially."

"Driving a Porsche probably helps. After all, I am the female version of Lewis Hamilton."

"Mum!" Neave called from upstairs. "Will you read us a bedtime story, please?"

"I'll be right up!"

"I should probably go." Cassie detected a hint of disappointment in her own voice.

"If you must," Siobhan said, walking her to the door. "You know you don't have to."

"I need to, but I should say thank you for a tolerable time." Cassie contemplated a hug but wasn't entirely sure how to initiate one. She took a step back just as Siobhan stepped forward, searching Cassie's eyes for permission. Cassie didn't exactly grant it, but she didn't withhold it either.

Enveloped in Siobhan's embrace, Cassie struggled to stifle a sigh. If she weren't careful, the restraints she had put in place would not only loosen; they would unravel.

"So, are we still on for quad biking tomorrow?" she asked when they separated.

"Absolutely," Siobhan said, her gaze sauntering up and down Cassie's body. "Weather permitting."

It took more effort than it should have for Cassie to turn and walk away. Restraint had never been her strong point and now that she was forced to rely solely on her self-control, she felt unbalanced. Siobhan did that to her somehow, tipped her axis and threw her out of kilter. She needed to get a grip, avoid any extreme reactions and most importantly of all, keep Siobhan at arm's length. Easier said than done.

CHAPTER ELEVEN

"Maureen Johnson's entrance in *Rent*, all leather and motorcycles, has nothing on me!" Cassie yelled over the roaring engine of the quad bike, the four wheels spinning in the mud, preparing to take on the range of terrains.

Siobhan couldn't hide her amusement at Cassie's enthusiasm, nor could she hide her excitement at Cassie's position: legs spread as she straddled the seat, fingers flexing as she clenched the handlebars. Here she was embodying a picture postcard of Siobhan's fantasies. Her hair was unkempt, yet the disheveled look suited her. Her leather jacket fit like a tight hug on a wintry day, and her jeans were aesthetically pleasing in their snugness. Siobhan swallowed the lump forming in her throat. Cassie was wreaking chaos on Siobhan's sex drive, one that had reintroduced its existence upon Cassie's arrival in her life and more specifically Cassie's arrival on her bike—Upheaval Knievel in all her glory.

"Earth to Siobhan!" Cassie whooped. "Are you getting on? Or too busy imagining things you shouldn't be?"

Flustered she'd been caught ogling, Siobhan took a step closer to the bike, realizing all too late this was going to involve very close contact.

Smirking, Cassie leaned forward onto the handlebars, and Siobhan swung her leg over the bike and shuffled forward until she brushed against Cassie's backside, the thrill of the contact bolting between her legs.

Cassie's knuckles knocked against Siobhan's helmet as if it were a door. "Just so you know, that won't protect you from lustful thoughts."

Her throaty chuckle made Siobhan's cheeks burn. "What about yours?"

"Mine is equally ineffectual."

"How do you know?" Siobhan teased her, Cassie's open admiration galvanizing her courage.

"Because when you rocked up in that figure-hugging jacket, which looks spectacular on you may I add, even my heart missed a beat. Let's not even go there with what happened when you mounted the bike. You look incredible."

Siobhan felt Cassie's eyes rove over her body and was glad she was wearing the helmet for protection. Her heart expanded at the compliment. Nobody had ever looked at her the way Cassie did, as if she were her own personal Bond girl, or made her feel sensations she didn't even recognize. "Perhaps we'd better put the brakes on," Siobhan murmured, as she reached around Cassie to squeeze the handlebars.

Cassie took hold of Siobhan's arms and manipulated them so they rested against her waist. Siobhan spliced her fingers, pressed her palms into Cassie's middle, and melted into the driver.

"Too hot to handle? Or we could live a little."

The quad bike shifted into action, the engine soaring into life, much like Siobhan's entire body, and then they were into the woods, whizzing past weathered trees rising from the undergrowth to brush against the gray sky. Spongy moss climbed up the dense tree trunks and pinecones were scattered across the dirt tracks, crushed easily under the wheels as they flew by, soaring over speed bumps. The scents of pine and wet dew hung in the air as Cassie took the track by storm.

"You okay?" Cassie called over the vroom of the engine.

"I'm pretty sure I just touched your breasts, so yes!" Siobhan cheered, knowing her response would go unheard as they sped through an opening in the forest. She made a mental note not to let Cassie lead Dylan's friends if she booked his party here. Then she remembered Cassie was only here to help her check out the place and wouldn't be present at the party—unless Siobhan could coax her into accepting yet another invitation. What would she do if Cassie agreed to come? Was she sending mixed signals if she kept asking Cassie round? No. She'd said she wanted a friend, and that's what friends did.

When the track smoothed out in front of them, Siobhan settled her chin on Cassie's shoulder, indulging in their proximity, reveling in the attraction, the arousal, the anticipation. Anything between them was impossible, but that didn't mean she couldn't enjoy herself anyway.

Before she could dwell on that possibility, Cassie pulled to a standstill. "Would you like to have a go at driving? You'll love it, and I might be able to breathe again." Cassie patted Siobhan's arms, and Siobhan realized she was still clinging to Cassie.

"Sorry," she said, letting go. "I wanted to live to celebrate Dylan's birthday. He'd be most annoyed if I died on a quad bike before he'd had a go on one. How about you drive us back to the start and we get our feet on solid ground?"

"You know, I'm familiar with this part of the coast. The scenery is beautiful around here," Cassie said, "not that you'll have seen any of it on that little jaunt through the forest. But if we take a steady drive over to Kingsgate, I can take you to my favorite place."

"The castle?"

"The lighthouse."

"From one adventure to the next," Siobhan said, her anticipation soaring at the chance to spend more time together.

❖

As darkness fell, the blue haze of the day lifted to reveal stars lighting the night sky like compact glow sticks. Cassie marveled at their beauty as she walked with Siobhan, perfectly in step, enjoying her company far more than fast driving, special sandwiches, or even cigarettes, which she suddenly realized she hadn't craved for a while.

"So has it always been about fast cars and a need for speed?" Siobhan asked.

"It feels amazing to roll the soft-top down and get out on the road, destination nowhere in particular. It's where I do most of my thinking, tunes blasting and all the time in the world. It's a good way to relax after a busy week at the office."

Siobhan gasped. "You mean having dinner at my place with two children desperate to impress you isn't relaxing enough?"

"You know how much I despised the delightful time I had."

"Is that what you were thinking about while racing through the woods?" Siobhan asked, dimples denting her cheeks when she smiled.

"I'm not giving away top-secret information." Cassie hesitated, allowing herself a moment to take Siobhan in. "Not even to you." She paused, considering the best way to suggest her idea.

"What?"

"Close your eyes."

"Why?" Siobhan asked even as she complied.

"Because I asked you to."

Cassie felt the grains of sand sink beneath her feet as she took Siobhan by the hand and guided her towards the best viewpoint of the deserted lighthouse, a whitewashed tower clinging to the barnacled rocks.

"You can open them now. Can you see the top of the old lighthouse?" Cassie pointed. "I'd like to take you up there. The view is stunning and it's an amazing place to star gaze. You up for it?"

"I'm always up for pretty much anything."

"Well then, allow me to lead the way." She mock bowed. When they had made their way up the twisted staircase, Cassie clasped Siobhan's shoulders and guided her to the gallery deck. "Take in that view for a moment." While she did, Cassie relished the expression of awe on Siobhan's face, the way her gaze mimicked the ivory moonlight sweeping across the bay, glistening like a blanket of molten silver and glimmering off the sand.

"So...do you come here often?" Siobhan asked.

Cassie licked her lips. "Helena and I used to come down to the beach after our wild nights out during the summer break from uni. We'd invent these ridiculous games and then try to remember how to play them when we were sober. There was one where we had to put on an accent and convince everyone we met it was genuine."

"Did you ever attempt an Irish accent?"

"Yes, and I was terribly unconvincing, got busted and had to down a shot or five. I can pull off a lot of things, but the luck of the Irish isn't one of them."

"So what you're saying is..." Siobhan exhaled. "It's best to leave the Irish accent to the natives?"

Cassie swallowed hard. Siobhan had amplified her accent, infusing her speech with musical intonations, and Cassie's heart began dancing in new and entirely unexpected ways.

"It tends to wear off when I'm not around other Irish people," Siobhan went on, tossing her hair over her shoulder. "You should hear how everyone talks back home in Slane. One hundred miles an hour and the Meath slang in full flow. You wouldn't understand a word."

"I wouldn't need to." She looked at Siobhan, then drew her gaze away. She opened her mouth to speak, then shut it before something sweet and genuine came out.

"We're not doing a whole lot of looking at the stars." Siobhan looked up. "Do you actually know anything about them?"

"Not really. I reckon if the future existence of sandwiches relied upon it, I could probably point out the plough."

Laughter erupted between them as they both looked skywards. It was then that Cassie's hand slipped around Siobhan's back and settled on the base of her spine, drawing her in closer. To her surprise, Siobhan didn't pull away.

"Come on then, which is it?" Siobhan asked.

Cassie drew the pattern with her free hand as accurately as she could, enjoying the sensation of Siobhan's body pressed so close to her own, her heart rate soaring. Eventually, Siobhan drew her eyes away from the sky to look at Cassie.

"Tell me about more of your uni antics with Helena."

"Bath being Bath, nights would often end with us dancing absurdly in the fountains, which escalated into water fights with total strangers. We'd end up catching the bus home looking like drowned rats. Well, she looked like a drowned rat. I can pull off sexy, even soaked from head to foot."

"Is there any look you can't execute to perfection?"

Cassie pretended to concentrate for a short amount of time and then shook her head. "No, I don't think so."

"What if I were to tell you that you have tiny specks of mud splattered all over your face? Here." Siobhan touched her just above her cheekbone and Cassie's eyes followed. "And here." She trailed a finger down to her chin. "And even a little just here." She ran a finger across the bridge of Cassie's nose.

Cassie was rooted to the spot, transfixed by Siobhan's touch. Her stomach flipped as Siobhan took her hand and guided her to other specks on her face. She could hear her own breathing, more audible as it quickened with every new touch. "How come you're not covered in mud?" she whispered.

"The perks of sitting behind a dangerous driver. The bruises I'm going to find on my backside tomorrow from being tossed around like a crowd surfer? Less perky."

"Your poor backside," Cassie said, dragging her teeth across her lower lip, her resolve waning. "If there's any support you feel it may need, you can count on me. I'm an expert on women's arses."

"I knew it!" Siobhan cocked her head, dropped her hand. "I just knew that if an expert in that field existed, it would be you." She reclined against the rendered wall, and Cassie followed her lead, glad of its solidity right now.

"This would be the perfect place to initiate a romantic interlude," Cassie said. The words escaped without intent and were followed by a whispered expletive as Cassie pressed her hand to her mouth to prevent more preposterous declarations pouring out. What if Siobhan misinterpreted the observation? Or worse, what if she didn't?

No sooner had the sentimental suggestion left Cassie's lips than Siobhan turned to her, pressing her lips to Cassie's.

Cassie found herself luxuriating in their warmth and softness. She longed to draw her in, to introduce the dance of their tongues, but she fought her impulses, though it took all her willpower to place her hand on Siobhan's chest and gently push her away.

Before Siobhan could apologize—*Sorry* was the first word she'd ever uttered in Cassie's presence, and Cassie didn't want it to be her last—Cassie took the lead.

"I can't do this with you," Cassie murmured, slipping her hand onto Siobhan's shoulder. To her surprise, Siobhan didn't pull away. "I like you too much."

Siobhan nodded and rested her forehead against Cassie's shoulder. "I like you too much too."

Cassie held Siobhan to her, knowing full well she should push her away, say something witty, break the tension. Instead, they stood beneath the stars, silent and still. She'd give herself this one perfect moment. Tomorrow they'd go back to being friends.

❖

"Why the fuck did I have to kiss her?" Siobhan flung herself onto the bed, her thoughts spiraling like the staircase they'd ascended in the lighthouse. It was a disaster of her own making. She'd allowed her impulses to erode her common sense, her arousal to overtake her rationality, and her need to be desired to eclipse any chance she had of remaining professional.

She ran her fingers over her mouth. She could still feel Cassie's lips on hers. Cassie's hand on her shoulder hadn't soothed her. It had triggered a throbbing that had started beneath her ribs and ended between her legs.

Siobhan couldn't recall the last time she'd had an orgasm. Now, she not only longed for one, she required the release. Although she was alone in the house, she ran Matthew's routine through her head. He and the kids would be gone for another few hours, at least. The last thing she needed was to get caught in the act in the bed she no longer shared with him. Or worse, to be forced to stop short.

Certain that her solitude would be preserved, she reached for the lamp, and when the room descended into darkness, she took that as her cue to give in to her craving.

Siobhan pictured Cassie's glossy golden hair, her velvety skin, her luscious leather jacket. She allowed her hand to steal inside her jeans and below her underwear. The wet heat she discovered surprised her—she had almost forgotten what desire felt like. Without further thought, she slowly slipped one finger inside herself, welcoming the sensation. It was easy to settle into a rhythm, despite not having pleasured herself in years.

Desperate for more, she slid another finger inside, thrusting with purpose, conscious of her breath coming in throaty gasps. She envisioned Cassie all over her: twisting, grinding, writhing.

Her body surged into sexual overdrive, sweat trickling down her neck as she pushed faster. She fondled her breast with her free hand, visualizing Cassie's fingers in place of her own, while the other continued to work towards her end goal.

Cassie's name was on the tip of her tongue, as her climax hit full throttle, sparking spasms that engaged her entire being.

"Shit!" Siobhan exclaimed, burying her head in a pillow, aching to do it all again but denying herself that luxury. Once, she could just about excuse, but twice felt a step too far. It was going to be difficult enough continuing their friendship, but if she continued like this, she'd never be able to look Cassie in the eye again. One spectacular time would simply have to be enough.

As her body and breathing calmed, panic set in, and she prayed she would wake up with some sort of clarity—or at least some good sense.

Their quad biking trial might have been over, but Siobhan was far from out of the woods.

CHAPTER TWELVE

If I suggest potential meetings for Tuesdays…" Cassie stopped pacing long enough to scribble the day down in her notebook, then frowned and scratched it out. "Not Tuesdays. Wednesdays. Wednesdays are good." She tapped her pen against her lip. "We could also try for Saturdays. That works best for me." She hopped up onto her desk. "Communication works fine as it is, but we'll need to look more in-depth at physical contact." She jumped down and resumed pacing, her excitement building. "Specific times and places, that's an obvious one, and—"

The shrill ring of her office phone almost compromised Cassie's concentration, but she ignored it. Why talk to someone else when she was conversing so eloquently with herself? She jotted down a few more details, then poked her head out of her office.

"Do you have that status report for me?"

"Give me ten minutes and we can look over it together."

Siobhan didn't look at her, but she looked at Siobhan, and the sight of her accelerated the ache Cassie had been feeling ever since *that* kiss. Was Siobhan so absorbed in the figures she couldn't even glance up from her computer? Or was she avoiding Cassie? The latter seemed more likely.

Cassie cleared her throat. "Are you still free tonight?" Siobhan didn't answer right away, and Cassie felt every nerve in her body tense. Rattled, she blathered, "*I* am, just in case you were wondering."

"I thought you might have made other plans, given what happened the other night."

Siobhan finally looked up, giving Cassie the distinct impression she was being weighed up, like a director assessing an actor's suitability for a role in their show. This is *my* show, I'm in charge, Cassie reminded herself.

But then Siobhan said, "I'm glad you haven't made other plans."

Siobhan's smile always extended to the rest of her. Cassie heard it in her lilting voice, in her deliberate selection of words, the way she visibly relaxed.

"Excellent. It'll give us an opportunity to address the elephant in the room." This time she neither required nor desired a response. "After work, we'll jump on the Tube to Little Venice. There's a fantastic waterside café I know."

"Let me guess. The sandwiches are out of this world?" There it was again, the knowing smile that tied her up in knots.

"Something like that." It was all Cassie could string together in her bemused state. She walked away—and straight into the Dracaena plant that had been in position longer than she had. "Shit," she murmured under her breath, hoping Siobhan hadn't seen.

"That plant must have dangerous designs on you," Siobhan called from her desk. "Either that or it finds you as irresistible as—" Siobhan stopped short.

Cassie took a deep breath. This discomfort would be the death of her. "I think I might need to stick an out-of-order sticker on my forehead and call it a day." She chuckled, wondering whether Siobhan could sense the artifice of her smile. *Not a chance.* Cassie played it cool for a living.

So why did being around Siobhan make her feel like she was always two steps behind?

❖

As they navigated the Rembrandt Gardens en route to the café, Cassie's heart pounded like a musical overture.

She led Siobhan down a series of stone steps, the moonlight bringing a refreshing elegance to the charcoal night and lighting the way ahead. When they reached a neon barge lit by twinkling fairy lights, Cassie indicated for Siobhan to walk along the gangway.

The deck was split into small, secluded areas, each with its own beanbags, blankets, and pyramid-shaped heaters. Cassie pointed to a section overlooking the water. "Shall we take that little area over in the corner?"

Siobhan began heading towards the floor table—meant for sandwiches, and the large fluffy beanbag—meant for sharing.

Cassie allowed Siobhan to sit down first before settling in next to her. But the beanbag left no room for distance. In fact, closeness was so compulsory, they were all but sitting in each other's laps at first. Shuffling and awkward laughter ensued as they tried to maintain a respectable distance. Cassie was glad when they succeeded and even more glad when a waiter appeared to take their order, providing a momentary reprieve from the way Siobhan had felt pressed against her: comfortable, warm, unacceptably distracting.

Hot chocolates with the full works and a sandwich platter ordered, Cassie sat back, looking up at the night sky. The stars were scattershot on their dark canvas, almost as haphazard as her mind.

"You're not your usual functioning self today. Is everything all right?" Siobhan asked, the hesitation in her voice evident but the hope in her eyes blatant. When Cassie looked at Siobhan, that hope seemed to spread into every part of her.

With delicate attention to detail, Cassie lifted Siobhan's chin, a quick touch, two fingers at her jaw. There, then just as suddenly, gone. She heard Siobhan take a tiny breath, like a sunflower opening up to first light. Cassie shivered, her hands trembling with a need to explore. "Yes," she said, "I've been contemplating a proposition for you and dwelling on how to approach it."

Siobhan's eyebrows arched. "A proposition?"

The waiter approached, served their sandwiches and drinks, then departed. Cassie went straight for a tangy pulled pork wrap, digging in with abandon, as if she weren't on the verge of vulnerability—and, potentially, stupidity.

"I was thinking we could come to some sort of arrangement whereby we agree to see one another, spend time together, maybe even have weekly…meetings."

Siobhan fumbled with a napkin. "Erm…is this your way of asking me out?"

"Absolutely not," Cassie said, moving into business mode. "There can be no thought of an actual relationship between us."

"Oh." Siobhan pinched her bottom lip, a pensive expression on her face. "You said you liked me. Too much."

"Which is why I'm recommending an illicit affair. No strings attached. We both get something out of it, something I believe we both need, and we follow a strict set of rules. That way, nobody gets overly invested."

"Just marginally invested?" Siobhan asked.

Cassie couldn't tell whether it was a challenge or a compromise. "There's *no* investment. Just two friends having an extra bit of fun on the side," Cassie clarified, defying Siobhan to dispute the accuracy of her statement. "Well?" she prompted her. "What do you think?"

Siobhan rolled her head back and launched into laughter. "You're not serious," she spluttered.

Cassie bristled at the magnitude of her mirth and waited for Siobhan to notice the lack of reciprocation. When at last Siobhan looked at her and saw that Cassie was sitting there, rigid and stony, she fell silent.

"You *are* serious. I'm sorry. It's just—the way you asked, like it's the most routine suggestion in the world, which by the way, it isn't. Why don't you inform me what these rules you're imposing consist of?"

The tension eased from Cassie's shoulders, and she sat up a bit straighter. "I want to see you every Wednesday and Saturday."

"The nights that work best for me. You really have thought this through. I'm impressed." She didn't look impressed.

Ignoring the backhanded compliment, Cassie said, "It could work. We're clearly attracted to one another and I admit that I find myself thinking about you way too much. This way we both get our physical needs met but we're free to go about our regular daily lives." Although it made sense, she had to admit that it sounded a little tawdry when laid out that way.

Siobhan wrapped her hands around her hot chocolate, leaning slightly away from Cassie. "Wow." Siobhan shook her head. "I can tell you've invested a lot of thought into this. I'm afraid I can't guarantee you every Saturday, even *if* I wanted to."

"It isn't ideal to have to rewrite the rules." Cassie frowned. "However, I can be content with Wednesdays and one night of the weekend. Is that manageable?"

"Not that I'm agreeing to anything here, but I think I could work that out."

"Good. Now, to ensure there is absolute clarity about the agreement, let's review: there will be no feelings involved. You won't expect anything more from me than what I offer. Sex is an absolute must, but there will be no kissing on the lips. It's far too intimate," Cassie stated, with both formality and finality.

Siobhan took a large bit of her cranberry and turkey wrap, as if she needed something else to chew on. Her whole body had shifted away from Cassie and she directed her gaze out onto the water.

"You don't have to give me an answer tonight," Cassie said, her confidence slowly fading in the face of Siobhan's silence. "Take your time to think about what I'm offering. I want you to fully understand what you're getting into, should you choose to get into it."

"And this is what *you* want?" Siobhan sounded skeptical.

"It's what I feel needs to happen," Cassie supplied. "It's the only way I can think of to deal with our mutual attraction."

"Or we could really push the boat out and agree to a few dates, see how it goes, spend time together and let things progress naturally. What you're putting on the table is like a business offer and I'm not sure I can do that."

"It's the best I can offer. I've made it clear from the start that I don't do commitment or relationships. You've always known that."

"Believe it or not, this was never my intention. I applied for this job to improve my career, not risk it. There's a lot to think about here, a lot at stake if things go wrong."

"If you're concerned about your job, it will be safe, no matter what happens between us. You have my word."

"That's as may be, but I'm still married. I have children."

"This doesn't involve them."

Siobhan shook her head, her lips pursed. "Sometimes you really do beggar belief. Of course it involves my children. Every decision I make involves them. Besides, you were the one who promised them a trip to the seaside at some point."

Cassie had neglected to factor in the kids, but if she confessed her negligence to Siobhan, the offer would be off the table faster than she could forget the name of a one-night stand. "I intend to keep that promise. I'm not opposed to their presence on occasion. Besides, it's not as though we'd be conducting our affair right in front of their eyes. I'm certain we could control ourselves."

"Because we've done a great job so far."

"That's what the rules are for."

"Right." Siobhan looked pale, her voice shaky. "I'm not entirely sure why you brought me to such a…This place is romantic, Cass. I don't know why you brought me here to make such a matter-of-fact proposal."

"It's a proposition, not a proposal." She paused, deliberating whether or not to even deliver her next words, considering the lump that had formed in her throat at the mere thought of saying them out loud. But she knew it was necessary for Siobhan to hear them, if only so she'd understand the noncommittal nature of the proposition. "Who knows, maybe one day you'll find that special someone to make a go of it with. Then you can thank me for preparing you in the best way possible."

Siobhan said nothing, but Cassie could hear her thoughts clattering louder than shutters in the eye of a storm.

"I'm going to get going," Siobhan announced after a moment, placing a ten-pound note on the table. "For my share of the sandwiches. I'll catch you tomorrow. Good night, Cassie."

"Good night," Cassie called after her.

Cassie could tell Siobhan felt conflicted, but given time she felt sure Siobhan would acquiesce. After all, Cassie knew the attraction went both ways and it *had* been Siobhan who had technically made the first move and kissed her. If that didn't speak volumes, nothing else would. Cassie wasn't in the habit of reading these situations wrong either, which meant she was confident Siobhan would come round to the proposition and agree to it, the benefits outweighing the concerns. If she didn't, which was highly unlikely, Cassie could bid farewell to their friendship. She tried to ignore the little internal voice that said it wouldn't be that simple.

CHAPTER THIRTEEN

"Hey, Mum, can we ask Cassie to my birthday party?" Dylan skidded to a halt at the kitchen table, running right into Matthew. "Oh." He looked sheepishly towards Siobhan. "I thought you'd gone to work after breakfast, Dad."

"Who's Cassie?" Matthew looked up from the back page of the newspaper.

"Cassie is Mum's *friend*," Dylan said.

"Well, that's a turn up for the books!" Matthew grimaced. "She's not one of your coworkers, is she, who dragged you off to the bar and convinced you to shirk your parental responsibilities?"

Who convinced you, she mused, answering him only in her head.

"She came round for dinner when you were away," Dylan said, all but sticking his tongue out at Matthew. "You should see the car she drives, Dad, it's—"

"I'm not interested in cars," he snapped.

Dylan's shoulders slumped. "Fine, I won't talk to you about them then. I won't talk to you about anything." He grabbed his school rucksack and trudged out of the room.

"If Dylan wants to invite Cassie to his party, then he can," Siobhan decided, reaching for Matthew's plate. In anticipation of his objections, she added, "You put me in charge of the guest list, remember? You put me in charge of the whole thing actually, if I remember correctly."

He stuck his nose back in his newspaper without answering her.

"Dylan's sulking on the stairs," Neave said as she entered the kitchen. She eyed her dad up and down, as though debating whether or not to speak to him.

Siobhan almost laughed. "He's not, sweetheart," she said, kissing the top of Neave's head. "He's just waiting for a lift to school."

"I'll bet he wishes he could show up to school in Cassie's car," Neave said. "Then everyone would tell him how *cool* he is."

Matthew's head shot up. "I don't want to hear any more about this Cassie or her wondrous wheels."

"You just want to spoil the fun," Neave muttered, storming out to join Dylan.

"What is going on here, Siobhan? Both stropping off like bloody teenagers, and Cassie this, Cassie that."

Siobhan considered how much more he would dislike Cassie if he knew her main motivation was to bed his wife. She turned towards the sink to conceal her smirk, making a mental note to chase up her solicitor when she got to the office, in the hope of speeding proceedings along. "They like Cassie. She's fun."

"They're not the only ones showing enthusiasm for her," Matthew said, his tone icy.

When she faced him again, he was standing, his hand on his hip. Typical argument pose.

"Go get in the car, kids. I'll be along in a minute," she called out, but if Matthew expected a squabble when they were out of earshot, he was in for a surprise.

Siobhan offered only cold silence. Now that the divorce was in motion, it was simply a case of holding things together for a short while longer. If that meant biting her tongue instead of biting his head off, then so be it.

"I'm just teasing you," Matthew said, as if disquieted by her calm. "I'm glad you have a friend." He went to touch her arm, but she maneuvered out of his reach. "I know I've got nothing to worry about. You'd never cheat or walk out on me. You're far too much of a soft touch for that. It's what I love most about you."

A hot brush of anger curdled in her stomach. She wheeled around, head held high, not even affording him the courtesy of a backward glance. "I have to get going."

"You seem a little flustered," he said.

Siobhan knew exactly what he was doing: pushing and pushing until she gave him the reaction he desired. She disarmed him with a pleasant smile. "I'm not flustered in the slightest. I'm just eager to get to—"

"Cassie?"

"—work."

It was only after she dropped the kids off at school that the eagerness emerged. The mere thought of seeing Cassie had her heart exceeding the speed limit. She pictured Cassie at her desk, wearing a patient expression of questionable authenticity. Siobhan knew she would be desperate for an answer to the proposition she had braved.

When she considered exactly what an affair entailed—sneaking around in the dark, returning home in the cold light of day, the injured party none the wiser—she wasn't sure she could go through with it.

Having grown up in Catholic Ireland, she knew adultery was a sin. Her upbringing hadn't been particularly religious, but she doubted her mother would look down on her immoral daughter with pride. The last thing she wanted was to be a disappointment, but then she remembered how much her mother had disapproved of Matthew and decided she would understand this choice, this need.

Would her children? What if they discovered her dishonesty? They knew she was unhappy with their father, but still, it was unfair to burden them with her deceitful decision. And what if they alerted Matthew, intentionally or accidentally? Of course, if he did find out, he might demand a divorce, and then they'd finally be on the same page about something.

She could always wait until after the divorce was finalized. Cassie hadn't stipulated a specific starting date, but she had specified that they would be having an illicit affair. If Siobhan were divorced, it would no longer qualify as an illicit affair. It would qualify as an involvement, which Cassie certainly didn't want.

Of the thousand thoughts bouncing around inside Siobhan's head like lottery balls, one stood out: she definitely wanted Cassie.

No sooner had she convinced herself to agree to the affair than she managed to talk herself out of it again. Could she abide by Cassie's unbending rules? Cassie hadn't just piqued her curiosity or revived her interest in women. When Siobhan was with Cassie, she felt giddy, senseless, aware. How could she handle a passionate liaison that required her to be dispassionate? The answer was simple: she couldn't. Therefore, her answer had to be no.

Temples throbbing with a banging headache, she pulled into her parking space. When she checked herself in the rearview mirror, she recoiled at her reflection. "The shadows under my eyes are darker than the shades of night," she muttered.

But when she encountered Cassie in her office doorway, lying—or at least leaning—in wait, Siobhan's resolve wavered.

"Good morning, gorgeous."

"I'm sorry?" She blinked rapidly, her thought process delayed. "Is it really wise to start addressing each other in such an overfamiliar manner?" She glanced around, expecting Julie to materialize like a genie from a magic lamp, notebook in hand, ready to report on their new dynamic to anyone who would listen.

"Each other?" Cassie quirked an eyebrow. "I don't believe you've assigned me an alias yet." She winked.

Siobhan felt her internal thermometer rise despite her bad mood. "I've had a shit morning." She rubbed the back of her neck. "Want to hear about it?" She fully expected Cassie to retreat at this point.

Instead, she said, "Come on through," and, when Siobhan complied, Cassie threw her a small tub of aspirin. "For your headache."

"You can tell?" Siobhan couldn't hide her surprise. Or her gratitude. Or her suspicions. She opened the lid and poured two into her palm. Cassie handed her a glass of water and while Siobhan took a swig to swallow them, she watched Cassie pull the blinds down and move towards the leather sofa in the corner of her office, which Siobhan had never seen her occupy before.

Cassie tapped the space next to her and Siobhan advanced with caution, certain she resembled a detective on a police procedural approaching an armed suspect. When she perched on the end of the sofa, Cassie immediately slid closer. "You look like you haven't slept," Cassie said, running her thumb down Siobhan's face, eliciting a soft moan.

Cassie's seeming sincerity scared her. Given the circumstances, she couldn't be sure if anything was genuine. "You're only being attentive because you want me to agree to the arrangement. I know you, Cassie Townsend."

Color appeared in Cassie's cheeks—an ill-tempered shade of red, followed by a frown.

"Think of all the showboating you'll be able to do: another notch on your almighty bedpost, courtesy of a married woman. Have you had one of those before or am I your first?" She couldn't help the angry words spilling forth. Everything was so confusing.

The moment she felt Cassie's arm wrap around her waist, she was lost. Instead of resisting, she melted into Cassie. Agreeing to this affair would be a terrible decision, one she'd make against all her better judgment, yet there was a combination of lust and belief that she simply couldn't ignore.

Her mind raced back to the lighthouse, to their kiss. It should have been hot and furious, but instead it had been short and sweet, nothing like someone only out for their next conquest. It should have been Siobhan's fingers in Cassie's hair, her teeth raking across Cassie's bottom lip. Siobhan imagined pressing her thumb to the corner of Cassie's lips, coaxing her mouth open to deepen the kiss. Right now her body was thrumming, her pulse fluctuating fiercely. They should have been so close together that there was no way to tell them apart, yet Cassie had pushed her away. That would never happen again if Siobhan said yes, since kissing would be off the table. She understood that if she accepted Cassie's conditions, she'd have to refashion her fantasies, but there were plenty of places for both of them to place their lips other than their mouths.

"I want you, Siobhan, and I mean *really* want you, as much as you want me." Cassie used her free hand to cup Siobhan's jaw, drawing her in. "I'll make your first experience with a woman so special. Additionally, you'll have someone to share occasional late-night conversations with, someone who will relish your company and not take it for granted." Cassie loosened her grip around Siobhan's waist.

Right away, she missed the comfort and heat of her touch. "Maybe so, and let's not forget that you get exactly what you want too: no emotions, no commitment—"

"Mind-blowing sex," Cassie added, killing with her a smile. "It's pretty easy to envision just what an illicit affair between us might look like, don't you think?" Cassie playfully walked two fingers up and down Siobhan's arm.

"Fuck. I don't know whether my head's buried in the sand or up in the clouds. There's a lot at stake for me here."

"Not if you abide by my rules." Cassie's clipped tone indicated there were to be no deviations from her expectations. "It really is that simple." She went to her desk, rummaged around in her drawers, and returned with a silver envelope, which she presented to Siobhan.

"Is this a bribe?"

"It's not a bribe. It's an invitation, which you are welcome to accept or decline, much like my original proposition. It's all down to you."

"And you're making it *so* easy for me.'

"I can't afford to get this wrong." Cassie's expression this time was sincere, her eyes clear with need.

To know Cassie wasn't as audacious as she had the world believe, somehow that mattered. Siobhan turned her attention towards the envelope, slowly peeling it back to reveal two tickets to see *Wicked*.

"I thought we might finally find out what those two are whispering about," Cassie said, clasping her hands to her chest as if she didn't know what to do with them. "Meeting night doesn't have quite the same ring to it as date night. I guess we could rename it that, if you'd like to come?"

"Date night. I *do* like the sound of that."

Cassie blinked, hovering over her like a spotlight. "Are you...are you saying what I think you're saying?"

"Yes." Siobhan took a deep, steadying breath. It was a mistake. One she desperately wanted to make.

"Completely no-strings?" Cassie asked, as if her life depended on it.

"Not even a kite string," Siobhan vowed. She could do this. She could feel wanted, enjoyed, for as long as it lasted. And when it ended? She pushed the thought away.

CHAPTER FOURTEEN

Y ou need a woman in your life."
Declaration delivered, Eva took a seat at the ridiculously expensive table Cassie had insisted on buying when she first moved in. Artfully positioned on the balcony, it brought a hint of unconventional elegance, but it still felt like a luxury too far. Her sister clearly thought as much, eyeing it up with mistrust. "If only to stop you wasting your money on revolting balcony furniture."

"How about ridiculous gadgets?" Cassie asked, placing two mugs of hot chocolate in front of them. "I just got a new Velvetiser."

"Indeed. Marshmallows, cream, rainbow sprinkles." Eva's grin peeked out from beneath her foam mustache. "This is so gay."

"Thank you." Cassie watched with satisfaction as the brightly colored sprinkles melted into the cream, producing a prism of radiance.

"All I need now is for you to light a cigarette and share it with me because it's a well-known fact I don't smoke."

"Neither do I." Cassie raised her hands in celebration.

Eva stroked her chin, a hint of suspicion in her eyes. "Since when?"

Cassie cleared her throat, avoiding eye contact. "Since I quit. Today. Again."

"Talk about longevity."

"I've come to realize I have *way* too many vices—"

"Said Cassie Townsend never. You quit with a view to…what? Improve yourself? Or impress someone?"

Cassie abandoned her overpriced chair and took up residence at the railing. "I quit with a view to enjoy this one," she said, sweeping her arm across the view of the city. "For as long as I possibly can."

Below, London was alive with lights, like someone had sprinkled glitter over the city as far as the eye could see. Cassie knew the route of the Thames below and could vaguely make out the outlines of boats running their familiar sightseeing trips. She imagined tourists looking up at where she now stood, appreciating the city as if for the first time.

"I can't imagine ever getting tired of sitting here and watching the world go by," Eva mused.

Cassie was grateful she had dropped her line of questioning—for the time being. "It's funny you should say that, because I often think I'd swap it to wake up by the ocean." She remembered how Siobhan had been enraptured by the coastal paintings in her office, drinking in every last detail on their first meeting. Then there was the artsy photo she had sent to Siobhan of Minnis Bay during her last visit to Eva. Then there was the lighthouse…

"You wouldn't last two minutes without the hustle and bustle of the city. In a small town like Broadstairs you'd get through all the available women in the blink of a…thigh."

Cassie tried to keep a straight face. "I reckon I'd give the unavailable ones a good go too."

"You are so not moving within fifty miles of my peaceful town. I've no desire to be part of one of your little scandals."

"I can see the headline now: *Sapphic Sister Scores Sex Scandal.*"

"That is *not* where I see my future heading."

There was a slight warning to Eva's tone that amused Cassie more than it advised her. Nevertheless, it was time to change the subject. Again. "Dad sent me a text. Did you have something to do with that?"

Eva blew her cheeks out, then released the air. "I had no idea," she said, but Cassie could tell by the way she busied herself with her spoon that she was lying. "Okay, I may have had a little to do with it."

"He shouldn't need you to remind him he has two daughters." Cassie clamped her teeth shut to avoid any harsher words. Although she hadn't read the text, the fact that it was sitting in her phone had meant something. Now that she knew it wasn't a genuine gesture from him, she wasn't interested. "Did you write it too?"

"Don't be daft. I know you were disappointed when he pulled off a disappearing act last time." Cassie opened her mouth to protest, but Eva didn't allow her the opportunity. "Don't deny it. I know you, Cassie. It was wrong of him to do that; I told him so at the time and I told him again afterward. Something obviously hit home if he decided to text you. What did he say to you?" Cassie shrugged. Eva extended her hand expectantly. "Hand me your phone right now."

Cassie seized her mobile phone before Eva could, just as a notification popped up: a message from Siobhan. She pulled it closer to her chest, resenting the rise in body temperature she experienced at the very notion that Siobhan had initiated contact. Despite the fact Eva was watching her with sisterly scrutiny, Cassie couldn't resist a quick glance, smiling to herself as she read the message: *I can't wait to see Wicked with you, but I'm wondering what the after show looks like.* Cassie's cheeks felt hot, and she imagined they matched the pink of the marshmallows melting away in her drink.

"Do I detect a twinkle in your eye?" Eva teased her.

Cassie cursed her sister's observant nature. "No." She swiped down to the message from her dad, making a mental note to reply to Siobhan later. *It seems we missed each other. Eva suggested we meet up and thrash this out. The wedding is coming up and nobody wants that to be awkward.* "Talk about priorities." Cassie lifted her eyebrow. "Your wedding means I have to toe the line."

"That's not what I said and well you know it. I put forward the idea that it might be good to talk, just the two of you, away from Mum."

"Now you're making *me* want a cigarette." Cassie folded her hands behind her head.

"Are you going to reply?"

To her credit, Cassie gave it a moment's consideration before responding. "I'm just not there yet." It was the truth. "I know you don't always understand me, but you invariably respect my decisions."

"That's a slightly mellower reaction than I was expecting," Eva said. "I'd have bet my life on your mug flying across the room, at the very least. What's gotten into you?"

"Absolutely nothing." Cassie closed down the conversation. "I don't suppose you still have my old drum kit by any chance?"

"That bloody blue sparkly thing?" Eva cringed. "You've not lost your penchant for bad taste! I'm pretty sure Danny put it in the loft when we moved."

"Do you reckon it's still playable?"

"Why? And don't tell me you're so desperate to relive your youth, that you're going all AC/DC on me."

"Christ, no!" Cassie's laugh came right from her belly. "Look, I know it's a long shot, but I was hoping you might be able to resurrect it for me? I promised Siobhan's daughter I'd show her a few beats, teach her how to spin the sticks. Nothing too ambitious." Cassie tried her best to downplay the whole thing, looking Eva directly in the eye as she spoke. It was a strategy she knew she wouldn't get away with but felt the need to attempt it anyway.

"Siobhan's daughter? Why would you be spending time with Siobhan's daughter? Or, for that matter, with Siobhan?"

"It's just a drum lesson." Cassie kept eye contact. *Nothing to hide here.*

"At my house, which is a definite day trip from London. A day trip with a married woman and her two young children. That doesn't sound like any sort of Cassie I know."

"Forget I mentioned it. I'll buy a bloody drum set if it's such a big ask."

"It's got nothing to do with that." Eva folded her arms. "Siobhan *is* the woman you were crushing on when we went to see Drake, right?"

"I hate that word. It's childish."

"Yet perfect for your situation," Eva pointed out. "What aren't you telling me?"

Cassie knew this wasn't likely to go down well, so she decided to rip the plaster right off. She drew breath and spoke. "We're having an affair. Well, she's *agreed* to an affair. We haven't technically done anything yet."

"Oh! That makes it all right then." Eva's expression darkened. "What the fuck, Cassie? I thought she was straight."

"So is spaghetti, until it gets wet."

"This isn't a joke, Cassie, and it won't end well, not for you and certainly not for her. This desire you have to be the womanizer, the seducer, I get it, I accept it, but this? This is selfish, even for you."

"You don't get to call me that," Cassie snapped. "You don't know what a difficult decision this has been for me."

"To think with your clit? I'm sure that was *very* challenging!"

Cassie stalked across the balcony. "I told you because you asked, not because I care about your opinion."

"Well, you *should* care. It's precisely because *I* care that I'm calling you out."

Although Cassie felt under fire, she refused to doubt her decision. "Siobhan knows exactly what she's getting into. I've created very specific rules and she's agreed to follow them."

"So it's not even a 'We'll fall into one another's arms at every available opportunity because we can't keep our hands off one another' affair?" Eva's pitch was on par with a world-class soprano. "It's premeditated?"

"It's necessary." Cassie bit back saying anything more, resenting her sister's primitive opinions. And resenting the slim ring of truth behind them, too.

"Well, the fact that you can control it, by imposing all these *very specific rules*, tells me it's entirely unnecessary. It's the most self-centered thing you've ever done and there's a pretty long list." Eva turned away from Cassie, as if she could no longer bear to look at her. "Where are your cigarettes?"

"Here." Cassie reached into her jacket pocket and flung the packet across the table. Eva lit the Marlboro with the candle from the center of the table and inhaled deeply as the tip lit up red. Cassie picked up an ashtray from the floor and slid it across to Eva. "Use this."

"Thanks." Eva offered her a drag, but as tempted as she was, she declined.

Cassie walked back inside her apartment, leaving Eva alone with her disapproval. She didn't need Eva listing all the reasons why it was a terrible idea. What did it even matter that Eva had taken exception to the setup? Unless she had a point? Cassie shook her head. No nagging insecurity was going to get the better of her. She would stick to her guns, regardless.

"It's getting cold out there." Cassie looked up to see Eva making her way towards the sofa. Her sister's tone and eyes had softened; her limbs seemed looser. Cassie knew the signs well: Eva was coming down from her agitated outburst.

"I'm not out to hurt anyone." Cassie steepled her fingers together, fidgeting with her thumbs. "Please don't think that of me."

"What if you're the one that stands to get hurt?"

"That won't happen." Cassie shook her head. "She's not mine to lose. There will be no feelings invested from either side. I can keep to that—you know how little I've devoted myself to anyone since university."

"And this is something to be proud of? She could lose her marriage, her home, her children—"

"She won't lose her children."

"You can see into the future? Because when her husband finds out, which he undoubtedly will, he'll have something to say about custody. Have you thought about that? I'm pretty sure you don't want two kids and their mother landing on your doorstep."

"It won't come to that," Cassie insisted, even as a small part of her resisted that certainty.

Eva shook her head but scooted closer. "Boy, am I glad I have Danny."

Cassie rolled her eyes, but she appreciated Eva's capitulation, however temporary.

"I just don't want to see you get hurt again. Not after what happened last time."

"That was a blip," Cassie cut her off.

"A blip that has you completely incapacitated when it comes to relationships."

Cassie grinned and threw a cushion at her. "Hence why I'm not investing myself into a relationship."

Eva clutched the cushion and sagged into the sofa. "It's not me you have to convince though, is it? It's the poor woman whose heart you're about to break."

"That's not going to happen. I know what I'm doing."

But did she? Of all the questions Eva had asked, why she'd made such a choice had never come up. Yet it was this question that still irritated her, especially when she couldn't find any answer that made sense. Deviating from one-night stands was huge in her world, especially when there was no clear rhyme or reason for it. Confusion fogged her brain as she tried to reason out her decision. Working it out seemed entirely impossible and no matter how hard she tried, nothing could justify it. This made her eternally grateful her sister hadn't asked the question she simply couldn't answer. Why change the habit of a lifetime for one woman?

CHAPTER FIFTEEN

"The expression *break a leg* only applies to the theater, you know!" Cassie exclaimed, dodging this way and that with about as much elegance as a rugby player on roller skates. Yet another delinquent whooshed past her, screaming in delight and causing her to question her sanity.

Standing in the woodlands, surrounded by overexcited boys, Cassie shifted from one foot to the other, unable to find any position that made her seem at ease, especially when kids kept charging right at her. She felt like she was performing a dynamic dance routine in the middle of a Shakespearean tragedy. Dylan made a beeline for her, dragging another boy along with him for good measure. She squeezed her hands together until her knuckles went white.

"This is Mum's friend, Cassie." Shoulders back, chest out, Dylan seemed to grow more animated and confident by the minute. "Cassie, this is my best mate, Liam. See the silver 911 over there, Liam? It's Cassie's!"

The boy's eyes went wider than flying saucers. "No way!"

Cassie fiddled with the zip on her jacket, glad she had gone with a practical one rather than her leather one today. The other adults in attendance were practically kitted out, so she had done well to blend in, even though she had never felt more out of place.

"Yes way!" Dylan's laugh boomed out. "You're not usually this quiet, Cassie," he said, shaking his head as if he were disappointed in her. Cassie tucked her hands into her pockets. "Well, seeing as you've lost your voice, just nod when I ask you this very important question,"

Dylan said. "You're coming out on the quads with us, aren't you?" The instant her head bobbed, Dylan turned to Liam and said, as if the information were confidential, "Mum says Cassie is crazy fast."

"Awesome! Have you ever raced cars?"

Finally, she found her voice. "I've raced a supercar around Silverstone, but not for many years."

"And your street credit is growing by the minute." Siobhan's Irish lilt washed over her as she joined them. "I wasn't sure you'd come." She squeezed her arm.

"Well, I washed my hair last week, so I was all out of excuses." She felt sure her smile betrayed nerves she didn't want Siobhan to pick up on.

Siobhan nodded her approval. "You made Dylan's day. And maybe mine too." Siobhan squeezed her arm again.

Dylan tugged at Cassie's other arm. "Any chance you can drive the two of us back home in your car?"

"Dylan," Siobhan scolded him. "Cassie's gone out of her way to join you today. Don't pester her."

"What are you talking about? She doesn't live *that* far!"

Cassie looked from Dylan to Liam and back again, the idea of driving them home way out of her comfort zone. She pulled on the zip of her jacket, up, then down again. Something about the way Dylan looked at her, full of enthusiasm and hope, reminded her so much of Siobhan, it was both heartwarming and hair-raising.

"Pleeeeeease."

"I guess so." Cassie rolled her neck as the boys jumped up and down and hugged one another.

"You do know you're going to have to actually let them in your car now?" Siobhan asked, a wry smile on her face. "There's no going back."

"It's okay. I've wrapped the back seat in plastic sheeting, serial-killer style." Cassie winked.

Siobhan brushed shoulders with her. "I need to sort everyone out for their ride. It would be too much to ask for them to fasten their helmets both independently and safely."

A small part of Cassie wondered if Siobhan would welcome some help with the helmets, but she hadn't asked, so—

"Which is yours?"

"I'm sorry?" Cassie looked to Siobhan for assistance but found herself beside another woman entirely.

"Which child is yours?" the woman beside her repeated. "I haven't seen you around school, so I wondered if you were from Dylan's football team."

"Christ, no!" Realizing she'd overreacted, she rubbed her sweaty palms against her trousers and tried again. "I'm Siobhan's friend. Dylan invited me. We're both car enthusiasts."

"See the lad in the blue hoodie? That's my Joe. He's been going on about this for weeks. I love the fact Siobhan has gone all out for Dylan's party. I know most of us would just book *Football Mania* for an easy life. Alice, by the way." She offered her hand.

"Right." Cassie shook it as Alice examined her, nodding slowly. Cassie began nodding as well, if only to avoid being upstaged by Alice's dashboard ornament dance. Her eyes darted towards Siobhan, and she wondered if she could send out an SOS signal and be rescued. No such luck. "Dylan doesn't like football."

"Which is crazy when you consider how football mad his dad is. He's never at home. We all comment on it, saying how well Siobhan does on her own, considering she's a single parent most of the time, or so Joe tells me. It's probably why you agreed to help today, right? Though apparently Matthew *is* here somewhere. He drinks with my husband, Ryan, and was moaning like mad about having to come here last weekend. Bloody men!"

Cassie let out a high-pitched laugh, suddenly hyper-aware that not only was she stuck in suburban hell; Matthew was around too. She sent out imaginary feelers to detect his presence, hoping to prevent any further surprises of the unpleasant sort. "I should go—"

"Word on the street is they aren't far off a divorce. Well, that's what Dylan says anyway."

"Dylan said that?" Cassie filed the information away. "Is it official, do you know, or just wishful thinking on his part?"

Alice nodded again, and Cassie couldn't decide whether to be grateful for the open-ended non-answer or annoyed by it. Nevertheless, she had no desire for participation in after-school gossip. "Please don't speak about Siobhan behind her back," Cassie said, with more tact than she thought herself capable of. Take a bow, Cassie, take a bow, she congratulated herself, delighted with her decorum, as she strode over to the children, who were listening to the instructor's safety briefing.

When Siobhan saw Cassie approaching, she smiled and threw a helmet her way, which Cassie caught in one hand, a most miraculous accomplishment, given that Siobhan's smile had completely disarmed her.

"Aren't you quadding too, Siobhan?" Alice asked, apparently having followed Cassie like one of those irritating pull-along toys that had survived the severing of its string.

"Siobhan Carney on a quad bike?" an obnoxious voice guffawed. "We're talking about the woman who thinks the rearview mirror is for checking hair and makeup. Don't worry, your kids are safe. My wife is a careful driver, she always slows down when going through a red light."

Cassie bristled, feeling the hairs on the back of her neck stand on end. A sideways glance passed between her and Siobhan, who visibly tensed at his disparaging comments. Nobody responded to the remarks, nobody laughed, instead waiting with bated breath for Siobhan to say something. She didn't.

Although Cassie had seen Matthew before from a distance, she was still surprised by his appearance up close. His face was a haze of grey stubble, and his dark eyes were too close together, supported by the dark bags beneath them. He cocked his head towards Siobhan, running his hand through his hair, causing several strands to spring up at odd angles. His smug, self-serving look was enough to put Cassie's temper on stand-by, especially when she saw Siobhan drop her shoulders and duck her chin.

Cassie picked up another helmet. "Siobhan's riding with me."

"Yes." Siobhan pulled the helmet on. "I am." Siobhan regarded her husband with a defiant gleam. Subject closed.

Matthew glared at her, his too-close eyes narrowing. "And you are?"

"Riding with her."

The parents around them tittered. Matthew shuffled away from the crowd, hands in his pockets, and Siobhan marched over to the quad bike, where she confidently positioned herself on the back.

"Squidge up," Cassie whispered, urging Siobhan towards the front. "You're driving." She flashed Siobhan a *You've got this* look before pulling her helmet down too.

"We can switch though, can't we?"

Cassie knew Siobhan hadn't particularly enjoyed the swift pace the first time around, but there was no way she would permit Matthew to make a fool of Siobhan in front of everyone.

"As soon as we're out of sight if you need to," Cassie said, before nudging Siobhan's waist. "You'll be fine though." She leaned forward to whisper directly into her ear, "Just follow Dylan—he's setting the pace."

"Mum!" Dylan beamed at her. "I thought you said you were just watching! You're the best!"

"See, not only have I rescued you from that arrogant dick, I've also improved *your* street cred with the kids," Cassie said, placing her hands firmly on Siobhan's waist and feeling an instant, intimate thrill. "Try to relax and enjoy the experience."

"Wedged between your legs, it will be hard not to." Siobhan leaned back into her.

Cassie scanned the crowd for Matthew, but he was nowhere to be seen. She imagined him sulking like a nominee without an Oscar, and her lips spread into a satisfied smile.

❖

They hadn't ended up swapping positions. In fact, Siobhan had enjoyed taking the lead. Granted, it was a child-friendly route, requiring stricter adherence to the rules than when Cassie had gone all Lewis Hamilton on them. She heard Dylan and his friends whoop as they approached another woodland bump, saw the joy on his face as he tackled the tricky terrain, and couldn't bring herself to worry about Matthew. The fact she was seated between Cassie's thighs went some way to alleviating her concerns too.

"Time to head back," the instructor yelled, to disgruntled shouts. "There's a couple of great bumps before we're back to the start." The boys cheered at this, their disappointment fast forgotten. Siobhan almost joined in.

"Why don't you go first?" Dylan hollered across at her. "Show Dad what you can do!"

"Come on then!" she called out, buoyed by her son's confidence in her ability. A wicked defiance swept over her at the prospect of irritating Matthew. "Follow me!"

Braving the accelerator a little more resulted in Siobhan mastering a slightly quicker pace, and when she stepped off the quad a short time later, cheers erupted from Dylan's friends. Dylan himself stood up on his bike to give her a standing ovation, cheering wildly as she shed her helmet and shook out her hair.

"Impressive," Matthew conceded from where he'd lounged in the sun, unwilling to join in the group fun, looking like he'd just battled a packet of sour candy and the sweets had won. "Howev—"

"Wasn't she just?" Cassie interrupted.

A lightness in Siobhan's chest accompanied the thrill of Cassie's absolute fearlessness in confronting him.

"Hey, Cassie!" Neave escaped the clutches of Bronagh's hand and ran towards Cassie. "Did you have fun? I can't wait till I'm old enough to do it too."

"Immeasurable fun!" Cassie replied. "Especially with your mum."

"This is the famous Cassie." Matthew scowled. "We've heard lots about you. I believe you intruded on our family dinner a few weeks back."

"She didn't intrude," Neave said with a little scowl. "She was invited." Tugging on Siobhan's trouser leg, she asked, "What's *intrude*?"

"It means she was somewhere she didn't belong," Matthew answered.

"Speaking of which...you know, you look awfully familiar," Cassie said, a wry smile on her face. "Were you that husband who dragged his kids around the London bar scene in search of his wife?"

"How else was he supposed to put the children to bed?" Bronagh, Matthew's mother, bristled, her thin mouth pressed together in disapproval.

"By himself, like a big boy." Neave stepped in front of her mum like a little bodyguard. "Except we don't need anyone to put us to bed. We're not babies. He just didn't like Mum going out, even though he goes out all the time."

Matthew's nostrils flared. "I had no intention of going out *that* night. I was being considerate by giving your mum a lift home."

"Like a good husband would," Bronagh added.

The comments were coming so thick and fast, Siobhan didn't know where to look. She placed her hand against a tree trunk to steady herself. This was going to ruin Dylan's party, but she couldn't bring herself to put a stop to it.

Siobhan was grateful for the intervention as Cassie stepped forward to kneel beside Neave. "I've promised Dylan and Liam they can ride home in my car. There's room for you too. Why don't the three of you climb in?"

The three kids raced off, and the tension dwindled as parents began sorting out their kids. Cassie gave Siobhan's hand a squeeze and then glanced at Matthew. "Lovely to meet you."

Cassie departed as well, hips swiveling in a swagger that sent Siobhan's nails raking down the tree trunk.

"Should they really be going with her?" Bronagh demanded. "She's obnoxious and abrasive and already rubbing off on Neave." Her eyes burned into Siobhan like an iron monger's furnace.

Matthew's mother was a formidable character from the Dark Ages, one Siobhan had spent her whole adult life appeasing or apologizing to. She wouldn't get *her* in the divorce, thank goodness.

A vision swept through her mind of what might happen if she declined to dignify Bronagh with a response. She imagined a town devastated by the elements: wrecks for homes with crumbling walls and collapsed roofs, trees upended from their roots and strewn across the streets, household appliances and debris scattered all over the place. It was time to step up, face Hurricane Bronagh head on.

"She's a good influence."

"Is it even safe for them to ride around in her pretentious car? I mean, she can only be driving that thing to show off."

She didn't care that her forced smile would come across as a grimace. "I trust her with my children."

Bronagh let out a quick, disgruntled snort, reminding Siobhan of the eponymous hero in *Babe: A Pig in the City,* one of Neave's favorite films. She chortled to herself at the mental image. Bronagh regarded her like she was something that had been left to go off at the bottom of the fridge, but Siobhan paid no heed, continuing to snigger, unable to stop.

"Well, I don't like her." Bronagh directed her comment at Siobhan, and Siobhan couldn't help but wonder if she were speaking about her or about Cassie. "She's arrogant and flashy," Bronagh blustered, as if to clarify. "Matthew thinks the same."

Matthew hooked his thumbs through his belt loops and took his mother's side without saying a word, thrusting his chest out.

"Thanks for the feedback." Siobhan simulated another smile, then turned away without another word and made her way over to Cassie, who stood leaning against her car.

"And I thought my family politics were complex." Cassie let out a low whistle. "I just hope I haven't made things worse for you."

On instinct, Siobhan pulled Cassie into a hug. "I'd say you showed remarkable restraint. Unlike Neave. That girl takes no prisoners." Cassie chuckled, but she also tensed. Not wishing to draw any unwanted attention, Siobhan released her, putting a respectable distance between them. "Matthew is heading to Birmingham tonight. I'm sure he'll be thrilled not to have to take us home first. Spurs are away tomorrow so no doubt he'll have arranged to catch up with his mates at the hotel later. We're lucky he gave us as much time as he did today. And by lucky, I mean terribly unfortunate. Give me five minutes to make sure everyone has my address and then we can head back. That is, if there's room for one more in your beloved vehicle? I know it's not your ideal way to spend a Saturday night, but I can offer you birthday cake and a children's sleepover. We might even squeeze in a U-rated film."

"How can I possibly say no?"

"With great ease, I'd imagine."

Cassie only hesitated for a moment. "I'm happy to be your companion for an evening of U-rated fun tonight," Cassie consented, leaning in to add, "After all, I can see plenty of X-rated fun written in our future. It would be rude to rush things."

CHAPTER SIXTEEN

"You coming?"

Siobhan looked up from her desk. Cassie had changed into fitted jeans, a sleeveless white shirt, and a navy blazer. She looked incredible and when their eyes met, she was thrilled to find Cassie's desire mirrored her own, her eyes dark and hungry. Sometimes, that gaze inspired tension. Other times, it delivered exhilaration. Now was one of those other times as a new vision ambushed her: a conflagration, the fire brigade bursting into the office, and Siobhan having to explain that the spark between them was the sole cause of the blaze.

"I said," Cassie repeated, flicking the thin strap of Siobhan's dress back up onto her shoulder, "are you coming?"

Siobhan hadn't even noticed the strap had slipped. "That depends where you're taking me: the theater or bed?"

"That's dangerous talk." Cassie stepped closer, stroking Siobhan's shoulder with one finger. "I thought I'd make an effort tonight," she said. "Helena's always telling me I should work the blazer look more often. I don't because as a lesbian libertine, it's hard enough fighting women off without adding a blazer into the mix."

"I'm surprised you don't walk with a stoop, carrying the weight of your big head every day."

"The struggle is real." Cassie palmed Siobhan's waist and Siobhan found herself transfixed by Cassie's lips, lips that held softness, passion and a smile that couldn't hide her lustful thoughts. "You, by the way, are absolutely killing it tonight."

"What are you two still doing here?"

Startled by Julie's intrusion, though she should have been used to them by now, Siobhan whacked her pencil pot, upending it and sending its contents scattering in all directions.

"Should I rephrase the question?" Julie smirked, plucking a pencil off the floor. "Where are you two sneaking off to together?"

"The theater," Siobhan mumbled at the same time Cassie grumbled, "Nowhere."

Julie's hawkish eyes assessed them. "The Theatre Nowhere? I thoroughly enjoyed their production of *Something's Going On.*"

"This, Siobhan, is what we lesbians call cliterference," Cassie said, returning the remaining pencils to their pot. "Essentially, it's when someone—let's use the office gossip as an example—gets in the way of the known lady-killer flirting. How does it feel, Siobhan, to be on the receiving end of a cliterception?"

"I'm splitting my sides over here." Julie tilted her head, her words accompanied by a round of applause.

"Well, let me entertain you then." Cassie executed a terrible twirl. "On second thought, I don't believe I could entertain *you* specifically. But if you'd like to ask me for a date, feel free. Then I can take great pleasure in turning you down."

"The only thing that's getting turned down is your mouth, because I'm not interested," Julie said. "I only came back to grab my umbrella." She made a great show of looking for it, but within seconds she shrugged in defeat. "It doesn't appear to be here."

"Good thing it's not raining." Siobhan leaned against her desk, her arms folded.

"Silly me," Julie sing-songed.

"Cassie." Siobhan put her hand on her hip and glowered. "I don't like this cavalier attitude you have around Julie. What if she reports us for inappropriate behavior? You promised not to jeopardize my job."

"Julie's harmless." Cassie shrugged.

"But are *you*?" Siobhan challenged, holding her ground. "On my first day here, she called you a poisoned chalice."

"Not poisoned. Just...spiked."

Siobhan felt her body temperature do just that, and not in the way it usually did when she was around Cassie. "Cass—"

"You're right, we should be more careful," Cassie conceded. "I have a tendency to get rather carried away. Just call me out on it and I'll stop. You have my word."

❖

Riveted as she was by the visual spectacle—sorcery, flying monkeys surging across the stage, the shambolic Wizard using his golden-faced contraption, all flashing eyes, cogs and gears, to yell for the guards—it was Elphaba's disillusionment that propelled Siobhan's heartbeat.

When Glinda accused Elphaba of having "delusions of grandeur" and the antihero of the story declared she was through accepting limits, Siobhan brushed her lips upon Cassie's ear, mimicking the musical's poster, and whispered, "You know, I think you and Elphaba would get on like a house on fire."

"She's not as easygoing as I am."

"Oh, is that how we're describing you these days?"

"If the broom fits."

A standing ovation ended the first act's flirtation.

Siobhan sat back in her seat, thinking that instead of spending one short day in the Emerald City, she'd rather spend one long night in Cassie's bedroom. With that thought in mind, she focused on the program in an attempt to regain a little equilibrium.

Out of the corner of her eye, she saw Cassie reach under her seat and pull out a bag of chocolate. "Malteser?"

Siobhan nodded, thankful for the distraction. Cassie poured the chocolates from the packet with a gleam in her eye. Chocolate in hand, her fingertips moved towards Siobhan's mouth, her eyes holding her gaze as she fed her a lustful bite. Siobhan watched as Cassie popped one into her own mouth and leaned back in her seat, totally composed. She wished she could say the same for herself, but alas, she and Elphaba were racing one another towards the final melting.

Cassie inserted another Malteser into Siobhan's mouth, then sucked the sugary remnants from her fingers, looking like she wanted to devour Siobhan along with the remaining chocolate. "Is there anything else you need?"

SKYE ROWAN

Siobhan fingered the collar under which she was hot, then drew her fingers over her chest, taking Cassie's gaze along for the ride. "Do you really want me to answer that question?" Siobhan breathed deeply, her lips close to Cassie's.

Cassie didn't have time to respond because the overture started up, the second half about to begin. She was forced to suspend their chocolatey dalliance. Siobhan felt all her nerves firing at once as Cassie shifted in her seat, throwing her a heated look that promised to intensify their flirtation.

Yet Cassie did no such thing. In fact, her lack of contact seemed deliberate. The way she withheld her touch, as if testing both Siobhan's patience and her willpower. Siobhan fidgeted in her seat all the way through the musical's love song, wondering if she too were as brainless as the Scarecrow.

When Elphaba flew into a rage over her continually thwarted efforts to do good, Siobhan's frustration was barely under control.

"Are you purposefully playing with me?" she whispered through shallow breaths, gently nibbling on Cassie's earlobe before moving away.

Cassie's lips parted as she continued to stare ahead, nodding towards the stage. "Concentrate on the ending. The whole show has been building up to this climax."

She did, the ending of the show as bittersweet as the unrealized conclusion to her craving.

"Well!" Cassie whooped, slipping her arm through Siobhan's as they exited the theater. "I never expected to feel so gutted for Glinda at the end. Elphaba walking off into the sunset should have been a happy ending, yet Glinda lost everything."

"She was definitely a little in love with Elphaba," Siobhan said, and Cassie gave a quick bark of laughter. "As you can see, I'm getting better at picking up on lesbian vibes."

"At last!" Cassie released Siobhan's arm, took a short run, and performed a classic heel-click-jump with moderate perfection.

Cassie returned to her side, and they stood facing one another, like scene partners at an audition. Cassie's entire demeanor had changed, suddenly she looked so small, her smile replaced with a look of apprehension.

"What now?" Siobhan asked, biting down on her lip in anticipation of Cassie's next move.

"We should get you home."

"Not back to your apartment?" Siobhan pushed, this response completely unexpected.

"It's a long way from here and not the easiest place to get to on the Tube."

"Easy enough that you'll manage to get home, I assume?" Siobhan folded her arms and eyed Cassie with a hint of suspicion. "Is something wrong, Cass? Because if you've changed your mind about all this you need to let me know."

"Jesus, Siobhan, it's not that," Cassie shook her head. "It's anything *but* that."

"Good. So, if your place is too far, we could go to a hotel and get a room."

Siobhan was aware she was beginning to sound desperate, but Cassie's behavior made no sense. From everything she had heard about Cassie, and everything she had learnt for herself, this purposeful retreat was out of character. Which could only mean one thing. Cassie was having doubts but couldn't find the words to articulate her feelings, especially having pursued what she thought she wanted so relentlessly.

"I don't want to get a hotel room with you."

"Way to make a woman feel special. Shall I pack my bags? Because I feel like I'm getting some sort of piss off."

"That was never my intention." Cassie looked away, awkwardly rocking back and forth. "I just can't do this with you, not like this."

"I just don't get you, Cassie. I thought tonight was amazing and unless I've misunderstood, non-committal sex was within the limits of your stupid rulebook. I'm pretty shocked you don't want to—"

"Tonight *has* been amazing, the best night I can remember having in a long time." Cassie ran her hand through her hair, looking pained. "Which is why I don't want to rush things within the constraints of what we have. I want to do this right."

"Excuse me?" Siobhan had to hold back her laughter because the look on Cassie's face was so sincere, laughter would be highly inappropriate.

"Don't make me say it again." Cassie rolled her eyes. "It was bad enough saying it once."

"I guess I'm just a little confused. I think I'm allowed to be. I never knew there was a 'right' way to conduct an illicit affair."

"Christ, Siobhan, can't you see?"

Siobhan shook her head, words failing her. Just when she thought she finally understood where Cassie was coming from, she threw the worst sort of curve ball.

"It's your first time with a woman. That's only something you've waited your whole life for—"

"Something I'm going to be waiting a little longer for, apparently." Siobhan didn't hide her frustration well.

"You trusting me with this, it's huge. I know what I said, the rules I've put into play, but that doesn't mean I can't make this special for you. It *has* to be special, that's my responsibility. I can't just ram you up against a wall and have my way with you because we can't keep our hands off one another." Cassie seemed to stop and think this over. "Though I'm sure we can make time for that further down the line."

Siobhan softened and her frustration eased. It was hard to stay irritated when someone was being so attentive. "You really are an enigma, Cassie Townsend, but I think I like it."

"Well, I don't." Cassie scowled. "You've given me a huge responsibility. But, if I can get myself together, how about we go for drinks next Wednesday and then if you still want to, we can go back to my place and take things from there."

"As much as it pains me to wait, I'm actually blown away by your thoughtfulness."

Cassie nodded, making no move to retreat, simply staring.

"You don't take compliments well when they delve a little deeper do you?"

"I don't think anyone's ever given me one about anything other than my fantastic backside or charming wit," Cassie said.

"Oh, we're going back to your safe place, banter and an air of cool no one else could ever master."

"Thank fuck for that, it's about time. I don't want you to get used to this, it's atypical."

"I've noticed." Not for the first time Siobhan thought, but that was the last thing Cassie needed to hear right now, having shown her softer side so willingly. It was Siobhan's turn to make Cassie feel comfortable, get her back to safe ground. "So…for tonight's parting, because part we must, will it be A) a hug, B) a handshake, or C) a fist bump?"

"That isn't the body part best suited for bumping." Cassie's eyes were dark, searching. Their familiar twinkle back in an instant as she hit the ground running. "I'll teach you about that next week."

"And here I was thinking you'd lost interest."

And for a terrible moment Siobhan really had thought the worst. Cassie's rejection was the last thing she had come to expect and according to the cascade of emotions that had flowed with it, the last thing in world she wanted. Siobhan wasn't sure what to make of that, so she chose to ignore the tiny flutter of her heart when she thought of Cassie wanting her to feel special, Cassie taking her time. Siobhan had never expected a music box melody with Cassie, she'd been willing to accept the bare minimum, but tonight something had changed.

CHAPTER SEVENTEEN

"So, welcome to your first ever lesbian bar," Cassie said as she led Siobhan through the throng of women, some lingering on the fringes of the bar, others pressed together on the dance floor.

"Talk about life goals," Siobhan replied, raising her voice to be heard over the music.

"Absolutely! And it's not just any lesbian bar. It's your first and my favorite."

"Because of the clientele?" Siobhan said. "Or because it's named after Florence's song 'Cosmic Love'?"

Aware of the significance of her answer, Cassie replied, "I adore Flo more than anyone."

A couple of women struggling to manage full glasses of drinks nearly smacked into them, but Cassie yanked Siobhan against her just in the nick of time, supplanting one collision with another, more desirable one. One that caused Cassie's stomach to swoop like the swirling font of the bar's neon sign.

When Siobhan's pupils—and, presumably her own—began to dilate, Cassie disengaged, in favor of the privacy provided by the cozy booth in the corner.

"I love the vibe here," Siobhan said as she looked at the lesbian icons staring right back at her from the walls, everyone from k.d. lang to Cassie's own heroine Florence Welch.

Gesturing to the surplus of framed photographs, Cassie said, "If you can identify three of them, I'll—"

"Pink, Lana Del Ray, Sharleen Spiteri of Texas, Skin of Skunk Anansie."

"You *do* know your lesbian culture," she said, squeezing Siobhan's waist.

"What's my reward?"

"I didn't get that far."

"Neither did I." Siobhan's eyes took in every inch of her. "Yet."

"Well, if it isn't Cassie Townsend, the lady-killer," a larger-than-life voice boomed.

A rather attractive woman Cassie had some distant memory of was now making a beeline for her. Cassie gulped and then plastered a wide grin on her face, curious what Siobhan would make of this situation. After all, it was common for Cassie to get accosted in such places. What wasn't customary and would likely take some getting used to, was the fact the woman she was having an affair with was there to witness it.

Before Cassie knew what was happening, the woman had brushed Siobhan aside and thrown her arm around Cassie's shoulders. "You never called."

At that moment, the fairy lights inside the jam jar on the table they hadn't quite made it to, weren't nearly as twisted as Cassie's insides.

Cassie felt another arm wrap around her waist.

"Hi, Cassie's with me tonight."

The fairy lights loosened. Cassie's jaw slackened as well. It alarmed her how alluring it was to see Siobhan stake her claim. Normally, she'd feel the need to back away. Instead, the sole need she felt was to back Siobhan up against the nearest wall and have her wicked way with her.

Only she wasn't supposed to be doing that, not according to the personality transplant she had suffered last week. Even now, Cassie wasn't sure what possessed her to make such a statement; it was wholly uncharacteristic. Especially since her goal since day one had been bedding the beautiful women on her arm. But was there more to it than that? Cassie often found herself avoiding that exact question, but her reaction to Siobhan tonight was purely sexual, of that there could be no doubt as her mind raced to the gutter. She was coming to her senses.

The woman looked Siobhan up and down, her lip curling. "I was with Cassie another night. I notice you didn't introduce yourself, so I'll return the favor. It's good preparation for when she's invoking your name and then promptly forgetting it."

Siobhan set her lips against Cassie's ear. "Do I tell her cliterference is banned tonight?"

"No," Cassie said, her hand homing in on Siobhan's backside, firm and tight as a kettle drum. "Though I do believe you just made it to the top of my to-do list." With Siobhan's arm still wrapped warmly around her waist, Cassie smiled at the woman. "It's nice to see you again, *Sophie*. Have a good evening."

"Causing your customary commotion, I reckon!" Helena seized Cassie's shoulders and dropped a kiss onto her cheek. "Hello, Ms. Come-Hither Coworker," Helena greeted Siobhan. "It's a pleasure to see you here of all places, with her of all people. This is Riley." Helena clutched her companion's arm like a bridal bouquet. "We've hit the five-date limit and she still likes me." Helena and Riley made googly-eye contact.

Cassie imagined herself shrinking before their eyes likes Ant-Man. Her best friend was once again putting her to shame and providing Siobhan with a perfect reminder that normal lesbians did in fact date, it was just Cassie that didn't.

"We've been here five minutes and have already heard what an unbelievable shag Cassie is at least three times," Riley said as they made their way over to the table.

"Just wait until Siobhan finds that out for herself," Helena chimed in, offering Cassie an impressed wink.

Cassie tried not to look embarrassed but gave it up as a bad job. She felt confident she could live up to Siobhan's expectations, and even more confident that she could exceed them. But how did Siobhan feel about it? She didn't miss the flicker of unease that passed in her eyes, but it disappeared quickly.

"I don't remember inviting you tonight." Cassie performed her usual eye roll. "I certainly didn't ask you along for a running commentary," she lowered her tone, "on my sex life."

Cassie hoped Helena would take the hint; after all, she cared a little what Siobhan thought of her.

Helena performed the zipping action over her lips. "Say no more."

"So how did you guys meet?" Riley asked, clearly sensing the need for a change in the direction of the conversation.

"Work."

Cassie didn't offer anything else, the pressure mounting as Siobhan's eyes met hers.

"I admire that. Working together and dating, that's got to be a challenge. I mean we're just starting out, but I don't think I could work with her too despite very much being in the honeymoon period."

"We're not dating," Cassie said.

Helena cleared her throat. "The honeymoon period is amazing, may I add. You know, Siobhan, the best sex you'll ever have is within the first three months of a relationship."

"We're not in a relationship," Cassie replied automatically, wondering if and when she had given Helena reason to think otherwise. Not that it mattered. Helena would draw her own conclusions regardless—or, more accurately, make her own assumptions. She contemplated catching Siobhan's eye, to gauge her reaction to Helena's assertion and Cassie's denial, but she was afraid of what she might see there. Instead, she ran her hand across Siobhan's thigh and said something ridiculous. "She knows *nothing* about lesbian sex."

"First, you start with a chat-up line." Helena held up her finger. "For instance, 'Your face is a work of art. You should frame it. With my legs.' A classy—sorry—a Cassie classic."

"It's better than 'I think the lipstick you're wearing would look great on me,'" Cassie retorted. "That was Helena's go-to line for years."

"Still is!" Riley said, resulting in raucous laughter. "Hey, listen, I know this roasting battle is just heating up, but we only came here for a quick drink before dinner. We're going to have to love you and leave you."

"Thank fuck." Cassie raised her glass to perform a toast of one.

When the two of them were alone again, Cassie felt Siobhan's breath dangerously close to her ear. "Hearing all these rumors about your sexual prowess, I think you've kept me waiting long enough. I don't know how much longer I can sit here and remain in control." Siobhan squeezed Cassie's knee purposefully. "You have no idea what I want to do to you."

Cassie's gaze roved over Siobhan with the urgency of a high-speed car chase. "You seem to understand my terms and conditions perfectly, but how well you comply with them remains to be seen."

Siobhan trailed her finger down Cassie's neck, teasing her top button open. "That's down to you to test out."

❖

Siobhan's breath caught in her throat, her heart pumping with uncontrolled excitement as Cassie slammed her apartment door shut. She could feel fire beneath her fingertips, not to mention Cassie's backside, which she was groping with urgency.

"All that warmth, wine, and wanting in the bar, I thought we'd never get home."

Cassie was finally standing right there, all hers, and Siobhan didn't know what she wanted to do first. So it was that her hands moved to frame Cassie's face.

"No." Cassie ducked under her arm, leaving Siobhan dissatisfied.

Slumping against the wall, Siobhan expelled her pent-up frustration in a loud sigh. "Do you have a cigarette?"

"You don't smoke," Cassie pointed out, sidling up beside her. "Let me guess the plan. I smoke a cigarette, taste like an ashtray and prevent you wanting to kiss me."

"I don't want to kiss you." Siobhan couldn't look at Cassie, not when Cassie would take one look at her and read the lie written in her eyes. Then the words had spilled out before she could slam the brakes on. "Actually, I've never wanted to kiss anyone as much as I want to kiss you right now."

"Siobhan, you know—"

"Don't worry. I have the message loud and clear. I know it's against the rules, but the rules are shit."

"Perhaps," Cassie conceded, shrugging. "But they're there for a reason."

Siobhan wondered whether Cassie would find this rule challenging at all. She thought she detected a tinge of disappointment in Cassie's demeanor, but she couldn't be sure.

"To ensure we eliminate all temptation, would you like me to devour a clove or two of garlic before we proceed?" Cassie stroked the back of Siobhan's neck.

"I'd like you to give in and kiss me," Siobhan almost begged as Cassie's fingers found the button on her jeans.

"Given time, I'm sure you'll find there's plenty of other ways to satisfy our needs," Cassie said and began to set a series of hot kisses against the tender flesh of Siobhan's throat. "That's if you're ready?"

"More than ready."

This, in essence, was the truth. However, Siobhan fretted about her natural ability—and whether or not she possessed any. Would she be able to turn Cassie on? Would her performance, which Cassie would no doubt analyze, be satisfactory?

There was no time for such thoughts as Siobhan came alive under Cassie's exquisite attention: goose bumps, heart thumps, a quivering she couldn't suppress. She took a deep breath, preparing to let go for the first time in her life.

Cassie unbuttoned Siobhan's shirt, and Siobhan reveled in the sight of Cassie's eyes drinking her in.

Cassie removed her bra with ease, while Siobhan ran her hands up Cassie's back and fumbled with the clasp.

"It's all in the art of the pinch!" Cassie informed her, but before she could try again, Cassie was cupping her breasts, and Siobhan's nipples were reacting in just the right way. When Cassie's tongue teased the tips, Siobhan made a guttural sound that came from somewhere deep within. Never had she felt so desirable.

"If we don't get into the bedroom now," Cassie said, "I'm going to throw you down on the floor. So either go there or come here."

"Come here," Siobhan murmured, and it was both a decision and a direction. She sensed the greed in her own craving as she sank to the floor and pulled Cassie down on top of her. She succeeded in tugging Cassie's T-shirt over her head, then failed again at unclasping her bra.

"Would you like some assistance?" Cassie divested herself of the garment quickly and threw it out of view. "Better?"

Siobhan's fingers curved around the points of Cassie's pert breasts. "It seems your nipples are accepting of my attention, even if your lips aren't," she mused, before covering the soft tissue with her lips. When she nipped Cassie's nipples, Cassie's head rolled back and she reached for Siobhan, her grip growing possessive.

"I need to get these off." Cassie tugged at Siobhan's jeans, her breath coming in throaty gasps as Siobhan lifted her hips in consent. "And these." Cassie ran her finger down the lace along Siobhan's thigh. When Siobhan arched her back, Cassie took the material between her teeth and with one impressive yank, Siobhan's underwear was no more.

Siobhan had never been so totally exposed in front of someone who was paying attention. It turned her on irrevocably, her arousal slipping down her thighs as Cassie's breathing grew faster and more audible as she ran her fingers over Siobhan's torso.

Cassie's skillful tongue was all over her hot, sweaty body, as if she were drinking in every new taste, reveling in every scent. Siobhan felt herself almost incapacitated as Cassie ran her fingers enticingly close to her core, using a provocative rounded motion to part her lips.

Without thinking, Siobhan reached for Cassie's lips once more.

"You've got to stop doing that," Cassie whispered, placing a finger over Siobhan's lips.

Siobhan settled back, still twitching towards Cassie's body.

"I wasn't trying to kiss you," Siobhan deflected, but it was the last thing out of her mouth before the moans hit fever pitch as Cassie worked her clitoris with both calculation and appreciation.

Dizzy with need and totally consumed, Siobhan's breathing grew shallow, and when Cassie pressed two fingers inside, followed by a thumb, she pushed against her to feel more. As much as she wanted to savor each moment, she deferred to her desire, her body convulsing in ripples as an earthquake of pleasure hit full throttle.

Siobhan flopped onto her back, her breath still coming in gasps, drained and delighted. "We need to do that again...and again...and again."

"Oh, I know." Cassie sounded breathless as well. "You know, my original plan did involve the bedroom. We could still try it out."

Once more, Siobhan found herself drawn to that bold mouth.

"Am I going to have to put the rules on repeat?" Cassie threatened her.

Siobhan didn't have time to make up another excuse as she was led to the bedroom. She allowed herself a moment to take in the rose petals spread across the cream bedding as Cassie dimmed the lights, lighting a small collection of tea lights, their flickering wicks dancing shadows across the room. Cassie's desire to make her first time special crept back into her mind and she felt her heart expand at the effort Cassie had gone to. They hadn't quite made it that far for their first time, but they did have all night.

"I did have big plans." Cassie swept her fingers through the petals. "Not to take you in the hallway." She almost managed to pull off sheepish, but not quite.

"Fucking hell, Cass. I have no idea how this no-kissing-on-the-lips rule is going to work when you're making me want to kiss you so badly. It's practically impossible."

Cassie's eyebrow arched. "I thought you weren't trying to kiss me."

"I think I'm going to have to hold my hands up," Siobhan huffed half-heartedly. "It's proving to be more of a challenge than I anticipated."

"My lips are pretty kissable. It's one of my many claims to fame."

"And mine is…" Siobhan crawled over Cassie on hands and knees. "Well, I don't have one at the moment. Shall we see if one emerges?" Siobhan hoped she sounded more confident than she felt.

But when Siobhan caressed Cassie's skin, from her neck to her breasts to her thighs, and Cassie moved in the most sensual way Siobhan had ever seen, all thoughts of anything else fled.

There was no hesitation in her touch, as she slipped her fingers inside, first one then two then three, applying and reducing pressure in accordance with Cassie's responses. Every time Cassie seemed about to go over the edge, Siobhan would bring her back with softer, slower strokes, until Cassie was a heated mess. The power was intoxicating, and her heart felt like it would explode. Cassie's body was exquisite, but more than that, they were sharing something special, whether either of them would admit it or not.

"I'm going to lose my mind if you don't let me come," Cassie growled, biting down on Siobhan's shoulder. Siobhan curled her fingers. "Oh fuck, Siobhan."

Siobhan smiled, feeling empowered, feeling that Cassie deserved to be devoured. Descending to the slick wetness of Cassie's center, she thrust her tongue against Cassie's wetness and was rewarded with sweetness and a guttural moan. She shivered, eager to explore more of the velvety flesh until Cassie shattered under her eager attention.

Silence descended upon them as they lay naked, entwined together, basking in the warm afterglow. Absentmindedly, Siobhan found herself twirling Cassie's hair between the fingers as a range of thoughts invaded her headspace.

She had waited her whole life for a moment like this. Sleeping with Cassie had been everything she could have wished for and more, but lying here with Cassie now, somehow this felt just as significant. Facing the reality of all she had missed out on suddenly felt huge. She had never appreciated how much she had given up until now.

But where did Cassie fit in the picture? Deep down, Siobhan knew it was dangerous to even ask that question because she already knew the answer. Cassie had stuck rigidly to the no kissing rule, just one of the stipulations of their affair, and it was clear there would be no deviation anywhere else on Cassie's part. She was there to show Siobhan a good time, to fulfil a need, but she could walk away at any time without an explanation. Yet Siobhan couldn't bring herself to regret it, even if part of her wished it could mean more than it did. It was a night she would remember for the rest of her life, regardless of the fact it meant nothing deeper to either one of them.

CHAPTER EIGHTEEN

Standing before the en suite mirror, Siobhan scrutinized her appearance for signs of change, something to indicate she was now an adulteress. Try as she might to see a difference, she was met with the same reflection, except her eyes were brighter, more animated than she could ever remember.

She smiled as she remembered all the ways Cassie made her feel: attractive, appreciated, authentic. For the first time in her adult life, she felt utterly unshackled. And soon, she really would be.

The rapping of knuckles on the door wrenched her from her reverie. "Are you okay in there?"

Hearing Matthew's voice caused a slight feeling of guilt to seep in, creeping over her like an ominous mist. She hadn't known she was truly capable of cheating until she'd gone and done it. Would Matthew be able to tell?

Siobhan threw the door open and walked past him to what used to be her side of the bedroom. "I'm okay," she said. "Thank you for asking."

She must have sounded too pleasant, too approachable, because he stepped closer and placed his hands on her waist. "I wanted to apologize for my behavior at Dylan's party."

"Thank you," she replied curtly, sustaining her smile as she stepped out of his grasp.

"So...what are you up to today?" Matthew asked, his Adam's apple bobbing as he bounced on the balls of his feet. He seemed to be anticipating some sort of invitation.

"Meetings, mostly," she said, running a brush through her hair and glancing at him in the mirror.

"No time for me, I suppose. Only time for Cassie? I mean, work?"

Siobhan sucked in a breath. "I'm working, Matthew. I have a job."

"I'm starting to think you like her more than me. Hell, I know the kids do." Matthew frowned. "Well?" he prompted her when she neither confirmed nor denied his accusation. "Do you?"

Siobhan returned the brush to the dresser, yet maintained her grip on the handle, needing something solid to ground her. "Are you asking me if I'm happier in someone else's company than I am in yours?" she responded, hoping her voice and her face revealed only the truth, not the treachery. "Because I think we both know the answer to that."

"Siobhan!" Matthew's shock seemed genuine, his panic real.

"If we're being honest with one another," Siobhan began, pressing the pad of her thumb into the bristles of the brush, "you're no happier in this marriage than I am. You're just afraid to admit it and unwilling to act upon it." She drew herself up to her full height. It was time. "But I'm unafraid, and I'm willing."

"Christ, Siobhan, anyone would think you're trying to get rid of me."

"I am," she blurted out.

For once, Matthew sounded more pitiful than apathetic. "Are you…leaving me?"

"I'm divorcing you." Siobhan suddenly felt rigid and relaxed at the same time. There was no escaping the words now that they were out in the universe. Wanting to ensure Matthew fully understood, Siobhan held his gaze.

He didn't look away, his gaze searching as if for an answer he'd understand. "Cassie put you up to this, didn't she?"

"This has nothing to do with Cassie." She was relieved to recognize the truth of her reply. She had made this life-changing decision long before meeting Cassie, but she welcomed the reminder. "This is about our dysfunction as a couple," Siobhan said. "It's about your failure as a father."

"My mother thinks I'm an excellent father *and* a good husband."

"She's not married to you though, is she? I am. And I wouldn't expect you to have any differing opinions from your mother. After all, I did marry her that day too, didn't I?"

"You know divorce is prohibited in the Catholic church. I don't want Mam to go through the shame of us getting a divorce—"

"We don't love each other, Matthew." She took a deep breath, knowing that her next words had to be delicate, accurate, and irrefutable. "You married me for noble and practical reasons, and maybe I should have considered that more at the time, but the truth is, we were never right for each other. We both deserve better, don't you think?" She softened her gaze. "You can't tell me you're happy, Matthew. Don't you want someone who looks at you like you're their everything?"

Matthew's forehead creased, and she could almost hear him contemplating the validity of her statements. "When you put it that way...you're right. I do deserve better."

Siobhan arched her eyebrows, and Matthew shrugged apologetically.

"We both do. The kids too."

She nodded, unfurling her fingers from the hairbrush. "I have a meeting with my solicitor today to discuss divorce proceedings, living arrangements, custody. These are all things you need to think about."

"Do you not think you should have alerted me to your plans before running full speed ahead with things? Do I not get a say in any of this?"

"I've just asked you to think about the important things."

"Fuck's sake, Siobhan! I meant about the divorce in general. You're acting like this doesn't mean anything to you." He slumped against the doorframe. "I mean, I know you're right, but, Jesus, it's like you don't have any feelings about it."

"I don't," Siobhan said as kindly as she could. "It's the right decision for everyone and deep down you know that. I don't even think it's a huge shock to you. When you're standing there telling me your biggest concern is what your mother is going to think, that's a surefire sign it's the right thing for us."

Matthew's face crumpled. Although he agreed with her, his hurt was still obvious. "You can keep the house and custody of the kids. Mam will take me in—once she recovers from the shock and the shame, and we'll have the kids over for tea every so often."

Siobhan grimaced. He didn't even care about custody. That was a blessing, but she knew it could still hurt the kids, finding out he didn't care. Upon reflection, she highly doubted it. This was exactly what the three of them wanted. "Thank you."

❖

"Wake up, sleepyhead!"

Cassie felt herself being pummeled by pillows. Pulling the covers over her head, she vocalized her displeasure.

"You sound like a cross between a singing dolphin and a grunting sea lion." Helena tugged on the blankets again.

"Go away," Cassie muttered, rolling onto her side, still unable to make sense of her current situation, considering she had gone to sleep alone.

"That's no way to welcome a woman into your bedroom." Helena flung herself down beside Cassie. "The expression is rise and shine, not rise and whine."

"What are you doing here?" Cassie grumbled, rubbing her eyes as she forced herself to sit up.

"What are *you* doing here?" Helena retorted. "I rang your office, and your always antagonistic, slightly sexy secretary said you were working from home this morning."

Cassie covered her ears. "Take out the slightly sexy and we can resume this conversation."

"Working from home, that's code for hookup hangover, right?"

"So you thought you'd come over with a recovery remedy?"

"It's my lunch hour and I wanted to check you weren't left handcuffed to the bed or worse, dangling from the ceiling. That happened to Riley once."

"Sorry to disappoint your vivid imagination, but I was just sleeping. Siobhan and I have a late meeting tonight. Time differences in the US can make it tricky, so I'm having the morning off."

"Siobhan too then," Helena deduced. "So, where is she?"

"Home with her husband, I'd assume. She didn't spend the night."

Helena reared back in mock surprise. "Are you telling me you sent the woman who spent all night making come-to-bed eyes at you home to her husband?"

"I'm telling you to put the kettle on and maybe, after a cup of very strong coffee, I might tell you about the most unbelievable sex of my life."

Helena let out a delighted chuckle and then rushed into the kitchen, stumbling over her own feet in her haste. "I shall return in a flash!"

Cassie threw herself back on the pillows, the now familiar scent of Siobhan stimulating memories of their incredible first night. She ran her hand across the bed covers, remembering how Siobhan's body had reacted to even her slightest touch. Somehow, Siobhan had woken a long-forgotten desire in her and yet here she was now, waking up alone, the same old story. Perhaps she should have written a *No leaving in the middle of the night* clause into their agreement, because waking up alone didn't feel so great for once. She shook off the thought and dragged herself out of bed to face Helena's inquisition.

But when Cassie joined Helena in the other room, it was she who posed the first question. "Why does my kitchen look like the Mad Hatter's tea party on stimulants?" she asked, situating herself at the breakfast bar.

"I'm making us pancakes," Helena announced, waving the frying pan, in which resided a floppy mess. "Revelations like these require them." Helena scooped the concoction onto a plate. "Here, I think it's cooked." She tossed Cassie the golden syrup. "Disclosures please, but first, congratulations are in order. Siobhan is great. By far the best woman you've shown interest in in a long time. If she weren't married, you two would be fantastic together."

"We're not together." Cassie poked at the mess on her plate. "And she is married. And I'm not available."

"But your vaginas *are* well acquainted?"

"*They* got together. We didn't."

"In that case, did your one-night stand see your nightstand? Or were you so desperate you took her right there on the floor in the hallway?" Helena gasped. "I didn't step in anything, did I?"

As Helena inspected the soles of her shoes, Cassie flipped her hair in annoyance. "She was desperate, not me. And it's not a one-night stand. It's an affair."

"I need a moment to compute that sentence. You're having an affair with her? You don't have affairs." Helena put her foot down. "That's practically commitment in your world."

"It's a two-night a week arrangement that gets me the best sex I've ever had—"

"Siobhan, with zero lesbian experience, is the ultimate shagmaster? Lock up the lesbians of London!"

Cassie blew out a noisy breath. "She only cheats with me. That being said," Cassie elaborated, lest she get the wrong idea—again,

"Siobhan is free to do as she pleases on the nights we're not together." She ate the final mouthful. "You know, that was almost edible," she admitted, swirling the coffee in her mug before finishing it off.

Helena was looking at her as though she was several layers short of a triple-decker sandwich.

"What?" Cassie suddenly found herself wishing Helena could only read her like a flimsy leaflet instead of a detailed book.

"I just never had you down for sharing, that's all. Then again, she *is* married..."

"In this case, sharing is *not* caring." Cassie took her plate to the sink. "Besides, she's not sleeping with her husband. They don't love one another. By all accounts, they never did. That reminds me: my dad texted me again at the weekend. He keeps suggesting we meet up."

Helena's cheeks expanded, then she popped out an exhale. "From one mind-blowing bit of news to another. What have you said?"

"I haven't replied. It's all for the sake of Eva's wedding. There's nothing genuine about it."

"You mum's probably terrified of one of you making a scene. The last thing poor Eva needs is you and your dad going ten rounds in the boxing ring while they're making their ever after vows."

"That's the point right there." Cassie began to pace. "This shouldn't be about Eva. If he's serious about wanting to make things better, he should be thinking about me. He needs to understand the impact of his behavior. This isn't something that can be worked out in ten minutes so we can all sit around playing happy families for the in-laws."

"The fact he's trying is a huge step forward. Or at least it has the potential to be. Just meet him for a coffee, somewhere neutral. Then if it all goes tits up, you can do a runner."

"He *disowned* me. I'm not sure he gets a second chance." Cassie hated the bitterness in her voice, but she hadn't felt anything else towards her father for years.

"What he did was wrong, you won't get any argument from me about that, but forever's a hell of a long time to stay mad at someone."

"But I'm *so* good at it," Cassie said with a small smile.

"You are," Helena agreed, "but don't you think one long-term grudge is enough?"

Heat rising in her cheeks, Cassie strode out of the kitchen. "I'm not holding any other grudges."

"Not even towards—"

"Don't bring her up. Ever." Cassie fought with her balcony door, trying to slide it open to no avail. It was times like these that she wished she still smoked.

"Sorry!" Helena held her hands up in a gesture of surrender. "But talk to your dad, see what he has to say. If it's a total train wreck, you can always seek solace in the shagmaster." Helena joined Cassie in her sullen staring out over the city. She squeezed her in the ribs until Cassie laughed, wriggling away.

"You need to give me my key back," Cassie groused. 'I can't be having all these unexpected interruptions from you."

"Not now you're having regular shag fests." Helena winked. "Or do you really want it for Siobhan?"

"She doesn't need a key."

"My mistake." Helena humored her, and Cassie was grateful for it. "Well, that's all the time I have today for you and your impossible love life. I have to get back to work, after which I'm meeting Riley for tea and sex toy shopping."

Helena slipped past her, but before she reached the door, Cassie snagged her arm and pulled Helena into a tight hug. "Thanks for checking in," she mumbled, refusing to resent how much she meant it.

"Love you," Helena said. "Have fun home wrecking, head wrecking, whichever it is."

Cassie was pretty sure Helena had been referring to Siobhan's head, but her own was in bits. The imminent conversation with her dad was playing on her mind but that wasn't what was eating away at her.

Waking alone had never bothered her and yet today it had her feeling cold, empty, and vulnerable although she couldn't explain why. Or she didn't want to. She didn't need to look too far to see what was becoming obvious. Having an illicit affair with Siobhan was supposed to be a solution to a simple need, only it wasn't a simple need, not for Cassie anyway. What she had with Siobhan felt dangerously real, tangible, and in truth, far from simple.

CHAPTER NINETEEN

L inking arms with Siobhan as the soft, glowing light from the day's sunshine swept below the horizon, Cassie moved with a spring in her step. In twilight the surface of the lake was as smooth as obsidian, the sweet aroma of summer blooms filled the air, and the welcome cool of the evening swept over her.

"I forgot how lovely it is to take a walk in the twilight," Siobhan said.

"I love Finsbury Park. The last time I was here was when I dragged Eva to a festival a couple of summers ago."

"Now tell me, what's on Cassie Townsend's playlist?"

"I think you can imagine who was headlining, but Eva seemed to know everyone. Ironically, I had to beg her to come with me, only to find she knew more artists than me. Her taste is shocking!"

Siobhan let out a throaty laugh, which sent Cassie reeling no matter how many times she heard it.

"Hence the Drake concert. What else is deemed shocking in your world?"

"I think it was the Weeknd, Gorillaz, and the Chemical Brothers at that gig. Can you believe she didn't want to spend all of Sunday crushed up to a fence at the front, awaiting the goddess that is Florence? Her dimples would almost give yours a run for their money…almost." Cassie left a quick, light kiss exactly where Siobhan's dimples were beginning to form, then whispered a profanity, considering the gesture far too affectionate.

"What about you? Musicals aside, what do you listen to?"

"When you have a six-year-old daughter, it's hard not to drown in chart music. The Weeknd is a particular favorite right now."

Cassie turned her back and made to walk off. "We can't even be friends, I'm sorry. It's over."

"If it improves my credibility any, I love Madonna."

"Modern Madonna or eighties Madonna? And before you make a choice, remember this is another of those future defining moments."

"Eighties of course, although 'Ray of Light' is…let me just phrase it as Neave would." Siobhan took a moment to fold her arms and lean to one side, amusing Cassie with her confidence. "An absolute banger!"

"I'm willing to accept your decision on Madonna, mainly because of your use of the term banger. Come on, I want to take you somewhere."

Cassie wrapped her arm around Siobhan's back, nestling her in and they fell into time together, following one of the footpaths through the woodlands, still humming with life into the late evening. The moonlight streaked through the tall boughs in brilliant beams lighting the path before them, whilst shadows danced in the background. It wasn't long before they came upon the open expanse of the boating lake.

"I totally forgot about the boating lake. I have some fond memories here."

A look passed over Siobhan's face that Cassie couldn't decipher. "If you're about to tell me Matthew proposed to you here, I'm preparing to leave for the second time in one night."

"Oh come off it. I used to bring Dylan and Neave when they were younger. It was ice cream from the retro ice cream van, which I could usually rely on one of the kids to drop, and then a pedalo out on the lake."

"So happy memories?"

"Very much so," Siobhan said.

"Though I can't say I'd be all that happy dropping my ice cream."

"I can picture you sulking now." Siobhan nudged her in that playful manner she was getting used to.

"So…" A cheeky grin spread wide across Cassie's face. "Do you fancy making some new memories?"

"The look on your face tells me I might not have a choice."

"How are your sea legs?"

"It's a bloody lake, Cass."

"Same difference." Cassie grabbed her hand and pulled her along an overgrown path, bringing them out by the old, wooden boating hut. "If I remember rightly, they always leave a couple out overnight, ready for the first customers."

Exactly as Cassie remembered, two row boats were tied up by the edge of the water. The one she chose was an old-timer, the wooden planks looking like they had seen better days, yet she was still seaworthy.

"This is a regular jaunt? Do you bring all your..."

Siobhan stumbled over her words and Cassie was alarmed by the fact she now found this endearing. "Were you going to ask if I bring all my women here?" Cassie asked, amused.

"If the shoe fits."

"It doesn't, Cinderella. You are the first and only woman I wish to steal away onto a row boat in the middle of central London."

"I'm honored."

"After you." Cassie mock bowed and held out her hand for Siobhan to climb in. The wooden boat rocked precariously from side to side. "You did that with such grace." Cassie winked.

"I've seen *Titanic*, you know. I know how romances on boats end."

Cassie untied the rope from a timber post and then thrust her breasts towards Siobhan, almost unbalancing the boat again. "Paint me like one of your French girls, Jack."

"Sit down, before you fall down." Siobhan chuckled, watching Cassie pitch from side to side. "You know, even Granuaile, pirate queen of Ireland, despised motion sickness. And capsizing. And drowning."

Cassie threw her head back and burst into laughter. "The only thing you're drowning in," she challenged, seating herself beside Siobhan, "is desire."

Siobhan expelled a long-suffering sigh.

Cassie gazed—first at the pearly beams of moonlight twirling gracefully over the water, and then at the woman glowing next to her, whose radiant smile lit up the night sky.

"The stars *are* out in abundance tonight." Siobhan looked upwards. "It was a night like this when I—"

"See those five stars shaped like a W?" Cassie interrupted, not ready for the reminder of their near kiss. "That's Cassiopeia."

"Were you named after it or was it named after you?" Siobhan said, though Cassie could tell from her tone that the playfulness was put-on.

"Queen Cassiopeia was a totally self-absorbed tyrant with a ridiculously high opinion of herself," Cassie said.

"Question answered!" Siobhan bit down on her bottom lip.

"*Her* ego was uncontrollable," Cassie continued, stifling a smile, "but King Cepheus adored her with his entire being. She got their kingdom into all sorts of trouble, boasting about her unrivaled beauty. One day Hera decided enough was enough, tied her to her throne, and launched her into the sky." Cassie pointed to the stars again. "Where she remains to this day. When Cepheus found out what had happened to his beloved wife, he cried like a baby, until Zeus couldn't listen anymore. He flung his friend upward with pinpoint precision, so he landed right next to his egocentric wife. His constellation sits just above hers." Cassie pointed at the sky. "See it? It looks just like a stick house."

Siobhan nodded, shifting closer, until Cassie could feel Siobhan's hair against her face, the soft strands caressing her cheek.

"And you once told me you didn't know anything about the stars."

"I made the effort to find out." Silence descended around them again, the only sound ripples on the water as Cassie took up the oars again. "I thought I'd start with a formidable woman."

"You're in dangerous territory tonight." Siobhan's eyes met Cassie's with an intensity she had yet to experience. "If you're going to insist on making those smoldering eyes at me, then I'm going to have to think of a creative way to show my appreciation. Words just won't cut it."

Cassie trembled in triumph, deciding she deserved at least partial credit for Siobhan's newfound audacity.

Cassie breathed in…out…then a split second later the space between them was gone and Cassie found herself powerless. Siobhan unzipped her jeans and pushed her hand inside, letting out a moan of pleasure upon discovering Cassie had gone commando as Cassie's slick wetness welcomed her. The effect she had on Cassie turned Siobhan on so much that she was insatiable, desperate for Cassie to take her too. Cassie's hips bucked in encouragement. Siobhan worked like an expert, following her instincts, and when Cassie felt the skillful flick of Siobhan's fingers against her clit, she gripped the sides of the boat.

And tipped an oar up and over the side. "Shit!" Cassie stared at the oar as it bobbed up and down on the water. "I think I can reach it."

"Leave it." Siobhan slid out of her, though.

Cassie leant over the side, her eyes and smile on Siobhan. The boat wobbled. Distracted, Cassie completely misjudged the distance, and went headfirst into the lake.

When she emerged from its depths seconds later, spluttering spectacularly, Siobhan had already rescued the navigational implement. She extended her free hand to Cassie, who reached for it just as a large piece of pondweed draped itself across her face. She scrabbled at it and chucked it aside with a grimace. "Gross."

Siobhan held the boat steady as Cassie clambered back in with all the grace of a newborn starfish.

Twenty minutes later, they'd made it back to shore in one piece. Cassie sat on the small wooden jetty picking a wide range of pond life from her hair, whilst Siobhan tied the boat back up.

"Never has the expression drowned rat been more fitting."

"I was doing so well." Cassie stood up, shivering a little. The evening was warm but the water had a life and temperature of its own.

"Smooth, real smooth." Siobhan nodded her agreement. "My *Titanic* analogy wasn't so far off the mark after all. Don't let go, Jack."

"You're fucking hilarious, you know that? You should do stand-up."

"And you have pondweed for hair." Siobhan leant forward and removed another clump, kissing her cheek as Cassie shivered again. "You're freezing." Siobhan untied the hoodie from around her waist and placed it over Cassie's head. "This should help."

Cassie huddled into the hoodie, soaking in the warm, cedar and orange blossom scent of Siobhan. "You do know you aren't getting this back any time soon?"

"Come here."

Cassie allowed herself to be enveloped in Siobhan's arms, instantly settling into the warm, comforting embrace. She listened closely to Siobhan's heartbeat and allowed her own chest to rise and fall in time. Here she was again, doing something she knew she shouldn't be. Her teeth supported this thought as they began to chatter with the cold.

Siobhan allowed her eyes to linger a moment. "I have to say, you do look pretty sexy soaked."

"I was born sexy, Shiv. You should know that by now."

"It's a long time since anyone called me that," Siobhan said, lowering her eyes. "I've always just been Siobhan."

"Siobhan it is then," Cassie smiled.

"Shiv was Mum's nickname for me."

"I'm sorry." Cassie wasn't sure what else she could say.

"Don't be, I've always loved the name. You using it makes it sound special again."

Cassie willed her chattering teeth to hold still long enough to smile and say, "It's beautiful, much like its owner."

It was happening again, Cassie's tongue running away with her when she was around Siobhan. Spending time with Siobhan had too easily become Cassie's favorite pastime, but there was something so warm, so genuine about the way they were together, Cassie could feel herself losing her senses. She knew walking away would be the best decision, especially when Siobhan looked at her with those beguiling eyes and she almost lost herself. Siobhan was getting too emotionally invested, that much was obvious. Cassie had nothing to give back. She was an empty vessel where relationships were concerned, yet here she was rooted to the spot, totally absorbed in a woman she had vowed not to care about.

This was purely sexual and deep down Cassie knew that. It was just that sometimes the lines became blurred, but Cassie could put a stop to that immediately and remind Siobhan of the limitations of their affair. After all, the fact it was purely sexual on Cassie's behalf was something Siobhan needed to know. So why couldn't she bring herself to say it out loud?

CHAPTER TWENTY

"Y ou have a visitor."

Cassie's jaw clenched. She was engrossed in overwhelming amounts of money and had only picked up the phone when its incessant ring became overbearing. When she did, it was impossible to miss the jubilance in Julie's voice.

"I don't have anything booked in for today," Cassie said, flicking through her diary, "unless you've not done your job properly."

"He's demanding to speak to you, and it doesn't look like he's going anywhere any time soon."

Cassie was sure she could hear Siobhan in the background, sounding agitated, but couldn't make out what she was saying.

"Tell whoever it is he'll have to make an appointment. I'm not at the beck and call of Joe Public, you know."

"I don't think he'll agree to that. He has the exact same petulant look in his eyes that you've spent years perfecting."

Next thing Cassie knew, Siobhan had crept into her office, taking the utmost care to shut the door behind her, as if she were in the middle of a mission for MI5. She was professional to the last at work, so it was uncharacteristic of her not to knock. When Siobhan began twisting her wedding ring, Cassie knew something was wrong. She hung up on her secretary. "I've got Julie being a blundering buffoon on the phone and you standing there totally awkward like a hedgehog in a nudist colony. What's going on?"

"The visitor..." Siobhan pulled her blazer across her chest, buttoning it.

"Spit it out, Siobhan." Cassie hated being on the back foot. "You know I can't bear ditherers."

"The guy asking for you…it's your dad."

"What?" Cassie's stomach dropped. "He can't be here." Her pitch was a little too high for her liking, so she consciously tried to calm herself down, leaning with her elbows on the desk and placing her head in her hands. "Tell him to go away."

"I can't do that." Siobhan's tone was firm as she crossed her arms.

"If you're not going to help me, there's little point in you standing there making the place look untidy." She didn't look up.

Siobhan approached Cassie, hand extended. "When I heard Julie speaking to you, I knew she was deliberately drawing out the truth. I wanted to come and tell you myself because I know what a shock it must be."

"I don't need your emotional support." She shrugged Siobhan's hand off her arm. "He shouldn't be here. I tell you, if I find out who let him in, heads will roll."

"Cass…" Siobhan reached out again. "Take a few deep breaths; you don't need to lose it. I get the impression he just wants to talk."

There was such kindness in her voice, it irritated the hell out of Cassie. "Look, just because we're fuck buddies doesn't give you the right to an opinion about my family."

Siobhan took a step back, frowning. "You assume too much. Buddies indicates something far more significant than what we have."

A wave of nausea crept over her as she realized this was the first time she had spoken to Siobhan with such disdain.

"I didn't mean to imply—"

Siobhan held a hand up, cutting her off. "Don't worry, I know *exactly* where I stand. There was no need to reiterate it so rudely. I'll send him in." With that, Siobhan was gone.

"Fuck!" Cassie regretted her harsh words. Siobhan had placed herself directly in the firing line, delivering the news in the kindest way possible, and Cassie couldn't even—

"Hey." Her father managed to both dominate and cower in the doorway.

"You've got some nerve," Cassie jumped down his throat. "Leave."

"Five minutes. If after that you want me to go, then I promise I will."

"Five fucking minutes? You think that's all it's going to take?"

"It's just a figure of speech." He held out his hands. "I want us to talk—on your terms, of course."

The sight of him standing there looking imploringly at her brought up every emotion she'd been hammering down for the last several years. "Has Eva put you up to this?"

"It's got nothing to do with Eva. This was my last resort. You've been ignoring me."

Cassie's blood boiled at his audacity. "Says the forever absent father. Washing your hair last time I visited, were you?"

"We need to move forward," he said, unperturbed. "The only way I can see us doing that is by having an open and honest conversation about the past. I want us to have some sort of relationship. This has gone on long enough."

Cassie let out a snort of laughter at the sheer gall of her father's claim. If she had ever felt the need for a cigarette since quitting, it was now. She pulled open her drawer, rummaged around inside, and found nothing more than an empty box. "You should know," she slammed the drawer, "I did compose a reply to your text. I just never sent it. In simple terms it said I'm not ready to talk. Turning up here, forcing me to see you, it's bang out of order. You of all people should understand how important it is not to bother me at work."

"It's the only way I could guarantee seeing you."

Cassie picked up a folder, focusing intently on it, though the words were a blur. She shouldn't even be considering conversing with him, not after the way he'd spoken to her all those years ago. Niggling away inside was the way she had spoken to Siobhan just moments ago. Her head was a mash-up of jigsaw pieces from differing puzzles, resentment battling something far worse rooted deep in the back of her mind: hopefulness. *If* she were going to actively participate in this conversation, she needed to pull herself together.

Rolling her shoulders back, she held her chin high and spoke with quiet assertiveness. "You're here now, so you leave me little choice. I'll speak to you, but make no mistake, this isn't what I wanted." Cassie looked towards the door, hoping Siobhan hadn't made a dash for an early lunch break. "Give me five minutes," she said. "There's something I need to do before we have *any* sort of conversation."

Cassie stepped out of her office and closed her father inside. She glared at Julie, who glared right back, then gazed at Siobhan, whose focus was fixed on her computer. "Siobhan, can I speak to you?"

Siobhan didn't look up, and when she answered, her tone was ice cold. "Of course."

"Can we go somewhere more private?"

"You can say anything you need to right here," Siobhan asserted, still unwilling to make eye contact.

"Actually...I can't." Cassie cocked her chin at Julie, who was gawping at them like a newspaper reporter about to get a huge scoop.

"Don't worry, I'll head out on my lunch so you two can finish your domestic in action-packed style." Julie raised her eyebrows, smirking.

Any other day Cassie would have risen to the bait. Today, she simply watched until Julie departed, her eyes glued to her phone while her fingers typed with unnatural speed, setting off the rumor mill, no doubt. Little did Cassie care as she plonked herself down on the end of Siobhan's desk and lowered her head. She sighed, twiddling her thumbs, the words thick in her throat. "I owe you an apology. I shouldn't have spoken to you like that."

Siobhan stopped what she was doing and looked up. "No, you shouldn't have," she said. "I'm not your whipping boy. However, I am aware of what a big deal this is to you. I'm sorry if I overstepped. My intention was to help you."

Cassie slumped down into the seat opposite Siobhan. "I know that," she said, her voice flat. "I screwed up." She rubbed her palms together. "I just feel so conflicted. I mean, how ridiculous is it that even a tiny part of me wants to feel optimistic that he's changed?" Cassie felt her chin begin to tremble and hated herself for it.

Siobhan squeezed Cassie's hand. "There's no rule against experiencing more than one emotion at once, especially about something like this."

"I hate him for how he's made me feel all these years and yet..." Cassie couldn't finish the sentence.

"I know this wasn't on your to-do list for today, and I know he hurt you, but—"

"He didn't hurt me," Cassie was quick to interrupt, unable to bear Siobhan seeing any weakness. "He pissed me off."

"Okay," Siobhan conceded. "And this is your chance to tell him how that made you feel."

Cassie scowled. "Thank you."

"Care to expand?" Siobhan asked, offering Cassie a genuine smile.

"For your advice," Cassie said through gritted teeth. "I appreciate it."

"You know, at this rate I could end up being indispensable."

"Not on my watch," Cassie muttered under her breath. "Now, if you'll excuse me," she voiced at an audible volume. "I can at least manage a sandwich and coffee before showing him the door."

❖

"The last few years have killed your mother."

Cassie's fork nearly catapulted across the table. "Last I checked, Mum was alive and well-versed in defending you. And you might want to choose your words more carefully. Not everyone is lucky enough to still have their mother around."

"Oh," he said. "Did someone you know—"

"We're not talking about someone I know. We're talking about me. And Mum, apparently."

Her father Mark nodded. "Between the two of us, we've put her in a terrible position. Eva as well."

"Ah, the conforming daughter, the one you acknowledge. And are you seriously laying the blame for this discord on my doorstep? Because—" Cassie saw their waiter weaving his way towards their table and stopped. Finally, some respite. She took a sip of the coffee, then propped her chin on her hand, giving the sandwiches her full attention.

"I'm not blaming you," he said quietly. "I was…I was actively avoiding you. I was wrong—to avoid you and to…and to reject you. When I finally realized that, I wanted to apologize, but I didn't think you would accept it. Too much damage had been done—*by me*. Too much time had passed, and I know it's supposed to heal all wounds, but I doubted very much that it would."

He looked directly at her, and for a terrible moment, she thought he might cry. Or that she would. Cassie looked away, unable to cope with the unusual range of emotions she was experiencing. She couldn't remember the last time she had cried and felt embarrassed now as she brushed away a tear. "You said some really hurtful things," she said, despite having denied the truth to Siobhan.

Her dad poked at a meatball in his sub. "I know and I can't tell you how sorry I am, how much I wish I could turn back time and take those despicable things I said back."

"You mean things like *dyke* and *rug muncher*?" Cassie watched him cringe.

"Your mum calls me out on it regularly, says I made you feel like…like…"

"Shit?" she supplied.

"I was trying to put it in my own words, but I don't know—"

"Since you don't know, I'll tell you. You made me feel like you never loved me."

He recoiled as though she had struck him. She hoped her words did hit him hard. In the gut, in the heart, between the eyes.

"That…that was never…I never…I should have…" His words dried up mid-sentence, as if he'd lost the will to continue. He squeezed his eyes shut, anguish etched across his face.

Cassie couldn't decide whether to feel vindicated or validated. She popped a wedge of bread into her mouth. "Why the sudden need for reconciliation anyway? Worried I'll make a scene at Eva's wedding?"

"No. Eva doesn't know I'm here. This comes from my regret, my desire to make amends. Eva's wedding has only made me realize how much of your life I've missed. We were inseparable when you were a kid, remember? It drove your sister crazy."

An image flashed in her mind: a walk on a wintry day, placing her Wellington boot-covered foot into her father's huge footprint and feeling in awe of him. A laugh bubbled up, and before she could stop it, it burst out against her wishes.

Her dad chuckled for the first time since they had been together. It was a comforting sound somehow, despite her resentment towards him.

Refusing to indulge him any further, Cassie cleared her throat and said, "Just because you're a recovering homophobic doesn't mean I accept your apology. You made me the mess I am today." Another surge of bitterness took hold, and she seized the handle of the coffee pot. She tilted it towards the mug, realizing all too late that she was pouring him a cup and not her. "You're welcome," she muttered, as if that had been her intention all along.

He swallowed hard. "I wouldn't consider you a mess. From where I'm sitting, you've done well for yourself—"

"Professionally, yes. Personally, no. I have trouble seeing the good in people, connecting with them. I tend not to get attached, lest they leave me when they learn things about me they don't like."

"I love you," he said simply. "I've never stopped. But I need to learn how to love you the way a father should. And perhaps you'd be...open to learning how to love me too? Perhaps we might get there together?"

"It's very early days," Cassie said, but she smiled before she remembered she shouldn't. "I guess we've taken the first step today, but this isn't going to be easy for me and I don't plan on making it easy for you."

"I'd expect nothing less." He mirrored what Cassie knew to be her trademark grin. "So, how would you rate the sandwiches?"

"The triple-decker steak is the ultimate winner of this lot."

"See, I'm all about the BLT."

"A traditionalist in more ways than one," Cassie said. "No doubt you put salt and vinegar on your chips too."

"Absolutely! Though I have been known to live on the edge and dip in gravy occasionally."

"Absolutely unacceptable! That's what I like about Siobhan. She's ketchup all the way. She also understands the importance of never ordering any sort of egg sandwich."

"Siobhan?" He raised a questioning eyebrow.

"A friend from work." Cassie couldn't believe she'd let that slip out, like she was talking about a girlfriend. "A good friend."

"Is she someone you're...seeing?"

Cassie glared at him in warning. "How about the crispy chicken sandwich? That's pretty good too."

"Happy to enjoy any sort of sandwich with you," he said cheerfully. "It means a lot."

The hope Cassie had harbored seemed to be justified. Here was her dad, trying to make amends in the only way he knew how. The anger hadn't subsided, it was still gurgling away in her darkest depths, but it was easing ever so slightly. Given time, she wondered if she might come to forgive him and find a way to move on with him being a small part of her life, something she couldn't imagine contemplating only a few weeks ago.

Barriers were breaking down, some of the strongest walls she had imprisoned herself within were crumbling. What she couldn't understand was why this was starting to happen now? Why now, when she was making more effort than ever before to avoid emotional connection, lest it be the unravelling of her?

CHAPTER TWENTY-ONE

"Behind every great woman is her backside," Siobhan observed as Cassie, who was on all fours with her arse in the air, fumbled around adjusting the bass drum pedal.

"I didn't come round here to be ogled by you," Cassie said from her place on the floor.

"It's an added perk." Unable to help herself, Siobhan reached forward and squeezed. Cassie turned towards her, eyes blazing like a forest fire and Siobhan tried to play the innocent. "What?"

"You're distracting me." Cassie moved closer.

"Is that a problem?"

"That depends on what you want me to be banging: you or the drums." Cassie's lips parted as her gaze veered to Siobhan's breasts.

"I think we both know the answer to that," Siobhan murmured, reveling in Cassie's gaze. Then, with more fortitude than she knew she was capable of, Siobhan redirected her thoughts from the source of her arousal. "It looks like you're all set up. Shall I call Neave down? She's going to get such a surprise."

Cassie was standing now, taking in her handiwork, a gleam in her eye. "I'm warning you, it's been a long time since I played. There could be carnage."

Siobhan shrugged and then placed a lingering kiss on Cassie's cheek. "Chaos and carnage are my specialties. Didn't I tell you? Neave! Cassie's here!"

Neave darted into the room, skidded to a halt when she saw the drum kit, and whooped with excitement. "You brought it!"

Cassie smiled. "A round trip to my sister's last Sunday and here they are. I did promise I would pick them up for you."

Neave bounced around the kit, taking everything in, spinning and twirling as she went. "The color looks a little like the Smurfs have puked all over it. I love it!"

"I'm delighted someone does." Cassie rolled her eyes. "My sister was always moaning about the color. To be honest, I think she was glad to be rid of the kit from her loft." Cassie looked at Siobhan. "It fills the space nicely."

"And permanently, it would appear." Siobhan settled on the edge of the sofa in the conservatory. "So, are we about to be treated to a performance?"

"I thought we'd get Neave going first." Cassie brushed past Siobhan as she reached down for a bag, then emptied its contents onto the sofa. "These are my original drumsticks." Cassie spun them up into the air, then failed to catch either, much to Siobhan's amusement. "You didn't see that," she whispered to Neave, whose stifled laugh came out as a snort. "Here, I thought you might like a set of your own."

Neave's whole face lit up. "They have my name on!" she exclaimed. "Look, Mum!" Neave thrust them in her face and Siobhan tried to just look impressed, when in reality she was bowled over by Cassie's thoughtfulness.

"Danny bought me these when I was a teenager. Your first drumsticks will always be special to you. These are still my go-to sticks."

"Was Danny your first love?" Neave asked, and now it was Cassie's turn to snort.

As her daughter awaited a response, Siobhan sat upright, uptight, her muscles twitching. Cassie was always one step away from overstepping.

"What's so funny?" Neave asked.

"Danny is my sister's fiancé," Cassie replied between chuckles. "I reckon you and Dylan would love him. He's a surf instructor."

"Sickage!" Neave yelled. "Thanks for the drumsticks!" She threw her arms around Cassie, and Siobhan was amazed to see her accept the hug, even if she did freeze like an actor suffering from stage fright, rather than fully participating.

"For future reference, drummers do high fives," Cassie said gently. "Now come and take a seat at the stool and we can get cracking."

Siobhan mouthed her thanks, appreciating the simple nod of acknowledgement Cassie gave her in return. She settled more comfortably into the sofa, curling her legs under her as Cassie shuffled the stool closer to the kit and pulled up a chair next to Neave.

"The first thing you need to know is that those awesome new drumsticks need to be held loosely in your hands. Don't grip them too tight. Like this." Cassie waved her sticks around and Neave copied her. "Now, if you're anything like I was when I got my first kit, you'll want to bash every drum going, right?"

Neave wiggled in anticipation of this very instruction. She had shown amazing restraint so far. "Can I?"

"Go for it." Cassie grinned at Siobhan. "Now is the moment for hands over ears. This could last a while." She moved her hands up onto her ears for protection. "Dylan's lucky he's in Watford. Out of hearing range."

"I'm not sure he'd consider himself lucky. Matthew's dragged him to a football match. The game isn't until tomorrow, but they're staying over with Matthew's friend and his son. He only agreed to go because the other boy is his age and Matthew promised to take Dylan to the cinema tonight. He had a face like a wet weekend when they left."

"Dylan or Matthew?"

"Both."

"Cassie, listen to this!" Neave used the pedal to make the bass drum boom into existence. "It sounds like elephants marching!"

"If you pass me your sticks, I'll show you another animal."

Neave immediately obliged and Cassie sat at the drum, quickly flicking the sticks onto the snare to create a rattling sound.

"You told me you didn't like the zoo," Siobhan teased her, sticking her fingers in her ears.

"Wait, what? You don't like the zoo?" Neave's forehead crinkled up. "What sort of adult are you?"

"A cagey one." Cassie chortled at her own wit, but Neave shook her head in dissatisfaction and continued to hammer the drums, showing no sign of letting up.

"You can make this stop, right?" Siobhan threw Cassie a pleading look.

"You are looking a little frazzled."

"Enough experimenting, time for some teaching." Siobhan raised her voice over the relentless din her daughter was making. "Neave, darling! Cassie is going to teach you a beat now!"

Neave stopped, pouting at Siobhan, until Cassie focused in on their lesson, looking every bit the pro.

"Count with me to eight. We're going to keep it equal and you're going to hit this one to every beat of the eight. It's called the hi-hat."

Neave followed the instructions to the letter, which both amused and confused Siobhan as Neave was normally determined to go about things in her own way. Neave mastered the beat quickly under Cassie's tutelage and soon Cassie was challenging her to quicken the pace, adding her own parts to the rhythm as they played together. A warmth crept into Siobhan's heart as she watched the two of them together, Cassie paying Neave the attention Matthew never had. She shook the thought away. Cassie wasn't the family type.

"Now we're going to add this drum, the snare, on three and seven, and in a minute you're going to need your foot."

"I don't think I'll be able to do two different things at once."

"Of course you will," Cassie said. "It just takes practice. Hear that, Siobhan? Lots of practice!"

"And lots of lessons," Siobhan added, winking at Cassie. "Hear that, Neave? Cassie's going to be around a lot more."

Their heads whipped up. Neave wore an expression of elation, while Cassie's expression was one of…consternation. Siobhan shook it off again, telling herself she was just imagining things, and that the difference wasn't so drastic.

"Sorry to spoil the party," she said, "but Mia's mum will be here in ten minutes and you've not even packed."

"Okay, Mum." Neave high fived Siobhan and Cassie and then hastened out of the room.

"About what I said…"

"I know what you meant," Cassie replied. "You just meant that she'll only be able to play—and play properly, at that—with me."

Siobhan could see her struggling to subdue a sincere smile and relaxed a bit.

"I may need to invest in some ear defenders or take up an interest in very long walks." Siobhan rubbed her temples. "I think I have a headache."

Cassie leaned in closer, her lips brushing her ear. "Ah, drum headaches, now that's something I *am* an expert in curing—"

"Mia's here!" Neave flew past them. "See you tomorrow!"

"I didn't even get a good-bye kiss." Siobhan pouted. Deciding to push her luck, she added, "Someone has to agree to kiss me, right?"

"You've got to work on the art of subtle, it really isn't your strong point."

Snaking an arm around Siobhan's waist, Cassie guided her out into the garden and towards the loungers, where they'd agreed to spend the afternoon sunbathing, amongst other activities that required them to be minimally attired.

Cassie whipped off her T-shirt and shorts to reveal a black bikini.

"Jesus, Cass…" Siobhan's mouth watered. The bends of Cassie's hips and the fullness of her breasts were perfection. Siobhan was transfixed as Cassie ran her hand through her hair. First she noticed her lean, capable arms and then allowed her eyes to roam over shapely legs.

"You didn't think I was going to sunbathe fully clothed, now, did you?" Cassie made her way over to Siobhan, who stood gawping. "Isn't it time you slipped into something more revealing?" Cassie complained, pulling playfully on Siobhan's T-shirt, and soon she too was similarly starkers, save for an orange bikini.

"You need sun cream." Siobhan waved the bottle.

"Is that the best foreplay you have to offer?" Cassie wiggled her backside in Siobhan's direction. "I suppose my arse is in particular danger from the sun's rays." Cassie wiggled it some more.

"It's in certain danger from me." Siobhan jumped up and playfully pounced on Cassie, pushing her down onto her front on the sun lounger and straddling her. "Can't have you burning, can we?"

Try as she might, it was almost impossible to ignore the desire pooling between her own legs. She spread sun lotion liberally, Cassie's pert backside feeling amazing beneath her fingertips as they roamed freely. Siobhan's hand moved over, under, and in between Cassie's bikini bottoms, whereupon she did indeed discover an abundance of arousal that rivaled her own.

When Cassie failed to stifle a moan, Siobhan began to explore further, pressing herself into Cassie's thighs, running her lips across Cassie's earlobe.

"Hey, Mum!"

Siobhan jumped like a toad in a thunderstorm, snatched her hand out of Cassie's bikini bottoms, and threw herself into the chair opposite.

"Dylan, what are you doing here?" she demanded, her heart thumping so loudly she was convinced everyone could hear it. She yanked Cassie's T-shirt over her head. "Where's your father?"

"Dunno," Dylan mumbled, walking towards them. He sat down next to Cassie on the lounger Siobhan had speedily vacated. "He said I was better off with you and then he sped off. What does he mean? He's right, but what does he mean?"

Siobhan sucked in her cheeks. She knew exactly what Matthew meant. He was referring to their divorce and the fact he was happy to give up his parental rights to Siobhan. What she couldn't figure out was why things had gone so wrong in the space of the couple of hours they had been out together. She also knew better than to bring it up now, with Cassie and without Neave. "He must have changed his mind about the match. He didn't want to force you to do something you weren't going to enjoy, so he's dropped you back off with me."

Dylan shook his head. "You're way off the mark, Mum. Dad changed his mind about the cinema, not the match. When we got to the hotel, he decided he'd rather watch the game on TV in the bar with Mike and Jamie, and he said I had to watch it with him, because he didn't trust me to be alone in the room. Then he said he was sick of looking at my sulky face and everyone found me unpleasant to be around. I think he wishes Jamie was his son." By the time he finished, Dylan was on the verge of tears.

"Hey, let's have less of that." Cassie ruffled his hair. "How could anyone pick some other kid over you? You're more than good enough, so don't try to conform to what your father thinks you should be. It takes a lot of backbone to be an individual."

"I've got guts coming out of my ears!" Dylan swiped at his eyes with the backs of his hands. "I'm glad Dad brought me back, Mum. I'd rather hang out with you and Cassie. "What were two doing anyway?" Dylan looked a little confused, his brows knitting together. "Wrestling?"

"Looking for my earring." Cassie was quicker than she could manage, throwing Siobhan's T-shirt over her head as she spoke.

Dylan seemed to take a while to process this information, inspecting Cassie closely. "You've just put Mum's T-shirt on, and your ears aren't even pierced."

"*My* earring!" Siobhan knew she sounded panicked. "We were looking for *my* earring. It must have fallen out."

"Whilst you were wrestling," Dylan laughed. "You've always been good at wrestling."

"Anyways, I'm going to go," Cassie said, and Siobhan's heart dropped. "I should leave you two to talk."

"You don't have to go." Siobhan reached for Cassie's hand, then pulled back, remembering herself. "I don't suppose you fancy the cinema tonight? I know it isn't the evening we had planned, but—"

"Please, Cassie," Dylan chimed in. "You can even pick the film."

Cassie put her hands on her hips, then crossed her arms, then wiped her palms on her thighs. Finally, she gave a weak smile. "Of course I'll come, but I'm leaving the selection to you."

"Why don't you go get sorted, love? I'm assuming you'll want to take that football shirt off."

"Why is everyone taking their shirt off today?" Dylan shook his head as he went into the house.

"Talk about cliterception," Siobhan said, trying to make light of the situation. But when she turned towards Cassie, she noticed her face was scrunched up like a discarded letter and her lips were pinched as if they'd been superglued shut.

"You look like you're going to lose it," Siobhan said gently.

"I'm just regretting the interruption," Cassie said.

"You could always come back after the cinema and stay the night," she offered, cautiously optimistic.

A pensive expression crossed Cassie's face. "And what would Dylan think of that?"

"Considering you're his favorite person in the world right now, I'd say he'd be delighted. You showed such empathy—"

"I'm not staying over. Not after what just happened."

"He didn't see anything. He thought we were playing a game—"

"But we're not playing a game. We're having an affair."

"Actually, right now we're having an argument," Siobhan said, unable to help herself.

Cassie's eyes pierced hers. Earlier, Siobhan had been enraptured by the intensity in Cassie's eyes. Now she felt intimidated.

"He may not have seen *everything*," Cassie said, "but he did see *something*. He simply didn't understand what he saw. It's a good job

Matthew didn't come storming in. I don't plan on spending the next few months defending or explaining myself to your husband."

Siobhan's breathing stuttered to a standstill. Slowly, she leaned back in the lounger. "You've put an expiry date on this already?" she asked, her tone steady and even, a sharp contrast to her heartbeat.

Cassie didn't meet Siobhan's eyes when she answered. "That's the thing about affairs. At some point, they have to end." She cupped Siobhan's face in her palm. "I'm going to head home."

Siobhan stayed in place, and soon heard the front door close. She closed her eyes and let the emotions swirling through her rise so she could pay attention to them. What had she been thinking, asking Cassie to go to the cinema? She was spending a lot of time with the kids, and Siobhan had grown comfortable with the situation, like it was normal. But it wasn't. Though she had been overly optimistic this might last longer than a few months, Cassie was right. At some point, this would end, and it was important she didn't forget that.

CHAPTER TWENTY-TWO

I am *not* fascinated by the ludicrous length of giraffe tongues," Cassie said. "I am envious of them." She observed Siobhan, awaiting the flush she felt certain would rush to her cheeks. It would be a pleasant change from the glum expression she had been wearing most of the day, especially when the kids weren't around. But Siobhan simply plastered on an unconvincing smile and Cassie knew she would have to change tactics. "Thanks for inviting me."

"It was the kids' idea. They love it here. Neave enjoyed serving as your mini tour guide." Siobhan looked over to the adventure playground, where her children were imitating the monkeys, swinging wildly from the climbing frame.

"Dylan thinks I was separated at birth from the spider monkeys, so all in all a successful outing."

Siobhan looked her up and down. "Noisy, cheeky—"

"Scratching their backsides," Cassie said, pleased to see Siobhan's head loll back in laughter. "Personally, I can't see the resemblance."

Cassie went to dig her playfully in the ribs, but Siobhan shifted to the other side of the bench. This wasn't the first time she had avoided physical contact today, but Cassie wasn't about to dwell on it. "When you first told me you were a serial zoo visitor, I was cynical—"

"Now *that's* an accurate way to describe you," Siobhan muttered. It was like a cloud had drifted overhead, such were her mood changes today.

"Is something bothering you?"

"Nothing at all," Siobhan said without looking at her.

"If this is about what I said the other day…" Cassie adopted a challenging tone, leaning on the arm of the bench, head against her hand. "It wasn't meant to unsettle you. I was just stating a fact."

Siobhan responded with a small intake of breath. "Is that what you think you've done? Unsettled me?" Siobhan's nostrils flared as she twisted her watch around.

"Not fiddling with your wedding ring today?" Cassie glared at the sparkly reminder of Siobhan's marital status.

"It seems to irritate you—either the fiddling or the wedding ring. I can't be sure which."

"Please tell me you haven't gotten emotionally invested. I didn't sign up for the silent treatment and mood swings. I usually enjoy myself when I'm with you. Affairs are supposed to be fun."

Siobhan stared at Cassie, and the force of her gaze knocked Cassie for a loop. She saw a whole world in Siobhan's eyes, ready to spill out. Cassie looked away first.

When Siobhan spoke again, her tone was lighter, and Cassie wondered if her eyes were as well, though she didn't dare check. "Well, just think how much more you'll enjoy yourself tonight, when we're alone. Good thing my kids have a better social life than I do, right?"

"I'll second that." Cassie inwardly cheered, pleased with, if not a little unsettled by, the change of topic. "What do you have—"

"Cassie?"

A woman Cassie knew all too well pushed a pram in their direction. With her heavenly white teeth, photogenic smile, and enticing blue eyes, she looked like she had been spun from the sunshine itself. As she spoke, a silky tone to her West Country accent, Cassie felt the color drain from her cheeks and her muscles coil with tension.

"It *is* you! I was telling myself it couldn't be, but here you are."

Cassie twisted her hands together, her gaze gravitating to the ground, but she rallied herself to look up, loath to let Siobhan see weakness. "Hi, Emilia."

"Let me introduce my husband, Ethan," Emilia said, draping her arm possessively around her companion and planting an overly affectionate kiss on his lips that seemed to last longer than necessary.

Cassie appraised the man. He had the sort of face that would stop a straight woman in her tracks and was holding a little boy by the hand. "Husband?" she choked on the word.

"You remember Cassie," Emilia said, but Ethan looked blank. "From uni."

His lips curled into a smile, then he emitted a snicker. "I *do* remember you."

Even now, looking at Emilia, it wasn't difficult to see why Cassie had made such a huge mistake. The display she was putting on, dangling off Ethan's arm in an embarrassing show of devotion, almost seemed natural. Perhaps nowadays it was?

As Emilia eyed Siobhan like an audience member trying to work out the final plot twist, Cassie couldn't read her. *Nothing new there.*

"This must be your partner?"

"Coworker," Cassie corrected her, scowling. She felt Siobhan tense slightly beside her.

"Right. Do you take all your coworkers out to London Zoo on a Saturday? Or has it happened again?"

"I'm Cassie's friend, Siobhan."

"Cassie must have the worst gaydar imaginable." Emilia pulled her sunglasses down and looked over the frames directly into Cassie's eyes. Emilia had always been a master of eye contact, unlike Cassie, who needed to look away, even now. "I'm Emilia. We were at uni together. I can't imagine Cassie talks about those days often."

Cassie watched as she offered a well-manicured hand, Siobhan accepting with an easy nod.

"She doesn't actually."

"For good reason," Cassie said.

Cassie found herself unable to make eye contact with either woman. The last thing in the world she needed right now was this painful part of her past dredged up. Emilia was the reason Cassie found herself incapable of any sort of relationship. The mess she was in today, that was all Emilia too, but Siobhan didn't need to know that.

"Nonsense! Bumping into her like this brings back a few interesting memories."

Dylan raced over, his cheeks red, his face looking hot and sticky, Neave traipsing behind. "Mum, please can we head to Liam's now? We need to finish our volcano project. Then next week we get to watch it explode!"

Never had Cassie been more relieved at a child's interruption.

"Are these *your* children?" Emelia scrutinized them, incredulous.

"They're mine," Siobhan stated, wrapping an arm around each of them.

"That gaydar really *is* faulty." Emilia's jaw tightened. "What happened to your proclamation about never wanting children? You said you'd never date any woman with kids. A dull pastime, that's what you called children."

"We're not dating," Cassie muttered through gritted teeth. "I told you, we're coworkers. And that's why the gaydar thing doesn't matter, Emilia."

"Dating!" Neave bounced up and down in front of Siobhan.

"They're not dating *yet*," Dylan whispered to his sister, loud enough for everyone to hear.

Cassie really felt like she'd walked into the lion's den, only without the benefit of being eaten.

Dylan looked towards Emilia and said, "If she didn't like children when you knew her, it was only because she hadn't met the right kids yet."

"The absolute best kids!" Cassie gave him a big grin, hoping nobody could tell how forced it was. "I had other pastimes back then."

"Anyway," Emilia drawled, looking unconvinced, "we'll let you get on with your afternoon. You look like you're having a lovely time. Congratulations."

Cassie mustered up what was left of her willpower to simulate another smile, waving as they walked off, her eyes following Emelia all the way.

"Why don't you two go and play for another ten minutes and then we'll make tracks?" Siobhan suggested.

The children took their cue and raced back over to the playground.

"The dark horse rides again," Siobhan said, also watching Emilia and her husband walk away. "You told me you'd never been in love."

Cassie let out a low whistle, her mouth going dry, her brain scrambling for an excuse. "What on earth makes you think I was in love?"

"I know you're devoted to denial, but it's written all over that sulky face of yours."

"Don't be ridiculous!" Cassie folded her arms, creating a deliberate barrier between them.

"It's not difficult to read between the lines. You were in love with her."

The accuracy of Siobhan's inference made her stomach queasy and her vision blurry. "I think I'm going to be sick." Cassie put her head between her legs.

"Talk about dramatic. Honestly, Cass, you're okay."

Cassie could tell an eye roll had accompanied that reassurance. Siobhan began to rub Cassie's back, working to soothe her, but then, without warning, the rubbing turned to patting, as though Siobhan were comforting a stranger. Then the comfort ceased completely, and Cassie felt Siobhan shuffle across the bench, once again putting a safe distance between them.

When she spoke this time, her concern was replaced with practicality. "Take a few deep breaths. You've had a shock, just relax."

Cassie stumbled up, her head spinning. "I need to go home."

"You're not going home," Siobhan said. "We're going to drop the kids off at Liam's like we planned and then go back to yours. I'll make you a cup of tea and then you can tell me why my wedding ring isn't the only one that's unsettling you."

❖

"My mum always said there wasn't a problem in the world that couldn't be solved over a cup of tea."

"Believe me when I say, no cup of tea is strong enough for this fucked-up situation. I need a cigarette." Cassie marched out of the kitchen and into the bedroom in hopes of hunting one down.

Siobhan busied herself making tea, her thoughts scattershot. Of course Cassie's callous comment the other night had hurt, even if it wasn't supposed to. Now that she had been accused of emotional investment too, were things just heading towards a natural conclusion? Was that what Cassie was trying to tell her? Had she made a mistake ever agreeing to conditions she couldn't meet, just to fall into bed with Cassie? Deep down there was a reason for all Cassie's choices, she knew that, but she'd never be allowed close enough to find out what they were, Emilia being a perfect example.

Cassie returned with a lit Marlboro in her mouth, puffing away like a blacksmith's bellows.

SKYE ROWAN

"I'll have that." Siobhan reached for the cigarette, and after a minor kerfuffle, succeeded in removing it from her hand. "You'll only regret it tomorrow when you wake up and your throat feels like you've swallowed razor blades."

Cassie huffed, clearly irritated that Siobhan was preventing her from drinking and smoking herself into a stupor.

"Here's your tea. Are you going to drink this straight or would you like some sugar?"

"I don't take anything straight," Cassie said, picking up her mug. "Or sugary."

"How about direction? Will you take that? Come sit with me." Siobhan led Cassie to the swing seat outside on the balcony and sat down cross-legged to face her.

Cassie mirrored her actions, crossing her legs, but then looked away. "I don't want to talk to you."

"This is what a Cassie meltdown looks like. Why don't you start with the obvious and tell me about Emilia? Something happened between the two of you, something you've never opened up about. Not to me anyway."

"I don't open up to anyone."

"Well, I think it's about time you gave me that courtesy, I think I've earned it."

"What's that supposed to mean?" Cassie threw her daggers.

"That I'm right here, Cassie, asking you to talk to me, asking you to be honest."

"Fuck." Cassie raised her eyebrows pointedly, then shook her head. "Helena warned me time and time again not to fall for Emilia, but I just assumed she was jealous."

"Wait, Helena liked you?" Siobhan rested her chin on her hands and leaned forward.

"Liked me? She fancied the pants off me." When Siobhan looked disbelieving, Cassie said, "Her words, not mine. But I fell for Emilia in a big way. I was never interested in Helena although she would've been the better choice. Somehow, I managed to delude myself into thinking Emilia felt the same way about me. We dated for three years and there's a part of me that still clings to the fact it was incredible."

"Yet the look in your eyes tells me it wasn't."

· 182 ·

"Helena told me time and time again, but I wasn't listening. I lost my senses to this woman. I didn't even mind that she would desert me at the drop of a hat when a better offer came along. It was me she went to bed with every night, me she woke up with, and nothing else mattered."

"That doesn't sound like the Cassie I know so well."

"She's the reason you're stuck with this shit version of me."

Siobhan took a sip of her tea. This was the first time she had ever heard Cassie be so openly disparaging about herself.

"I'd never even considered the fact she wasn't gay, or even that she was bi. Why would I? Imagine my surprise when one day I come home to find her in bed with Ethan, the future fucking husband."

"So that's what the award-winning performance was all about today? I did wonder if anyone could really be *that* in love."

"Or *that* straight," Cassie said. "Though she did tell me she never wanted to be with a woman again. I guess I ruined that experience for her. Maybe I should have warned you too."

Siobhan shook her head, the threads of Cassie's past irreversibly unraveling to make sense.

"Look, this isn't an easy plaster to rip off, but she crushed me that day. To think someone is your whole world and then find out they were using you for a bit of fun, it's not easy. Add to that the fact your best friend told you this all along and there you have your explanation for the woman who won't commit to any relationship ever again." Cassie's cheeks seared scarlet.

"It goes a long way to explaining how you feel. Between what happened with Emilia and the struggles you've had with your dad, you've not had an easy time," Siobhan said. "It seems she's in denial now with all that talk of faulty gaydar, I can see why that bothers you. Just so you know, I'm only interested in women. Despite my mistakes. I've only ever been interested in women."

"Right." Cassie looked doubtful.

"I'd like to kiss you and make it better. Is that still not allowed?"

"No, it isn't. Remember, you're not a rule-breaker like me. I broke the first rule of any relationship: never fall for someone who cheats on you."

"So you weren't just infatuated with her. You were in love with her."

"I never said that."

"You said you fell for her."

"Fine," she grumbled. "Maybe I did have some feelings for her, but that's all in the past now. I won't ever allow myself to fall again, not in the present, nor in the future. Never. It was a one-time thing, a bit like this is a one-time fling."

"There are plenty of women out there who are lesbian or bi and able to be faithful. Closing yourself off that way because of one woman is extreme."

"I was only stating the obvious." Cassie began to pull on her shoelaces, untying them, then fastening them again. "It's not like you're not going to leave your husband, as unpleasant as he is, for me. Not that I want you to. Obviously."

Siobhan contemplated how best to interpret the look that passed over Cassie's face: fright, or elation. Both, she decided. With Cassie, much like the two of them, neither feeling was mutually exclusive. Nevertheless, she took a deep breath. "It may surprise you to find out that I *am* going to leave my husband, and for one reason alone. For *me*."

Cassie jumped up and leaned against the railing of the balcony.

Siobhan watched her look out over the cityscape. "Don't even think about impaling yourself on the Spire. Not even you could pull that look off. And just to provide you with some clarification, I made my decision to leave Matthew long before you came along."

Cassie shifted her elbows onto the railing. "That parent at the party said something, but I thought it was just gossip."

"Why didn't you ask me?"

"I was…"

"Afraid to hear the answer?" Siobhan asked.

"It was none of my business," Cassie said, sitting back down. "Now I know it's true, I need to think. I need time to take this in. I mean where are you and the kids going to go?" Her face blanched. "You're not thinking you can move in with me, are you?"

Siobhan's stomach dropped. She'd gotten too close to Cassie, if a simple question like that hurt so much. "Our living arrangements don't concern you, but you have nothing to fear."

"You still should've discussed it with me."

"Why would I discuss my divorce with my coworker-cum-fancy woman?"

Cassie regarded her as though Siobhan had been the one to impale her on the Spire.

Having gained the upper hand, Siobhan let out a deep, satisfied sigh. Cassie went to great lengths to point out the status of their relationship, so it was her turn to relish the opportunity.

"I thought we were also friends," Cassie murmured. "Friends with a wide range of added benefits."

"Don't do that," Siobhan warned her. "And don't expect me to talk to you on an emotional level when there are no emotions involved. *Your* rules."

Cassie reached for Siobhan's hand. "Look, Shiv—"

Siobhan withdrew. "Don't call me that. And don't touch me like that either. Couples hold hands, we don't."

"Since when?"

Siobhan glared at the hand she'd abandoned, then turned her glare on Cassie. "Kissing is too intimate for you. I feel the same way about hand-holding."

Cassie moved her hand onto her knee, positioning, then repositioning it, like it didn't even belong to her own body, and Siobhan almost felt bad for her.

"Look, Siobhan, whether or not you intended to divorce Matthew doesn't change things for us." Cassie took a sip of her tea, her eyes focused on the mug, and Siobhan wondered what she would see in those eyes if Cassie faced her. "I've made my feelings clear from the very start—"

"You don't have feelings, remember?" Siobhan couldn't help the anger that was forcing its way out.

"I *do* have feelings."

"For me?"

Siobhan watched Cassie's throat undulate, watched Cassie press her fist against her trembling lips. Siobhan refused to break eye contact first; Cassie needed to feel this pressure. Her whole life felt like it hinged on Cassie's answer, and if she were to be let down, she had to maintain her dignity until the bitter end.

"Right now I just want to keep things simple."

"Right now?" Siobhan asked. "So there might come a time when things progress beyond simplicity?"

"I can't give you the answer you seem to be looking for." Cassie's eyes met hers now.

Siobhan could feel the fire and fear simmering there, and it sent tremors across her skin. "Well, there's no question what has to happen." Siobhan closed her eyes and rubbed her temples, taking a moment to clear her head. When she spoke again, her voice was crisp, clear, confident. "This has to end. Now. For you. For your benefit. No-strings is your style. Who am I to cramp it?"

"Siobhan..."

"No. You gave this an expiry date." It took a momentous effort for Siobhan to turn her back on Cassie, but she did it with her head held high. "I'm just bringing it forward."

She stormed from the apartment with as much dignity as she could summon, but once she was in the car, she let the tears flow. It wasn't Cassie's fault, not really. She'd made it clear right from the beginning where she stood. But Siobhan had let her in. She'd spent time with the children, who adored her, and it had given Siobhan such a wonderful feeling of peace and belonging, that she'd allowed herself to fall down the rabbit hole.

Walking away was the last thing in the world she wanted to do, but the only right decision. She dropped her head onto the steering wheel, tears streaming down her face as she faced up to the reality that this was over. But if she was going to save her heart and keep her kids from being hurt, walking away really was the only option.

CHAPTER TWENTY-THREE

Your old love interest and your new love interest facing off at the zoo." Helena shook her head. "It's like some doomed romance novel from Stephen King."

"May I remind you that Stephen King writes horror?" Cassie informed her.

"My point exactly."

"May I also remind you that I have no interest in love, with or without Siobhan?"

"Right." Helena picked a flat stone off the sand and handed it to Cassie, who hurled it into the ocean. "And here I was thinking love might only be a stone's throw away."

Cassie swallowed hard, bending down to pick up another stone. It felt smooth and cool between her fingers, a welcome contrast to the raging inferno in her mind. She moved backward, perfecting her angle, and then flicked the stone, watching it bounce once, twice, three times, before disappearing under the water.

"Speaking of throwing things away...I ended it." Even to her own ears, she sounded anything but casual, unaffected, uninvested. It was also a lie. Siobhan had walked away, and Cassie had spent the time since brooding over Siobhan while denying that she was upset.

"Are you insane?"

"As much as I value your opinion," Cassie rolled her eyes, "I've made my decision and fully intend on keeping to it."

"But you two were getting on so well. Hell, I even liked her."

"What does that matter to me? I'm not going to change my mind because you approve."

"Common sense is like deodorant," Helena said. "The people who need it most never wear it. I'm including you in that category, in case you were wondering."

Cassie threw another stone, aiming her frustration and anger at the water, a sympathetic and silent stand-in for her best friend, who just didn't know when to leave well alone. "It was only ever a silly affair."

"One that made you the happiest I've seen you in a long while. Don't tell me seeing Emilia stirred up feelings—"

"Nothing like that," Cassie cut in. "I had no choice but to end it. Siobhan failed to follow the terms and conditions."

"You mean she developed feelings for you?" Helena gasped in superficial surprise. "How awful!" She squeezed Cassie's waist. Cassie squirmed away from the contact, tugging at her T-shirt to put it back into place.

"I stipulated from the start that it had to remain a feelings-free involvement." Cassie looked down at the oatmeal-colored grains beneath her feet, knowing if she met Helena's eyes right now, she'd be able to read her thoughts.

"All I'm saying is, if you look at this from the point of view of a reasonable human being, there are worse things than a seriously hot woman falling for you and...you for her."

"Christ, you sound like her. Clearly this isn't something we're going to agree on, so can we just leave it?"

"My lips are sealed." Helena completed the motion. "Though I think you're making a terrible mistake."

"Something else I excel in."

"How are you feeling about today's family reunion?" Helena's eyes were softer now, and Cassie appreciated the change of subject.

"I'm feeling ready," Cassie answered, "or not." She squeezed Helena's hand. "I'm grateful for your support, immoral as it may be."

That was the most honest she had been all day. Heading to her parents' house for dinner was never going to be easy. Coupled with the fact she had originally asked Siobhan to go along, she was feeling fragile. Unsure of the welcome waiting for her, her stomach churned with the range of possibilities. Her dad had begun to put the pieces of their fractured relationship back together, but this day was huge and relied on her playing her part too. The only problem was the fact she didn't feel like herself at all anymore, not since Siobhan.

❖

"Who wants pancakes?" Siobhan forced a smile into her voice as she placed a plate onto the kitchen table beside a bowl of blueberries and a bottle of golden syrup. Dylan and Neave raced into the kitchen, cheering and whooping. Dylan grabbed a fresh pancake and shoved the whole thing into his mouth.

"Where's Dad?" he asked, flecks of food flying as he spoke.

Siobhan almost managed a chuckle. "I thought I raised children, not zoo animals."

"One child, one zoo animal," Neave clarified, sticking her tongue out at her brother. "Dad's staying at Grandma's, Dylan, remember?"

"Forever?" Dylan asked.

Neave offered a sad smile. "Is that why you've been crying, Mum?"

Siobhan had done everything in her power to hide her tears, saving them for her pillow when she was alone at night, but of course her eyes were red and blotchy this morning. She told herself those tears would be the last she would cry for Cassie.

"I haven't been crying."

Dylan and Neave subjected her to identical looks of *Yeah, right*.

"I have been crying." Siobhan began pouring orange juice for everyone, the carton shaking because she didn't have a steady hand this morning. "Which is why we need to talk." Despite her absent appetite, Siobhan dished out a portion of pancakes for herself and took a big bite. She would need all the strength she could get. "Your dad and I, we just don't love each other. I'm not sure we ever did." She took a breath. "We certainly don't belong together. That's why we're getting divorced."

"So you're leaving Dad for Cassie?" Dylan asked, his eyes lighting up at the prospect as Neave sat forward in her seat, ready for more information.

Siobhan's mouth fell open. "What?"

Neave grinned. "Why do you look like a dying goldfish?"

"She doesn't, she looks like Dopey discovering he actually has feet under that long robe!" Dylan hooted.

"How did you...? Why would you think that about Cassie and me?"

"She likes you, you like her. You two go together like bangers and mash, the ultimate combo!" Dylan licked his lips, this being his favorite meal.

"Two women *can* get married," Neave added, her grin widening. "Dale, in my class, has two mums. One has the most amazing hair; it's five different colors! He brought in pictures of them wearing rainbow flags for the Pride parade. Their dog even wore a rainbow lead and collar."

Siobhan's thoughts were swirling so quickly, she couldn't keep up. "I didn't realize I was in the company of such astute allies?"

"We do Diversity Week at school, Mum." Dylan took Siobhan's hand.

His touch helped to ground her, although she did detect a hint of haughtiness in his tone. "I'm so proud of you two."

Neave gave Siobhan's shoulder a patronizing pat. "Different kind of pride than the one we're talking about, Mum, but thanks."

This time, Siobhan did manage a chuckle. But then she remembered the gravity of the conversation and cleared her throat. "I'm not leaving your dad for Cassie. It's important you know that. Your dad and I both deserve to be happy, and we can't be happy together."

"But you *are* going to be with Cassie, right?" There could be no mistaking the fact that Neave's question was actually a direction.

Siobhan had to remind herself that in addition to her marriage, she and Cassie were through too. Even though Cassie had almost admitted to harboring feelings of some kind for her, Siobhan knew she'd be a fool to think Cassie would come around. After all, if Cassie could seek out the worst in any situation she found uncomfortable or unfamiliar, why shouldn't Siobhan do the same? Self-preservation worked both ways.

"Can we invite Cassie round?" Dylan asked. "I bet she loves pancakes."

Siobhan reached for her glass of orange juice, desperate for something to hold on to. "We might be seeing less of Cassie from now on."

Siobhan wondered whether that would make any difference to Cassie's life. Would she miss the time she spent with the kids at all? Or would she be glad they weren't around to interfere in her life anymore?

Despite wanting to think the worst of Cassie now, looking at her kids, she knew they'd have seen right through any act. She liked to think she would have seen through it as well, but she obviously lacked her children's observational skills.

"You've had a row, haven't you?" Neave said, not missing a trick. "Be a big girl and say you're sorry."

"She'll accept," Dylan said, standing taller as he faced Siobhan squarely. "She loves you."

"Now you're just being ridiculous," Siobhan said. "And how do you know so much about relationships, may I ask?"

"He fancies a girl in his class," Neave said.

Dylan looked like he wanted to run his sister over with one of his remote-controlled cars. "I do not!"

"He asked her to go out with him, but she said she'd rather date a sausage!"

Dylan blushed as Siobhan smiled. Apparently, her son was experiencing as much success in his love life as she was in hers.

"She doesn't know what she's missing out on." Siobhan ruffled his hair, turning her *That's enough* face on Neave. "Though I do happen to believe primary school is a little young to be considering serious dating. You should wait till you're at least sixty. By then, you might know what you're doing."

"*You* don't and you must be nearly that age." Dylan nodded, his eyebrows raised.

She inhaled deeply through her nose and exhaled through her mouth, determined to steer the conversation back on track. "Let's not focus on Cassie. Let's focus on how you feel about what I've just told you about your dad and me. It's okay to be upset by it, and you can tell me if you are."

Dylan glanced across the table at his sister, then began picking at his fingernails, not bothering to even fake being upset. "I'm...grateful," he said, turning kind eyes onto Siobhan. "I mean it, Mum. You don't ever smile when you're around him, and he's not very nice."

Damning as it was to hear Dylan talk about his father like that, he was spot-on. Siobhan hated to think what damage their strained relationship had already done to the children, but they were resilient. Her too. This was the best decision she could possibly make, for all their sakes.

"I don't think Dad's very happy either," Neave added. "No offense, Mum. You just don't belong together, like you said." She frowned. "We'll live with you, though, right?"

Siobhan nodded, a surge of pride and relief rising in her chest at how her children were handling this news. "Of course you'll stay with me. Just remember it's your dad's unhappiness that comes out in unhealthy ways, that's why he sometimes comes across as unpleasant." Siobhan didn't want to excuse his behavior, but at the same time, she didn't want his children growing up hating him. "I think you'll find things will change for the better now that we're no longer together."

"They certainly will," Dylan said, "once you and Cassie make up." He lifted an eyebrow in expectation.

Siobhan saw his raised eyebrow and raised one of her own. "We're friends," she insisted, although she wasn't even sure this was true anymore. "I'm sure she'll keep up the drum lessons, maybe even take you go-karting or bodyboarding in time, but we need to concentrate on us right now, not your father and certainly not Cassie. This is our time to be strong and face the changes together, okay?"

"Okay, Mum." Neave got up from her seat and made her way around the table to Siobhan. She wrapped her arms around her in a warm embrace, one that Siobhan hadn't realized she needed until she was in the midst of it.

Dylan hopped off his chair and commandeered Siobhan's other side. "We'll focus on us right now," he agreed. "But if you don't ask Cassie out within a reasonable amount of time, we're going to do it for you."

Siobhan closed her eyes, and that's when images of Cassie's disarming smile and piercing eyes invaded her privacy. But Siobhan refused to let her in, erecting a dam to hold the influx of intrusions at bay. Cassie had cast Siobhan from her mind, as was her style. She had taught Siobhan well, and Cassie knew better than anyone that Siobhan was a quick learner.

❖

"You've noticed, she's not here." Cassie gave her sister a quick hug on the doorstep, choosing to address the issue before Eva could ask for details. "Take what you want from that, or should I make it easier and just say you were right all along."

"Maybe come back to Siobhan later," Helena whispered, placing a kiss on Eva's cheek. "It's great to see you."

"Even if she wasn't the first name on the list," Cassie added, automatically going on the defensive. "You told me having an affair with her was a terrible idea, and it must be satisfying to know you're always right." Poised like a battleship ready to take fire, Cassie stalked away from Eva and towards their parents' kitchen, leaving both Helena and Eva shaking their heads.

"Cassie!" her mother exclaimed, intercepting her in the hallway, beaming from ear to ear. "Come here."

Cassie felt arms wrap tightly around her in a warmer and more genuine welcome than any she had received previously.

Her mum pulled back, studying her closely. "You look worn out. Have you been sleeping?"

"I'm fine." Cassie shrugged her off. How typical of her mother to notice the one thing wrong with her, although she had to admit her mother's concern sounded sincere.

"I hope you're not too tired to tour the photo gallery?" her mum asked, leading a considerably confused Cassie into the living room. Her gaze wandered to the photos on the bookshelves: a picture of her graduation that Eva had provided them with; a picture of Cassie painting Eva's nails; and in pride of place, a photo from a childhood trip to Florida—that included all four Townsends. No visitor to the house would be forgiven for assuming they had only one child.

"It may need a little updating." Cassie felt light-headed.

"You made a valid point the last time you were here," her mum said. "We decided to address that long before your dad took it upon himself to visit you."

With her eyes teary and lip quivering, Cassie knew she looked anything but photogenic right now. Without further fuss, her mum grabbed her hand and guided her into the kitchen, where her dad, clad in a ridiculous flowery apron, grinned at her.

"Delighted to see you made it!"

"You too," she said softly.

Her dad pretended to pierce his heart with the handle of a wooden spoon. Then he winked at her. "I'd give you a hug, but I fear I may smell like a giant Yorkshire pudding," he chortled, turning his attention back to the oven.

"Did someone say Yorkshire pudding?" Helena approached her mum and dad, giving them both a kiss on the cheek.

"Weren't we expecting Siobhan?" her mum asked, and Helena harrumphed. "You're always welcome, Helena, you know that. I think we were just interested in someone Cassie deemed important enough to bring home." She looked towards Eva, who gave her the way-too-soon-to-broach-this-subject head shake.

She regretted mentioning Siobhan, but at the time it had seemed like a good idea. Even though Siobhan was just a friend and a fling, Cassie had thought she could at least give her parents the pleasure of the illusion that their fickle daughter had gotten serious with someone. She should've known better.

"She couldn't make it," Helena said. "Something came up with her kids." She made it sound so insignificant, Cassie almost thanked her for it.

Her mother looked startled. "You're seeing someone with kids?"

Her dad chipped in, rescuing her. "There's a couple of bottles of wine in the fridge. Who wants to do the honors?"

"I'll do them." Cassie leapt up, glad of the diversion. She didn't want to talk about Siobhan or her kids. Dining here as a family for the first time in such a long time, it really hit home how much she missed them all. Neave with her excessive enthusiasm, Dylan with his wicked wit, and Siobhan...

Cassie couldn't even begin to list all the things she missed about Siobhan, and this troubled her as much as it upset her. She poured large glasses for everyone bar herself, opting for orange juice instead. "I'm driving, she's drinking." She nodded towards Helena, who offered her an apologetic look.

Sitting at the family dinner table, surrounded by her newly nearest and dearest, a strange sort of comfort crept over Cassie. Comfort and familiarity. It was almost too easy to remember how much she had enjoyed sitting round Siobhan's kitchen table, enjoying the food, the conversation, the sense of belonging. There would be no more of those opportunities now, except with her own family, whose company she found...pleasant, for once.

Her mum was like a different person, as if the abated tension between her husband and daughter had changed her entire being. Conversation flowed easily between Helena, the life and soul of the party as she had always been, her mum, keen to catch up on Cassie's life, and Eva, brimming with delight that things were working out so well. And when her dad called Cassie outside after the main course for a smoke, she accepted the invitation willingly.

"Believe it or not, I've actually given up for good," she said as she waved away the offered cigarette. "Siobhan kind of inspired me." Cassie kicked herself for bringing up Siobhan rather than leaving her where she lay: not in Cassie's bed.

"Sometimes it pays to be a quitter."

Cassie scoffed. She didn't need advice on her love life from an absent father. All her problems had started over an argument about divorcing an absent father. Well, that and a lack of emotional connection.

"And sometimes," he continued, "we just don't know when to let go of ideas about ourselves that may not be true, especially when we're being stubborn about someone who really matters."

"I wouldn't know anything about that."

"What? Being stubborn or the fact Siobhan really matters to you?" he pressed.

"You don't know that." This conversation needed a swift change in direction. "Thanks for having us over today," she interjected, and was relieved to realize she meant it, and that it felt good to say.

He nodded, appreciation and quite possibly—although she wasn't ready to look too closely—affection in his eyes. Then he fell silent, and she wondered if he were trying to get his next words just right, so he wouldn't offend her, and she felt a bit bad for taking his remarks so personally.

"Thanks for coming, for trusting me," he said, then slipped into silence again. The next time he opened his mouth, nothing came out. Cassie laughed. "What?"

"You look like an actor who's screwed up his lines," she teased him.

"I never did know the right thing to say, did I?" he mused, sounding more regretful than anything else. "It means a lot that you're prepared to let me in, Cass. *Back* in, would perhaps be more accurate."

Cassie's heart expanded in her chest, although hearing her father utter Siobhan's nickname for her caused it to shrink slightly.

"I should say I'll wait until you two finish talking to contribute my two pennies, but I'm afraid my input requires interruption." So saying,

Eva plopped down on the bench beside Cassie, who scowled at her with as much good nature as she could muster. "Did I overhear you two talking about Siobhan?"

"See if you can get her to confess her feelings for her love interest," her dad stage-whispered to Eva. Then he stubbed out his cigarette, hardly touched, and pressed his lips to Cassie's cheek.

Cassie stared after him, mouth ajar, as he made his way back into the house. She looked at Eva, who was just about picking her own jaw up from the pavement.

"You let him kiss you," Eva said, sounding a little too pleased for Cassie's liking. "A first step away from cold and calculated."

Cassie begrudged her a nod.

"Speaking of cold and calculated…don't you think you ought to at least reconsider with Siobhan?"

"You were the one telling me how selfish I was being for having an affair with her."

"That's before I realized you're in love with her. You know this, right?"

Eva's eyes were trained on her with such veracity she felt compelled to tell the truth. Or at least avoid it really well. "Why does everyone keep saying that?"

"Because it's true."

"I don't have feelings for her. *She* has feelings for *me*."

"Feelings don't have to be mutually exclusive," Eva commented, not without condescension. "They can be mutual. And exclusive to one person. There's no shame in admitting that—or in opening yourself up, just like you did today with Dad. You have the opportunity to turn your life around, embrace what you've evaded for so long: a relationship with Mum and Dad, a relationship—not an affair—with someone who's good for you, and vice versa. If you want Siobhan, go and get her, but ditch the ridiculous rules."

"My daughter's a rule-breaker, not a rule-maker." Cassie was alarmed to see her mother coming to sit down on the bench next to her. "There's not a person here who doesn't want what's best for you."

"I guess Helena's been talking to you too. She's clearly filled Eva's head with all sorts of nonsense. She's a liability, divulging things I'd much rather were kept private."

"I'm not a liability," Helena piped up from behind Cassie. "I just can't hold my tongue. And seeing as I'm the only one who's witnessed you and Siobhan in the throes of coupledom, it's up to me to vouch for how preposterously compatible you are." Helena squeezed her shoulders. "You and Siobhan go together like chips and ketchup."

"In case you're wondering, Cass," her dad added, taking up a position beside her mum, "you are the recipient of a family intervention. This Siobhan and I have something in common: a relationship with you that's worth repairing."

Cassie couldn't decide whether to feel besieged or appreciative, but found herself leaning towards the latter. The fact that they seemed ready to accept she had fallen in love with another woman, even though she hadn't, was huge progress. It was like a weight she hadn't even known was pushing her down had been lifted.

"Whatever you decide," her dad continued, "just remember that a good woman won't stand around waiting for you to come to your senses. Besides, someone needs a date for Eva's wedding, doesn't she?"

Cassie sighed in exasperation. "I'm not in love with her and nothing you guys can say will convince me otherwise." An arsenal of eyebrows arched in her direction. "I mean, I don't think I even said that I want her as my wedding date."

"You didn't have to." Helena nudged her. "We *know* you."

Not well enough, Cassie thought. The last thing she wanted was to turn up to her sister's wedding with Siobhan on her arm. There really would be no stopping her family then. They'd get all excited and then when things went tits up, which inevitably they would, given Cassie's track record, they would be even more disappointed in her than ever.

Siobhan had ended things with good reason, and she had to accept that and move on. She'd busy herself with the string of women ready and willing for their one night with her. Apologizing, changing the rules, these were things Cassie couldn't do, not when all roads led to the same ending—rejection.

CHAPTER TWENTY-FOUR

"Julie!" Cassie yelled through to the outer office. "Ask Siobhan if she's got the Garnier pitchbook. I need to see it before tomorrow's meeting."

Julie's head popped in, as if her body preferred to remain on safer ground. "She's only out here," she answered through her teeth, with what could only be described as forced restraint. "You could always ask her yourself."

"If I wanted to ask her myself, I would have done so," Cassie snapped. She had been more demanding than usual this morning, she knew, having arrived at work in a foul mood. In a poor attempt to restore her professionalism, she cracked a terrible impression of a genuine smile. "*Please* just get on with the task. These figures won't calculate themselves."

Julie disappeared and Cassie tried to focus on the numbers in front of her, but her productivity was at an all-time low. She focused in on her breathing, closing her eyes and picturing herself zipping down the Thanet Coastal Road, soft-top down, wind soaring.

Although the reunion with her family had gone better than she could possibly have expected, their compassion meant she'd gone from thinking about Siobhan every minute, which was bad enough, to thinking about her every second. Between these thoughts and her total incompetence in the office, her emotions were bubbling like the Coke and mint imperials Dylan had used to create his model volcano.

It didn't take long for Julie to reappear, this time walking into the room and meeting Cassie head-on. "Mrs. Carney doesn't have the pitchbook," she said, sounding more than a little amused.

"Don't…" She stopped herself, clenching her jaw. What else did she expect Julie to call her? After all, she was still Mrs. Carney. "What do you mean she doesn't have it?" Cassie narrowed her eyes. "Why doesn't she have it?"

Julie rocked back on her heels, squinting right back. "I don't know."

"Well, go and ask her. I needed that pitchbook two hours ago."

"Then why didn't you request it? Look, I don't know what sort of bust-up you two have had, but I'm not your go-between. Just have your lovers' tiff—"

"We're not lovers!" Cassie was shouting now, but Julie chose to take no notice of her.

"The sooner your disagreement is out in the open, the sooner I can spread the word and we can all get on with our jobs." Julie pivoted on her heel and exited.

Cassie stalked out of the office behind Julie, determined to give Siobhan a piece of her mind this time. There was a fluttering feeling in the pit of her stomach that changed into a churning the closer she got to Siobhan.

"Siobhan, may I have a word?"

"Of course." Siobhan made no attempt to move, her attention drifting over to Julie, whose texting wasn't in the least bit surreptitious.

One day Cassie was going to ask Julie exactly who it was she needed to notify of Cassie's every move, but today was not that day. "Why don't you have the Garnier pitchbook, Siobhan? I need it for tomorrow. Have you even done it?"

"No." Siobhan wouldn't meet her eyes. "You said you were doing it."

"No, I asked you to do it."

"You absolutely did not. I think I'd remember."

"*I* think you'd remember to act like adults." Julie dropped her phone onto her desk with a conspicuous clunk. "Not hormonal teenagers having their first breakup."

Cassie folded her arms. The office gossip had spoken the truth for once. "The pitchbook needs doing. We could potentially be in Paris soon, completing one of the biggest investments the company has ever seen. We have to land this deal; failure isn't an option," Cassie said, trying to keep her tone as temperate as possible. "We shouldn't let our personal lives compromise our ability to do our jobs. Would you agree, Siobhan?" Cassie hoped she sounded adequately apologetic without losing the upper hand.

Voice devoid of emotion, Siobhan replied, "Yes."

"Then please come into my office. We need to work on this together if we're to get it done in time."

Siobhan picked up a pile of folders and entered Cassie's space, shutting the door behind her.

The next two hours were filled with insufferable silence. Cassie gave up barking orders, since Siobhan ignored them anyway, and because Siobhan knew exactly what she was doing.

But it was what Siobhan *wasn't* doing that drove Cassie mad. She wasn't speaking to her, except when necessary and only about the project. Siobhan wasn't flirting with her. She wasn't smiling at her. She wasn't even looking at her.

Cassie had to rely on her memories to make the experience bearable. She thought of Siobhan's face when she was happy. Her eyes always laughed first, but the rest of her followed swiftly. "I miss your smile," she murmured without thinking.

Siobhan's head snapped up, an intriguing but indecipherable expression on her face. But it flatlined before Cassie could contemplate what her sentimental slip of the tongue meant to Siobhan.

"I think that's a job well done, all things considered," Siobhan said, clicking *Save* on the screen. "I'm going back to my desk."

"Don't go." Again, the words escaped Cassie's lips before she could stop them. "Can we go somewhere to talk? Somewhere more private? I think we've both earned a break."

Siobhan looked Cassie up and down, but there was neither trust nor desire in her eyes. "If we must," she said.

Normally, Cassie would have responded with some sort of risqué banter, but she could tell Siobhan wasn't in the mood, and she didn't dare risk having her speaking privileges revoked. "How about I take you up on the roof?"

"You can take me *to* the roof," Siobhan stipulated before Cassie could backtrack, and Cassie knew she had no choice but to accept someone else's terms and conditions for once.

❖

"Allow me." Cassie pushed the door open and swept her arm across her body, inviting Siobhan to precede her. If Cassie thought this gallantry would impress her, she was sorely mistaken.

Cassie shoved her hands into her jacket pockets and walked over to the edge of the building, looking out over the domineering London skyline. "What an incredible view."

Siobhan fussed with the buttons on her jacket, impatience starting to get the better of her. "I'm assuming you didn't bring me up here to talk about how wonderful the view is. You said you wanted to talk," she reminded Cassie.

"Yes, would you like to start?"

Siobhan let out an infuriated groan and marched over to where Cassie was trying to be aloof. What maddened her more was that when Cassie reached for her hand, Siobhan found herself incapable of resisting, relishing the touch instead. "Don't start with that," she warned, withdrawing her hand.

Cassie looked down at the ground, where one foot jittered in agitation. Siobhan hovered between sympathy and satisfaction. "What scares you more, Cassie? Saying the wrong thing? Or saying the right thing?"

Siobhan watched as Cassie's lips opened and closed without ever emitting a sound, as though she were starring in a silent movie and going rogue with the script.

Then her lips were moving again, so swiftly that Siobhan couldn't contain the gasp that escaped when Cassie's mouth met hers. An overwhelming craving expanded inside her, flourishing like a newborn rose bursting upward to claim the sunshine. Cassie clasped Siobhan's face, thumbs caressing her cheekbones as their breathing harmonized into one melody. Cassie took fistfuls of Siobhan's hair in her hands, pulling her closer so their lips met again and again.

Cassie backed her up by the door, engaging her in a fiery, impassioned kiss. Siobhan could feel Cassie's heart hammering as Cassie pressed frantically into her. Another sensuous moan escaped Siobhan as the gentle flicks Cassie applied with her tongue worked to send her into rapture, her body quivering like the strings of a violin. Before Siobhan could maintain any self-control, Cassie was all over her, as they disintegrated into a series of long, fervent kisses, hungry and aching, their lips moving effortlessly in time.

"Please let me touch you, Shiv," Cassie murmured between kisses.

"No." Recalling all the reasons Cassie was wrong for her, but still finding Cassie's magnetism impossible to resist, Siobhan made a momentous effort to pull away. She concentrated on her ragged breathing and allowed herself a rare moment of contemplation. "And you can call me Siobhan."

Cassie's body sagged as she let out a monumental sigh of dejection.

Siobhan ran her fingers over Cassie's lips. When they'd first stepped onto the roof, her lips were the color of cotton candy. Now, bruised from kissing, they were the color of amethyst. "Fuck!" Siobhan pushed herself away from the wall, moving to sit down on one of the rattan sofas, half-hoping Cassie wouldn't follow and half-hoping she would. "I love your mouth. But I hate what comes out of it sometimes."

"I thought this was what you wanted." Cassie ran a hand through her hair. "I don't usually get rejected...twice."

"I made it crystal clear to you that our affair was over. What I want—what I deserve—is an explanation. After everything you've said, all the rules you've gone out of your way to enforce, you just fucking kissed me?"

"Maybe the rules need to change."

"Why?" Siobhan demanded. "You shouldn't have done that."

"Truthfully?" Cassie raised an eyebrow as Siobhan leaned closer in anticipation. "I have so many feelings for you that I don't know what to do with them."

"Then *please* elaborate and tell me what you're feeling."

"Shit."

Siobhan had to laugh. One expletive wasn't nearly enough for the monumental fuckup Cassie was making of the situation. Cassie sighed, then tried again, wrapping her arms around herself, as if she needed comfort to continue. "There's something there, something I don't know how to describe," she confessed, pulling on her shirt. "It's more than... Well, it's...non-physical. It's based on more than attraction."

"You'll recognize what I've been struggling with then." Siobhan offered a warming smile. "Not exactly an easy day out at the beach, is it?"

Cassie shook her head. "You deserve to be with someone who can invest in you and the relationship emotionally," she said, running her fingers down Siobhan's face. "I'm not that woman, Siobhan. I feel all kinds of crazy things for you, but I'm just not that woman. And yet, I can't seem to walk away from you, either."

She hunched over in disappointment. "*Why* aren't you that woman?"

"Because I don't know how to—"

"You could be that woman." Siobhan paused before pulling Cassie's hands into her own. "I know you could be. Besides, I don't want to rush into anything with you right now. Believe me when I say that I'm no more ready than you are. We need to take things slow, get to know one another properly, that's if you think I'm worth leaving your comfort zone for?" Cassie remained silent. "Can we at least agree to that?"

Cassie seemed transfixed by their joined hands. "Holding hands is for couples," she said, her face lighting up with cautious hope, as though the penny didn't just drop; it plummeted. "You're not writing us off?"

"I probably should, but I don't see how I can. I was pretty upset about..." Siobhan slammed on the brakes, recognizing the need to alter her approach. There was no way she was playing into Cassie's hands, not when *she* was the one holding them. "My *kids* were pretty outraged at the prospect of not seeing you anymore."

"They said that?"

"Essentially. They were very much Team Cassie."

"I imagine Dylan was talking about the car rather than the driver."

"Don't bank on it. He loves spending time with you; they both do." Siobhan sighed. "And that worries me, Cass. I don't want my children hurt."

"You know, my family is rooting for us too." Cassie brought her hand to her mouth and tutted, like she knew she'd said too much.

"I'm not sure how I feel about being the hot topic of your family reunion. How was it? I didn't dare ask."

"It went better than expected. Taking Helena was a genius decision, although she let the cat out of the bag within thirty seconds of saying hello. My family have some pretty strong opinions. They seem hell-bent on the opinion that we belong together, even though they've never met you."

Siobhan let out a deep sigh. "You're good for me, but just sleeping with you isn't good for me mentally. And it isn't good for you either. Is it?"

"It isn't," Cassie conceded. "Not in the slightest. We can't go back to how we were before, can we?"

"Absolutely not," Siobhan said. "You were almost right when you said the rules have to change. What they need to do is be chucked into the North Sea. We need time and space to deal with what we're both dealing with. And maybe some of that time can include each other."

At this Cassie laughed. "I'd very happily give you more of my time. If we land the Garnier deal tomorrow, we'll be heading to Paris in a few weeks…that's if you still want to come? I know we can get things right."

"Mixing business and pleasure, that could be dangerous, but of course I still want to come. I've never been to Paris and I imagine you could be a pretty decent tour guide." Siobhan smiled, and Cassie's eyes flickered with recognition. "But for now we're going to explore this non-physical something between us slowly, simply and in our own time. That's all I want: a chance to see where this takes us. But you must promise me one thing. One new rule." Siobhan looked deeply into Cassie's eyes. "You have to be real, present, and allow yourself to feel again."

Cassie cleared her throat. "I just don't think—"

"You've got to try Cass, defenses are not the way to go. Promise me?"

"I can try."

That would have to be enough for now. Siobhan was going against her better judgment, knowing how likely Cassie was to withdraw when things got too difficult, but when she thought back to that kiss, nothing had ever moved her like that had. No one was ever likely to kiss her like that again. It was the sort of kiss that came once in a lifetime, the sort that almost spoke of forever. Siobhan quickly brushed that thought from her mind, that was a risk too far.

CHAPTER TWENTY-FIVE

The last light of day passed beyond the horizon as Siobhan looked up to the sky, dazzling shades of sunset painted across it like a canvas. The towering trees of Ruislip Woods were silhouetted against the fiery sky, quite remarkable in their presence. Siobhan had to wonder why she had never noticed the beauty of this place before.

"Are you sure you don't want to eat?" Cassie asked, waving a menu at her. "Surely I can tempt you to a bowl of chips?"

Siobhan let out a slow breath, wondering why her stomach had been performing wild, acrobatic somersaults all day. After all, this was just another date with Cassie, yet it felt vastly different to anything that had been before. It was exactly as she had requested. Cassie felt real and present and right now she was pressed so close it was scrambling her brain.

"I'm just not hungry, but you go ahead."

"You know I'll always share my chips with you." Cassie took hold of her hand, the touch gentle and sincere. "Is everything okay? Would you like me to get you a soft drink?"

"Honestly, I'm fine." She took a sip of wine to reassure Cassie and looked up to meet Cassie's questioning eyes. "Actually, full disclosure here, I'm a little nervous."

Cassie blew out a long breath of her own, a smile tugging at the corners of her mouth. "You have nothing to be nervous about. Why don't we scrap the chips and take a walk around the reserve instead? It won't be long before the stars are out and I know you enjoy gazing at them, comfort zone and all that."

"I'd very much like that. I know it sounds silly but—"

"It's okay, Shiv," Cassie trailed a finger down Siobhan's face. "I get it. Just remember we've done this so many times before. Nothing's changed."

"Come on then." Buoyed by Cassie's simple reassurance, Siobhan finished her drink and linked her arm through Cassie's, leaning in towards her. "Let's go make out in the forest."

Stepping into time with one another was so easy that any apprehension Siobhan felt began to dissipate with the familiarity of Cassie's warmth, Cassie's touch, Cassie's laugh. Nothing had changed between them after all, unless you counted how much she was counting down the moments until they kissed again, because kissing was now very much in the rulebook.

Darkness had fallen as they walked off the beaten track, the haze of the sun's last rays disappearing to reveal stars lighting the night sky like shimmering snowflakes.

"This place reminds me of Hampstead Heath," Cassie said. "Many a night Eva had to go out there looking for me when I was a teenage tearaway. She must have been out of her mind to take me in when I left home."

"How old were you?"

"I moved in with Eva when I was fifteen. She'd only just met Danny at university and I came knocking on the door in the middle of the night and never left."

"I didn't realize you actually ran away."

"I didn't run away. I told my mum and dad exactly where I was going. They never tried to stop me. I think Mum recognized we were past the point of no return. It was tough at home from the moment I came out, the atmosphere was poisonous. She knew how close Eva and I were. I guess it made a weird sort of sense to her."

"That's tough though, you were very young to make such a huge decision."

"It never seemed like a big decision to me. I love my sister fiercely, I always have. She's always felt like home. I know Dad and I are on the road to recovery now, but I can't tell you how heated the disagreements were when I refused to conform to his expectations."

"I can't imagine you ever conforming to be a crowd pleaser."

"I certainly wasn't going to pretend to be someone else just to please him. Leaving was easier, though I don't think my mum has ever forgiven me or stopped battling her guilt about what happened."

"From what you've told me, it sounds like they're ready to accept some responsibility now."

"I guess they are, it just takes some getting used to. I mean I'm not sure my path would have crossed Dad's again at all had it not been for the bank. The arguments we had there were explosive. We were terribly unprofessional to the point where it was the final straw for me. Julie would have had a field day. I had to leave because I couldn't hold it together any longer. I've never admitted that out loud. It was tough and I never thought we'd be where we are today."

"You've come a long way. The way you handled your dad's visit to the office was impressive all things considered, even if you were a complete cow to me." Siobhan nudged Cassie playfully, "Don't worry, I won't hold it against you."

"It's three strikes and out, that was only number one." Cassie held her hands up trying to protest her innocence.

"I don't think we should get into counting the number of strikes you've had with me, Cass."

"You may have a point."

"I bet Eva's over the moon with how things have started out with your dad. It can't have been easy on her."

"She's always been stuck in the middle. I mean she's a pain in the arse and an absolute disapprover of affairs, but I owe her everything. You know both her and Danny left their flat share to rent a house so that I could live with them and still go to school. They put me through uni too, though I often wonder if Mum had a sneaky hand in that. Of course, I'd love to resent that but can't really considering where I am today."

"I can't wait to meet your sister. She sounds like an amazing woman with her head screwed on. I imagine we'll get on well."

"She's exceptional and a lot more level-headed than me. She's lived through every trauma with me and dealt with them a hell of a lot better than I have." Cassie shook her head, smiling.

"Including Emilia?" Siobhan pushed. She'd never quite managed to get an honest answer about Emilia.

"We're really doing this aren't we?"

Siobhan nodded.

"Fine," Cassie sighed, stopping to face Siobhan. "Seeing as I'm so bloody obvious, you're right. I was in love with her."

"Finally…" Siobhan paused for dramatic effect, "the truth."

"I haven't talked about this with anyone, you should know that."

"If it's too difficult, we don't have to—"

"Actually, we do." Cassie's tone was firm, like she'd finally accepted the importance of this conversation herself. "It doesn't feel so difficult here with you, though it's not easy to admit the one woman I fell for was the one woman who managed to elude me."

Siobhan could tell Cassie was trying to play it cool and hide her battle scars, but she needed to understand it was okay to be vulnerable.

"You don't have to do that you know."

"What?" Cassie raised an eyebrow, not quite mastering oblivious.

"Pretend it doesn't matter. It clearly does. This woman has had a huge impact on your life, whether you care to admit it or not. I want to know more about her, more about you. I think it will go a long way in helping me understand you."

"I get that, but it's not pretty."

"I never imagined it would be. It doesn't mean I don't want to hear about it." Siobhan left a lingering kiss on Cassie's cheek. "Talk to me."

"In the three years I dated her I would have done anything for her. Looking back, I know she didn't treat me well. She had so many flaws, which Helena was all too quick to point out, each of them valid, but I didn't want to know. I also don't know whether you've noticed, but I have a fair few flaws of my own, so who was I to judge? She's the only woman who has ever held my heart and she literally crushed it. I see that now. I'm in a better position to understand those feelings. I've never dealt with her loss…or gotten over it."

"Which explains Cassie the womanizer, Cassie the conductor of emotionless affairs. It makes sense to me. You should have opened up to me sooner."

"I find it difficult to trust people."

"Which also makes perfect sense considering your dad let you down badly and the woman you loved cheated on you." Siobhan paused, hoping she hadn't overstepped the mark. "She doesn't know how lucky she was."

Cassie shrugged her shoulders. "She ruined everything. I can't give myself to anyone because of her. I can't feel."

"I don't think that's true." Siobhan placed a hand over Cassie's heart. "You felt, with me, up on that rooftop. At least I'd like to think you did."

"I guess there may have been the slightest twinge of feeling."

Siobhan lifted their intertwined hands and kissed Cassie's. "I'll take that for now."

Cassie pointed to a small gap in the fence, clearly looking for a distraction. "If we duck under the fence here, we can go sit over on that rock. It looks like a perfect spot for stargazing."

"Or a romantic interlude." Siobhan squeezed Cassie's hand in anticipation, remembering the last time Cassie had uttered those words.

She allowed Cassie to guide her across the makeshift path, towards a rock just big enough for the two of them to squeeze on. Siobhan watched as Cassie sat down, discarded her shoes, and moved to a position where she could dangle her feet into the cool blue.

"Careful." Siobhan reached out playfully. "We don't want another boat rescue."

"That depends if it involves mouth to mouth." Cassie grinned then tapped the space next to her, which Siobhan immediately filled.

Cassie began to slowly untie Siobhan's trainers, paying great attention to detail as she removed her socks, massaging her feet to warm them up before she encouraged her to dip them in the water. Siobhan splashed her feet, enjoying the cool that lapped around them as she leant closer into Cassie.

"So, what about you?" Cassie asked. "I've just told you about my first love, I'm assuming you had one too."

"Now you are digging." Siobhan used her foot to splash Cassie, who wiped a drip from her nose, smirking. "I'm not sure I really had one."

"When was your first kiss then?"

"That one I can do. Nathan Kelly when I was fourteen. He had a sort of edgy look finished off with a wild Mohican hairstyle. I think I liked him because he had unique fashion sense and didn't listen to the same conventional music as everyone else. He was great until he laid me in the garden, kissed me and I didn't know where to begin."

"I find that hard to believe."

"Maybe I wasn't as enthusiastic about kissing Nathan as a certain other person I know. I think the moment my lips met Nathan's my suspicions were confirmed and I realized I wasn't attracted to men."

"Yet you took that information and married Matthew."

"There were a few other insignificant kisses in between, just to highlight how much I wanted to kiss a woman. Then I decided to wait the best part of fifteen years to do it."

"Do tell, was it worth the wait?"

Siobhan allowed herself a moment to reflect on the question whilst taking in their surroundings. She lowered her head onto Cassie's shoulder, her gaze wandering over the water. The lake shimmered underneath the tinted light of the moon, ripples dancing from her depths to create whispers upon the shoreline. The idyllic scene almost stole her breath.

Looking into Cassie's eyes, they fizzled like the ocean flickering and colliding with the shore, they were so expressive and full of unsaid emotion.

"I could do with a gentle reminder."

"Is that so?" Cassie's stare punctuated her last line of defense, her breathing shallow as she prepared to capitulate. "Come here."

There was fire beneath her fingertips, on her tongue, in her racing heart as Cassie's lips met hers in a fiery, impassioned kiss that seemed to stretch out for days. She closed her eyes and allowed herself to get lost in the moment, amazed by what Cassie could communicate with a kiss, until some time later she emerged, leaning in so their foreheads were touching.

"Definitely worth the wait." Siobhan still sounded breathless as she tried to slow her racing heart, concentrating on the beat of Cassie's.

"Do you know what else I thought might be worth the wait, if you're feeling brave?"

"Go on."

"With everything that's happened recently with my family, I've been thinking a lot about your mum," Cassie said, pulling Siobhan in closer and pressing a tender kiss to the top of her head. "I'd love to see where you grew up, visit some of the places from your childhood, perhaps even see the farm."

"You'd want to do that?"

Of all the things she'd been expecting from Cassie, she had not seen this coming. She'd buried Slane in her past, a past she continued to block out. She'd left with Matthew all those years ago and returning had always felt like an impossibility. Her kids had no idea where their Irish roots lay and she'd always been okay with that. Yet Cassie's suggestion didn't fill her with the horror she expected.

"I'd love to go back with you, but only if it's something you want to do. I know how difficult it must've been for you and I know how much you loved her..." Cassie trailed off, momentarily looking uncomfortable, before she pulled it smartly back together. "I'd like to share the experience with you."

"It's not something I've wanted to do—"

"Is that true? Or is it more something you've never wanted to do with Matthew? You can be honest with me if you really don't want to."

"It's Matthew, of course it is. I hate to think how disappointed she'd be in me for marrying him—"

"I think she'd be pretty proud of the remarkable woman sitting next to me right now." Siobhan felt her heart race again as Cassie cupped her face and pressed an affectionate kiss to her lips. "The one who *is* embracing her identity."

"All her friends are still there, most of my school friends too. I feel like they'd all know how stupid I was to run off with Matthew and marry him. I can't bear that judgment, even now."

"They might like me." Cassie raised an eyebrow. "I can play up to an audience."

"You can play up to your audience of one any time. I'm not sure about a bigger fanbase."

"You're not dead set against the idea then?"

"Quite the opposite. I know that the kids would be thrilled to visit. They're always asking me questions about Slane. I also think it would do them the world of good to get away for a few days with everything that's going on."

"I wondered about next weekend if it doesn't seem too soon? It would be great to do something with the kids before Paris. I'm sure I can put a plan together, if you think that's something that might come under the remit of taking it slow."

"Taking it slow." Siobhan smiled as she repeated the words, appreciating their value. Cassie had opened up more tonight than she'd done in all the time they'd known one another, and it filled her with hope. Hope for what she wasn't sure. "A little bit of honesty and I understand you so much better. I realize why you struggle with your feelings; it makes sense."

"I'm sorry for freaking out about the divorce. I don't know why I did that."

"I do. You assumed you were the catalyst. You couldn't be more wrong. The reason I went for the higher paid banking job in the first place was to ensure I could be self-sufficient when I divorced him. I'd already set the wheels in motion. Sadly, it's not something you can take any credit for."

"You mean I didn't sweep you off your feet and whisk you out of the clutches of the tyrant's grasp?" Cassie chuckled as she pulled her feet out of the water and began to dry them with her socks. "I'm disappointed. I'm also sorry I overreacted. In the spirit of full disclosure, I'm pretty thrilled you're soon to be a divorcee."

"Is that so?"

"Given time, I might even ask you on another date."

"I shall eagerly await your invitation. Honestly, I can't wait to have someone to share things with. There are so many new places I'd like to see, so many experiences I'd like to share with..." Siobhan hesitated.

"It's okay." Cassie squeezed her hand. "You can say it."

"There's a lot I'd like to share with you." Relief washed over her as she said these words out loud. "Travel has always seemed so far away with Matthew. I've never wanted to go anywhere with him."

Cassie focused solely on her shoelaces as she spoke. "That's because he's not your person, or so Helena would say."

"My person?"

"Helena has this ridiculous theory that everyone has their one person floating around somewhere in the universe. The person you're destined to be with. You just have to find them and the rest is simple or so she'd have you believe. There's even talk that Riley might be her person, though how she knows that after a few months, I'll never know. I don't know that I even believe in her theory, but if I did, it would be safe to say Matthew isn't yours."

"I think we can both agree on that." Siobhan smiled wistfully, relaxing in Cassie's arms once more.

They had come such a long way in this one evening together. Cassie making a huge breakthrough with her openness after all this time and Siobhan asking the questions playing on her mind. For so long she had been trying to make sense of the woman she was wholly invested in, but tonight was the first time she had made inroads. Cassie wasn't an easy woman to figure out at first glance, but delve a little deeper and so much became understandable.

This evening Cassie had laid the foundations for a wonderful time visiting Slane as a family, putting Siobhan's needs first and considering exactly what they might be. Then they had Paris to look forward to, somewhere she had always dreamed of visiting, but had pretty much given up on. The thought of visiting with Cassie excited her. Now they were both embracing the whole taking it slow concept, it felt like mountains had moved and oceans parted for them. Siobhan could relax, embrace every moment. Finally they were moving in the right direction.

CRAVING CASSIE

CHAPTER TWENTY-SIX

I s this it?" Dylan lifted a single eyebrow.
"I did tell you that you wouldn't be impressed." Siobhan
tousled his hair. "But this is Tulach Farm. It means little hill in Irish—"
"Which seems pretty ironic considering the hill we've just walked
up," Cassie said, wiping her brow in melodramatic fashion.
Neave scratched her head. "It looks worse than Dorothy's farm in
Kansas and I'm talking *after* the tornado."
Dylan spun around, looking out in all directions. "I can't believe
anyone could live here. Where are the shops?"
"The town is just over that hill." Siobhan pointed in the direction
of the road as visions of the rolling green hills and stone walls made her
heart ache with old memories. How she wished her mum were still here
to meet her children. They were embracing the trip, thrilled at the sights
they had been shown so far, but she still felt her mum's absence. As if
reading her mind, she felt Cassie's hand slip into her own.
"You're doing great."
Siobhan nodded, both touched by the gesture and impressed with
Cassie's intuition. This was exactly what she needed to hear right now.
"Who looked after all the cows?" Dylan asked. "It stinks around
here!"
"Believe it or not, I used to whip my wellies on and muck in
when we moved the herd. You haven't lived until you've tried to shift
a stubborn herd of cows. They make working with Cassie look easy."
"You're going to have to expand on this new information," Cassie
said, gawping at her, then the cows, then back at her. "*You* worked with
them?"
"Woman of many talents standing right here."

Cassie took a seat on the fence, blowing out her cheeks. "No wonder you like giraffes so much." Cassie tapped the space next to her and Siobhan jumped up, balancing just as she had as a child. "I mean, it looks great fun I suppose, but when all is said and done, it's still you chasing around a herd of cows. I'm trying my best to picture it." Cassie shut her eyes, a wicked smirk spreading across her face.

Losing herself in Cassie's smile, Siobhan was surprised when a voice she immediately recognized broke her reverie.

"Siobhan Kavanagh, is that you?" Siobhan turned around to see a familiar woman leaning on the fence, squinting at her through rectangular-framed glasses. "I was wondering who was in my field."

"Kendra? What are you doing here?" Siobhan cursed her inept greeting. But it was hard to think straight with her schoolgirl crush right next to her in wellies and a wax jacket. She jumped down from the fence, almost losing her balance.

"I've been living here all my life. We bought the farm a few years back when the family you sold it to moved on." Kendra let out a hearty laugh, it was still the same warm-hearted, sincere laughter Siobhan remembered from all those years ago. "You, however, haven't been back to Slane in forever. If you had, you'd have known that. How on earth are ya?"

Cassie practically vaulted from one side of the fence to the other in her haste to join them. "Hi there," she said, offering Kendra a hand. "Cassie."

"This is Kendra Lynch." She watched as Cassie's eyes widened, prompting Siobhan to give her the don't-you-dare glare. "We went to school together. We were good friends."

"It's O'Connor now. I only went and married yer one, Ayden the baker's son. D'ya remember him? You should; you spent enough time hanging round his shop."

Siobhan had to laugh. Kendra really had no idea that Siobhan had been there for her.

"Was the baker's shop near the post office, by chance?" Cassie asked, earning a no-sex-for-a-week-if-you-say-anything glare this time.

"Right next to it," Kendra said. "Siobhan must have told you a lot about me if ya know I'm the girl from the post office. I'm flattered."

Siobhan waited with bated breath, recognizing the playful glint in Cassie's eye and wondering if she had the self-restraint to stop herself.

"She's had a few tales to tell for sure."

Siobhan breathed a sigh of relief.

"I'd love you to fill in a few extra details for me though. Do tell, what was she like as a child?"

Kendra adjusted her glasses. "I remember us rocking up to church on a Sunday. We'd be sat in our Sunday best listening to the sermon and Shiv's mam would be out round the back looking for her. She had this habit of disappearing during the first bloody hymn and never returning."

"Where was she?" Cassie asked, her eyes lighting up.

"Round the ice cream van. She'd be found with a melting ninety-nine in her hand, Mr. Whippy all around her face and strawberry sauce dripping down the cone."

"I used to save the ice cream man, Joe, my red lemonade bottles. He was building a den for his grandkids and using bottles to construct the windows. I helped him collect them and I bloody hated church. I mean, ice cream or church, what sort of choice is that?"

"The priest used to get thick with her, but no amount of giving out would make her listen. She was even worse as a teenager, never where she was meant to be, telling her mam she was at the hurling club, when she was hanging round the post office."

"I can't think why she'd be there." Cassie's eyes twinkled. "Sounds like you were just as much a rebel as I was." Cassie smirked. "I'm curious. What was it with the post office? Were you a big stamp collector?"

"Siobhan's always been a bit of a dark horse. You won't get any sense from her, I never could. Anyway, tell me about now? How many kids? We have five and another on the way." She tapped her expansive belly. "What about you?"

"The two swinging upside down from that tree over there are mine. Dylan and Neave."

"And Matthew? Is he here too or have you left him home alone?"

"Slightly complicated." Siobhan blushed.

"Slightly?" Cassie looked to be stifling a grin.

"Sounds like a conversation to be had over a bottle of wine, not that I'm drinking. You *must* all come over to the farm tonight. Ayden's in Dublin at some farmers' market, so it's just me and the kids. He'll be gutted he's missed ya. Say you'll come."

"We'd love to." Siobhan smiled.

"We haven't touched the old farm cottage where you lived. Ayden's converted the largest of the old barns into our home, it had to be a complete renovation for our brood. Just follow the dirt track and you can't miss us."

"Shall we say around seven?"

"That's grand. Bring the kids up this afternoon, they can meet my gang and get to know them. I'll catch ya later, looking forward to it."

"And there goes the most gorgeous girl in all of Slane." Cassie fell to her knees and thrust her fist at the sky.

"Not while you're here," Siobhan said. She watched Kendra strut back across the field. How different would her life have been had she chased Kendra instead of going off with Matthew?

"How are you feeling? Is your love rekindled?" Cassie asked, her grin widespread. "Do I have competition?"

"I thought you relished a challenge."

"I just never thought it would come in wellies and a wax jacket."

"I'll have you know, it's a skill pulling off that look. I should know, I mastered it in my teenage years herding the cows."

"Was that before or after the ice cream around face stage?" Cassie chuckled. "I might have to ask Kenda for photographic evidence."

"I must have terrible taste in women!"

"Shocking!" Cassie pointed to herself. "You're all right with going round tonight?"

"I am." Siobhan appreciated every subtle move Cassie made to check she was doing alright, knowing what a big deal this was to her. "I'd like to go. We were good friends growing up so it will be interesting to catch up. Coming back, it seems remarkable I've stayed away so long. Thank you enough for pushing me. It feels like I was always meant to be here with you. Does that sound strange?"

"A little."

Siobhan could tell Cassie was uncomfortable with her gratitude. It was typical of her to be unwilling to accept thanks, but the way it flummoxed her made Siobhan want her all the more.

"You're bloody gorgeous when you're avoiding how much I appreciate you."

"I'm doing no such thing," Cassie chuckled. "I'm glad you're enjoying yourself. Just pre-empting tonight, I have a feeling there might be more questions about Matthew."

"I'll tell Kendra the truth. I have nothing to hide. I'm *very* glad to be here with you." Siobhan linked in with Cassie as they walked back towards the children. "I wouldn't be here without you."

The realization that Cassie's presence was the overriding difference felt big in some way, but she wasn't ready to process that yet and she certainly wasn't going to make any further grand proclamations. The weekend was going well, Cassie had been the perfect companion, intuitively knowing what Siobhan needed at any given point. The children were enjoying themselves, full of questions and enthusiasm. Most significant of all, the memories were happy, fond memories. The fact that it no longer felt painful showed her just how far she had come with Cassie by her side.

CHAPTER TWENTY-SEVEN

Siobhan felt her heart pounding against her ribcage as she knocked at the front door. The fact they were back in her village, visiting her childhood friend, going out together in her world for the first time, led to a strange mix of both anticipation and trepidation. They weren't a couple, but this felt like the closest they had ever been to one another emotionally. Things were finally heading in the right direction, she didn't want anything to panic Cassie, the taking it slow model working brilliantly for them at this point.

Dylan and Neave had already met the O'Connor children that afternoon and been introduced to the old Irish art of wellie wanging, so that was one less thing on her mind. Dylan was excited about playing Scalextric with their only son and Neave was thrilled to find the other four girls were as enthusiastic about creating dance routines as she was.

"Come in, come in. It's good to see ya." Kendra pulled both children into a warm embrace like she'd known them all her life. "Let me take you guys through to the snug. My gang haven't stopped talking about their plans for tonight. I believe they involve doughnuts and ice cream."

"And dancing." Neave performed a quick cartwheel as if to confirm this.

"Shane's going to race his Formula One cars with me. Cassie will probably want to join us later, she loves cars!"

"I should probably confess right here and now that I would love a go." Cassie offered Siobhan an apologetic look. "I haven't played Scalextric for years."

"Come on, you two." Kendra took Dylan and Neave by a hand each and Siobhan heard them chattering away as they were led to the snug.

"I can't believe I now have to compete with a car racing game for kids."

"It's only right I give you and Kendra time to become reacquainted." Cassie winked and then took a seat in the kitchen. "You couldn't write this."

Siobhan sat down next to her at the large kitchen table, immediately taking a trip back down memory lane. The warmth from the aga reminding her of nights sitting round the table at home with hot chocolate. She and her mum would put the world to rights, always busy making plans for the future. She wondered how her mum would see things now.

Kendra bustled back into the kitchen and before Siobhan knew what was happening, she had been swept up in a warm bear hug. "It's been far too long." Kendra pulled back, keeping hold of her shoulders as she studied her from top to toe. "You look amazing! You're practically glowing!"

"It must be the light." Siobhan brushed the compliment off awkwardly.

"Nonsense. It's so good to see ya. I don't think we thought we ever would again." Kendra hugged her once more, squeezing tightly and then looked towards Cassie. "Do tell all then. Matthew isn't here, I can't help thinking that's significant somehow. How do you two know each other?"

"We're close friends." Siobhan struggled to think of anything more to say considering their current situation. "We work together." She looked at Cassie, who responded with a warm nod and smile, then quickly turned on the charm offensive.

"I've been training Siobhan in the wonderful world of investment banking." Cassie grinned. "We soon discovered a mutual love of theater and star gazing and now here we are." Cassie wasn't exactly playing it cool, but Siobhan found her affability endearing.

"You missed out sandwiches."

"How could I forget all the nights we've spent with them!" Cassie brushed her shoulder against Siobhan's and the contact went straight to Siobhan's head. It always amazed her that no matter how much time they spent together, just one touch from Cassie could leave her yearning for more.

"Never mind your sandwiches, do you both drink white?"

Siobhan nodded and Kendra busied herself pouring two large glasses and an orange juice for herself.

"It would have been grand to get pissed with ya, but I always seem to be pregnant. Let me just take these through to the kids," she indicated to a tray of drinks, "then I'll be back and you can tell me more of your news."

"She's got a great personality and she can talk for Ireland, I'll give you that," Cassie said. "But your taste has improved with age."

Cassie leaned forward and kissed the smirk from Siobhan's lips. Siobhan kissed her back deeper, closing her eyes and dissolving entirely into Cassie's caress. For a moment, Siobhan allowed herself to be swept away in the sensations of softness and sincerity, only pulling away when she heard Kendra's footsteps approaching.

"The kids are getting on like a house on fire in there. Shane has taken Dylan up to his room and the girls are creating some sort of human pyramid to end their routine."

"There was Neave telling us she's no longer into dancing. Cassie's been teaching her to play the drums."

"She's pretty good actually and has natural rhythm," Cassie said. "I imagine she's much like Shiv, can do anything she puts her mind to."

Siobhan noticed Cassie's pupils dilate, a mixture of longing, passion and intrigue written in her eyes. Siobhan basked in their familiar chemistry and felt her own body temperature shift gears in sync with Cassie's.

"That doesn't surprise me. I can imagine your daughter been a force of nature, just as you were. We spent a lot of time together growing up, Cassie. I have to say, I never understood the whole Matthew thing, that took a lot of us by surprise, considering everyone thought you were in love with Ayden."

Siobhan needed a moment to compose herself. After all, this was a little surreal. She was sitting here with the wife of the guy everyone assumed was her first crush, her actual first crush and then there was Cassie. How could she even begin to explain how she felt about Cassie?

"It's a shame he's not here to clear up that misconception," Siobhan chuckled.

"I had my own suspicions, even back then." Kendra's eyes sparkled with a wicked glint.

"It's lovely of you to have us over." Siobhan almost fell over her words to dodge the conversation. Maybe she wasn't as self-assured as she wanted Cassie to believe. "I think the future may hold more trips back to Slane, the kids love it."

"So, what does bring you back? I mean it must be at least five years—"

"Nine actually."

"Christ, where did all that time go? And why do you look ten years bloody younger than me these days?"

"I'm trying to keep her youthful." Cassie winked. "I don't want her to fall over the precipice at thirty. It's a dangerous age.".

"Life begins at thirty. Is that why you've kicked Matthew into touch?"

Siobhan leant back in her chair, running her hands through her hair, trying to put together a response. She felt a hand squeeze her knee under the table, it was a subtle move by Cassie, but it was good to feel such a reassuring touch. She pulled herself together, self-assurance found.

"We're in the process of getting divorced. I don't think that will come as a great surprise to you." Siobhan took a large gulp of her wine. "I'm moving on with my life."

"Righto." Kendra looked as if everything was falling into place. "Then let's hear more about you, Cassie." Kendra was digging. "You two seem close."

"We are."

Siobhan felt breathless, weak and there was chaos in her chest. In the presence of someone else, to hear such an acknowledgement from Cassie was huge.

"Siobhan applied for a promotion within the company and we ended up being thrown in together at the deep end. I don't usually work with anyone else." Cassie paused, looking to Siobhan, who seemed to blush a darker shade of red. "You see, I'm a bit of a pain in the arse, but the two of us get on insanely well. Siobhan's an exceptional woman."

Joy sparkled in Kendra's eyes. "I'm glad she's found someone to spend time with who appreciates her."

"Oh, I definitely appreciate her." Cassie raised her glass. "How could you not?"

As more wine flowed, the evening flew by and Siobhan settled comfortably into conversations on several weird and wonderful topics. It turned out she and Kendra had a lot to catch up on, but Cassie joined in like she had known them all her life. Kendra was as warm and funny as she had always been and Siobhan had to admit, the thought of visiting Slane more often was starting to appeal.

Every so often Cassie would catch her eye and give her such a heartfelt look that butterflies would take off in her stomach. It was at these points she would have to force herself to remember they were still taking things slow. Sometimes that was so easy to forget.

"Can you point me in direction of the Scalextric?" Cassie stood up. "I promised Dylan I'd give him a race. Show him what the pros can do."

"Just through the hall and up the stairs. Shane's is the first room to the left. You won't miss them; they'll be up to ninety in there."

"Busy and enthusiastic," Siobhan translated, seeing the look of confusion on Cassie's face.

With Cassie off to challenge the kids, Siobhan knew exactly where their conversation was heading. To her credit, Kendra hadn't pushed things all evening, but she knew her well enough to know she was going to make the most of this short opportunity.

"Are you going to tell me what's really going on?" Kendra asked. "I know I haven't seen you in an awfully long time, but I know you."

"Which means you'll appreciate that Matthew and I were going nowhere."

"I couldn't believe it when you left with him in such a whirlwind. You were pregnant right?"

"Everyone knew?"

"There wasn't really any other explanation for it. Besides," Kendra took a careful pause, "it was the only thing that made sense, considering I always thought you were interested in women." Siobhan tried to look confused but Kendra gently touched her arm. "Yes, I knew, even back then." Kendra pushed gently, "I take it Cassie—"

"We're good friends." Siobhan couldn't meet her eyes. She didn't know what to say, especially when what was going on between them was so difficult to define.

"Come on, Siobhan, I'm not blind. Tell me if I'm speaking out of turn, but there's something between the two of you isn't there?"

"I don't know what you mean." Kendra gave her such a dubious look that she immediately relented. "Is it that obvious?"

"Well, I wish Ayden looked at me the way Cassie looks at you. She thinks the world of you, it's written all over her face."

"Believe it or not, she's on the down low tonight, we both are." Siobhan crinkled her nose as she realized how silly that sounded.

"The down low." Kendra shook her head in disbelief. "If this is the down low, then there's no hope for you. I don't think Cassie can help it, it just radiates out of her."

"Your imagination is running a little wild with you. We're not together, we're not in a relationship. It's not a big deal." Siobhan tried to brush it off, not even believing herself anymore.

"You keep telling yourself that if it makes you feel better, but I can see it a mile off. She's totally in love with you."

"What are you two talking about?" Cassie reappeared at the most inopportune of moments. Especially when Siobhan wanted to throw a million different questions Kendra's way, including how she had noticed something that still eluded Siobhan.

"The weather," they both replied at once, laughing.

"Did you win?" Siobhan asked.

"I wouldn't exactly call it winning. But I claimed second place or last place, depending on how you look at things."

Siobhan chuckled. "Such a sore loser. You should've known the undisputed king of racing cars was going to beat you." Siobhan stood up and went to give Kendra a hug. "Tonight has been great, Kendra. I promise that we'll do it more often."

"You should come over to London for a visit after the baby's born," Cassie said.

"I think we'd all love that. I might even get Ayden away from the farm for a weekend."

"We have an early start in the morning as we're going to the beach in Bettystown. Cass, please will you go and shuffle the kids along." Siobhan needed just a few more minutes alone with Kendra. Her words echoed in her head like a melody she had been waiting a lifetime to hear.

Kendra's gaze followed Cassie until she left the room. "She's great by the way."

"She is, isn't she?" Siobhan agreed, relief washing over her as the truth found its way out.

"I very much approve." With that, Kendra gave her a final squeeze. "Your mam would love her too. She brings out the best in ya and wow, you don't half look happy!"

"I'm not sure she had any idea that I was into women."

"I think you'll find she did. I used to hear her talking with my mam in the post office and she always said you'd end up with a woman one day, once you opened yourself up."

"Really?"

Time seemed to stop momentarily as Siobhan took in Kendra's revelation. Had her mum always known? It made sense considering how close they were, but she'd never had the chance to confide in her. The fact she had always known was comforting to hear, even now. Especially now.

"Absolutely!" Kendra confirmed. "She was always my favorite customer to eavesdrop on. She had wonderful craic and a heart of gold and believe me when I say, she would very much approve."

Siobhan's mind was whirling as they said their good-byes and the children made their own promises to keep in touch. Siobhan slipped her hand into Cassie's as they made their way back to the cottage they had rented, two exhausted children in tow. Her own brain was working overtime, Kendra's words resonating as she felt the connection between them.

She's totally in love with you.

Could there be any truth in Kendra's words? With every day that passed, they were becoming closer, but they never discussed their feelings. Cassie wasn't hiding anymore and they were naturally gravitating towards each other, but Siobhan knew Cassie wasn't ready for any sort of conversation on this level. It was too soon, too final. Yet Kendra had seen something Siobhan was missing or more likely, something Siobhan didn't dare dream might be true.

She's totally in love with you.

CHAPTER TWENTY-EIGHT

I had no idea the Moulin Rouge would be a distasteful building in such a dodgy area."

"You have to admit the windmill is weirdly impressive," Cassie said.

"I can totally see the connection: flour grinding in the mill, girls grinding on the stage. It all makes perfect sense."

"Ah, yes, topless girls, the best of what Paris has to offer." Cassie handed Siobhan a tissue as she rubbed at her nose.

"I wanted to see where the inspiration for the film came from."

"You're quite the fan of the doomed romance, aren't you?"

Siobhan caught a sneeze. "I'm not a big fan of illicit affairs."

"And *I* am?" Cassie flitted her eyes in a poor attempt at innocence.

"Considering the words 'I'm a big fan of illicit affairs' once passed your lips, I'd say so yes."

"I've moved on from that stage of my life," Cassie said. "Now, speaking of lips, come here and let me kiss yours." Cassie amazed herself every day finding new ways to kiss the woman next to her; tonight it was soft and chaste. "You dazzled those clients today, which is quite remarkable when you think how we hardly uttered a word to one another when we put that pitchbook together."

"Ah yes, back when I was frosty."

As if on cue, Siobhan's nose spasmed and she sneezed again.

Cassie stroked her arm. "Are you feeling okay?"

"It's nothing. Just a sniffle." Then she "sniffled" once, twice, three times, until her nose was glowing like Rudolph. "I'm fine. When you have kids, you have this inbuilt autopilot to keep going."

"Which isn't required here," Cassie said, genuinely concerned.

"If my eyes weren't streaming right now, I'd roll them," Siobhan said. Then she yawned and sneezed at the same time, which Cassie hadn't even known was possible.

Cassie placed her palm against Siobhan's forehead. She felt heat coming off her skin, yet Siobhan was clammy to the touch. "We're going back to the hotel."

"You want me to do my dying dog impression bedridden?" she offered, smiling, but it was weak and watered down. "I don't want to ruin your evening."

"There's only one woman I want to see scantily clad prancing around in Paris." Cassie stood up as Siobhan sneezed yet again. "But I can wait."

As it turned out, she would have to, because the first room Siobhan entered upon their return was the bathroom, not the bedroom.

"No need to panic." Siobhan groaned as she hung her head over the toilet bowl. "I'm not pregnant." She wiped her mouth with the towel Cassie handed her. "We're only bringing up the two."

"Thank fuck for that. I know I'm a one-woman woman these days, but I can't be bringing up a horde of kids. I'd never remember all their names." Cassie inwardly marveled at the magnitude of Siobhan's statement, although she did wonder how much stock to put in it, given Siobhan's present state. Kids hadn't ever been in her plan. Jesus, how those plans were changing.

Siobhan leaned over the toilet again, Cassie kneeling beside her, holding her hair away from her face and rubbing her back. Siobhan leaned back against the bath and accepted the glass of water Cassie handed her. "I'm so sorry. You really didn't need to see that."

"You didn't quite reach the dizzy heights of *The Exorcist*."

"Disappointing." Siobhan laughed, but it turned into a coughing fit. She wrapped her arms around herself, shivering.

"Can you make it to the sofa? I recommend it over the bathroom floor." Cassie guided Siobhan into the living space, where she had already laid out a duvet and pillows.

"Give me about three hours to work out the hot drinks machine in there and I'll be back," Cassie said, deciding it best to give Siobhan a little time to regain her dignity. After faffing about with the overly complicated machine, she managed to produce two warm drinks.

She searched through the collection of packaged biscuits, eyeing up the chocolate ones before popping one into her mouth, and then she grabbed something that might help.

"Tea and possibly the worst biscuits of all time." Cassie placed two steaming hot mugs on the table, along with a plate of rich tea biscuits. "Helena swears by them for a hangover. Let's hope they're versatile." She looked over at Siobhan, who was snuggled up in the duvet, head resting on a pillow. "Are you warm enough?"

"Yes, thanks. I'll see you later."

"What?"

"Go out and explore. I'll be fine here on my own."

"No way," Cassie said, sitting down at the opposite end of the sofa. She absentmindedly reached under the duvet for Siobhan's feet and began massaging them in a slow, circular motion. "I'm not going anywhere."

"I honestly don't mind you going out. I'm sure there's some great Parisian gay bars you could entertain yourself in."

Cassie huffed. "I don't want to go out."

"And I don't want to be responsible for spoiling your fun. I trust you not to pick up women," Siobhan insisted, her hand creeping over to Cassie's. "Well, at least not more than one."

"Is that what you think of me?" Cassie let go of Siobhan's feet, rolling her shoulders and leaning back.

"You know I'm only teasing, but you could be out enjoying all Paris has to offer, instead of watching me puke my guts up."

"I'm staying here because I want to. You asked me to allow myself to feel again and I'm starting to, which means you have to accept that I want to stay and look after you." With that, Cassie withdrew her hand from Siobhan's, folded her arms across her chest, and drummed her fingers against her forearms, building up to the final admission. "I care for you, Siobhan."

A silly grin materialized on Siobhan's pale face. "Did you just admit that out loud?"

"Shit." Cassie started at her nails. "What are you going to do about it? Turn me in?"

"Well, I'm certainly not going to turn you on," she said, nudging Cassie's calf with her foot so that Cassie resumed her massage. "I can't imagine I'm a very attractive prospect right now."

"Do you really want me to answer that?" Cassie needed to regain her equilibrium, so she focused intently on kneading Siobhan's feet.

"You're pretty good with your hands," Siobhan murmured. "If this is the attention to detail I get, I should be ill more often."

"Not on my watch."

"You do know you'll have to look after me when I'm ancient and need pushing around in a wheelchair."

"You're pushing your luck there."

"No. You'll be pushing your luck, literally." Siobhan gave a faint chuckle and then reached for her mug to take a sip of the milky tea, wincing when she sat back.

"Is your back hurting?"

"My neck is aching, and my head feels like a dead weight."

"Come over here." Cassie indicated the space between her legs. Siobhan filled the gap immediately. Cassie smiled. "Rest your head against me and close your eyes," she said, gathering the duvet around Siobhan again. She began massaging her shoulders. "Is that better?"

Siobhan nodded, her eyes closing.

Cassie moved her hands beneath Siobhan's shirt but maintained sole focus on massaging and relieving Siobhan's aches. She tried not to notice Siobhan's body, all soft edges and defined curves, or how her raven hair flowed towards soft breasts dappled in freckles. To her surprise, she found she didn't have to try all that hard, realizing all she wanted to do was look after the woman before her, the woman she was trying so desperately hard not to fall for.

Cassie let out a sigh. Her feelings were all over the place right now and she had expressed them far too easily.

"I can read you like a book. You're struggling with what you just said." Siobhan looked up into her eyes. "Please don't. You must know I care for you too."

"You're delirious." She twisted a strand of Siobhan's hair around her finger absent-mindedly and then she pressed her lips to Siobhan's shoulder. "Siobhan—" Cassie hadn't even touched her tea and already warmth was rolling through her. "Do you think we might be able to extend our stay in Paris? I'd love to explore the city with you when you're feeling better. Depending on the kids of course."

"Matthew's taking the kids to his sister's on Friday for the weekend as they have a training day. I was surprised they didn't complain when he suggested it. They enjoy spending time with their cousins, so I think that has a lot to do with it. It will do them good to spend time together doing something fun and not football related."

"I think you're right."

"Which means I'd love to share more of Paris with you," Siobhan said, snuggling deeper into the duvet and, by association, Cassie.

"Are you feeling any better?"

"Snuggling into you feels amazing," Siobhan mumbled, her eyes closing sleepily whilst her nose twitched.

As Siobhan slept, Cassie allowed herself a rare moment to truly study her beauty, stroking back a strand of stray hair. Moments like these were ones she had never experienced before and once again she had to remind herself of the conscious effort she was making to slow things right down. Still, she felt a lightness in her limbs as she pressed her lips to Siobhan's forehead. Siobhan snored gently in response.

❖

Siobhan slipped her hand into Cassie's, entwining their fingers as if it were the most natural thing in the world. Her head was still a little cloudy, but Cassie's exuberant company had perked her up considerably. So far, Cassie had flitted from one piece of artwork to another, no methodology to her journey, just sheer excitement at being here. It was refreshing to see her so impressively improvisational.

They stopped to stare at a painting depicting the French Revolution called *Liberty Leading the People*. Siobhan tilted her head, smiling in anticipation of Cassie's appraisal.

"See, that's what I don't get. Here we have a powerful French woman leading the revolution, waving her tricolor, and what is she wearing?"

"Next to nothing." Siobhan quirked an eyebrow. "I'm actually surprised you haven't taken me to more art galleries."

"Mona Lisa is most definitely fully dressed," Cassie said.

"Funnily enough you haven't taken me to see her yet!"

"If you're trying to trick me into telling you you're the only woman I enjoy seeing starkers, you might as well give it up as a bad job this very minute." She squeezed Siobhan's hand. "Now, how about we go find Aphrodite, take a few selfies and then head outside. You'll like her—she's topless too!"

"You're making me blush now!" Siobhan focused on the map and happily trailed along after her exuberant tour guide.

"You know, I bet the pyramid looks incredible all lit up now that it's dark. I might also treat you to a flashing Eiffel Tower replica if you're lucky."

"I might be about to have a relapse. Besides," Siobhan lowered her tone, "there's only one woman whose flashing I welcome, and it certainly isn't the Eiffel Tower, as feminine as she is."

By the time they left the Louvre, Siobhan was all art galleried out. After two days stuck in their hotel room, she relished the fresh air. There was no question, though, that it had been wonderful to be so taken care of while sick. Cassie had been attentive and kind, teasing and at ease. She'd taken care of meals and drinks, and not once had she seemed the least bit put out by it. Siobhan couldn't remember the last time someone had cared for her that way.

Silhouetted against the velvety sky, they walked hand in hand in companionable silence, traversing the banks of the Seine, following what seemed to be a rarely used but defined footpath.

Eventually, Siobhan noticed the trees becoming denser and was surprised to find herself in a peaceful, star-lit clearing, with only Cassie and the enchanting moon for company.

Cassie sat on an old bench covered in the carvings of timeless lovers and beckoned Siobhan to join her. "I have something for you."

"I'm intrigued and terrified in equal measure," Siobhan said, downplaying her anticipation.

"I picked this up here in Paris."

"You *did* leave my side while I was sleeping after all." Siobhan tutted, grinning.

"I did," Cassie said. "You were doing such a magnificent impression of Snow White's bestie, Snorey, I didn't want to wake you." Cassie made a ridiculous snoring noise that made them both laugh. "How could I? Here." Cassie pulled out a tiny box from her leather jacket pocket. "This is a little gift to say…" She trailed off, squirming slightly. "I'll just let the gift speak for itself."

Siobhan untied the lace ribbon, feeling Cassie's attentive eyes on her the whole time. She opened the box to reveal the most exceptional handcrafted necklace, made of white gold, with a pear-shaped diamond.

Her heart expanded in her chest at the gesture, and the lovely romance of the moment. It was a beautiful gift, thoughtful and sincere, exactly like Cassie these past few days.

"Turn it over," Cassie said.

"*Inevitable*," she read out loud. "Is this in honor of how you tried your level best to avoid the inevitable?"

"We have to honor it somehow," Cassie played along.

"I guess there wasn't room for: *I tried everything in my power not to kiss you, but you were far too irresistible.*"

"I'm saving that for a Christmas T-shirt—you know, one of those ones couples take selfies in on Christmas Eve."

Siobhan raised an eyebrow. "Couples?"

Crimson graced Cassie's cheeks. "A slip of the tongue. It's your fault for getting all sneezy and enchanting," she murmured, deflecting Siobhan's scrutiny by focusing on the necklace, which she attempted to unclasp in an adorably uncoordinated manner.

"As someone once told me, it's all in the art of the pinch," Siobhan said.

"Turn around," Cassie instructed when she'd pinched the clasp properly. Siobhan complied, lifting her hair off her neck so Cassie could fasten the delicate chain.

Siobhan turned back around. When she looked into Cassie's eyes, she could tell there was more Cassie wanted to say but couldn't find the words for. There was no need to push right now. Exhaling, Siobhan cupped Cassie's face in her hands. "Thank you. It's beautiful."

Cassie nodded in acknowledgement and turned her face towards the sky.

"Are you going to tell me another romantic story about the stars?" Siobhan asked, following her gaze to the blanket of constellations.

Cassie fiddled with the zip on her jacket. "Look, Shiv, I know I'm still learning how to be with you, but being with you is what I want. And I want you to teach me how."

"Who's training who now?" Siobhan teased her, but her pulse was racing as she leaned in. "We take this slowly, one day at a time."

Siobhan softly set her lips on Cassie's, warmth blooming inside when Cassie returned the kiss, as she brushed Siobhan's hair back with one hand while sliding the other around Siobhan's waist, pulling her deliciously closer.

Cassie's mouth brushed her lower lip, her tongue following suit, and Siobhan's lips parted to allow Cassie's tongue in. She twined her fingers through Cassie's hair, losing herself in the rush.

The reminder about time had been as much for herself as for Cassie. It seemed like Cassie was finally getting herself together, expressing her feelings in a way that Siobhan could deal with, but it was early days. Cassie was predisposed to pulling back, and she could still perform a complete U-turn without a moment's notice. Siobhan knew it may only be a matter of time before they were facing this sort of difficulty and although she couldn't pretend that didn't concern her, she felt better equipped to deal with it than she ever had before. Knowing Cassie cared, despite what she might show or say in a moment of panic, made the world of difference.

CHAPTER TWENTY-NINE

"Sacré bleu, does Gay Paris agree with you!" Julie joked, faking a French accent that made her sound like an unemployed standby in *Beauty and the Beast*. "Cassie tells me you were quite ill in France, but you're certainly glowing now. You both are."

Cassie patted Siobhan's shoulder as platonically as possible. "I'm glad you're feeling better, Mrs. Carney."

"I'm assuming Cassie gave you all the TLC you needed to make a full recovery?" Julie shuffled forward in her seat.

Cassie picked up a folder from Julie's desk and hid behind it under the pretense of reading its contents. "Siobhan's more than capable of looking after herself."

"That's a new necklace, *Mrs. Carney*," Julie remarked. "Has it replaced your wedding ring?"

Cassie's eyes shot to Siobhan's ring finger, which was, for the very first time, beautifully bare. Her eyes lifted to Siobhan's face and lingered, accepting the affectionate gaze she received in response.

"I wonder if your next marital marker will have more staying power." Julie appeared to be commenting to herself, shuffling a stack of folders into alignment. "I did call this."

The comment should have riled Cassie. Instead, it confused her. And intrigued her. "What?" she squeaked. Clearing her throat, she said again, "You called what?"

"I knew exactly what was happening, even if you two didn't," Julie said. "Being the nosiest person in the building comes with a certain degree of excess knowledge. Besides, this is the first time I've ever seen you pine for anyone."

"I haven't been pining." Cassie knew this was an outright lie, but her cool demeanor was quickly unravelling.

Julie held up a hand in a warding-off gesture. "Oh, please. I've been calling this since the day Siobhan walked in all legs and heels. There's potential in this. I should know, I've been keeping tabs on you both."

Cassie widened her eyes and blew out her cheeks, spluttering like a sprinkler system. "I thought you were merely the office gossip. I thought you despised me."

Julie grinned in a manner Cassie couldn't read. "I can multitask. Now, if you'll excuse me, I have a range of things to get on with that won't be nearly as exciting as watching you two dance the 'will they, won't they?' tango. Oh, and, Ms. Townsend, a word of advice. Your reactions have been far too slow." With that, Julie flounced off, probably in search of newer and more interesting gossip.

"What the fuck just hap—"

"She's right you know. About one thing at least: your reactions. Even if the rest was *entirely* unexpected. I also feel the need to add that there's so much more to me than legs and heels." Siobhan laughed. Cassie didn't. "Are you okay?"

"You're not wearing your wedding ring."

"I returned it to Matthew after Paris. It felt like the right time. I realize we're taking things slow, but I can't wear something that represents my old commitment to him when I have…" Siobhan paused so that it was obvious she was picking her words carefully, "feelings blossoming with someone else. That isn't me."

Cassie felt her knees weaken. As if anticipating her needs, Siobhan leant over and propped her up. "You have feelings for someone else? Do I need to up my game?"

"This isn't a game, remember?" Siobhan teased her. "But if it were, I recommend you play to win."

"Listen, if you're feeling up to it, I wondered about that trip to the coast I promised the kids. We could go this weekend. It seems like the perfect time for you to meet Eva. Two birds, one stone and all that."

"I'd love to meet your sister." Siobhan beamed. "I think we can safely assume the kids will be well up for a trip to the seaside too."

Cassie needed a moment to comprehend what had just happened. Julie's U-turn was one thing, but Siobhan removing her wedding ring was next level significant. Whether she knew it or not, Siobhan had raised the stakes for both of them. For someone as closely guarded as Cassie, this felt huge. Siobhan was committing to her, even if she had caught herself before she said the actual words. Cassie had lived her life insistent that nobody would ever want her enough to commit, enough to love her and yet Siobhan felt dangerously close. It was all Cassie could do not to sweep Siobhan up into her arms and try in her not so eloquent way to express what this meant to her. Instead, she held back. In typical Cassie style, she wasn't giving anything away just yet.

❖

"Did you just splodge ice cream on my face?"

Siobhan smiled at the smear of cerulean blue coloring Cassie's nose. "I was just being considerate. I know it hurts when someone says the words *Wake up*."

"I wasn't sleeping."

"Ah, so that drool was just a figment of my imagination."

"I was not drooling!" Cassie dabbed at the corners of her mouth, not looking in the least bit dignified as she did so. Next, she drew her middle finger down the bridge of her nose, then licked her finger clean. "Great choice, by the way."

"Seems we're both getting better at making those," Siobhan said, reaching over to wipe the rest off Cassie's nose. She took a taste. "Delicious."

Cassie's eyes smoldered. "Me or the ice cream?"

"Before I gag…" Eva exchanged a knowing look with Cassie, then pulled her sunglasses back down over her eyes. "Please stop with the taste testing. I feel like I've entered some alternate universe. I liked it up to the near exchange of bodily fluids."

"Cassie, please can you help with the moat?" Dylan pointed to the fortress Cassie had helped the kids construct, a disgruntled look on his face. "Every time we add water, it just sinks back into the sand."

"Sand will do that. Give me five minutes to eat this ice cream before your mother rubs it all over my face, and I'll see what I can do."

"It seems your skills are needed elsewhere. There is a God!" Eva raised her hands to the sky.

"Mum!" Neave yelled. "We have an ice cream incident!"

"Another one?"

Siobhan looked over to Dylan, whose cone had face-planted onto their fortress. His top lip quivered. She nudged Cassie. "What did I tell you about kids and ice cream?"

"Come on!" Cassie said, jogging over to Dylan. "Let's go sort out a replacement together. I'll even see if I can wangle an extra flake." Dylan's face lit up as Cassie helped him up and brushed the sand off his face.

"She's really good with them," Eva said, as they watched Cassie and Dylan traipse hand in hand across the sand. "I did *not* think I'd be saying that, let alone witnessing it for myself."

"They adore her. I had a near mutiny when she and I..." Siobhan trailed off, unsure how much Eva knew.

"I'm glad you worked things out. I've never seen her the way she was when you two fell out." Eva looked a little sheepish. "She didn't go into the ins and outs of the situation, but she was devastated. You mean a lot to her."

"So far we've not had an easy ride, but we're working it out together, day by day."

"I'm glad to hear it. She's like a different woman today, relaxed, happy and she's totally at ease in your company. That's something I've never seen with Cassie. Sometimes I forget what good company she can be, especially when I'm so used to her being off somewhere sulking or rebelling."

Siobhan smiled. Conversation flowed effortlessly with Eva, and it was gratifying to hear someone who really knew Cassie talking so positively about their flourishing relationship. "We're not rushing into anything," she said, adjusting her sun hat, "but I think we're finally heading in the right direction. She's slowly letting go of her hang-ups." She didn't mention that things were good because she was finally working to be the person she wanted to be, too.

"Cassie got me a double flake!" Dylan brandished his cone like a sword, much to Neave's disapproval.

"Don't worry, you can have mine." Cassie pulled out the extra flake that had appeared in her own ice cream and bobbed it into Neave's mouth, much to Siobhan's amusement.

"Since we got back from Ireland, Mum's shown Dad the door for good!" Dylan said, plopping down in the sand. "You know what that means, Cassie."

"I…" Siobhan felt her cheeks burning. "Erm…I…" She looked from Cassie to Eva and back again. "I was going to tell you later, but the finalized divorce papers came through. He just needs to sign them now."

"It means you can officially start dating Mum." Dylan stated it so matter-of-factly, he might as well have added: "And that's an order."

Siobhan drummed her fingers against her knees, trying to hide her smirk. "I did warn you they were very much Team Cassie."

Cassie ruffled the children's hair. "Do I get a say in the matter?"

"No, because Mum's totally in love with you," Neave declared. "You *have* to be together."

"Neave!" Siobhan willed the ground to open up and swallow her. The last thing she needed right now was her children making giant proclamations when she was trying so hard to keep things slow and steady.

Siobhan watched as Cassie ran a hand through her hair, as if by smoothing it out, she could also smooth over what had just happened.

"I'm sorry, Cass. It seems my children are a little prone to getting carried away and spilling state secrets."

"I'm not sure I find it entirely objectionable," Cassie said, looking out across the beach.

"Right. That's good to know then," Siobhan said, watching Cassie closely for any sign that she might be hiding more complex feelings. "I'm glad we cleared that up."

Eva gave a single, hearty clap. "Any moment now Cassie's going to burst into song with the seagulls backing her up, flitting their wings in a spectacular dance routine as the crabs provide backing vocals."

"That would be amazing!" Neave exclaimed. "Mum could do the moonwalk!"

"Embarrassing!" Dylan groaned.

"But entertaining," Eva said.

"Are you okay for a little bit if we head for a short walk?"

Siobhan got the distinct impression this was something Cassie had already agreed with her sister. Cassie received a quick thumbs-up from Eva along with a beaming smile, so closely resembling Cassie's own.

"No worries." Eva pulled Siobhan in close to whisper into her ear. "Safe to say, she *really, really* likes you."

Cassie took Siobhan's hand in her own as they ambled along the shore, white foam from the waves gently creeping up on them like thieves in the night.

"I've been dying to get you alone all day," Cassie said.

"Yet I'm not sure this is a private enough beach for you to pounce on me." Siobhan feigned mild disappointment. "Still, you have my undivided attention."

"You had to mention the pouncing?" Cassie bit down on her bottom lip. "Here I was thinking now was about the right time to do at least one thing properly."

"This isn't another of your wild propositions, is it? I think we've both lived through enough of them for one lifetime."

Cassie shook her head. "Actually, I wanted to ask if you'd come to Eva's wedding with me, you know, as my date?"

Siobhan stopped in her tracks as she felt her heartbeat take on a life of its own. She took one, two, three deep breaths to calm herself as she looked at Cassie, who was hovering on the spot, pretending that this wasn't a big moment.

When she didn't reply straight away, Cassie raced straight into a ramble. "You might think it's too soon, but we've never been in such a good place. At least I don't think we have. It feels like the right time to do something significant." Cassie turned towards the ocean, forming a steeple with her hands. "I've spent hours considering where we go next, wondering if there's any such thing as a right time. I've also run through every reaction you might have but this makes sense. Well, it does to me anyway." Cassie looked baffled by her own incompetence. "Christ, I'm practically incoherent."

It was Siobhan's turn to bite her lip, trying to hide her amusement. She wanted to cheer from the rooftops, she wanted to cartwheel along the surf, but she reined in her excitement to focus solely on Cassie. This was a bold move from Cassie and Siobhan's mind raced with the possibilities of where this might be going. Cassie was finally acknowledging them as a couple. She was so swept up in her racing thoughts and absolute delight that she forgot to offer Cassie a reply.

"This is the moment where you put me out of my misery and say yes." Cassie nudged her. "Pick up your cues, Shiv!"

"I'd love to go to the wedding with you."

Before Siobhan could register what was happening, Cassie had swept her up in a passionate kiss, leaving the imprint of soft warm lips upon her own.

"Gross!" Dylan said, running across the beach towards them, but his grin negated his revulsion.

"Where did you spring from?" Siobhan asked, amazed to see Neave right behind her too.

"I'm sorry." Eva arrived to complete the picture, holding her hands up. "They were not to be detained a moment longer."

"We needed to check you said yes." Neave bounced up and down, excitement getting the better of her. "You did say yes, didn't you?"

"Of course she did! The fact they're kissing says it all." Dylan scrunched up his nose.

"You're so unromantic." Neave shook her head as if her brother were hopeless. "One day you might have to kiss a girl."

"No way! I'm leaving that to Cassie."

"Good choice." Siobhan nodded her approval. "After all, she is the expert."

"An expert who doesn't need an audience," Cassie said, glaring at her sister, who shrugged apologetically. "Now come here and let me kiss you again."

That was Dylan and Neave's cue to head back to their sandcastle, Eva following closely behind. Siobhan felt Cassie's lips linger on her own, seeking permission to deepen the kiss Siobhan felt like she had been waiting a lifetime for. Finally, she was going to be the woman on Cassie's arm, the one she introduced to her family, the one she took back to her hotel room and spent all night making love to. It was hard to rein in her wildest dreams when her lips were locked with Cassie's, but she took back her final thought considering it too much, too soon. For now, accepting this invitation, attending the wedding as Cassie's plus-one, would be more than enough.

CHAPTER THIRTY

*M*aybe, just maybe, one day I could descend to my knees for her with a ring.

This thought had been the catalyst that derailed Cassie's performance as a bridesmaid, something she was still cringing about, mortified at having embarrassed herself over such an unexpected thought.

"I can't believe I forgot to accept the bouquet. I had one job. If anyone other than Eva noticed, I'm laying the blame at your feet."

"Cass, I'm pretty sure there's at least a handful of witnesses who saw Eva battling her bouquet while Danny tried to put the ring on her finger. Thank goodness your mum stepped in."

"I was distracted." Cassie was determined to leave it at that.

Siobhan leaned in close, nearly nuzzling her nose. "I'd love to know what the distraction was. Am I to blame?"

"Maybe you can coax it out of me later."

Eva had compromised with her on everything except being a bridesmaid, and she had still botched it up. Now, she longed to retreat to her hotel room—one, to get out of her bridesmaid costume, a silver floor-length dress with a slit and spaghetti straps; and two, to devour Siobhan, who looked unforgettable in her midnight blue dress and soft curls. Cassie was instantly drawn to Siobhan's neck, where the pear-shaped diamond that had sealed their feelings hung gracefully.

"How about we steal away to the terrace while they finish the photos?" Siobhan suggested. "Assuming your part is done?"

"It most certainly is." Cassie tugged at the dress, following her out. "There's only so many times you can say *sausages* while smiling, without wanting to eat one in a bloody great sandwich. Now I'm going out on a limb here to say that sausage sandwiches aren't on the menu today." Out on the terrace, away from the hustle and bustle of the wedding guests, Cassie kicked her heels off. "I'm ditching these at the first available opportunity," she said, scrunching up her face in distaste. "Though you look exquisite in yours. Now I know why they call them fuck-me heels."

"I see weddings bring out your romantic side," Siobhan whispered, her lips tantalizingly close to Cassie's ear.

Cassie's heart beat like a snare drum, her body responding to the lovely lilt of Siobhan's voice and the sweet scent of champagne on her breath. "I don't have a romantic side," Cassie said, reaching for her hand and interlocking their fingers. "Our lighthouse looks amazing over there silhouetted against the sunset."

Siobhan followed Cassie's gaze into the distance, where their lighthouse stood, untouched by the passage of time. "Ah, yes, the lighthouse, where we didn't share our first kiss."

Siobhan allowed Cassie to pull her into a tight embrace and coax her head onto her shoulder. They stayed that way for a long time, breathing as one, until Cassie began to trace soft kisses down her neck.

Siobhan seemed short of breath, leaning forward so their foreheads were touching. Cassie's hands worked their way slowly up and down Siobhan's back, and she marveled at the softness of the skin there. Cassie leaned closer, and the moment their lips melted together, tiny sparks of static danced across her skin, and she deepened the kiss until only they existed.

"Knock it off!" Eva's voice cut through their kiss, reality kicking back in. "Whose wedding is it anyway?"

"Have you quite finished with the pretentious poses?" Cassie kissed her sister on the cheek.

"Have *you* introduced Siobhan to Mum and Dad yet?" Eva shot back.

"Give me a chance! We've been kind of busy watching you get married."

"It was gorgeous," Helena said, appearing out of nowhere. "I've never seen two people make eyes at each other for so long." Helena grinned at Cassie, a wicked glimmer in her gaze. "And I'm not talking about the bride and groom."

"I was thinking—"

"About getting down on one knee yourself?" Helena cut in, and Cassie watched Siobhan's cheeks flush. "Because that's the only reason I can see for your small misdemeanor."

"Yeah, thanks for leaving me laden with flowers, Cassie." Eva chuckled.

Cassie stood rooted to the spot, unsure how to respond and feeling seriously out of her depth.

"Congratulations to both of you," Helena said, smiling at Eva before turning to face Cassie. "And to you two." With that, she was gone, probably to search out Riley and plan their wedding—or hers.

"It was a beautiful ceremony." Although Siobhan was speaking to Eva, her attention was focused on Cassie.

Cassie met Siobhan's gaze. She swept a stray curl behind Siobhan's ear and reached for her hand, a combustible current coursing between them. "Come on then, seeing as it's a wedding, let's go introduce you to the in-laws."

Siobhan knew the stakes were high as they approached the Townsends, Cassie holding tightly to her hand. The loss of both parents, coupled with the terrible relationship she shared with her mother-in-law, had made her long for something more, something she'd never deemed possible. Cassie was in the process of reconnecting with her parents and Siobhan loved the thought of being part of that journey. She only hoped the Townsends approved of her. They stopped in front of Cassie's mum and she made the introductions.

"So you're the woman responsible for the changes in my daughter?" Maria gave her the once-over, eyebrows furrowing and then releasing.

Siobhan wondered if she was upset, and it was all she could do to remain standing under such close scrutiny. She felt Cassie wrap her arm around her, offering both support and encouragement and she leaned into her, grateful. Then something changed in Maria's demeanor as a smile burst across her features, her eyes crinkling at the corners. "You've had quite an impact. Thank you."

"She may have made a little leeway herself too," Siobhan said, squeezing Cassie's hand.

Maria wrapped her arms around Siobhan, pressing a kiss to her cheek before pulling back to admire her outfit. "That dress looks sensational on you." Maria glanced over at Cassie, put an arm around Siobhan to pull her close, and whispered, "Tell me she isn't carrying her heels."

"I wish I could." Siobhan offered Maria a knowing grin.

Chuckling, Maria called, "Mark!" and made a fuss of waving him over. "This is Cassie's date, Siobhan."

"Ah, the plus-one! Delighted to meet you." He kissed her cheek before turning to Cassie, beaming. "I see you and the shoes got off on the wrong foot."

"Dad." Cassie groaned.

Maria tugged on her husband's arm. "Do you think you might be able to persuade your daughter to put her shoes back on?"

"Nonsense! She can wear what she likes. Or not wear what she doesn't like. I'm sick of this thing too." Much to Siobhan's amusement, he undid his tie, looped it over his head and then, not quite daring to ditch it on the ground, hung it over his chair.

"I'm taking that as Dad's permission to get out of this bloody dress." Cassie's familiar smirk made a welcome appearance and Siobhan adored her even more for accepting the good-natured banter from her dad.

"I'll be ten minutes, no more." With that, Cassie disappeared.

"Come, sit down." Mark patted the seat next to him.

"I couldn't. I'm not top table material today." Siobhan didn't want to feel like she was intruding on the family. They had welcomed her with open arms, but she wasn't a permanent fixture—yet. She was conscious that today was all about their family, one she was very new to. "Plus, I'm pretty sure Cass has her own chartered agreement for not sitting at the top table. She probably made Eva sign it in blood." She fiddled with the straps of her dress, realizing how ridiculous this sounded.

Mark leaned forward and took her hand. "Shall I let you in on a secret? I know Cassie had no intention of sitting at the top table, but I've overruled her. Not because I want her on show to everyone, like she thinks, but because I want to sit next to my daughter. I'm pretty sure your place setting is next to hers. But why don't you keep her seat warm until she gets back?"

Siobhan felt warmth spread through her as if she'd just had her first sip of a fresh hot chocolate. She made her way around the table and there, just as he'd said, was her name written on her place setting. In keeping with the seaside theme Danny and Eva had chosen for Kingsgate Castle, her name was framed by local shells.

She appreciated the simple elegance of Eva's wedding: the charming shades of blue that comprised the color scheme, the unique handwritten messages in bottles put out for favors, the miniature lighthouse tea lights.

Mark popped the cork on a bottle of champagne. It bubbled freely, alongside the lively buzz that filled the air as he poured her a glass. "You know, Maria did all the favors herself." He picked up one of the little bottles. "She walked every beach in Broadstairs to find the right shells and stones."

"The lighthouses were Cassie's idea," Maria said. "Do you think she'll be all right with the surprise seating arrangements?"

Siobhan had an inkling that Cassie would be agreeable, despite her previous demands. If not, Siobhan could talk her down. "We'll soon find out," she said, nodding towards Cassie, who was heading their way.

Cassie had changed into fitted black trousers, a sleeveless satin top the color of her bridesmaid's dress, and a light blue blazer. Siobhan practically had to hold her jaw up, especially when Cassie momentarily turned around to greet someone, presenting Siobhan with her showstopping arse.

She stood up, reaching across the table to kiss Cassie's cheek and lingered longer than necessary.

"Are you lost?" Cassie said. "Do you need a map back to our table?"

"About that," Mark intervened. "I'd like you to take your seat at the top table next to me, with Siobhan beside you."

"You know," Cassie began, her voice even but not edgy, "I did the dress *and* the speech under the specific agreement that I wouldn't have to sit at the top table." Her gaze swept over the table's occupants, landing on Siobhan last. Cassie's eyes laughed first, and the rest of her followed swiftly. "Scoot across."

Siobhan placed her hand on Cassie's knee. "Look at you, taking it all in your stride. Seriously, Cass. Have you always been this agreeable and I just never noticed?"

Cassie leaned back, folding her hands behind her head. "Laid-back is my middle name."

"Right. And the Queen is starring as Frank-N-Furter in the Christmas production of *Rocky Horror*."

"Hanging around me has improved your sense of humor no end!" Cassie laughed, but then her face fell. "It looks like the speeches are about to begin." She clasped her hands and cleared her throat.

"You can do this! All else fails, just turn around and waggle your arse at them. In those trousers, it's next-level hot."

"Cassie, are you good to go?" Mark asked, handing her the mic.

"No, but I guess it's now or never," she murmured, removing a folded piece of paper from her trouser pocket.

Siobhan settled back in her seat, ready for Cassie to dazzle.

"Hi, everyone. I'm Cassie, Eva's sister, enigmatic and entertaining, the one no one talks about. I think we can all agree it's been a fantastic day, but unfortunately that ends right here with my speech. When I first heard Danny had proposed to Eva, I was a bit like: whoa, what is he thinking? Does he know she always packs three pairs of knickers for each day of a holiday? Did someone tell him about the time she drove a hire car into the Atlantic Ocean pretending to be James Bond? Or how she spent the next three hours picking crabs out of the car bonnet with her sister, who was absolutely thrilled to be involved in such an epic event? Sorry, Eva, but your driving is hopeless even if your taste in men isn't! Danny is everything you were looking for and more: handsome, intelligent, charming." Cassie paused, a puzzled expression crossing her face. "Sorry, Danny, but I can't read the rest of your handwriting!"

Although it would have been inconspicuous to anyone else, Siobhan noticed when Cassie bit down on her lip, a surefire sign she was going off script and about to get sentimental.

"My sister is an incredible woman." Cassie turned to face her sister. "No matter what's been going on in your life, you've always been there for me. You've worked hard to keep me grounded and you've kept this family together by loving unconditionally. I'm incredibly grateful and immensely proud of you. You deserve all the happiness in the world, both of you, so can we all raise our glasses in a toast? May all your ups and downs come only in the bedroom!"

Siobhan glided her glass into the air, and they sat together listening to the rest of the speeches, none stirring the crowd quite like Cassie's.

"You should sing my praises more often," Eva said before wrapping her arms around Cassie. "You were fantastic!"

"It's almost time to cut the cake and then the first dance." Maria was so excited she reminded Siobhan of Neave in a moment of unbridled joy.

"Cake, yes. Dancing, no." Cassie blew out a long sigh. "Honestly, Eva, I don't know how you're going to do it. All those people staring at you in such an intimate moment."

"It's the first dance, not the wedding night." A wicked grin, not dissimilar to Cassie's, spread across Eva's face. "Nobody's going to be watching *me* anyway. Danny dances like a gorilla in a snowstorm."

"Thank goodness! And if all else fails, Siobhan's claimed an epic moonwalk!" Cassie teased as Mark offered Siobhan his hand.

He pulled her up, twirled her, and spun her around to face—

Someone whose praises nobody would ever sing.

Matthew Carney.

CHAPTER THIRTY-ONE

Out in the reception, they faced off.
"I thought you'd want these sooner rather than later."
Matthew's hunched form oozed a drunken hostility like gasoline: scorching, deadly, formidable. He shoved the divorce papers into her hands. She didn't have to look to know he'd signed them.

Siobhan narrowed her eyes. "And how did you know where to hand-deliver them?"

"Mum asked the children where you were and Neave told her."

I'll bet Bronagh bullied it out of her, she thought, but if she wanted to handle this quickly and quietly, approachable would have to be her middle name.

"Thank you for bringing these," she said, keeping her voice and face as neutral as possible. "It was very thoughtful of you to go out of your way for me."

"If you wish to thank me properly, you'll introduce me to your plus-one." Matthew baited her, raising one side of his mouth in contempt. Siobhan felt as if she'd been thrown under the bus, and not just any bus: a huge double-decker bus full of tourists visiting the capital city.

"My date?"

"Yes, Dylan said you were going as someone's date." He turned his nose up. "Some ridiculous nonsense about being asked on a beach."

Siobhan watched, horrified, as he barged past her, making his way into the main room, where the first dance had just finished. He helped himself to a glass of champagne and sat down at a table, looking every bit like he was supposed to be there.

This was more disarming than if he'd come in all guns blazing. Matthew's coolly dispassionate look left her cold and clammy. It was only a matter of time before he erupted. He was keeping her on tenterhooks for his own pleasure.

Siobhan followed him, heart hammering inside her chest. She felt like a hunted fox running for its life. She glanced around, noticing a few people had paused their conversations to glance at them. Her patience was beginning to wane, but she had to keep him calm. If Matthew made a scene at Eva's wedding, the Townsends would never forgive her.

"Please don't ruin someone else's wedding day."

"A wedding day is just that, Siobhan. A *day*. It's not like I'm ruining their marriage or anything. I have no experience doing that. That's *your* area of expertise."

The statement knocked her for six. She swallowed, rubbing at her throat, tension surging through her as she willed herself to prevent this situation from escalating. "You agreed to this, Matthew. We talked it out. We said we'd go our separate ways."

"Yeah, well, I didn't know you'd be dating someone else before the papers were even signed."

"We can talk about Cassie, but not here." *Shit*, she thought, regretting, for the first time, how easily Cassie's name tripped off her tongue. Closing her eyes, she pinched the bridge of her nose.

"Ah, so it is Cassie. I always had you down as far too much of a coward to commit adultery, especially with a woman. Guess I gave you far too little credit!"

A scene was no longer avoidable, as he'd raised his voice so that more than a few people were nudging one another and looking on with interest. Fury and embarrassment assailed her.

"I can't imagine anyone inviting you as their plus-one." Cassie appeared by her side without warning.

"Why, if it isn't the famous fuck buddy."

"I'm not her fuck buddy." Cassie turned to Siobhan, and her eyes were so different in this moment, softer than Siobhan could ever remember. Despite the horrible state of affairs, her insides ached at the sensation of genuine affection written in Cassie's eyes, but even she wasn't prepared for what came next. "I'm in love with her."

Siobhan's world came to an absolute standstill, but she had no time to absorb this new information because Matthew's outrage was coming thick and fast.

"And *I'm* her husband! Or I was until you came along. I fixed her and you brainwashed her." He pointed a finger at Cassie with such vehemence, Siobhan thought his arm would detach from its socket. Then he thrust that finger at her. "You couldn't have waited until all this was finalized? What am I supposed to tell people? What do you expect me to tell my *mother*? She's going to disown me. How long has this been going on?"

By now their little scene had developed into a full-blown production with a captive audience.

The truth was the only way out of this now. "We've been together for quite some time."

"In my house?" Fury blazed across his twisted face. "You brought her into my house to fuck her?"

"It wasn't like—"

"Did you fuck her in my house?" His eyes nearly popped out of his head.

"I'm not answering th—"

"Did you fuck her in my house?" he boomed.

She glanced down at the floor, then up into his face, determined to look him square in the eye. "Yes."

Murmurs of approval, disapproval, and everything in between sauntered through the crowd, which had doubled in size and, to Siobhan's horror, now included Cassie's mum and dad.

Cassie took hold of Siobhan's hand, squeezing tightly.

"You get your filthy fucking hands off her."

"Don't speak to her like that." Cassie stepped forward. "She's the mother of your children and you need to speak to her with the respect she deserves."

"Clearly, you don't know the meaning of that word, and Siobhan certainly doesn't."

Next thing she knew, Cassie's father was bursting through the crowd to tackle Matthew head-on. "Why don't we tone it down. I don't care what you think she's done. I don't care what she's actually done. The way you're speaking right now needs to stop, and you need to leave."

"You must be father of the dyke," Matthew sneered.

"She's already heard that from me. She doesn't need to hear it from you. I've apologized because it's derogatory and downright wrong. I strongly suggest you do the same or we're going to have a problem."

Face red, knuckles white, Matthew took a step closer to Siobhan. Siobhan didn't budge. At the last moment, he diverted his attention to Cassie. "How many times have you fucked her?" he demanded, the smell of whisky wafting off him in waves.

Mark opened his mouth to speak, but Cassie shook her head and stayed silent.

Matthew turned back to Siobhan. "And Dylan? Neave? What exactly is it you think you're going to tell them?"

"They already know the truth."

"Well, congratulations! You've fucking outdone yourself this time, telling the kids before me. Fucking spectacular!"

"I've always been honest with them, you know that."

"I will not have my children being brought up by a—"

"Lesbian?" Siobhan's insides were churning despite her bravado. "Better a lesbian than a no-show. You really should consider what full custody of the children means, before you threaten me. They would be all your responsibility, even on football days. Every day, every hour, every second."

She must have struck a chord because he looked her up and down, like he was battling some internal decision.

"We don't need to make any decision right now. For the moment they're probably better off with you. I'll drop them off tomorrow before the…"

"Spurs game."

"I don't want to disrupt their routine," Matthew said. "I want to do what's best for the children. This isn't their fault." He glared at Cassie. "It's *her* fault. I don't want *her* around them."

"You don't get to dictate to me or the children."

"When she fucks off in a few months because she's had her fill of you and the children, you'll be begging me to take you back. She doesn't know the first thing about children or bringing them up."

Cassie stood tall, shoulders back, head high. "It may come as a surprise to many people in this room, but not only do I love Siobhan, I care about her children just as much."

Siobhan glanced away from Matthew so he wouldn't see the tears gathering in her eyes. The last thing she wanted was for him to have the satisfaction of thinking he'd put them there. He gave them a final glare as he turned and slammed his way out of the hotel.

Before she knew what was happening, someone guided the two of them out of the room and into the quieter space of the reception. When they were away from prying eyes, Cassie eased her into a chair.

"What a super impression I've made." Siobhan shook her head, allowing Cassie to wipe away her tears.

"We're not going to judge you by his behavior," Cassie's dad assured her as she sniffled and shrugged. "As someone who has fucked up pretty spectacularly as a father, I do have a bit of advice to give," Mark continued, taking a seat across from her, "you can't leave things like this with him. Give him time to calm down and then try to discuss the important things as maturely and rationally as possible. You need to think about what you want, what both of you want and get that across in the simplest terms."

"He's right," Cassie said, "as much as it pains me to admit."

"I've ruined the wedding." Siobhan put her head in her hands.

"You have not." Cassie enveloped Siobhan in her arms and stroked her hair, encouraging Siobhan to cry herself out.

"I'll leave you two, but please don't stay out here all night. The party will be more than ready to welcome you back when you're ready."

"I did try to stop him, Cass. I'm so sorry. You should never have invited me."

Siobhan felt Cassie's hand underneath her chin, lifting her face so they made direct eye contact.

"I'm glad you're here with me. I'm also glad you didn't have to go through that alone."

"Your family are going to think I'm nothing but trouble." She sniffled and dabbed at her eyes. "I am nothing but trouble."

"Have you met me? You're a breeze compared to me; you'll get no arguments from anyone on that. Besides, don't you think we should be focusing on the positives?"

"There are some?" Siobhan was embarrassed and deflated. Right now it was difficult to see the wood for the trees.

"You have signed divorce papers in your hand and Matthew knows about us. You've been honest and have what you need to move forward."

"What you said to him." Siobhan wiped a tear from her eye, consciously trying to pull herself together. "I wasn't expecting that."

"I'm not really sure how that happened," Cassie said.

Siobhan noticed Cassie's hands were moving of their own free will in that awkward way they did when she was uncomfortable. "We should get back to the wedding before anyone misses us."

The party was in full throttle when they returned. Siobhan was glad her drama didn't seem to have affected the mood, and she was even more delighted that most people seemed to have forgotten what had happened. She and Cassie made it to the dance floor without falling victim to any unwanted comments.

"Are the two of you okay?" The question came from Eva, much to Siobhan's surprise.

"We're okay," Cassie said, brushing shoulders with Siobhan.

Siobhan reached for Eva's arm. "I'm so sorry. I had no idea this would happen. I should never have—"

"I think we're all just glad he's gone," Cassie's mum cut in, wrapping her arm around Siobhan, "and that you're back in here smiling."

Siobhan blinked back tears. When Bronagh spoke for Matthew, it always seemed controlling, but when Maria spoke for Eva, it just seemed affectionate.

Eva's friends dragged her off then, plying her with more champagne, as Danny shimmied over, swinging what looked like a pair of fluffy handcuffs over his head.

"I don't know about you," Cassie said, inviting Siobhan into her arms, "but I've had my fill of restraints."

"Does that mean we can talk about what you said to Matthew?"

"Oh that." Cassie playfully shrugged, having had time to pull herself together. "After this song, I thought we could sneak off to the lighthouse. It seems like the perfect place to talk. I doubt anybody will miss us now that it's getting messy."

Once again Siobhan allowed herself to get all wrapped up in Cassie, and Cassie seemed content to hold her for as long as she needed. Cassie stroked Siobhan's hair, the strain and tension dissipating with every touch. Finally, they were together honestly. All the months of affairs and duplicity were over, and she found herself taking pleasure in the rawness of this reality.

CHAPTER THIRTY-TWO

It didn't take Cassie long to lead the two of them back to their picturesque cove, taking Siobhan's hand as they made their way up the twisted staircase towards the gallery. This was the place where they had shared their first kiss, brief as it may have been. That felt like an age ago now, but Cassie still wondered how she had mastered the willpower to resist. She couldn't remember ever wanting to kiss anyone the way she wanted to kiss Siobhan, especially after she put the almost laughable no kissing rule into place. If anyone had told her where the two of them would be now, she would never have believed them, never deemed it possible. Yet here she was, real and present in the moment, everything Siobhan had wanted and she had needed without ever knowing it.

Ivory moonlight flooded in through the hollows of the gallery, bathing them in its luminous glow. The sky threatened gentle rain, but nothing was going to stop her now. Cassie felt Siobhan move closer and lower her head onto Cassie's shoulder.

"Are you okay?" Cassie shook her head. She already knew the answer. "Stupid question. I know you're not okay. It's been a shit show of epic proportions tonight, but we have somewhere to go now. Next steps to take together. I know it seems like we're still a long way off, but I think my dad was right. It's all about what you want now."

"I'm going to collect the kids first thing tomorrow. I know we had plans, but they'll only be worrying, especially if Matthew arrives home still angry," Siobhan said.

Cassie nodded her agreement, thinking back to a time when she may not have been as amenable and wondering why she had spent so much of her life being hard work for other people.

"I'm going to sit down with Matthew when he's had a few days to recover and talk things through. I need to make my expectations clear, let him know what I want. First and foremost, he's going to have to treat me with respect in front of the children, regardless of what he thinks of me. That's important."

"You know exactly where you're going and what you want. I know it seems difficult to believe now, but some good can come out of this shitty situation."

"I just wish he'd had the good sense to pick his timing better."

"I know it isn't going to make you feel any better, but I genuinely believe everyone is on your side. Nobody is going to judge you for his poor decision making." Cassie pressed a soft kiss to the top of Siobhan's head. She didn't have the heart to express her concern over what her family might think as Cassie found herself bang in the middle of yet another scene. Now was not the time for that. "I think you handled things in the best way possible. You were pretty incredible to watch, dignified and truthful even when it wasn't easy to be so."

"I just hope your family will forgive me, especially Eva."

"She will, I promise."

A comfortable silence fell between them and for once, Cassie felt no urgent need to fill it. A lot had happened in a short space of time that evening, none of it easy. Siobhan needed some time to breathe, to relax and take everything in. It amazed Cassie how she knew Siobhan well enough to recognize this, having fully invested in their emotional connection. It felt good to be this connected and Cassie allowed herself some time to really feel it. This was a big moment for her too. She concentrated on the rhythm of their heartbeats, settling as one as she looked out over another amazing starlit sky.

Siobhan was the first to break the silence. "They're beautiful aren't they, Cass?"

"They really are," Cassie said. "Just like you."

Siobhan took Cassie's face in her hands, so that their foreheads were resting together. "Cass...I..."

"Don't." Cassie placed her finger over Siobhan's lips, knowing she owed Siobhan this moment. "Let me say it." She watched as Siobhan's lips began to tremble, her entire body following suit. "You're shaking."

"It's nothing."

"It's something." Cassie took the time to gather Siobhan up in her arms, amazed how their bodies instinctively molded together. "But you don't have to worry."

Convinced she had conquered the trembling, Cassie pulled back to ensure she was looking directly at Siobhan. She had to work harder than usual to gain eye contact, even as Siobhan did her best to avoid it, and she finally settled on cupping her face so that she couldn't look away. Despite her obvious nerves, the warmth radiating from Siobhan's eyes was like nothing she had ever known.

"Siobhan, I'm totally in love with you." Cassie paused, watching emotion ripple through Siobhan like the waves below creeping steadily towards the moonlit shore. "I've tried everything in my power not to fall in love with you, but fuck, it's just not possible."

Cassie waited, her eyes shutting momentarily, not sure what she expected to happen next.

Siobhan let out an audible sigh, which to Cassie sounded like it had been contained forever.

Still, she waited.

Until she was unable to wait any longer.

"Shiv, are you okay?"

"I'm just taking a moment to savor those words. You've no idea how long I've waited to hear them from you, and how I've been worrying that you might not feel the same."

"The same?" The corners of Cassie's mouth tugged upwards as realization dawned.

Her greatest fear, that of giving her heart away to someone who would never love her, was something she could leave firmly in the past. The warmth that went with this recognition wrapped itself around her.

"The exact same. I've held my tongue for so long because I wasn't sure how you'd react. I think I always knew you had to get to a place where you were ready to say it first. I just assumed you'd let me know before you casually announced it to the world." Siobhan laughed. "*That* was entirely unexpected, but it definitely got my attention."

"I know I should have told you before, but you know me, hopeless with words." Cassie frowned. "That doesn't mean I don't feel things, I just can't express them."

"Or you're scared to."

"I suppose it's pointless to deny it." Cassie held her hands up in defeat. "You were never just a casual affair to me. You must know that?"

"You worked your hardest to make me feel like I was. There were times you even had me convinced. But then I'd catch you looking at me, especially when you thought I wasn't paying attention, and it would send my head reeling again. You're a difficult woman to read, Cass, but that's just one of the many reasons I love you."

Hearing Siobhan speak so openly about her feelings after all this time and knowing she could do the same, felt liberating. Cassie took a moment to look up into the soft rain, before she ran her hand through her wet hair. The stars hung above them as if they were threaded on invisible strings, illuminating the two of them underneath the night sky. Siobhan's beauty was simply ineffable right now, which did nothing to quench Cassie's heated desire, so she focused in on another story about the stars, something that had always connected them.

"You see just there?" Cassie pointed out a constellation that she knew would be vaguely familiar to Siobhan. "That's Cetus the sea beast, just there under our friend Queen Cassiopeia. Unsurprisingly, she was responsible for him too, irritating the sea nymphs until they couldn't listen to her conceit anymore. They begged Poseidon to stop her boasting, so he sent Cetus to destroy the villages of her kingdom as a punishment."

"Another of your unique stories. I believe I first started falling in love with you around the time you introduced me to Queen Cassiopeia."

"I've always been in love with you."

With these words, Cassie finally realized the truth. It had always been Siobhan; she'd just been far too stubborn to admit it. In her whole life nobody had come close to making her feel the way Siobhan did: wanted, needed, loved.

Cassie's heart swelled in her chest as she leaned forward to kiss the droplets of rain from Siobhan's lips. As always, she was astonished by the unspoken dialogue that passed between them in just one kiss. How could she have held off kissing Siobhan for so long, when it was all she wanted to do forever? Forever: a word that had once scared her with its finality, now felt like it could never be long enough.

CHAPTER THIRTY-THREE

Cassie basked in the sunlight flooding in from the delicate glass dome above her. Taking a sip of freshly squeezed orange juice, she braced herself for the aftermath of Siobhan's disastrous introduction to her parents. Last night she had done well to convince Siobhan things were going to be just fine, but in truth, she felt nervy. She hadn't been reunited with her family long and yet here they were, entangled in another drama, with Cassie as the headliner. They *seemed* understanding, sympathetic even, but what if they'd been putting on an act for Siobhan's benefit? And Eva's? What if they were planning a confrontation—

"Good morning!" her dad said, taking the seat next to her, her mum sitting down opposite. "How are you?"

"I'm okay," Cassie said, keeping her guard up.

"No Siobhan?" Her mum reached for her hand. She didn't pull away.

"Not today." Cassie squinted, rubbing the bridge of her nose. "She drove home early to be with the kids."

"Is she all right?"

Cassie sighed deeply, reflecting on Siobhan's embarrassment. "Of course not."

"She will be." They remained silent as her dad poured three cups of coffee. "I was extremely proud of you last night. You handled yourself admirably."

"Thank you. It wasn't necessary though, was it? He didn't need to cause such a commotion. I can't believe how he behaved."

"He was irrational," her mum said, before slowly adding, "and he was hurt."

"Please don't tell me we're having a vote of sympathy for him this morning." Cassie folded her arms.

"I think we can all make assumptions about what sort of man he is." Her dad took a sip of his coffee, his expression blank, which Cassie knew meant he was trying to keep a range of things hidden from her as he thought. "I think what your mother is hinting at is whichever way you look at it, he's the scorned husband. However dysfunctional they were as a family, he was part of something, and now, quite simply, he isn't. He's lost his wife and kids to you."

"I hope you appreciate the importance of the decisions you and Siobhan have made," her mum put in. "Where children are involved, you can't and won't come first."

"You think I don't know that?"

"I think you do know that. I just think perhaps you haven't thought this all the way through. I'm not questioning your feelings for Siobhan. I'm—"

"Questioning my commitment?"

"Parenting isn't easy." Her dad blew out his cheeks. "I can attest to that. I can't imagine co-parenting being a walk in the park."

"Look, I know I deserve this grilling. Only a few weeks ago I was despairing at your house about losing Siobhan. Add to that the fact I've never managed to master a relationship and I get where you're coming from."

Her mum nodded. "It's important you understand the gravity of the decisions you make."

"I want to be involved in their lives. I'm under no illusion that Matthew's going to make it easy, but it's what I want. It's what we both want." As the statement left Cassie's mouth, she realized it was something they had never really discussed. Car rides, drum lessons, and seaside trips didn't equate to co-parenting.

"As long as you understand the commitment you're making and how they'll fit into your lifestyle." Her mum still looked serious.

"Clearly things are going to be different," Cassie said. "Matthew's outburst was unexpected, but I knew she'd filed for divorce. We haven't had a chance to discuss the future. Things have moved quicker than we anticipated. In some ways he's forced our hand, but I'm resolute in what I want: Shiv and the kids. I can't tell you what that looks like because I don't know. What I do know is that I love her. Christ, I never thought I'd hear myself saying that."

"Despite the fact we told you so," her dad said before he turned to her mum in what Cassie knew to be an attempt to lighten the mood. "You know, we should really consider special nicknames for one another. How about Marykins for you?" he said, and Cassie felt a warm glow rise to her cheeks. She wasn't used to being teased on such sentimental matters.

"Only if you agree to Marcos." Her mum chuckled. Addressing Cassie, she said, "You'll work it out together, I'm absolutely convinced of that. Plus, I get grandkids out of the deal. Nobody would ever have predicted we'd be getting them from you before we got them from Eva."

"Am I the new favorite?" Cassie clutched at her chest, holding still in mock expectation.

"It depends on what the kids decide to call me. Grandad sounds old. Now, Grandpops—I could get on board with that." Her dad stretched his arms out in front of him and gave a deep, gratified sigh.

"I can imagine you and Siobhan being a pretty good team," her mum said. "How was it that Helena described the two of you? 'Preposterously compatible'?"

"And she was ludicrously right." Eva took the seat next to their mother, holding an arm up to block the light.

Cassie pushed her sunglasses across the table. "These might help."

"Thanks." Eva settled them on her nose, wincing. "I've witnessed her in action with Dylan and Neave too. It's quite remarkable what a reasonable human being Cassie can be given the right company."

"Are you all set for your honeymoon?" her mum asked.

"Danny's just nipped home because he forgot our passports. I can't complain too much—he did turn up on time with the rings yesterday. Anyway, I thought I'd join you for a hangover cure before we leave."

"We were just going to take a stroll before breakfast." Her mum nodded towards her dad.

"We were?"

Her mum hoisted him out of his chair. "We are."

"Oh, I get it. We're going to bugger off so the two of them can have a sisterly heart-to-heart."

As Cassie watched them scuttle off, she shook her head with fondness. "I think we've been set up." Cassie waved politely at the waiter. "Please can we have some very black coffee?"

"Yes, please," Eva said. "Turns out, one too many Screaming Orgasms does not lead to one too many screaming orgasms."

Cassie grinned, but she tried to control her smirk. "Do they blot out hideous incidents involving your sorrier than sorry sister?"

"You owe me big style, Cassie. I shall accept weekly deliveries of apology flowers and the occasional invite to dinner."

"I'm not sure I know how to keep two women happy at once, but I'll try." Cassie poured Eva a cup of steaming coffee. "I don't think anyone could've predicted what happened last night," she said, shaking a sugar packet into her sister's cup. "But I truly am sorry. We both are."

Eva steepled her hands, resting her fingers on her chin. "Yesterday wasn't your fault, but it was your making, you and Siobhan. If you truly want my forgiveness, what I want to hear now is that this really is the start of something meaningful, that the debacle last night was worth it. You don't let her go again."

Cassie felt her eyes welling up, and she wished she hadn't shared her sunglasses so freely. Her sister's selflessness never ceased to amaze her.

"I won't," Cassie replied, never having meant anything more.

"Now don't get all teary-eyed on me this morning. I can't cope with this new range of emotions you seem to have picked up."

"I'm not teary-eyed." Cassie brushed a tear from her eye.

"You can tell Siobhan there's a serious amount of groveling required before I agree to any babysitting." Eva winked.

"I know I haven't always appreciated Mum, but it will matter to Siobhan more than anything what she thinks, having lost her own mum."

"I don't think you have anything to worry about." Eva poured herself another coffee, having downed the first cup. "Mum's seriously impressed. She thinks Siobhan has integrity in abundance, and that she's fiercely in love with you. Truly one of a kind."

"She said that?"

"I did indeed." Her mum appeared from the archway she had apparently stashed herself behind. "To Eva," she clarified, "who wasn't supposed to tell you." She folded her arms and tapped her foot, smiling. "Gob Almighty."

"So you *do* approve." Cassie could barely contain her grin.

"How could she not, when you two were locking lips on the dance floor? For what seemed like an unnecessary amount of time, may I add." Eva dropped her head on to her folded arms and looked up at Cassie. "I'm glad you finally told her how your feel."

Cassie turned to face her dad. "I'm truly grateful for the way you stuck up for me last night."

"I know I haven't done my job properly as your dad, but I fully intend to make up for it now."

Cassie found herself wrapped in her dad's tight embrace. His arms were strong and protective, exactly like she remembered as a child.

"Eva's right," her dad said. "It's a good thing that you've overcome your demons to open up with Siobhan. You've come a long way and I feel incredibly proud of you. We love you, Cass."

"I love you too," Cassie blurted out, delighted to discover she really meant it.

❖

"Shiv?" Cassie pushed the front door open, knocking no longer required.

Siobhan seized her T-shirt, pulling her inside. Lips met her mouth, greeting her like they had been away too long, Cassie feeling momentarily senseless with uncontrolled need. Before the kiss could escalate, Siobhan pushed Cassie back. "Neave's snoring away, but it's taken me all night to get Dylan off to sleep. He'll go off like a firework if he realizes you're here. Can you do quiet?"

"I can learn. How are the kids?" That this was her first concern was a true indicator of how far she had grown as a person.

"Extremely apologetic. Neave was devastated that she might have gotten us into trouble. I think she was awake most of the night worrying about it."

Cassie rubbed Siobhan's back, wanting for all the world to go upstairs and give Neave a hug too. "I can't believe the pressure she's been put under, especially to feel that way. And Dylan?"

"He's checked in with me a few times, but he doesn't know what went on. I think he surmises what happened, but his main concern, and what he's nagged me relentlessly about, is seeing you again." Siobhan blew out an exaggerated breath. "I'm slightly worried that I'm going to be last in line for your attention."

"You could always make an appointment," Cassie kidded, kicking her trainers off and relaxing into the sofa, arms stretched overhead.

"I'll call Julie," Siobhan said, settling in beside her. "I'll have her schedule an appointment with Matthew too while she's at it."

"He's agreed to sit down and talk things through already?"

"Yes, provided his mother can accompany him. I dread to think how that conversation is going to go. Divorce is already a step too far in her Catholic rulebook, but a lesbian for an ex-wife? I don't think lead balloon quite covers it."

"It doesn't sound so bad to me..." Cassie trailed off, biting her bottom lip.

Siobhan pulled the hood from her hoodie over her head, sheepish. "I'm not remarrying for a long time."

"That's good to know. Dressing me for such an event would be like a thorn in your perfect backside, irritating and impossible to shift." Cassie wasn't ready for that step, either. But then, she hadn't been ready for a relationship not that long ago. In the future anything could happen, she was no longer closed off to the possibilities.

"I'd be more than happy for you to dress yourself, based on last night's choice."

"Is that so?" Cassie reached for Siobhan's hood and gently tugged it down. "How are you feeling?"

"Have you eaten?"

"Sorry, did what I just said not come out of my mouth? Or are you avoiding the question?"

"I was going to offer to stick a pizza in the oven first. Partly because I haven't eaten since yesterday, but mainly to avoid having to think about your mum and how she feels about me now."

"Please don't worry about that. Besides, Eva might have let it slip that Mum thinks you're one of a kind, which I happen to agree with."

Siobhan breathed a heavy sigh of relief, as if she were expelling all the fears that had been racing through her mind since the Matthew spectacle. "She's not pissed off?"

"Apparently, our family doesn't do pissed off anymore. Forget last night's debacle. Both my parents think you're great. And me? Well, I think you're funny, kind, intelligent, gorgeous." Cassie paused, moving her hands up to Siobhan's face and traced a finger down the side of her face. "Unbelievable in bed. But they don't need to know that."

For the first time that night, Siobhan cracked a genuine smile. Cassie felt privileged to have put it there.

"So essentially, what you're saying is: with the exception of my marriage and our illicit affair, I'm a pretty good catch."

Feeling a sudden giddiness at everything they had to look forward to, Cassie fixed Siobhan with a smile and replied, "Essentially...yes!"

Siobhan pulled Cassie in for a slow, sensual kiss, instantly intensifying the mood between them.

"I still wish I'd made a better first impression. Glinda's introduction floating down in a bubble in Oz has nothing on me."

"We should organize another theater date. I feel in need of some new references."

"*Rent* is opening in London next month. I'd love to whisk you away for another night full of innuendo at a musical."

Cassie jumped off the sofa and launched herself onto the coffee table. "Are you going to take me?" she asked, in what she hoped was an inoffensive imitation of Idina. "Or leave me?" she said, swinging her backside as provocatively as possible.

"Leaving you is *so* not an option," Siobhan vowed, reaching out to pull Cassie down on top of her. Displaying a wide grin, she elaborated, "In fact I'm going to take you to bed and leave you begging for more. But first..."

"Pizza!" they both exclaimed at the same time.

There was *nothing* preposterous about their compatibility.

CHAPTER THIRTY-FOUR

How could you do this to him?"
From across Bronagh's kitchen table, Siobhan regarded her soon to be ex-mother-in-law with a combination of sympathy and apathy. Bronagh's own eyes reflected only animosity. Determined to convey as much confidence as she could, Siobhan urged her shoulders back and her head up. "I didn't come here for an argument. I came to talk about the kids. Where is Matthew?"

Bronagh looked like a lion ready to pounce on hopeless hyenas. "He's here and he's heartbroken."

Matthew blustered into the room. "I knew the moment I set eyes on that woman that she was no good for you. She's brash and impetuous. She was downright rude to me at Dylan's party."

"I understand you're angry, both of you. You have every right to be, and nothing I can say is going to change that. But Cassie and I fell in love."

"Oh, spare me the proclamations—"

"No! You need to understand something. I went all around the bloody houses trying not to act upon my feelings, but sometimes what two people feel is just too strong. Matthew and I never had that."

"*You* never tried," Bronagh insisted.

"You think Matthew did?" Siobhan wanted to shake Bronagh, wake her from the distorted reality she was living in and let her know what her son was really like.

"I think," Bronagh said, "you were sleeping around behind his back when you should have been looking after the children."

Siobhan steadied herself, taking a calming breath and imagining herself back on a rowboat, floating gently up and down on the waves. "People get divorced all the time."

"Not in the Catholic church." There it was, Bronagh's real issue with the whole situation: the fact she was going to have to tell her church friends and, worst of all, her priest, that her son was getting divorced—from a lesbian, no less. "You made a lifetime commitment."

"I did." Siobhan sighed. "But I didn't want to, and neither did Matthew, not really."

"What are you saying?" Bronagh demanded, and Siobhan realized this was something Matthew had never told her.

"I was pregnant. That's why we got married. It wasn't some fairy-tale romance with a whirlwind wedding. I was pregnant and told by your son that we needed to act quickly."

"You're lying." Bronagh's eyes were wide.

"Actually," Matthew murmured, hunkering down in his chair beside Bronagh, "she's not."

"You got her pregnant out of wedlock?" Bronagh began pacing the kitchen. "What if people had found out? What would they have thought of me?"

"You can appreciate my dilemma then," Siobhan said softly, and Bronagh stopped in her tracks. Siobhan considered clarifying that she was speaking about her own mum, but decided that in this instance, it wouldn't do any harm to let Bronagh believe what she wanted.

"It's irrelevant now," Matthew said, his arms crossed.

"Hardly." Siobhan shook her head, amazed that he could still be oblivious to the facts. "It goes a long way to explain why we've ended up here."

"Then what I don't understand is," Bronagh said, startling Siobhan with the gentleness in her voice, "if you were a…"

Siobhan held her breath, wondering what word someone with such blinkered views would use to describe her.

"…woman with no interest in men, why did you go out with Matthew in the first place?"

"I was young and foolish. I didn't know any better, but I was *always* honest with Matthew. Even way back at the start, he knew that I was interested in women. He's always known, but—"

"What?" Bronagh's high frequency could have shattered the glass of the Louvre Pyramid. "Matthew, is she speaking the truth? Did you know that?"

Matthew squirmed, sliding farther down in his chair. "I thought it would pass."

"These things never pass!" Bronagh erupted, and Siobhan almost accused her of being an ally. "You should have told me this all those years ago. I would *never* have let you marry her. And now there are not one, but two children involved in this entanglement who don't seem too fond of you either. Dylan! Neave! Come in here right now!"

Although Siobhan hadn't wanted them to be involved in this conversation, she knew it was the only way Bronagh would accept the truth. They were young, but their honesty could be brutal, which was exactly what Matthew and his mother needed right now.

The children came running in. Dylan skidded to a halt by the table and sat next to Siobhan and Neave jumped up onto her knee.

Bronagh cut right to the chase. "You both enjoy spending time with your father, don't you?" she asked, and Siobhan could tell from her tone that the children were expected to answer in the affirmative.

Dylan's brow furrowed. Neave's nose creased. They both looked to Siobhan, as if seeking permission to speak their minds. She granted it with a simple nod.

"Well?" Bronagh prompted them. "Do you enjoy spending time with your father?"

"No," the children chorused.

Matthew's face dropped like Icarus falling from the sky.

"Dad doesn't like us," Dylan said.

Siobhan was painfully aware of how harsh this was, and the fact Dylan didn't bat an eyelid when saying it saddened her. He had come to accept this as the truth, and it no longer bothered him.

"But you know who *does* like us?" Neave added. "Cassie! And she likes Mum, which is good, because Dad definitely doesn't."

"Oh, Matthew." Bronagh shook her head, teeth gritted. "Your children speak more highly of a woman they hardly know than they do of you." She turned back to the children. "There must be *something* you like about your father."

Neave shrugged. "I like that he's not around *that* much."

Dylan blinked. "I've got nothing."

"You're both being ridiculous!" Matthew's expression was far more hurt than angry.

"Are they?" Siobhan asked. "Or are they being painfully honest and it hurts you to hear it because deep down you know they're right?"

Matthew didn't answer, choosing instead to focus on his fingernails. That was answer enough.

"How could you do this to them?" Bronagh's face resembled a withered dishcloth, and Siobhan was delighted to discover the comment was directed not at her, but at Matthew. "I knew you weren't always the *best* father, or even the best husband, but—"

"You told me I was a good father."

"I have to say those things. I'm your mother. But everyone else seems to think otherwise, and I'm inclined to believe them."

"I only got married—and stayed married—because you made me feel like I had to!" Matthew's defense was weak.

"Don't you dare put this on me! It's on *you* that your marriage failed and that your children are now going to grow up in a home with lesbians for parents! I can only imagine how much more damage *that's* going to cause."

"It hasn't damaged me yet," Dylan said, frowning. "I already liked girls way before I knew Mum did."

"What if Neave picks it up?" Bronagh said, her chin raised.

"Mum and I are way different."

"Don't worry." Dylan chuckled, forever the wind-up merchant. "There's still time."

Siobhan fought the urge to high five her children. Instead she said, in favor of staving off a mutiny, "We can sit here and toss the blame around all day, but Dylan and Neave have expressed how they feel. They want to stay with me. I hope you can accept that, both of you. Like it or not, Bronagh, I'm always going to be the mother of your grandchildren."

Bronagh glowered at Matthew. "You need to change your ways, and quick. I'll not have it said that two gay women can bring up my grandchildren better than their incompetent father." With that, Bronagh stormed out of the room.

"Mam!" Matthew looked as though he couldn't decide which would be the safer option: to go after his mother, or to not go after his mother. Sighing, he said, "Dylan, Neave, please go out and play in the garden. I'd like to speak with your mother."

"Okay, but…we get to live with Mum, right?" Dylan asked, and Siobhan could tell from his tone that Matthew was expected to answer in the affirmative.

Neave crossed her arms, swung her foot under the table, her trainer squeaking against the floor.

Matthew was totally defeated, his whole demeanor deflating. "Yes. You get to live with Mum."

At this, both Neave and Dylan cheered, then proceeded to make a grand exit, Neave performing a stylish cartwheel, begging Dylan to have a go too. Surprisingly, he did, badly.

Siobhan couldn't bring herself to smile. It would be petty and childish, and she had no desire to rub it in Matthew's face.

"Siobhan, you must know I care for them."

"I'm afraid I don't know that, and they don't either."

Matthew was silent for a moment, dragging his thumb across the tabletop. "Do they really hate me?"

"They don't hate you; they dislike how you treat them. And just because the children will live with me doesn't mean you can't rebuild your relationships with them. If you want them to change their opinion of you, you have to change your opinion of them."

Matthew gave a subtle nod, which was progress as far as Siobhan was concerned.

"I'd like that," he said, then reiterated, "*I'd* like that. Not just Mam." He took a deep breath. "Do *you* really hate me?"

"I don't hate you. I regret putting up with you so long, but I only want to move forward now. You can make it incredibly difficult for everyone, yourself included, or you can do right by your kids." Satisfied she had said everything she needed to say, Siobhan pushed her chair back and rose to her feet. "I can't make that choice for you."

❖

"Look at that photo!" Cassie said, angling her phone towards Siobhan when she paused at a red light. "It was all I could do to keep Helena from coming over to throw a party. Fortunately, I talked her down to a double date."

In truth, Helena's over-exuberance at their relationship finally taking flight had kept her amused and distracted while Siobhan tackled Matthew. She studied Siobhan's face as she took the photo in. In it, Helena and Riley wore bright smiles and even brighter cone hats. Helena was puffing a party blower in Riley's face. Siobhan's smile unfurled like one. "Look how happy they are for us."

"I know two little people who are over the moon too!" Cassie said.

"So over the moon they couldn't wait to get off to their sleepovers, leaving us a free night to celebrate. They're so considerate."

Cassie shifted in her seat as Siobhan shifted into first gear. "You have a plan going forward?" She didn't want to apply extra pressure, but she was keen to know what had been decided in conversation with Matthew.

"He's going to have them Wednesday nights and every other weekend. I'm not sure Dylan's going to go for that, but I have to give Matthew the opportunity to change."

"As someone who's had father issues of her own, I get what you're trying to do and I respect you for it." Cassie was surprised to find there was no resentment in her voice, all she felt was pride and admiration towards Siobhan. "He's never going to be top of my Christmas card list," she admitted, "but you're right. I only hope he doesn't let them down. I mean nobody expected a musical with a purple puppet called Mrs. Thistletwat to be popular, so I guess anything really *is* possible."

"I still can't believe you thought we could take the kids to see *Avenue Q*. You have a lot to learn." Siobhan chuckled. "Do you think you can live with those arrangements for now?"

Cassie shrugged. "Wednesdays were always ours anyway." She slid her hand onto Siobhan's thigh and began stroking it.

Beside her, Siobhan's arms stiffened against the steering wheel.

"What's wrong?" Cassie was so tuned in to Siobhan's emotions these days it was exhilarating that she could read them before they were even out in the world.

Siobhan kept her eyes on the road, her leg jittery in Cassie's grasp.

"Look, Shiv, I get why you're nervous, worried even, but please don't be. We'll make it work. I don't have any expectations of you or the kids, unless you count wildly racing quad bikes or beating the drums loudly and out of time."

Siobhan pulled into a parking space, and the moment she turned the engine off, she reached for Cassie's hand and laced their fingers together.

"A lot's happened over the last few days. Sometimes it takes a while to sink in that we're actually here, together. You've changed so much and I'm not the same woman I was when I walked into your office. It's a lot to take in."

Savoring the heat of Siobhan's palm against her own, Cassie drifted closer, arching her eyebrow ever so slightly when Siobhan traced her fingertip down her neck. Warmth pooled in her stomach and Cassie closed her eyes as sultry lips ran across her shoulder, up her neck, then across her jaw towards her ear.

"Do you keep expecting to come to your senses?"

"Hardly."

Their eyes locked, their lips following suit, Siobhan claiming Cassie's mouth time and time again as Cassie was hit with the irrepressible feeling that everything in her life was much better now Siobhan was beside her.

But when Siobhan's hand wedged between her thighs, Cassie grasped her wrist. "We should get inside."

"I'm trying." Siobhan flexed her fingers against the seam of Cassie's jeans.

"The bar." Cassie laughed as she swung open the car door. "We should get inside the bar. Our friends are waiting. You don't want them to come looking for us, do you?"

"No," Siobhan agreed, stepping out of the car, "although I wouldn't mind *you* coming before they find us."

Cassie laughed again, opening Siobhan's car door and offering her hand. "Easy, tiger! We have all night for that."

No sooner had Cassie opened the door to the bar for Siobhan than party poppers went off with a bang over their heads, the radiant streamers bursting out like shooting stars. Cheering and whooping ensued from the unruly crowd of two.

Helena pounced, pulling Cassie into a bear hug. "Thanks for keeping us waiting! I can't think what you were up to!"

"Thanks for…" Cassie's head swiveled around, "inviting Julie? Please tell me that isn't her over there." She groaned, having spotted their secretary with a woman who was the absolute double of herself, making far too many accidental touches to not be flirting shamelessly.

Helena held up her hands. "I didn't invite her, but now you know she's here, you should at least say hello. She *has* been in your corner in an unorthodox sort of way."

"And on my nerves." Cassie rolled her eyes. "She's an irritant. Back me up, Shiv."

"I thought that description was reserved specifically for me." Helena pouted.

Cassie grinned and squeezed her best friend's shoulder. "You're *the* irritant. It's different."

"Nobody is taking top spot, from me," Helena said. "Anyway, she seems to be entertaining herself. How did you two come to have such a sexy secretary?"

"You have a girlfriend," Cassie reminded her.

"So do you!" Helena whooped before squeezing her waist.

Cassie squirmed into a range of unnatural positions, trying to escape Helena's wild enthusiasm.

"I've already agreed that should the opportunity arise I'd be willing to threesome in this particular case," Riley said.

"Yes, we decided we'd be prepared to allow Julie into our love bubble for a short while." Helena batted her eyes at Riley, who gave her a thumbs-up and a wink.

"Thank fuck for that! For a dreadful moment I thought you were referring to us!"

"Hey, my favorite love bugs have come in!" Julie waved wildly at Cassie and Siobhan, clearly inebriated.

Try as she might, Cassie couldn't see anything but genuine happiness and a good deal of alcohol consumption in their secretary's face. Their supposedly Sapphic secretary. "Did we know you were gay?" Cassie asked.

"It would appear you did not." Julie tilted her drink at them. "Don't beat yourself up over it. Not everyone can be as nosy as I am." She brushed shoulders with Siobhan. "I know what you're thinking," she said, looking pointedly at Cassie. "And no, I never had a thing for you, nor Siobhan come to think of it, sorry to disappoint." Julie seized the hand of the woman who was a carbon copy of herself, and shimmied away.

Cassie blinked. "Did she just walk out on us?"

"No, I'm pretty sure she just *came* out to us."

"God, you two look good together," Helena said in a voice that could wake the dead. "I mean, Riley and I look exquisite, but at least you've got something to work with." She squeezed into the booth and sat down opposite Siobhan, pulling Riley with her.

"Is this relentless teasing going to last much longer?" Cassie asked. "If so, I've got my sumo suit in my handbag."

"Just a short while longer, hang in there," Helena assured her. "We don't have all night, you know. We have to get home to Alexa."

Siobhan's eyes widened. "You have a daughter?"

"I have a virtual assistant," Helena said.

"Yeah, and we spent all last night trying to give Alexa an Irish accent," Riley shared, "but Alexa—or Roisin, as we now call her—was having none of it."

"We've decided to try again tonight. If it's another epic fail, we're going to compromise by having leprechauns do the sat nav instead!"

"I'd volunteer my voice, but I often feel like I've lost a lot of my accent to London, which is a shame because Cassie loves it. You should have seen her mooning when we were in Ireland."

"Your accent *is* perfect," Riley said with a big grin.

"Still, I'll leave it to the leprechauns. They'll be slaying it."

Cassie almost choked on her wine, spitting it back into the glass, the heat in the bar turned up a notch or two. "Do you want to record my sat nav?"

"Certainly." Siobhan cleared her throat. "Turn left at the traffic light. No, your other left," she directed, accentuating her accent in a way that sent arousal rippling through Cassie. "Any other instructions you might need a hand with?"

"Uh-oh. We'd better get out of here before it gets any hotter in here," Helena said. "Cassie Townsend, you live a charmed life to have the fuck of the Irish. Enjoy!"

And that's exactly what Cassie planned to do.

Looking back, it was hard to pinpoint exactly when she had fallen for Siobhan, but studying her, she couldn't imagine ever wanting anything else. Siobhan had expanded her world in ways she never knew were possible, in ways she had intended to fight, but fighting such strong feelings would have been impossible. She saw that clearly now.

Children had never been in her plans, yet she adored Dylan and Neave. Finding herself a girlfriend had never been on the cards, yet here she was with Siobhan at her side, allowing her to feel content in a way she never thought she could be. Opening herself up to change, to Siobhan, hadn't been easy but as she gazed with affection at her now, she knew she would never love anyone so completely. She would do it all again in a heartbeat for Siobhan.

CHAPTER THIRTY-FIVE

"I think you may have overdone it slightly." Siobhan doubled up, taking a fork from Cassie and holding up a cremated chunk of meat. "Anyone want a burger?"

"That looks like an ancient cow pat," Dylan said, wrinkling his nose. "You're the best on the road, Cassie, but you're bottom of the list when it comes to cooking."

"Hey, my sausages haven't poisoned you yet."

Siobhan gazed down at the bin bag, where the children had carefully disposed of their sausages, while Cassie continued to incinerate burgers. Amused, she looked on at Dylan, who was inspecting the salad with interest. When he glanced up at Cassie, he burst out laughing. Neave and Siobhan promptly joined in.

"What's so funny?" Cassie raised an eyebrow towards her disheveled hair. Below it, her eyes sparkled and her skin glowed pink with the heat from the grill.

"Your face," Siobhan responded, her heart racing a little faster. "If it were any hotter, we could toast marshmallows on your forehead."

"They'd taste better than these burgers!" Dylan said, poking at the meat.

"That's it, I'm downing tools." Cassie whipped off her apron in melodramatic style and threw herself into the sun lounger next to Siobhan.

"I love you," Siobhan said before subtly squeezing her hand.

Neave ran up to Cassie and launched herself on her. "Please can we have another game of badminton?"

"Only if I win!" Cassie jumped up and joined her.

As Siobhan watched Cassie run around the garden, expending copious amounts of energy, she considered how lucky she and the children were to have Cassie. This was what she had longed for her whole life: a lively, joyful family home.

Life was brilliant. Finally, she had a future to look forward to. Matthew was armed with the truth, the divorce papers had been signed, sealed, and delivered to her lawyers, and Bronagh seemed to have him toeing the line. There were lots of difficult decisions on the way, but right now, every time she met Cassie's eyes, she experienced pure contentment.

And now that Cassie was entirely hers, she also experienced pure desire. It could be quite maddening at times. If she weren't thinking about work or the children, she was busy picturing Cassie naked, yearning, ever-present. At the mere thought of what she was planning do to Cassie later that night, she was moist.

A second later, she was soaking wet...literally.

"Watch out! You're under attack!"

Dylan came racing through the patio doors with a huge water gun, squirting everyone in equal measure.

Chaos ensued as they all charged around, full of energy and life—as well as energetic threats against Dylan's life, courtesy of Neave. Cassie filled the watering can from the outside tap, made a beeline for Siobhan, then changed course and drenched Dylan instead. Screams of delight and happy laughter filled the air.

"Yeah! Soak him!" Neave cheered.

Siobhan hid behind one of the chairs, only to have Cassie instantly invade her hiding place and her personal space. Cassie's lips were warm and inviting and Siobhan was instantly consumed by the kiss, desperate to begin fumbling with Cassie's clothes, but she somehow summoned her strength and pulled away. The children would only be occupied for so long.

"I need so much more than a kiss," she said, feeling like a crescendo on mute. "When the kids are dried off, I'll make them a hot chocolate and get them to bed."

"We may have to delay our sex fest." Cassie glanced away. "I accidentally promised to read them a bedtime story in my best animated voice...which I could use to talk dirty to you with later."

Siobhan clutched her stomach, giggling at the ridiculous voice Cassie had put on: a cross between Marge Simpson on helium and a honking duck. She loved her all the more for it.

"I was actually hoping you might help out with that," Cassie said, burying her face in Siobhan's neck, kissing her up and down. "The bedtime story," she clarified. "And the dirty talk," she clarified further.

"In what way?" Siobhan asked, wiping her eyes.

"I haven't a clue where to start with bedtime stories."

"I think now's a great time to tell them ours," Siobhan suggested. "But let's leave out the juicy bits."

"We can reenact those when *we're* in bed!"

Half an hour later, Shivering Shelley and Cassandra Tantrum had been forced together on an important mission, ridden jet skis across the ocean, eaten a range of exotic sandwiches, almost drowned in an old rowing boat, and found their way home from an abandoned lighthouse.

Siobhan was perched on the end of Dylan's bed, as engrossed as everyone else in the pirate tale Cassie had whipped up, as Cassie delivered her closing line.

"So it was that Cassandra Tantrum and Shivering Shelley rode off into the sunset on a towering giraffe with a tongue longer than the River Nile."

Both children sat up, giving Cassie a well-earned round of applause.

"That was the best story I've ever heard," Dylan said. "You'd make a great pirate."

"Me?" Cassie feigned puzzlement.

"You are Cassandra Tantrum, Queen of the Seven Seas!" Dylan laughed, holding his sides. "You missed one important part though," Dylan said, shaking his head, as if feeling put out at having to point it out.

"I did?"

"Yeah! The bit where I told Mum you were in love with her—"

"And I told her to apologize." Neave thrust her chest out. "You missed out the romance."

"I don't think we need to go into *any* of that right now," Siobhan intervened, noticing how embarrassed Cassie looked.

"You will take us to school on Monday, won't you, Cassie?"

"Of course."

He high fived her. "What about the other days?"

"The other days?" Cassie gasped in mock horror. "They do know about my morning struggles, right?"

"We know you drool worse than Beethoven the St. Bernard when you're sleeping!" Dylan laughed as he snuggled down under his duvet.

"Or like a cow munching its way through a field of grass!" Neave danced about on Dylan's bed, clearly delighted with her form.

"Or like a hungry hippopotamus lounging in a mud bath, waiting for snack time!" Dylan added, and so it continued, until they were all out of comparisons and energy and were ready to begin drooling like Cassie Townsend with ice cream splodged on her nose at the seaside.

❖

"You need to come here," Cassie said, pulling Siobhan into a tight embrace. Siobhan immediately reached for her backside, and she longed to melt into the touch.

"I'm not quite sure why you set us up as pirates. You know their adventures never end."

"That *was* a bloody long story," Cassie said. "I'm all yours now." She squeezed Siobhan's arse. "Although I can't guarantee I'll be fully functioning."

"You'd better be," Siobhan said, pulling Cassie down onto the sofa with her so they landed closely entwined.

"I'm knackered." Cassie chuckled, shutting her eyes. "Kids are exhausting!"

"Then we won't have any more," Siobhan said. "Unless *you* want more?"

Cassie sat bolt upright, suddenly very much awake.

"Don't panic, I'm only joking. I know it's too soon for that discussion."

"I never imagined we'd be having *that* discussion." Cassie sank back. "A Townsend progeny has always been Mum's ideal rather than mine. But with you…" She ran her finger along Siobhan's shirt collar, then stopped before she let her feelings run away with her. "Considering even far-into-the-future children is mind-boggling right now, don't you think?"

"It's not a deal breaker, though?" Siobhan asked.

Cassie sat up, smiling tenderly to soften her expression, as she traced circles on the back of Siobhan's hand. "I've never even considered children of my own."

"And it's not something you need to consider now." Siobhan ran a hand down Cassie's face. "But you'd make an incredible mother."

"To a primary school kid, maybe. Someone less self-sufficient? I'd be far too dangerous with a pushchair." When Siobhan didn't smile, she could tell there was something else pressing on her mind, especially when Siobhan began fiddling with her necklace.

"Matthew doesn't want the house. He's going to live with Bronagh. Although they are most welcome to one another, he hinted at me buying him out. I'm not sure that's what I want."

"You don't want to live here?" Cassie's heart fluttered like she had a butterfly in her chest. She'd never voiced her hopes for the future, afraid of what they meant and uncertain of their success, but somehow this conversation felt right.

"This house is the only remnant of my marriage," Siobhan said. "I don't want to be here, and I'd certainly never expect you to want that. Matthew and I can sell this place and I can put the money into…" Siobhan stumbled over her words, "into something else. Something *we* want." Siobhan let out a heavy sigh. "I don't even want to stay here in the meantime. It doesn't feel right."

"Listen, I know it's not ideal, but you and the kids could move into my apartment. It's only a short-term solution, of course, but it gets you out of the house. We can start thinking about what happens next when the dust settles, after which…I wonder how you'd feel about us hunting for our own place. I'm sure it's too soon, but—"

Siobhan's lips silenced Cassie.

Siobhan brushed her fingers across Cassie's cheek. "I'm more than ready to start mapping out our future. I just didn't expect you to get to the same place so soon. I would totally understand if you needed to stand back for a little while."

Cassie kissed her. "I'm ready to start making epic plans with you." She rested her head against Siobhan's shoulder. "We joke a lot, but I hope you know that our love is louder than words. I love the way I feel about you, and how you've made my life so much bigger than I ever thought it would be."

Siobhan beamed. "Then I happily support your decision."

"Speaking of future plans, Eva called from her honeymoon. They're having an unbelievable time. Apparently, Iceland is full of volcanic geysers and rugged women! She's invited us all over to Broadstairs the weekend after next. Mum and Dad are keen to meet the kids."

"So, I did get a family callback. All is not lost."

"Certainly not, although I'm sure we could all live without the angry husband invasion this time."

Siobhan's laughter slipped into a sigh as Cassie swept her hair back from her shoulder and began to nibble her neck. Cassie's entire body was ready to give in to the hours of pleasure guaranteed.

Siobhan pushed Cassie onto her back, the tempting warmth of Siobhan's body almost agonizing as her gaze scorched. Cassie's whole frame shuddered as Siobhan let her tongue roam freely over any exposed flesh. Cassie found herself incapable of returning anything, basking in Siobhan's touch, recognizing the heated desire in Siobhan's eyes.

"Upstairs, now," Siobhan said, and Cassie's entire body ached in anticipation.

Getting to the bedroom proved challenging, as parting from one another proved almost impossible. Hands roamed, tongues thrashed, bodies surged. Until Cassie finally felt the relief of the bedroom door shutting as Siobhan reeled her in.

Cassie lifted her hips inches off the bed so Siobhan could tug her trousers over her hips and off until they lay crumpled on the floor. Soon the only thing on her was Siobhan.

"Is this an urgent matter?" Cassie teased throatily.

"I've done nothing but think about ripping your clothes off all day."

"Then let's not slow down."

Siobhan trailed her tongue along Cassie's torso and gently slid a finger inside as Cassie thrust up to meet it. She pulled Siobhan's head down, and when Siobhan eased her tongue inside of Cassie, her own head rolled back in delight.

But at this angle, she couldn't see Siobhan, so she tilted her chin down and when she opened her eyes, Siobhan's were waiting to meet hers.

Their gazes locked. In moments like these they loved with their eyes as much as their bodies.

Siobhan picked up the pace, and soon everything in Cassie felt tight and light and glorious. She came in a taut crescendo, pushing and tensing against Siobhan, desperate for more. Siobhan wrapped her arms around Cassie's hips and held her securely, encouraging her to ascend into oblivion.

CHAPTER THIRTY-SIX

Cassie! We've missed you!" Dylan hurtled across the beach to meet her. "You should see the waves we've tackled. I managed to kneel on a bodyboard for, like, five seconds! Danny said I was awesome!" Dylan turned his attention to her mum, edging closer to appraise her. "Hey. You must be Cassie's mum. You don't look much like our grandma. She wears flowery stuff and a great big scowl!"

"He's talking about Matthew's mum," Cassie said, then added, in a stage whisper, "a modern-day Audrey Two."

Her mum cracked up. "Now, if I ever get to the stage where you're comparing *me* to the flesh-eating plant from *Little Shop of Horrors*, plonk me by the sea and leave me for the fish."

"Promise."

"We're sitting over there." Dylan pointed across the sand. "Everyone is busy. Well…" Dylan paused, looking over at his mother. "Except Mum. She's having a rest."

Cassie walked across the sand to join the rest of her family. Eva and Danny were competing at beach tennis; her dad was buried up to his neck in sand, with Neave sitting on top of him, adorning him with shells; and Siobhan, well, she seemed to be lounging around doing nothing more than looking drop-dead gorgeous.

"Highly riveting and notably free wedding entertainment here," Siobhan announced, waving them over. "Can also be booked for birthday parties, engagements, and retirements."

"Retirements, eh?" her mum mused. "Did you hear that, Mark? She's ready whenever you are."

"Can't hear you, sorry. I've got my head buried in the sand."

"Your head's the only thing you've *not* got buried in the sand," Cassie teased him.

"Finally!" her mum said, then turned her attention to Neave. "What have you done to my husband?"

"Oh, you mean this guy?" Neave pointed to the lump she was sitting on. "We might release him later, but he's pretty funny."

"We're having a shell-ebration!" Her dad nodded towards his body, where the pods of past marine life had been fashioned into a bikini top.

"Told you he was funny!"

"He certainly is! But do you know what would be an improvement?" Neave shook her head. "If we gave him a mermaid's tail."

"Or a sea monster's tail!" Dylan dropped into the sand. "That would be epic!"

"Come on then, let's get to work."

Much to Cassie's enjoyment, her mother got down on the sand, snatched up a spade and dug in. She hadn't expected her mum to be so spirited, and her expression must have said as much because in the midst of molding the sand, her mum looked over at her and asked, "What?"

"Just admiring your resting beach face." Cassie turned towards Siobhan. "You look rushed off your feet."

"Apparently, I'm surplus to requirements. Your dad hasn't stopped since we arrived. I'll do an ice cream run in a bit, just so I feel I've played my part."

Neave came to stand by Cassie. "What do you think?" she asked, evaluating the weird and wonderful shapes they'd created. "Would Cassandra Tantrum be able to fight this sea creature?"

"Is Cassandra going to follow me around for life?" Cassie chuckled, not entirely averse to the idea. "She can take on anything!" Cassie put her hands on her hips and stood tall. "With a little help from her crew."

"I wouldn't rely on Mum. She's been sleeping." Cassie wished she'd been drooling too, so she could tease her about it. Neave poked Siobhan like she was a fire waiting to be stoked. Siobhan crackled to life.

"Busted!" Her dad laughed, pointing at her, before he burst out from the sand with a roar.

"You can't catch me!" Dylan yelled. "I'm too quick for you!"

Dylan sped across the sand like a sprite, dodging both of her parents nimbly, until her dad managed to catch up with him and tackled him. Her mum tickled his feet and soon Dylan was squealing in high-pitched delight.

Cassie watched as Neave ran down to the water's edge and equipped herself with a bucket of icy cold seawater. "I have big plans for this bucket!" she announced, thrusting it into the air by the handle and sending sploshes over the rim and onto her arm. And then she was off and running, bellowing, "Targets in sight!"

Naturally, she began barreling towards Siobhan, who'd been participating not as a spectator, but as a supporter. Cassie would know. She'd been watching her. In fact, she'd been so busy basking in Siobhan's fondness for her family, by the time she registered Neave's last-minute change in direction, the window in which to warn her mother had passed.

Her mum leaped off the sand like a kangaroo racing to the foliage bar.

"Neave!" Siobhan cried, horrified. "I'm so sorry, Maria. I thought she was heading for me."

"So did I," Cassie said.

"Wakey, wakey," Dylan yelled, tipping a bucket of icy seawater over his mum's head and bouncing up and down as Siobhan jumped up letting out a shriek.

"I had nothing to do with this," Cassie held her hands up, before handing Siobhan a towel. "I'm merely enjoying my time at the beach."

Cassie plucked a piece of seaweed from Siobhan's hair. "This looks strangely familiar."

Siobhan tilted her head back over her shoulder, posing. "Do I wear it as well as you pull off pondweed?"

"Without a doubt...you wear it better!" Cassie kissed her.

"You're not mad?" Neave swung the bucket at her side, her expression wary.

Her mum shook her head. "Not in the slightest! I think it's time for a family photo, let's update the album! Come on, everyone, gather round!"

Although it wasn't the most poised family photograph they could have produced, everyone was either chuckling, draping seaweed over

Maria or pulling off untested dance moves, as a bystander snapped them up.

"That's taking pride of place in our living room," Mark said.

Her worries doused, Neave darted over to Dylan and her dad, who were sculpting a race car together. "I'm doing the wheels!"

Her mum flopped onto the sand beside them. "Your children are quite fantastic. You almost forget how energetic kids can be, especially at the beach. Cassie was a real handful wherever we took her."

"That should come as no surprise to anyone here." Cassie chuckled. "They're a real credit to you."

Siobhan's cheeks reddened beneath her sun cream. Cassie felt her heart swell, knowing she would be eternally grateful to her mum for these words of kindness. It was exactly what Siobhan needed to hear right now. She squeezed Siobhan's hand.

"My kids adore you, Maria. You and Mark both. They haven't had an easy time of it recently, but this is exactly what they need right now. I'm very proud of them."

"Just like I'm very proud of Cassie, though she'll hate to hear me admit it. It's a mother's prerogative. We're pretty over the moon for her."

Cassie watched the two of them share a moment of comforting, steady eye contact and found her lower lip trembling. She pulled it between her teeth, but it kept quivering, completely undeterred.

"I'm going to take a stroll."

"Shall we walk back up to Eva's, have a cup of tea in the garden?" her mum suggested, and when her mum touched her face, Cassie found herself unable to speak.

"Cassie?"

She managed a nod.

Cassie's mum embraced Siobhan as if she were her own daughter. Then she looped one arm through Cassie's. "We'll see you back at the house in a bit."

❖

"You're overwhelmed," Cassie's mum stated simply, placing a mug of tea down in front of Cassie. "Tell me, what's big enough to overwhelm my resilient daughter?"

Cassie breathed in slowly through her nose, counting to ten, and then out through her mouth. "I don't think I understood how much I missed you until today," she confessed, her body shaking, overcome with emotions she didn't know what to do with. She battled fiercely against them, gripping onto her mug with two hands, as she tried to regain control.

"It's okay to cry." Her mum gently took the mug out of Cassie's hands, holding them tightly instead.

There was no judgment in her eyes, only love. Before she knew it, her mum was out of her seat, arms encircling her and Cassie was hugging her back. Her face buckled and tears began to roll from her cheeks onto her mum's shirt.

"You let it all out." Maria stroked her hair. "You're far better for being in touch with your emotions."

Cassie pulled away, her lip still trembling as she wiped her eyes, a smile breaking through. "My previous self would be fuming after a display of emotion like this."

"This has been as huge for you as it has been for Siobhan," her mum said.

Cassie shrugged. She hadn't considered that. "I have an important role to play for Dylan and Neave, and parenting...well, like you said, it's not easy, is it?"

"You're doing loads better than I ever did."

"It's not all on you, Mum," Cassie said. "I've been a terrible daughter. Seeing you with Dylan and Neave on the beach today, it's brought home how much I've missed out on. I was so stubborn and selfish, but I'm not that person anymore. You've got Siobhan to thank for the transformation. She's an amazing woman."

"She must be. I can't imagine you'd fall in love with just anyone— or, for that matter, that Siobhan would. Which means you're a pretty amazing woman yourself, Cass. You need to give yourself some credit. It takes a lot of courage to admit your mistakes and even more courage to learn from them."

Her mum squeezed her shoulder, and Cassie realized she was still standing with her arm wrapped around her mum. "But I can't praise you for accepting responsibility for your actions if I don't do the same," she continued, and Cassie braced herself for what might come next. "Cassie, I hated myself for letting you go when you were a teenager.

You may have been better off with Eva, but raising you wasn't her responsibility, it was mine. I've apologized to your sister so many times. And now I'm apologizing to you. I should've fought harder to have a relationship with you, Cass, regardless of what was going on between you and your dad. I love you, and I'm sorry."

Emotion choked Cassie's throat as she took in all her mum was saying. "Being with Siobhan, letting Dylan and Neave into my life, it's been wonderful, and so much more than I ever thought I was capable of. It's also made me see how precious family is. I don't want to waste another minute arguing or laying blame or apologizing."

"It seems I have my daughter back, although you must promise to never lose your charismatic stubbornness. There's nobody else we can get our fix of that from."

"Dad might be able to do a good job?"

"He's not nearly as charismatic."

They laughed along together, and Cassie felt like the cloud swirling above her had finally been lifted. Now she could focus on the positives. There was so much to look forward to, so much to share with her family.

"I can't wait to move forward as Team Townsend."

"That team has quite a few new recruits."

Cassie looked through the window, where Siobhan and her children were making their way back towards the house. Siobhan had stopped them to point out a constellation now it was getting dark. Cassie hoped it was hers. She turned back to her mum. "It will be great for Dylan and Neave to have you in their lives, Mum. They've not stopped asking questions about you since they found out we were coming here."

"Don't they have any grandparents?"

"Well, on their father's side, there's the mean green grandmother from outer space; and on Siobhan's side...there's no one. Her father died before she was born and her mum when she was still young."

Her mum gave a heavy nod. "It sounds like it will do her a world of good to have some new and approachable extended family," she said, her genuine warmth filling Cassie with such excitement for the future. Her mum wiped a tear from her eye, then she wiped one from Cassie's.

Then she tutted and shook her head. "Just when I finally get a handle on mothering, you go and throw grandparenting into the mix!"

CHAPTER THIRTY-SEVEN

The first time Cassie had taken her to the lighthouse at Kingsgate, she had fallen in love with the view. There could be no finer place to watch the ocean breathe, rising and falling with rhythmic ease. The stars were scattered like speckled moondust in the sky and the lighthouse itself was exactly as she remembered, rustic and mysterious, like it had stories of its own to tell. This was their special place, ready to welcome them back with open arms.

"What do you think?" Siobhan wrapped her arms around Cassie from behind, linking their hands over Cassie's middle.

"You want to move here? To Broadstairs?" Cassie asked.

At Siobhan's suggestion, the corners of Cassie's mouth turned up, inspiring Siobhan's to follow suit.

Nothing had ever felt more right.

"Why on earth not? I've never seen you so happy, Cass. Everything you need and everything I want is right here. We can find an old cottage, turn it into our little project. We love the sea, the kids love it, and I can't honestly think of a better support network for us." She brushed shoulders with Cassie, hoping she didn't sound too eager.

"We'd be in danger of U-hauling," Cassie mused.

"You know I have no idea what you're talking about, right?"

"Lesbian terminology."

"Like the sapphic strut or cliterception?" Siobhan looked out over the ocean, resting her head on Cassie's shoulder.

"Sort of. Basically, lesbians go from dating to cohabitating full tilt."

"How fast?"

"Three dates, tops."

"We've had more than three dates," Siobhan was quick to point out. "Does that have us married and pregnant by Christmas?"

"And divorced by Easter," Cassie said as she pulled Siobhan closer.

"Scrap that." Siobhan gave Cassie a peck on the cheek, letting her lips linger. "If you think it's too soon, just say."

"It's not that. There's lots to think about, like work," Cassie said slowly, and Siobhan looked out over the ocean, wondering if this was Cassie's way of holding back. "We're a long way from London, even on the train. Commuting is possible though." Cassie smiled warmly at Siobhan.

She realized that this wasn't Cassie holding back, this was her taking responsibility for something bigger than herself. "I'm sure it's workable. The company isn't going to want to lose you."

"They aren't going to want to lose you either. We're pretty much their dream team. If you think about it," Cassie continued, "there isn't all that much we can't do from a base outside London, other than meetings, which can be held anywhere anyway. I'm just not sure how Julie would cope without us, now that she's chief bridesmaid."

"We could always put her in the shed at the bottom of the garden."

Cassie's tone turned serious. "We need to consider schools too. Moving out here would be a big change for the kids. We'd need to talk it through with them."

Hearing Cassie put the children's happiness before her own, without a second thought, caused Siobhan's heart to expand in her chest. "They've made themselves at home remarkably quickly this weekend. I also have it on good authority that they've organized a sleepover at your mum and dad's place over the summer holidays. They might even suggest the move before we do."

"How do you think they'll feel about changing schools? Or moving away from their friends?"

Siobhan paused to really give this some consideration. "The last year has been tough on Dylan and Neave, tougher than I'd ever imagined, but they're happier now than I've ever seen them. I'll make sure they don't lose touch with their friends, which means you might have to tolerate a weekend of delinquents descending on us from the big smoke every so often."

"Now, you know I haven't touched a cigarette in ages. We don't want a relapse," Cassie said, leaning in to nibble on Siobhan's ear, then dancing kisses down her neck.

Siobhan struggled to remember what they were talking about. Fortunately, Cassie hadn't forgotten. Interrupting the stimulation, she said, "What about Matthew?"

"He's starting to speak to me civilly to arrange things, and Bronagh seems onboard too."

"Now that she's stopped seeing things through rose-tinted spectacles." Much to Siobhan's amusement, Cassie pulled her lips wide and failed to show off her fangs. Her impression of Bronagh was always a crowd pleaser.

"One day your face will stick like that!"

"Spoken like a true mother." Cassie winked at her.

"We'd only be a couple of hours away from him, so we'll be able to organize weekends for the kids. And since he seems to be making more of an effort—and the kids seem somewhat receptive—I think them having regular contact is important." Siobhan felt her nerves tap dancing inside her stomach. "So…what do you think?" She fidgeted with the pendant on her necklace as she awaited Cassie's response.

"Well…" Cassie clasped her hand and kissed it. "Eva once forbade me from moving within fifty miles of her 'peaceful town.' But that was back when I was benched. So…if this is what you truly want…"

"I want to be with you; it really is that simple. I know how you adore simplicity."

"Well, relationships *aren't* hard work if you're in the right one. That's something I've come to learn. I also happen to think this would be a wonderful place to bring the children up."

Siobhan wanted to fist pump the air and jump for joy, her heart soaring as she realized exactly how ready and willing Cassie was to co-parent with her. But she held it together.

"You know, you've made such a difference to their lives," Siobhan said. Cassie made to wave off the compliment, but Siobhan clasped her hand and kissed it. "I'd love to bring them up here with you. Imagine waking up every day to the ocean on our doorstep."

"Danny will have them running for surf champions in no time."

"It beats bloody drumming." Siobhan rolled her eyes.

"Be under no illusions. We'll still be doing that!" Cassie began to drum on her own knees.

Siobhan's eyes widened. "In moderation."

"Do I look moderate to you?"

"That's something we've all got to look forward to then."

"Yes, well, since we're making plans, I have something I'd like to ask you."

"Of course. It's only natural that you outdo me."

"How would feel about a reenactment?" Cassie met Siobhan's eyes, and when she did, Siobhan basked in their luminosity. Cassie caressed her cheek before she deftly began working her fingers up and down Siobhan's leg. "The first time we were here, you kissed me."

"I did," Siobhan said. "Is that the reenactment you're after?"

"In the form of a live action replay of course."

Siobhan felt Cassie's fingers entwined in the dark tresses of her hair, then Cassie's mouth was upon hers, insistent, invigorating, impatient. Even now, it still amazed Siobhan how Cassie always managed to kiss her exactly as she needed to be kissed: soft and moist, hot and breathy. There was no battle between them, only union.

Cassie delivered intricate kisses down her neck, nipping and sucking at her skin, and her nipples reacted to Cassie's tantalizing touch. Siobhan whipped off Cassie's shirt in desperation, her moonlit breasts now on full display. As Cassie's hands rode her helter-skelter curves, Siobhan's set to work on Cassie's trousers, insatiable in her desire.

When she felt the liquid lust between Cassie's legs, Siobhan struggled to control her breathing, as she removed the rest of their clothes, desperate for closer proximity.

Cassie must have heard her thoughts, because she twined her legs with Siobhan's and cruised along her thighs until their centers connected. Siobhan craved it all: their urgent flutters, their desperate collision, their unrelenting connection.

Siobhan bit into Cassie's shoulder in an attempt to stifle the scream that surged forth as the moist swell between them crested and erupted, leaving them both breathless.

Laying her head on Cassie's chest, Siobhan let her eyes roam the night sky, tracing the constellations where she recognized them. At the sight of the spectacular scenery, it hit her. The beauty she was now experiencing was all for her. Cassie had picked this special place for them to share. Out of everyone in the world, Cassie could take her pick, yet she had chosen her. Not on a whim, but with a declaration of love.

"Are you okay?" Siobhan probed, when Cassie's breathing hadn't calmed.

"Slightly more than okay. Over the fucking moon just about describes it."

"Still like me too much?" Siobhan asked.

"We *could* even throw the word love in there. After all, me loving you, you loving me, it's always been exactly as I said in Paris." Siobhan felt Cassie's hand cover both the pendant around her neck and her heart. "Inevitable."

Siobhan leant back and allowed Cassie to wrap her in a warm embrace, head reeling and skin tingling from their astonishing lovemaking. She always had and always would love Cassie and knowing Cassie felt the same, she was complete. Nothing had ever felt as right as being held in Cassie's arms. Looking up to where the stars were gathering in the clear night sky ready to put on their private show, it felt amazing to be present in this moment, sharing it with Cassie. This lighthouse was their special place, even if it had been where they shared that disastrous first kiss. Back then, if anyone had told Siobhan where they would be now, she would have never believed them. Yet it seemed unlikely there could have ever been another ending to their story. Their destiny was to find one another, learn from each other and in the simplest of terms, to love. But this wasn't just any love. This was a love that went to the very core of their being, a love to last a lifetime, a love that in Cassie's words, had always been inevitable.

About the Author

Skye Rowan lives in the village of Allerton Bywater in England with her three naughty yet loveable Romanian rescue dogs, Tatty, Ziggy, and Kylo. Her interests lie within the worlds of theatre and music, and she can often be found frequenting the West End to watch a musical, including her favourite, *Wicked*. She is an avid football fan and is proud to support the mighty Leeds United, cheering them on through thick and thin. Skye loves attending concerts and counts Florence and the Machine, The Sea Girls and The 1975 amongst her favourites. She loves to spend time travelling with her friends and counts New York amongst her best-loved cities. Skye is most happy when she is spending time with her partner, Nic. Together, they love to visit the beach for long dog walks, sing along to indie tunes on a road trip with the kids, or relax, toasting marshmallows around a campfire with a cup of tea.

This is Skye's first novel, and she is extremely excited about the prospect of readers getting hold of a copy of her first book.

Books Available from Bold Strokes Books

Almost Perfect by Tagan Shepard. A shared love of queer TV brings Olivia and Riley together, but can they keep their real-life love as picture perfect as their on-screen counterparts? (978-1-63679-322-1)

Corpus Calvin by David Swatling. Cloverkist Inn may be haunted, but a ghost materializes from Jason Dekker's past and Calvin's canine instinct kicks in to protect a young boy from mortal danger. (978-1-62639-428-5)

Craving Cassie by Skye Rowan. Siobhan Carney and Cassie Townsend share an instant attraction, but are they brave enough to give up everything they have ever known to be together? (978-1-63679-062-6)

Drifting by Lyn Hemphill. When Tess jumps into the ocean after Jet, she thinks she's saving her life. Of course, she can't possibly know Jet is actually a mermaid desperate to fix her mistake before she causes her clan's demise. (978-1-63679-242-2)

Enigma by Suzie Clarke. Polly has taken an oath to protect and serve her country, but when the spy she's tasked with hunting becomes the love of her life, will she be the one to betray her country? (978-1-63555-999-6)

Finding Fault by Annie McDonald. Can environmental activist Dr. Evie O'Halloran and government investigator Merritt Shepherd set aside their conflicting ideas about saving the planet and risk their hearts enough to save their love? (978-1-63679-257-6)

Hot Keys by R.E. Ward. In 1920s New York City, Betty May Dewitt and her best friend, Jack Norval, are determined to make their Tin Pan Alley dreams come true and discover they will have to fight—not only for their hearts and dreams, but for their lives. (978-1-63679-259-0)

Securing Ava by Anne Shade. Private investigator Paige Richards takes a case to locate and bring back runaway heiress Ava Prescott. But ignoring her attraction may prove impossible when their hearts and lives are at stake. (978-1-63679-297-2)

The Amaranthine Law by Gun Brooke. Tristan Kelly is being hunted for who she is and her incomprehensible past, and despite her overwhelming feelings for Olivia Bryce, she has to reject her to keep her safe. (978-1-63679-235-4)

The Forever Factor by Melissa Brayden. When Bethany and Reid confront their past, they give new meaning to letting go, forgiveness, and a future worth fighting for. (978-1-63679-357-3)

The Frenemy Zone by Yolanda Wallace. Ollie Smith-Nakamura thinks relocating from San Francisco to her dad's rural hometown is the worst idea in the world, but after she meets her new classmate Ariel Hall, she might have a change of heart. (978-1-63679-249-1)

A Cutting Deceit by Cathy Dunnell. Undercover cop Athena takes a job at Valeria's hair salon to gather evidence to prove her husband's connections to organized crime. What starts as a tentative friendship quickly turns into a dangerous affair. (978-1-63679-208-8)

As Seen on TV! by CF Frizzell. Despite their objections, TV hosts Ronnie Sharp, a laid-back chef; and paranormal investigator Peyton Stanford, have to work together. The public is watching. But joining forces is risky, contemptuous, unnerving, provocative—and ridiculously perfect. (978-1-63679-272-9)

Blood Memory by Sandra Barret. Can vampire Jade Murphy protect her friend from a human stalker and keep her dates with the gorgeous Beth Jenssen without revealing her secrets? (978-1-63679-307-8)

Foolproof by Leigh Hays. For Martine Roberts and Elliot Tillman, friends with benefits isn't a foolproof way to hide from the truth at the heart of an affair. (978-1-63679-184-5)

Glass and Stone by Renee Roman. Jordan must accept that she can't control everything that happens in life, and that includes her wayward heart. (978-1-63679-162-3)

Hard Pressed by Aurora Rey. When rivals Mira Lavigne and Dylan Miller are tapped to co-chair Finger Lakes Cider Week, competition gives way to compromise. But will their sexual chemistry lead to love? (978-1-63679-210-1)

The Laws of Magic by M. Ullrich. Nothing is ever what it seems, especially not in the small town of Bender, Massachusetts, where a witch lives to save lives and avoid love. (978-1-63679-222-4)

The Lonely Hearts Rescue by Morgan Lee Miller, Nell Stark, Missouri Vaun. In this novella collection, a hurricane hits the Gulf Coast, and the animals at the Lonely Hearts Rescue Shelter need love, and so do the humans who adopt them. (978-1-63679-231-6)

The Mage and the Monster by Barbara Ann Wright. Two powerful mages, one committed to magic and one controlled by it, strive to free each other and be together while the countries they serve descend into war. (978-1-63679-190-6)

Truly Wanted by J.J. Hale. Sam must decide if she's willing to risk losing her found family to find her happily ever after. (978-1-63679-333-7)

A Good Chance by Ali Vali. Harry, Desi, and Desi's sister Rachel are so close to getting everything they've ever wanted, but Desi's ex-husband is coming back to get his revenge and rip apart their chance at happiness. (978-1-63679-023-7)

A Perfect Fifth by Jaycie Morrison. Streetwise pianist Zara Keller and Lady Jillian Stansfield couldn't be more different; yet their connection brings a new awareness of who they are and what they truly want in their lives—including each other. (978-1-63679-132-6)

Catching Feelings by Ana Hartnett Reichardt. Andrea Foster expected to catch a lot of pitches from the Alder Lion's star pitcher, Maya, but she didn't expect to catch feelings. (978-1-63679-227-9)

Defiant Hearts by Lee Lynch. In these stories, you'll find your lovers, friends, and lesbians you wish you knew—maybe even yourself. (978-1-63679-237-8)

Love and Duty by Catherine Young. All Princess Roseli wants is to marry her three lovers, but with war looming, she must instead marry Princess Lucia to establish a military alliance between their planets. (978-1-63679-256-9)

Murder at Union Station by David S. Pederson. Private Detective Mason Adler struggles to determine who killed a woman found in a trunk without getting himself killed in the process. (978-1-63679-269-9)

Serendipity by Kris Bryant. Serendipity brings jingle writer Annie Foster and celebrity pop star Bristol Baines together, and their undeniable attraction keeps them close, but will their different paths drive them apart? (978-1-63679-224-8)

The Haunted Heart by Jane Kolven. A ghost, a ring, and a quest to find a missing psychic—it's a spell for love. (978-1-63679-245-3)

The Rules of Forever by Nan Campbell. After reconnecting at their high school reunion, Cara and Lauren agree to embark on a textbook definition friends-with-benefits relationship, but trying to keep it uncomplicated is harder than it seems. (978-1-63679-248-4)

Vision of Virtue by Brey Willows. When virtue and desire come together, be prepared for sparks in this next installment of the Memory's Muses series. (978-1-63679-118-0)

Cherry on Top by Georgia Beers. A chance meeting leaves Cherry and Ellis longing for a different life, but when Ellis's search for truth crashes into Cherry's insta-filter world, do they have any hope at all of a happily ever after? (978-1-63679-158-6)

Love and Other Rare Birds by Angie Williams. Ornithologist Dr. Jamie Martin and park ranger Rowan Fleming are searching the Alaskan wilderness for a bird thought to be extinct and they're about to discover opposites really do attract. (978-1-63679-108-1)

Parallel Paradise by Mayapee Chowdhury. When their love affair is put to the test by the homophobia of their family, community, and culture, Bindi and Rimli will need to fight for a chance at love. (978-1-63679-204-0)

Perfectly Matched by Toni Logan. A beautiful Cupid named Hannah, a runaway arrow, and just seventy-two hours to fix a mishap that could be the best mistake she has ever made. (978-1-63679-120-3)

Royal Exposé by Jenny Frame. When they're grouped together for a class assignment, Poppy's enthusiasm for life and love may just save Casey's soul, but will she ever forgive Casey for using her to expose royal secrets? (978-1-63679-165-4)

Slow Burn by Missouri Vaun. A wounded wildland firefighter from California and a struggling artist find solace and love in a small southern town. (978-1-63679-098-5)

The Artist by Sheri Lewis Wohl. Detective Casey Wilson and reclusive artist Tula Crane are drawn together in a web of passion, intrigue, and art that might just hold the key to stopping a killer. (978-1-63679-150-0)

The Inconvenient Heiress by Jane Walsh. An unlikely heiress and a spinster evade the Marriage Mart only to discover true love together. (978-1-63679-173-9)

A Champion for Tinker Creek by D.C. Robeline. Lyle James has rescued his dad's auto repair business, but when city hall condemns his neighborhood, Lyle learns only trusting will save his life and help him find love. (978-1-63679-213-2)

Closed-Door Policy by Erin Zak. Going back to college is never easy, but Caroline Stevens is prepared to work hard and change her life for the better. What she's not prepared for is Dr. Atlanta Morris, her gorgeous new professor. (978-1-63679-181-4)

Homeworld by Gun Brooke. Headed by Captain Holly Crowe, the spaceship Velocity's crew journeys towards their alien ancestors' homeworld, and what they find is completely unexpected—and they're not safe. (978-1-63679-177-7)

Outland by Kristin Keppler & Allisa Bahney. Danielle Clark and Katelyn Turner can't seem to stay away from one another even as the war for the wastelands tests their loyalty to each other and to their people. (978-1-63679-154-8)

Secret Sanctuary by Nance Sparks. US Deputy Marshal Alex Trenton specializes in protecting those awaiting trial, but when danger threatens the woman she's falling for, Alex is in for the fight of her life. (978-1-63679-148-7)

Stranded Hearts by Kris Bryant, Amanda Radley, Emily Smith. In these novellas from award winning authors, fate intervenes on behalf of love when characters are unexpectedly stuck together. With too much time and an irresistible attraction, anything could happen. (978-1-63679-182-1)

The Last Lavender Sister by Melissa Brayden. Aster Lavender sells her gourmet doughnuts and keeps a low profile; she never plans on the town's temporary veterinarian swooping in and making her feel like anything but a wallflower. (978-1-63679-130-2)

The Probability of Love by Dena Blake. As Blair and Rachel keep ending up in the same place despite the odds, can a one-night stand turn into forever? Or will the bet Blair never intended to make ruin their happily ever after? (978-1-63679-188-3)

Worth a Fortune by Sam Ledel. After placing a want ad for a personal secretary, a New York heiress is surprised when the woman who got away is the one interested in the position. (978-1-63679-175-3)